RESURRECT

ALSO BY THE AUTHOR:

Callsign: Deep Blue (with Jeremy Robinson)

RESURRECT

KANE GILMOUR

Quickdraw Books

For Perttu Santeri Aho,
my brother in arms at Pearl War.

ACKNOWLEDGMENTS

Any time an author writes a first novel and it sees publication, they are indebted to many people, and usually, these comments make sense only to the intended recipients. I'll probably leave someone out, but if I do, know that you are still in my heart.

Thanks to Perttu Aho for undying friendship and brotherhood across the miles and years, for providing a fleshed out spook for Quinn's dad, a CIA jacket on the man, and a prototype cover based solely on the first prologue that served as inspiration to me for years. Also for excellent feedback on the first part of the book and damn good intentions to get to the rest.

To my best bud, Tim "Bubba" Conley, for his decades of friendship, loyalty, and green funk. He also provided invaluable comments and feedback on everything. And he nudged me for years to get it done.

Special thanks to J.T. Ellison for excellent feedback and for believing I could get it right.

Thanks to the following folks for friendship and encouragement: Jennifer Bagdigian, Alana Renfro, Robert Satchell, Chas Vale, Terry White, Jean Twombly, Daisy Midman, Sunimalee Perera, Sonia Marzuki, Vis Perera, Razmi Farook, Tanya Uluwitiya, Kami Witmer, Kati Takacs, and Scott P. 'Doc' Vaughn.

Thanks are owed to Claude Florin and Jimmy Harris, both of whom allowed permission for their photographs to be used on the cover—even though only Claude's shot of mountains ended up getting utilized in the final product. Thanks also to Stan Tremblay for encouragement, excellent formatting, and Photoshop tricks that saved me a lot of time in designing that cover.

Thanks to my mom, Eileen O'Grady, for reading the manuscript and offering suggestions, as well as for offering her eagle-eyed proofreading skills. Thanks to my uncle, Richard Shaw, for his much-appreciated beta reading, as well as for years of support and love. On the subject of support and love, my thanks also go out to Joyce Shaw, Kris Gaudette, Cyndi Cassani, Emily Esce,

Samantha Tarantola, John Nee, Tracy Stober, Brian & Ingrid Milinazzo, Barb Wagamon, Shannon Gilmour, and Eòin Gilmour.

I am particularly thankful for Dr. Nancy Blechle's years of friendship, for showing me that math was not the devil's tool, and for keeping me sane in the TAP days. Her feedback on RESURRECT was invaluable, and she was the first true Jason Quinn fan out there. Keep strong, "Doc B", you are well loved.

Finally, I owe a Herculean heap of thanks to Jeremy Robinson. For his boundless generosity, encouragement, mad Photoshop skills, artistic suggestions, beta reading, story feedback, and an *amazing* blurb! I owe him huge thanks for introducing me to industry folks, for reams of insider knowledge, for offering me the opportunity to participate in the mighty Chesspocalypse, and for the chance to place a sample of this book inside the e-book of the novella I did with him, CALLSIGN: DEEP BLUE. He's given me everything and more that a new author could ask for from an established mentor. From the depths of my heart, Jeremy, thank you, thank you, *thank you.*

Kane Gilmour,
Montpelier, VT, Dec 2011

RESURRECT

HIDDEN

My hand grasps the killing power in Heaven and Earth.
—*Hong Xiu Quan*

Guo Cheng was startled in the darkness. It was quiet in the barracks, but Cheng almost shouted in surprise when he saw Commander Xiang standing over him.

"There is a secret mission," Xiang whispered to him. "I'm taking only two soldiers for it."

"When?" Cheng started to ask, still wiping the small crusty bits of sleep from his eyes.

"We leave right now. Only your weapons and your warmest clothes." Xiang had cut him off, his normal joviality replaced by a dour demeanor. Cheng had grabbed his clothes and after quickly stuffing them into a sack, he grabbed his long, tasseled spear from the rack against the wall and followed Xiang out the door of the barracks.

He saw that Xiang had also chosen Wu Xiao Jin for the mission. There were few soldiers stationed in Nanjing that Cheng did not know personally. Xiao Jin was one of the ones that kept mostly to himself. Rumors abounded that he was a ferocious fighter who had single-handedly won more than a few battles near Canton. Xiao Jin and the burly commander stood waiting in the dark. They were both packed and ready to go.

"I'll explain when it's safe," was all Xiang offered them as they started walking toward the northwestern edge of town. They walked in silence for hours until they were well into the countryside.

Near dawn, Xiang called a halt to their march and suggested they set up a camp well into the woods, away from the road. They sat on the hard ground eating cold precooked rice. Xiang told them it wasn't safe to make a fire. When they had finished, the tall and lithe Xiao Jin asked, "Commander?"

"Yes. Time to explain. The prophecies have come true. Our Lord has fallen." Commander Xiang said solemnly. Both Cheng and Xiao Jin were flabbergasted at the news.

"We will meet with a small group of pious holy men, who will be carrying His holy remains. We will travel for many days to the northwest frontier. There, He will be interred in a special tomb, far from the control of our enemies. We three are the escort. We are a small group. We move fast and travel light, so we may avoid the enemy troops as we pass through the western provinces." The commander, older than both Cheng and Xiao by only a few years, seemed far wearier than a man his age should.

"And after the entombment?" Cheng asked slowly. Commander Xiang didn't answer, and both Cheng and Xiao realized that no answer would be forthcoming.

They traveled only at night, and camped by day, taking turns on watch. After three nights of long quiet hours placing one foot in front of the other down the dirt and mud roads, with no words passed between them, they came across the priests. There were six of them, and they carried the shroud-wrapped body in silence. The priests would only speak when the group made its camp—and then only in whispers. Xiao kept mostly to himself, and he clearly took his task of guarding the group seriously. Commander Xiang rarely spoke either. Cheng resigned himself to being vigilant, spending long nights walking with the group, and dreaming of the farm he always wanted to own. Somewhere in beautiful Hunan province, far from the fighting, would have suited him fine.

Inevitably, they were set upon by bandits somewhere west of Xi'an. Bandits roamed the region, usually seeking silver and traveling in unwashed groups of eight to ten. The fighting was fierce, but with the assistance of the priests, who were very good at unarmed combat, they prevailed battle after battle.

Until they didn't.

In the last battle with bandits, they lost Xiao. He had been killed taking down five of the Mongols all on his own. Commander Xiang was wounded in the same fight, and now the man limped whenever he thought Cheng wasn't looking. The loss of even one of their small team on a mission so dire, as they felt pursued by their enemies and the elements, was a crushing blow to an already damaged morale. The remaining nights of their journey were uneventful, but filled with quiet sorrow.

Now, that dream of the farm was looking bleaker all the time. It was nearly three weeks later, and the puddle of urine Guo Cheng had deposited on the frozen ground outside the tomb was beginning to freeze. He looked at it in astonishment. He had relieved himself less than a minute before. He scanned the hills that ringed the valley for any sign of Qing troops or Barbarians. As usual, he found nothing but the howling wind, as it ripped through the mountains and across the beautiful frozen lake.

"No one will ever find this place," he said to himself.

The tomb was set into a small hollow in the earth, just at the top of a hill and at the foot of another beyond it. Cheng the stood outside of the stone structure. Xiang and the priests were all inside. *Performing the rituals*, Cheng supposed, but he wasn't really sure. Even though they had journeyed for weeks to reach this desolate place, he was not permitted inside of the tomb. He was just a soldier, as Commander Xiang had reminded him when they arrived.

A light snow began to fall, and Cheng wrapped his cloak around him a bit tighter. He still had about two hours to go before the commander would relieve him on the watch. He squatted down and leaned against the wall of the tomb, hoping to lessen the impact of the wind against his body.

He tried to remember the last time he had truly felt warm, and then he scanned the horizon for any sign of movement once more. He kept his eyes open, even when he wasn't on duty. Whenever he closed them, he would see Xiao Jin's contorted death face. Although Cheng hadn't gotten to really know Xiao Jin, he wished it had been one of the priests that had been killed in the battle instead. For the rest of the journey everyone had been in foul spirits, paranoid, and on edge. Finally, they had reached the tomb. Xiang had explained how a separate group of priests had journeyed ahead of them to prepare the structure. Cheng saw no sign of the other priests when he arrived and wondered where they had gone, but he thought better of asking the commander.

The snow was starting to fall heavier now. Just as Cheng was wondering where Commander Xiang was, he heard a noise behind him and turned to see Xiang in the doorway to the tomb. The look on Xiang's face was now even more severe than it had been at any time during their travels.

"Come to relieve me?" Cheng asked, knowing that was why the Commander had stepped out into the cold. What other reason would there be? Xiang wasn't one for idle chatter.

"No, Guo Cheng." Xiang replied. "The tomb is to be sealed now. The priests and I are to remain inside with our Lord. The priests told me you should be locked in here with us as well, but I gave them the excuse that I wouldn't permit it, because you are such a low soldier. You know I don't really feel that way, I hope. I don't know how well you'll fare out in the cold, my friend, but it will be a better fate for a soldier than to be locked in here. Take all your belongings. Leave no trace that we were ever here. It doesn't matter where you go, just get as far from here as you can. You are a free man now, no longer a soldier. Good luck, Cheng. Remember: *He* is with you."

Cheng looked at the commander aghast.

"Step back now, Cheng," the commander instructed.

As Cheng did so, Xiang stepped back into the doorway and placed his hand on a spot on the inside of the tomb wall. A massive stone door fell into place from above the doorway, landing in the snow and sealing the tomb with a heavy thud.

Cheng was stunned.

He was unsure whether to feel more horrified for the priests and Commander Xiang, destined to starve to death in the tomb with the remains of their master, or for himself, abandoned to the cold. He stood staring at the dark stone door for several minutes. He wasn't sure what he was expecting. Perhaps the door would open again? But no. Cheng knew from the look on Xiang's face, that this was no joke. Seven years in the rebellion army now meant nothing. They had lost the war. Their leader was dead. Cheng was now a free man.

He left the front of the tomb, and walked to the place where he and Xiang had camped the previous day. He buried Xiang's few belongings in the sandy soil beneath the deep snow, and then collected all of his own belongings. After hefting his sack onto his back, Guo Cheng took one last look at the frozen lake and the snow flurries that swirled across the ice. Then a thought occurred to him. He would be in danger every minute of his life from the Qing forces, if he even made it back to China. He would now be looked upon as a war criminal. All soldiers from the losing side always were.

"Where then?" he asked out loud.

Only the howling wind replied, its moan giving no advice.

Then, he turned to his left and began walking deeper into Tibet. It would have to be distant Lhasa. There would be no farm in Hunan for him. *But perhaps*, he thought as the wind whipped around him screaming, *perhaps a new life in Tibet. If I last that long.*

THE FINAL EXPEDITION

*This time, it would no longer be a matter of merely getting
acquainted with Central Asia.*
—*George Kish*

The old man sat on the bed for a moment, and tried to decide whether he was up for the task at hand. He was 87 years old, and he was about to embark on a journey that he felt only a younger, more vigorous man should undertake. More than 4,000 miles lay ahead of him in the coming weeks, but he felt fresh and full of passion for the notion of returning to the desert, one final time.

He looked around the room at his familiar antique furniture, and at the shelves lined with hundreds of books. *All of my worldly possessions*, he thought. No hint of longing or regret in the thought, and it quite surprised him.

"So be it," he said aloud.

The man walked quietly to the parlor and assessed the items laid out on the table.

"Very little scientific equipment," he observed.

He scanned the clothing, the array of pencils, maps, compasses, and leather satchels that filled nearly every part of the table's surface.

"Very little equipment of any kind."

But this will not be a scientific journey, he reminded himself. *This will be a spiritual journey.* "How odd it shall be, to travel with only a caravan of solitude. One man carrying all he requires. Surely, this is freedom."

He began to place the items on the table into the three leather satchels he had had a tanner in Uppsala make for him. "That man is a genius," he said. "He was able to implement all of the design elements I requested, and he even managed to improve on the design of these arm loops." The old man studied the loops for a few moments, tugging on them and rubbing them between his fingers, before returning to packing. He packed carefully and methodically, examining each item and reevaluating his need of it before placing it into the bag. In the end, he had not discarded any items. He smiled, smugly acknowledging to himself that he had planned well in laying the items out the night before.

The thought occurred to him that he might want to bring along two other items. He returned to the bedroom and picked a blank, leather-bound book from one of the shelves.

"A fresh journal," he said aloud. "The old one must remain." Then, he crossed to a small writing desk in the corner of the room and opened the small cherry-wood box that sat near the lamp. Inside was a tiny, very old pair of spectacles. He hadn't needed them in three years, not even for reading. His eyes were perfect since the cataract surgery, and he had reveled in that fact every day. *Still,* he thought, and placed the glasses in his inside vest pocket.

Just in case.

On the bottom of the wooden box, under where the spectacles had lain was a tiny, yellowed photograph not much larger than a postage stamp. The man took the photo, closed the box, and glanced at the picture's subject. The woman in the photo was young and very beautiful. After just a brief look, he tossed the picture onto the table and walked back into the other room.

A quick look out of the window confirmed that he still had some time before the dawn. He went into the kitchen and fixed a cup of tea, then sat in the parlor with his packed bags. He took his time in sipping the tea; he was in no hurry. He would be in Germany by the time Lars made the announcement. He thought that Lars would handle all the aspects to the deception quite masterfully, perhaps even better than he could have done himself. The deception was necessary, the old man reminded himself, because the press would have jumped all over his proposed journey. *And once the communists got word of it...*

No. Lars would handle things. The foundation would be set up, the newspapers would write their editorials, and he would be on his way to the Taklamakan, with no one the wiser.

The tea was finished. On a whim, he went into the bedroom and placed the cup on its side on the floor by the bed, spilling the last drop of tea with its black specks onto the carpet. The man looked at the cup and smiled again, this time broader.

"A nice touch," he said. Then, he strode purposefully into the parlor, stuffed the fresh journal into the oversized pocket of his coat, picked up the bags, and left the apartment. He walked down the stairs and out onto the street bristling with barely controlled excitement. As he walked though the snow to the train station, watching the gray light come up over the harbor, he thought that for this trip, his greatest expedition of all, no one would ever know.

But he was wrong.

BOOK ONE:
THE PROJECT

CHAPTER 1

> *But at the end of five days the route enters another province*
> *whose name is Tibet.*
> *—Marco Polo*

The mountains were too close. Way too close. The plane was out of control, and Dr. Eva Rayjek watched out the windows across the fuselage as the battered old plane's starboard engine coughed and then quit. The propeller haltingly finished its last revolution as Eva looked on. *Not a DC-3, but an Ilyushin*, she recalled with mounting panic. *A Russian plane. What was it Malcolm had said about it being thrown together by trained monkeys?* She looked to the front of the plane and saw that Malcolm and David were just now kicking in the door to the cockpit. *What could have gone wrong?* she wondered.

Eva was still feeling disoriented from her long nap. She had woken feeling uncomfortable from the sun on her face as she dozed in a passenger seat. She, David, and Malcolm were the only three passengers on the ancient Xinjiang Airlines flight from Xinning to Guangzhou. Once in Guangzhou, they would have to take a train to reach Hong Kong. They had been at the dig site 25 miles northwest of Xinning for five months, and they were all looking forward to a week's vacation in Hong Kong before they headed back to their respective universities and institutes.

There had been a palpable feeling of energy as the three archeologists, the only passengers, had boarded the pitiful looking plane on the tarmac of Xinning's one-horse airport. David had commented on how lucky they were to be flying in the DC-3 instead of the only other plane on the blacktop, a war-scarred Russian Antonov AN-2 complete with its top-mounted gunner's turret. Malcolm had been quick to note that their plane was in fact an Ilyushin Il-14, which was a Russian knockoff of the infamous American-made Douglas DC-3. David had looked like a child who had just dropped his ice cream cone, when he was shown up on his miniscule knowledge of aviation. Later they had all laughed and joked while Malcolm discussed in his thick Australian accent the things he would show them in *Hongers*, as he liked to refer to the Hong Kong Special Administrative Region, since it had reverted to Chinese ownership in 1997.

After the plane had left the ground however, each person turned their thoughts inward, and Eva spent about an hour mulling over the finer details of the buried city they had discovered in the Taklamakan Desert. Five months at the site wasn't nearly enough, considering all the delicate scraping of toothbrushes involved, but it was all the Chinese Government had been prepared to allow them on their visas and digging permits. Now they would have to return to the U.S. (and Malcolm to Australia), where they would send a barrage of letters to the Chinese embassies and the recently formed People's Ministry of Archeology in Beijing, requesting permission to return to the desert. This was an old game the archeologists were used to playing with the Chinese. The Chinese gave a limited length of time on the visas and the scientists returned to their own countries to resume the barrage of paperwork. While that was going on, the Chinese government sent teams to the site to loot whatever needed to be looted (a process which was inevitably blamed on "Capitalistic Barbarian Pirates"). Then the communist government would finally relent, and allow the scientists back in, and another few months of work could be accomplished, provided the bribe money that kept the on-site officials happily drunk every night, didn't run out.

The trio, working with a team of Chinese laborers, a few students from Chongqing University, and the omnipresent and ever-vigilant team of bureaucrats and military personnel, had managed to uncover quite a few artifacts that would go to the museums in Beijing. They had found a number of items that gave them the impression that the city had been constructed sometime in the fifth century, but it had also been used as recently as the 1800s. What had frustrated Eva, more so than David or Malcolm, was that there was no historical evidence of the city's existence. As far as Eva could tell, there had never been a city there, at that place in the desert. There was no hint of a town there in any records she could find, and yet it had existed for over a thousand years before becoming partially covered by the shifting sands in the last hundred years or so, perhaps even in the last twenty.

She had slept in the uncomfortable aircraft chair until the sun on her face woke her and some elusive thought nagged at her subconscious. When she awoke, she looked to the other two, who were also asleep in their chairs. Her mind took some time to focus on her surroundings and remember the flight to southeast China. That was when it had occurred to her. She was sitting on the left side of the airplane. *And the sun is on my face.* A quick look out her window confirmed her fear when she saw the snow covered mountains below them. They were flying west. Hong Kong was to the southeast. That was when she called to David and Malcolm, telling them what was wrong.

Dr. Malcolm Brewer was a big man. He had banged on the door to the cockpit of the aircraft only twice. When he received no answer from the pilot, he threw his bulk foot-first into the flimsy door that separated the cockpit from the cabin of the plane. Dr. David Arlon was right behind him, looking like the frightened, wiry professor that he was. The door burst inward and Malcolm took in the sight in a fraction of a second.

There was only a pilot, no co-pilot. The pilot had no shirt on but was wearing a leather World War II flying helmet. The man had stabbed a large knife into his own stomach, and dragged it upward through his chest, spilling his intestines into his lap. There was a large tattoo of two Chinese characters on the man's carved open chest. He was obviously dead, and had probably been dead for at least part of the flight because his body was cold to Malcolm's touch. Malcolm's eyes swept slowly upward from the gaping wound to the instrument panel, where he saw several gauges and the liquid compass above the windshield had been smashed, and the fuel gauges read well below empty.

Somewhere in the back of Malcolm Brewer's consciousness, he heard the starboard engine quit. Finally his eyes continued their sweep to the view out of the stumbling aircraft's canopy windows. What he saw was a lot of snow and a lot of rock. All of it was big, and all of it was close.

"Oh, bloody hell," he said, loud enough for Eva to hear him.

CHAPTER 2

A large snowflake was gently swaying as it clung to Eva's eyelash like a man scrambling at a cliff's edge in a bad 1970's made-for-TV movie. When her eyes finally fluttered open, the delicate structure of the flake was disrupted, and the remains quickly turned to water on her cheekbone. There was blood in her right eye, and she groggily pawed at it. A few more blinks and her eyes were able to focus.

Eva's first thought was that she was outside. But that wasn't right. She was still in the passenger chair with her seat-belt fastened, and she was still in the plane, but she was also outside. The front half of the aircraft simply wasn't there. In fact, the seat that had been in front of hers wasn't there. She looked down to see the jagged tear across the floor of the plane's fuselage. Ahead of her was only a long sloping valley of snow between two hills on either side. She tried to stand, forgetting the seat-belt, and found that she couldn't. After unleashing herself, she stood and turned to look to the rear of the plane. Some snow was inside, but otherwise it looked normal. Then, she turned back to face the front of the plane and saw that it still was not there. No plane. No propellers. No cockpit. No David and Malcolm. Just *outside* and snow.

"Mal?" she called.

She took a step forward, and she was out of the aircraft. The wind was so strong it nearly knocked her down. She had been somewhat aware of the cold, but she had been completely sheltered from the wind in the plane's rear half. Struggling against the wind, she walked to the side of the broken plane and around the edge of the shredded metal skin. She could see what had happened immediately. The plane broke apart when it hit and her segment, the tail, had slid down the icy slope before spinning to a stop with its opening facing away from the rest of the wreckage. There was a wide trough in the snow where the tail had turned, and Eva thought of children making snow angels. Then, she looked up the long vista of snow-covered mountains and saw the blackened trail from where the plane had come, skidding and leaping as it must have. There was a trail of debris stretching off into the distance, but no single chunk of it was recognizable. She desperately scanned the distant hills for a sign of the other half of the fuselage, or a wing, or David.

"DAVID!!!" she wailed, but her voice was lost in the wind immediately. Regardless, she tried again. "MALCOLM!!!" Nothing but the fierce shriek of biting wind in her ears.

I'm not panicky yet, she told herself, but she knew that she would be. It was only the shock that was keeping her calm, if a little loopy. *That and maybe the concussion,* she thought as she raised a hand to touch the clotted blood on her forehead above her right eye. The area was tender and already swollen so much that it felt as if her forehead had grown a bony knee.

She looked wildly at the trail of wreckage and realized that it probably stretched for several hundred yards. Maybe more. *But you have the biggest part of the plane. Yes. First things first,* she thought. She headed back into the shelter of the fuselage fragment, and immediately felt warmer. *Bastard wind,* she thought and realized that her mind was starting to clear. Hopefully that wouldn't also mean she would start to panic and scream like a lunatic. She looked behind her seat and saw that her carry-on was still there. *Amazing,* she thought. Then she saw why, when she tried to lift it. The strap had caught on the bottom of her chair. *Thank God for the small things.*

Inside the bag, Eva found her Gore-Tex jacket and pants, as well as a fleece pullover. She quickly threw these things on, and then she pulled the purple fleece ear-band out of one of the jacket's pockets and slipped it over her head. *Great,* she thought, *keeps the ears warm and staunches the flow of blood on one's forehead too!* Sarcasm was better than panic any day, but she still felt it uncomfortably close to her like a leering uncle with bad breath. She also found her fleece gloves and an energy bar. Those were pretty much all the useful items she had. Eva then searched the rest of her half of the plane, looking for anything else that might be of use. There really wasn't that much. A small first-aid kit had some matches, which she hoped would be able to start a fire for warmth. Some of the chairs were still intact, and she thought she could burn the seat covers and the foam cores. Granted, it would stink to high heaven, but better the carcinogenic fumes than hypothermia.

A look at her watch revealed it was nearly two in the afternoon. Thing still worked. *Damn, Timex* does *take a licking,* she thought. Maybe three or four hours before nightfall. And she would still need time to start her fire. Okay. Two hours. That's what she could spare for a search. She would hike up the wreckage trail for one hour looking for David and Malcolm, before she'd have to turn back. She knew her chances of finding them were not very good. She also knew that the chance of finding parts of them was better than of finding them safe and well, but she refused to let her mind dwell in the morbid zone. She grabbed the thin fleece Xinjiang Airlines blanket that was still sitting on her chair and wrapped it around her head like a shawl. *Please let me find them*, she prayed, and then she stepped out into the gale.

CHAPTER 3

There hadn't been that many fires. There hadn't been much fuel left in the plane. She tried to keep her mind on the task at hand: finding David and Malcolm. But her mind kept wanting to leap ahead in the process.

What are you going to do when you find their bodies, and know you're all alone? What then, huh? Oh, a fire. That's good. How long will seat covers burn? Maybe until morning? And then? What are you gonna eat? How long will it take for a rescue team? This is China! Will there even be a rescue team? How long until—

Stop it, she told herself. *One thing at a time. One. Only one. Find them. They'll know what we should do. Malcolm will know.*

Eva trekked up the slope through the snow for forty minutes. Along the way, she would stop occasionally to look at a chunk of wreckage. She was looking for anything that might be of use to her in the hours or days ahead. There was no sign of either of the men, and there hadn't been a sizable chunk of plane in a while, when she came across a nylon bag. It was David's carry-on bag. There was a gash in the side, but it was otherwise intact. She quickly opened it and riffled through for more layers of warm clothing. She found a sweater that she took, and also his Swiss Army knife. The rest was books and folders. She left them. They didn't matter now.

The wind had died down some, but it was still plenty cold. She took off her jacket and threw David's sweater on over her fleece, and then put the jacket back on. She felt a little bulky with so many layers, but the warmth felt good. She checked the time, and then trudged on toward the next chunk of plane she could see in the distance. It was a portion of wing, she saw as she approached it. It was mostly covered by snow, which was why she hadn't seen it at first. She passed it and headed up a particularly slippery part of the slope to the crest of the hill. The view was better here than it had been back at her half of the plane. Most of the rest of the plane was here on this small plateau. The daylight was fading already. She had used up her hour just making it up to this plateau where the bulk of the fuselage and wreckage lay. She called out one more time.

"Malcolm!!! David!!!" She waited for a response for nearly a minute, then she started to cry softly as she walked across the plateau.

It took her longer to get back to the plane's tail than it had to walk away from it, and by the time she reached her shelter, the light was leaving the sky quickly. She made quick work of the seat covers with David's knife, and decided to start her fire in the rear of the fuselage. She would stay between the fire and the open end of the plane, trying to get as much fresh air from the wind, and as much warmth from the fire as possible. Luckily, the seat cover lit quickly and easily, and the foam worked too. She figured if she needed to, she would also light the fleece blanket and the sweater, and anything else that would burn.

Darkness fell abruptly and soon after the wind died almost completely, but the temperature plunged, and she found herself edging closer to the fire before long—noxious fumes or not. She sat on the aluminum base of one of the passenger seats, and slowly ate half of the energy bar she had. The other half would be for the next day and the really hard work.

She planned to leave the wrecked plane the next day. On the plateau, she had found Malcolm's body. She noticed the gray color of his skin, long before she saw that one of his arms was missing. Its arm was torn out at the shoulder (she had a hard time thinking of the mangled corpse as 'Malcolm'). After awhile, she thought she should bury him, but then realized she had no shovel, and the ground was frozen anyway. She needed to keep moving because there would be no one to bury *her*. Eva had searched the body, and found another Swiss knife and a packet of peanuts from a bar in Hong Kong. Malcolm had also been a smoker and she found his Zippo lighter. She pocketed the smooth silver lighter, said a brief prayer, and then continued on her way.

She ate the nuts as she looked for David. She didn't find him, but did find one of his hiking boots. Thankfully, there was no foot in the boot, but the boot was all she needed. They were both dead. She didn't need to see David's body to know that. There was a sports water bottle in her carry on, and she filled it now with snow, and held it close to the fire until the heat melted the snow. *No, I won't die of thirst*, she thought.

Eva wondered, not for the first time, what had happened. Why had they been going *west*? Why had they crashed? Why had there been no sign of the cockpit on the plateau? Where was that damn pilot? Did he crash the plane on purpose? She had to assume so, because they were going west before they crashed. She looked at the ridiculous fire she had made and saw that it would be time to light another seat cover soon. She knew there wouldn't be a rescue team. She would have to leave the plane and the wreckage behind if she was going to survive. She knew that. *Which way to go*, she mused. Where was she? If she was in Tibet, as she suspected, then most directions would be fatal. She would die long before she found civilization.

South then. Sooner or later, south will mean warmer. If I live long enough, warmth will be all that will matter. Eva laid down on the floor of the aircraft, and fell asleep in minutes.

CHAPTER 4

Eva woke early because she was cold and the wind was howling loudly. The fire had long since dwindled out, but the daylight was back now. She checked her Timex, only to find that it had stopped. *Figures*, she thought. She got up and slowly stretched her neck to the left until there was a loud popping sound from her cervical vertebrae realigning themselves. She stepped to the edge of the plane and looked at the sky. Clouds and gray, but not snowing.

"That's something at least."

She looked back into the fragmented fuselage and thought of making another fire with some of the remaining covers, then dismissed it. *Might as well get going.* She stepped back into the tail to collect the fleece blanket, which she hadn't gotten around to burning yet. She paused and thought about staying. *No, Eva, just go.* Then she walked out into the wilderness.

She had trudged through snow and slipped across patches of ice for what she guessed to be about three hours when she needed to rest, and she stopped to finish what was left of the energy bar. She thought she was heading south. She hoped she was heading south. The clouds obscured the sun for most of the day, but there were times when she could tell from the whiteness in the sky, from where it was that the source of light was emanating. She rested until the water in her sports bottle was gone, along with the last bite of chocolate-peanut butter something-or-other.

"No more food then," she said aloud. "I wonder if I can catch and kill a yak? Hell, I wonder if I'll even see a yak."

She filled the water bottle with snow and placed it inside her fleece against her t-shirt and under her breasts, hoping that her body warmth would melt the snow. Her head ached and she rubbed at the lump occasionally as she started once more. She told herself that sooner or later she'd likely come across a source of water like a river or creek. She'd then follow it south, hoping that she would eventually end up in a town or come across a road.

The temperature was dropping. She was cold, but her own heat from the exertion of hiking in the mountains was keeping her warm, if not hot at times. She tried to stay in the valleys between the hills as she went. The snow on the ground was deeper now and once she fell in up to her waist. She cursed herself for not thinking of trying to make some kind of snow-shoes out of plane parts or the seats, but it was too late for her to turn back now.

It was all still snow and rock. She hadn't seen a single plant or creature. Not even a bird. Barren was the only word that kept repeating in her head. *Barren,* but beautiful. Towering rock hills and mountains, with snow sprinkled on top. They looked absurdly like ice cream to her. Every time she had a thought like that, she wanted to turn to David or Malcolm, the men she had worked with for the last half year. The men she had joked with, laughed with, and shared her excitement of archeological finds with. Then, as her mind would start to crumble and she would be on the verge of tears, a different part of her mind would take hold. The drill instructor part of her mind. Steroid Eva. *Go! Keep moving, girl. Walk! Survive. That's all that matters. One foot in front of the other.* That would be enough to clear the watery edges of her eyes and sober her up. She would focus again on the task for maybe an hour before thoughts of the dead man with only one arm returned.

In spite of the concussion that she was now pretty sure she had, and the lack of food and the dead body, she still thought she would be alright. All she had to do was find a town. She figured that she was in Tibet and hoped that there would be some little towns, or maybe some nomad yak-herders near by. *Someone.* But then it started to snow.

In a couple of minutes, Eva was convinced that the storm would be big, but she had no idea just how big it would be. She carried on, stopping for a rest when she needed to catch her breath, but not drinking. She had forgotten she had the water bottle against her stomach. In what she guessed to be less than a half an hour later, she was in what was definitely a blizzard. The flakes were huge—at least one and a half to two inches in diameter, and the wind was sending what looked like full panels of snow across her path. It was hard to continue walking against the wind, but she kept moving forward. *It'll let up soon*, she told herself.

It didn't. She was now in a total white-out condition, and she was breathing heavier through the fleece blanket she was using as a sort of balaclava. Then she tripped and fell into a drift of snow that covered her entirely. She panicked and thrashed until she was free of the drift, but the snow was coming down so hard that she wasn't sure that she *was* free of it. When she got to her feet and began to walk again, she was going back in the direction she had come from. She was walking parallel to her original set of tracks, and apart from them by no more than a few feet, but she was completely unaware of them—at just a yard away, she couldn't see them. She fell a second time and hit her head on a rock, buried under the snow. A streak of pain ripped through her head and down her spine, and she thought it would never end. Finally, the pain subsided a bit, but she stayed in place, lying in the snow. The drift was high enough to block some of the wind. *Maybe I'll just lie here and take a nap*, she started to think, then… *NO!!!* The Steroid Eva took hold, and she was back on her feet, moving forward so quickly through the snow that she might have looked like she was running.

The blizzard slackened a bit and she could see the mountains around her again between gusts of biting wind. When Eva stumbled the next time, her Steroid self was gone. She lay in the snow for a moment looking up at the sky, wondering what she had done to deserve a fate like this. The tears poured from her eyes, and her sobs came in deep gulping sounds that reminded her of a horse drinking water from a trough. That thought made her cry harder, then the sound of her crying became more of a rasping noise. Suddenly it was the funniest thing she had ever heard, and she started cackling with laughter, fresh tears springing from her eyes.

She forced herself to sit up as the last of the giggles were subsiding, and she looked on into the swirling white madness and saw something move.

Her giggles were gone instantly and a feeling of dread filled her from her top to bottom, as if someone had just used her as a container and poured ice-water into her. Every nerve tingled with alarm. Then she saw it again. It was light colored, maybe white. *Could it be a… no, no, no, that's ridiculous*, she scolded herself. She didn't think there were bears in Tibet, but it did look a bit like a bear. She peered harder into the wind and flakes, and she caught another glimpse of it. It was definitely tall, and it looked like two legs—maybe it actually was a bear. Then a new thought occurred. *Not a bear. The Yeti. A bigfoot. Wasn't that the legend in the Himalaya? Yeti?* Her mind began to swirl like the storm around her as the creature approached. It was huge. At least twelve feet tall she guessed, and it was waving its arms at her as it rushed her. It was yellow she observed with a detached attitude. Darkness was creeping in at the edge of her vision, and her panic had been replaced by a wooziness that made her feel as if she were drunk. The creature had a dark face and a yellow body coated with shaggy hair. It was coming right up to her. She thought it would feast on her. It would eat her meat and pick its drool-covered teeth with the bones from her fingers as if they were toothpicks. The last thing Dr. Eva Rayjek saw, as the creature came in close and wrapped its huge arms around her, was its chest. It was directly in front of her eyes. It wasn't a hairy chest, and she was confused by the embroidered words she saw as she passed out:

The North Face.

CHAPTER 5

"Are you awake?"

Eva's eyes flicked open as if she had received a jolt of electricity. She was looking into the face of a woman with a dark tan. She was about to sit up when she felt a hand grab her shoulder and force her down.

"Oh no," the woman said. "Don't get up, it'll probably hurt your head if you sit up. Just lie there for a while and take it easy, okay?"

Eva saw the smile in the woman's eyes and decided to stay put. There was yellow everywhere, and Eva was vaguely aware that she was in some kind of tent, but it looked huge to her. She saw a nametag on the yellow jumpsuit the woman with the long dark hair was wearing: CRUZ.

"Cruz…?" Eva started to ask.

"Yeah, sorry. My name is Valentina Cruz. I'm from Mexico. You can call me Val."

When she said Mexico it sounded like *Meh-hi-co*, but otherwise, the woman's accent said Southern-California-sunshine.

"And you are…?" the woman asked.

"Dr. Eva Rayjek. My plane crashed in the mountains." Eva told her.

"Yes. I know. Jason found you out in the snow. Take it easy, Doctor. You have a concussion. Are you thirsty?"

Eva nodded, and Val handed her a plastic bottle and told her to sip from it. The liquid tasted like Kool-Aid to Eva. While she drank, Val answered some of the questions Eva wanted to ask, as if she already knew what Eva would want to know.

"You're still in the mountains. This is an engineering project camp. We heard the plane go down, and Jason and Curtis went to look for it. I'm sorry to say that they didn't find any other survivors. They brought you back here and you've been out of it for several hours. I was starting to get worried. I'm a seismologist, but I have some first aid training and that makes me the team medic by default. Don't worry, we'll get you back to civilization." Val's smile was soothing and Eva listened without interrupting while she slurped the rest of the sweet drink from the plastic straw in the bottle.

"Where exactly are we?" Eva asked.

"South of Qamdo, in Tibet" Val said, her pronunciation of Qamdo sounding like *Cham-do*.

"I want to sit up."

"Then do it slowly, Doctor," Val cautioned her.

Eva did and was surprised to find that her head felt fine. She smiled slowly, and Val smiled back at her.

"Okay?" Val asked her.

Eva nodded, the smile still on her face. She would be fine now. She looked around the room and saw that it was, in fact, a large yellow tent that she was in. Her first instinct was right—it was a *huge* tent. She was on a cot, and there were five other olive drab canvas cots like it in the tent with her and Val. There were large plastic cases that looked like the one Eva's brother, Lewis, kept his camera equipment in, and in the center of the room was what looked to Eva like a futuristic wood stove. Instead of the typical black cast iron, this thing was made of plastics and titanium-like metal. It was definitely a stove though. It was warm in the tent, and the thing had a long cylindrical shaft that went up to the ceiling, and out. The tent was round and maybe twelve feet tall at the center, where the stove's exhaust pipe led. To her right, there was a tunnel leading out of the tent. Eva started to get up to her feet, and Val looked alarmed.

"Are you sure…?" she started.

"I'm fine, Val. Thanks. But I need to pee like a racehorse." Eva smiled, but squinted a bit as she did so. They both laughed hard, and Val began to lead her toward the tunnel.

"This way," Val chuckled.

CHAPTER 6

"...the fuck should *I* know what it means?"

Eva heard the man before she saw him, as Val led her into a large cavern carved out of rock. The camp seemed massive to Eva. There were several interconnected gigantic, yellow, dome tents—all manufactured by The North Face, Eva noticed. Each one was capable of sleeping probably twelve people she guessed. They had mostly been full of futuristic looking equipment and large gray plastic cases like the ones in the tent she woke up in. Val had led her through most of the tents on their way to the portable toilet stall, and was now bringing her to meet the man in charge of the project: Jason Quinn.

"You're the China expert," said a tall man with blonde hair and a calm, almost bored look about him, who was against the far wall of the cavern. He was wearing a yellow jumpsuit like Val's, as well as a climbing harness. He was feeding rope out of it and up the rock wall of the cavern. Eva's eyes followed the trail of the pink and black rope as it arced across the ceiling of the cavern, which Eva guessed to be at least 50 feet up. The rope led through several anchoring aluminum carabiners that had been fixed to the ceiling somehow, and at the other end of the rope was Jason Quinn.

Eva's first impression was that the man was like a giant spider. He had to be, to be stuck onto the ceiling like that. She couldn't see his features beyond his head of dark, shoulder-length hair, because he faced the ceiling he was climbing. He was extremely tan, and wearing only black spandex shorts under a climbing harness, despite the cold in the icy cavern. The muscles in his back and calves were visible from where she stood looking up.

He wore a small chalk-bag on a belt around his waist. It swung back and forth on a small carabiner. His hands were coated in the chalk, and because of the chalk, they looked skeletal compared to the rest of his tanned body. His fingers were pinching what seemed to Eva to be little more than flakes of rock. On his feet, he wore lime-green rock climbing shoes with sticky rubber soles that seemed to be held to the rock ceiling by magic.

Eva was amazed to see him above her moving across the ceiling, with what looked to her like ease. He wasn't even sweating as he continued his conversation with the man belaying him.

"I know quite a bit about Chinese history, but I don't speak the language, Curtis," he said while reaching for another hold on the ceiling. "Maybe we should ask Eric. He's from Singapore, but maybe he can read characters."

Eva wasn't sure what kind of abdominal muscles it took to keep your center arched up against a curved ceiling as you held on by your toes and wrists. She was doubtful if she could do it for even a minute. Quinn had obviously been up there awhile.

"No good," the man named Curtis said, as he casually leaned against the far wall looking up with mild interest at Quinn. "He speaks Cantonese, but doesn't read characters. I already asked him. Guess we're gonna have to send them on to Marge."

"Watch me," Quinn cautioned, then sprung laterally off of his toes through the air a few feet before grabbing another larger hold. His legs came swinging off the ceiling as he did so. Eva was certain he would fall, but he raised his legs up and planted them onto the rock ceiling as if they were weightless.

"Already done," he said, resuming his conversation. "I uploaded the pics to Marge an hour ago. Now it's just wait-n-see."

"Hah-hmm!" Val cleared her throat to get the attention of the climbers.

Grinning like a Halloween Jack-O-Lantern, the man named Curtis intentionally let the rope slide through his hand, just as Quinn was making another move and fell. Quinn plunged toward the ground, and the rope made a zipping sound as it slid quickly through the anchor system. He came to a bouncing stop about three feet from the ground, and directly in front of the two women, his body suspended horizontally over the ice covered floor by the harness and rope. Curtis had closed two fingers over the rope as it slid through his belay device, and he had stopped Quinn with a fraction of a second to spare. He was still grinning at the ladies.

"You must be our Dr. Eva Rayjek," Quinn said with a lopsided grin of his own. "Jason Quinn. Welcome to Sunnydale."

He held out his hand from his horizontal stance, still swaying slightly.

Eva looked aghast. This man had nearly died. Or so she thought. Eva would later come to know that the whole fall had been orchestrated by the two men. The sort of thing these jokers did for fun. Curtis let go of the rope and Quinn fell to the ground with a thump. He then released a locking carabiner on his harness, freeing himself from the rope, and sauntered over from where he had been standing.

"Curtis Drake Johnson. It's a pleasure," he said as he shook Eva's hand. Quinn picked himself up off the floor, chuckling to himself.

"You guys…" Val said, with a stern look. "Little boys, *I swear.*"

CHAPTER 7

Later on, over a dinner of Mexican enchiladas in a huge yellow mess tent, Quinn answered some of Eva's questions. Seated around them at a collapsible full-sized picnic table, were the rest of the project's crew. Including Quinn, Johnson, and Cruz, there were ten of them, but they had all been introduced to Eva so quickly that she couldn't remember their names. Most were engineers.

Eva had told Quinn her version of the crash, and of her trek through the storm. He and Johnson detailed their search for the wreckage. They mentioned that they had found the cockpit and the pilot's body. They explained that he had committed suicide (although they left out the gruesome details), and told of the Chinese characters tattooed on the man's chest. Unfortunately, Eva was unable to help with the deciphering, as she had studied Greek and not Mandarin in grad school. Her interests in China had begun later and she had yet to find a reason for learning the language. David had been the linguistic expert.

"So that was you in the yellow suit that found me?" Eva guessed.

"Yes," Quinn answered. "It's an all-environment suit designed for outdoor work in the kind of cold we get around here. It's called a Yeti Suit."

Eva found that ironic, but was too embarrassed for thinking that Quinn had been an actual Yeti, to tell them about that part of her ordeal.

"The suit is designed with heating elements much like deep water dive suits," Quinn went on. "The faceplate of the helmet has a digital camera built in. That's how I was able to take a picture of the pilot's tattoo and send it on to my boss in Colorado. It's basically a spacesuit for mountaineers."

"So what exactly are you all doing here?" Eva wanted to know.

"Besides climbing?" Quinn asked with a smile. Eva thought he had a wonderfully winning smile. She liked the look of his sea-green eyes as well, but she wondered what kind of man unnecessarily risked his life to climb the ceiling of a cavern.

"You guys aren't, like, CIA or something are you?" she asked.

"No." Curtis smiled. "We're building a tunnel."

"A tunnel? In the middle of nowhere?"

"For a railroad from Chengdu to Lhasa. We're starting in the middle of the route, roughly, tunneling through the mountains that the rails can't go around." Johnson explained.

"I thought the Chinese had abandoned the idea of a rail line to Lhasa with tunnels through the mountains, after they consulted the Swiss, who said it was impossible. The Swiss are supposed to be the best tunnel builders in the world." Eva said.

Quinn and Johnson exchanged a quick quizzical look with raised eyebrows, then started to laugh.

"Oh shit, the lady knows her stuff," Johnson said, laughing.

Jason turned to Eva and explained. "Yes. The Chinese did ask the Swiss. And the Swiss did say it was impossible. That was why the Chinese initially went with a railroad from Golmud up in Qinghai instead."

"But the Swiss ain't the world's best tunnel builders." Curtis said, and his laughter ended abruptly. Everyone seated at the table joined Johnson in a chorus. "We are."

"And just exactly who are you?" Eva wanted to know over the cheerful laughing.

Jason told her when the laughter had died down a bit.

"ARGO is a small, private organization headquartered in Empire, Colorado. The name is an acronym. It stands for Alpine Research and Geographic Observation. Founded by Teddy Roosevelt in 1902, and named after the ship from his favorite Greek myth, ARGO was originally a small division of the U.S. government meant to handle all manner of scientific studies relating to alpine climates, as well as vulcanology, glaciology, and geographical anomalies. Roosevelt himself headed up the organization, and the original headquarters consisted of one small room in Washington D.C." Quinn took a hearty bite of his enchilada, swallowed, and then resumed his tale.

"After two years his presidential duties intensified, and Roosevelt appointed John Tower, a noted Canadian back woods explorer and mountaineer, as the new director. For nearly seventy years, ARGO quietly collected data and engaged in expeditions to remote parts of the globe. Our funding was cut under the Carter administration, and the decision was made to privatize. By that point, John Tower's son, William, had already taken over the position of director. William Tower was a shrewd and canny businessman and by the eighties, ARGO's fingers extended into GIS, engineering projects like tunnel building, product development for mountaineers, special projects for different governments, and even an occasional treasure hunt.

"The current organization has five hundred employees. We hire the best and the brightest from a variety of different fields, and they get paid an extravagant annual salary. ARGO was originally funded by U.S. government claims to half a dozen silver mines in Colorado. Today our projects, patents, investments, and the occasional salvage rights or treasure repatriation fees help to keep the organization funded. Additionally, we receive money from the Pentagon's fabled Black budget, for our assistance in training the military in alpine tactics, although it's hardly a secret that we train them." He smiled.

"In 1984, William Tower set off on an expedition to map a crevasse network in Antarctica. He never returned. ARGO sent a search party out, but no sign of the man or his three fellow explorers was ever found. His last will and testament named his wife, Margaret Tower as his beneficiary, and as the new Director of ARGO, in the event of his untimely demise or disappearance. Marge is our boss. She's turned ARGO into a multimillion-dollar corporation by bilking the government for additional funding and cleverly investing our profits. She had also hired me in 2004 and made me ARGO's Director of Asian Projects four years later. This railroad tunnel project is my third as D.A.P."

"I've never even heard of ARGO," Eva said.

"Not many have," Quinn answered. "But it's been around a long time. ARGO consulted on the construction of the Panama Canal. Since the fifties, we've trained the U.S. Marines in detecting tunnels at the South Korean border and we train Special Forces teams in alpine survival. ARGO was a part of the rescue team for that disastrous Everest expedition in '96. We even help NASA from time to time—we do all kinds of stuff. Basically, when something like the impossible tunnel from Chengdu to Lhasa needs to be built, we get a call and prove that it wasn't that impossible after all," Quinn said.

"Then what's Sunnydale? You said *Welcome to Sunnydale* before."

"That's what we call our little camp here, since Eric over there," Quinn pointed to the Asian man seated at the end of the table, "said he thought the North Face tents look like eggs: sunny side up."

Eric said, "I still wanna whip up the biggest damn omelet you've ever seen, Quinn."

More laughter.

Quinn took on a serious tone, as things quieted again and said, "Dr. Rayjek, I'm sorry about the loss of your colleagues."

"Eva, please. Do you think there's any chance of finding David?" she asked.

"Then make it Jason, and no. I'm sorry, but no. We didn't see any sign of him." Quinn told her.

After a moment of quiet, Eva asked "So. When do we start?"

Quinn just looked puzzled.

Johnson spoke first. "Uh… start what?"

"On the trek back to civilization?" Eva said.

"Trek?" Johnson seemed skeptical.

Quinn spoke up, "We have a supply chopper coming. You won't have to hike back to Hong Kong, don't worry."

"Great!" Eva was relieved. "When's the flight?"

"About a week from now."

"What?" Eva's face drooped and her relief was gone.

"We have a regularly scheduled chopper coming in a week. We could have gotten it here sooner, but Marge thought it best if we kept to our regular schedule, just in case there are more unfriendly folks like your tattooed pilot lurking around that want to off you. So, it seems you'll be our guest for a while. But don't worry, we're not going to put you to work." Quinn explained.

"Actually, I think I might appreciate some work, if I'm going to be here for a week. It'll keep my mind off of what happened."

"Okay," he smiled. "Let's see what we can do."

CHAPTER 8

Quinn seemed to be avoiding Eva during their week together, and she wasn't sure why. She found herself attracted to the man, and although she caught him looking at her a few times, he rarely spoke to her and seemed uncomfortable around her. She ended up talking with Johnson more, although he seemed odd to her as well. Johnson wasn't distant like Quinn, but he chewed over his own words in his mind before speaking, as if he were checking them against the lexicon in his head to make sure they were the exact words he wanted.

Curtis Johnson was a good looking man, with short blonde hair and piercing steel gray eyes that always seemed to be scanning for something recorded on the back of her retinas, when he spoke to her. He told great stories of the climbing adventures he and Quinn had been on in Switzerland, and he had a gift for recalling minute details. Eva was enthralled whenever he began a climbing story, but somehow unnerved when he would lapse into silence for uncomfortable periods of time examining her. At least, she noticed, he did that to everyone when he spoke to them. She also got the impression that Johnson felt protective of Quinn, and she noticed that Johnson was very careful in his stories about not revealing too much personal information about Quinn. She wondered if maybe Curtis was being deliberately vague because of his *own* attraction to Eva. But if that was the case, she saw no indication of it in Johnson's actions.

Mostly the week passed with work. The ARGO crew were among the hardest working people she had ever known. They would all be up before she was and well into the day's work. The second day she got up early and they hadn't started work yet, but Quinn and Johnson were climbing the cavern ceiling again. They were all up, laughing and having a good time late into the night, each night as well. She guessed that they all might sleep for three hours a night, but she saw no signs of strain on any of them.

There was a small tractor-like vehicle in the cavern called a SnowCat. Eric would drive it in and out of the tunnel opening at the back of the cavern all day. When he came out of the tunnel shaft, the 'Cat was loaded with large chunks of rock, and Eva, Curtis, and Val would unload the rock and toss it into a pile outside the camp. Jason and some of the others were working deeper down the shaft, where she was not permitted. Curtis told her that they were constructing supports. The work went on all day, with everyone telling jokes, and no one complaining. They stopped for a half-hour lunch around noon each day, and finished around eight. It was some of the hardest physical work Eva had ever done, but she was enjoying being a part of this jovial group. The first day she didn't realize how sore her muscles were until she lay down on her cot at nearly midnight. By the third day, she didn't feel sore at all. Most importantly, she was keeping her mind off the horrors of the plane crash, her dead colleagues, and the idea that someone had intentionally tried to kill them.

Shortly after lunch, the day before the helicopter was due to arrive, disaster hit. Curtis was in the cavern fixing a tread on the 'Cat. Jason was in the Comm Room—the tent at the exact center of the camp. The team kept their sat-linked computers there, as well as their radio equipment. Quinn was there to check on two of the team members he had sent out that morning. Jakes and Henrickson were on a nearby mountain, surveying and checking weather. The others were scattered around the camp. Val was in the Sleep Room, where the group all slept on cots, monitoring three laptop computers she had hooked up to seismic tremor detecting spikes which were fired out of a pneumatic handgun. She had fired them into the rock below the camp on their first day at Sunnydale. The rest of the ARGO team were clearing the helipad of snow and enjoying the sun, which had put in a brief appearance. Eva was on her way from the cavern to the Comm Room, when Jakes's voice came over the radio next to Jason.

"Hey Quinn, who's on top of Shan? I thought you were going to hold off on a summit attempt. 'Too easy', you said." Jakes's voice was clear over the radio.

"What are you talking about, you crazy Texan? No one's up on Shan." Quinn responded. *Shan* was the name the team used to refer to the mountain they had burrowed into. It was Chinese for mountain. The actual name of the peak was a Chinese name that only Eric could pronounce properly, so they all just called it Shan.

"Well, it sure as hell looks like there's two guys up near Shan's summit. If it ain't you then who is it?" Jakes sounded amused. Quinn was not.

"What are they doing up there, Jakes? Can you get a good look with your scope?" The Yeti Suit faceplate's digital camera also included zooming software, which allowed the wearer to enhance distant objects as if the lens were attached to one of the most powerful telephoto lenses available for regular single-lens-reflex cameras.

"What the hell? They're laying bangs. Jason, they're planting explosives above the camp. Why the...? Oh crap. Oh shit. Jason..." Jakes's voice went from confusion to dismay to panic in seconds.

The rumble of the detonation shook the little camp hard. Val's eyes started to glow as she initially thought she was getting an earthquake. As a seismologist, she was completely involved in her laptop as soon as she felt the first twitch in the ground. She had just enough time to wonder why the tremors were coming from the mountain, but not enough time to form the thought in her mind of the word Jakes was suddenly screaming into the radio in another tent.

"AVALANCHE!!!"

Thousands of cubic yards of snow flowed down the side of Shan like eerie white surf on some tropical island as its breakers curl into a prefect pipe before shattering against the reef. But there were no surfers on this wave of ice and snow. The two Chinese men who set the explosives were killed in the blast and their ragged bodies were swept away in the crushing snow. It took exactly 43 seconds from the time the high explosive charges set near the summit of the peak detonated until the time the massive surge of frozen water obliterated its way to the valley below, completely covering the camp and removing any sign of it, as Jakes and Henrickson looked on in horror from another nearby peak.

CHAPTER 9

Quinn knew. As soon as Jakes had said explosives, Quinn knew. Before Jakes had gotten the first two syllables of 'avalanche' out of his mouth, Quinn was sprinting from the Comm Room tent down the tent corridor toward the rock cavern, the only place that might be safe. Eva was between him and the cavern and he just grabbed her as he ran. He had taken one long step inside of the cavern just as the shockwave preceding the snowfall hit. He leapt with Eva deeper into the cavern, and then everything went black.

A blaring neon green light filled the cavern as Quinn activated a luminescent light that lined the seams of the yellow ARGO jumpsuit he wore. Parts of the cavern's ceiling had collapsed inward, and the area that had been the entrance to the cavern was now a pile of huge chunks of ice and rock. He saw that Eva was okay, if dazed. He activated the green light on her borrowed jumpsuit, then he started to look for Johnson, who he knew had been in the cavern. After a few seconds, he saw Johnson's boots extending from a three-foot high pile of ice and snow. He quickly grabbed the boots, and pulled with all his might. Curtis Johnson's body slid out of the snow and the heap collapsed inward slightly, once his body was no longer supporting it. Curtis coughed a few times and indicated he was fine with a dismissive wave of the hand.

Quinn then headed over to where the entrance to the cave had been and started to dig frantically at the snow. He hit solid ice all too soon, and with a frustrated grunt, he ran across the cavern and returned with an ice ax. Eva watched silently, beginning to understand what had just happened. Quinn chopped and sliced at the ice as fast as he could, thinking that he had to get the others out as quickly as possible. Chips of ice were flying through the air as if he were some famous Scandinavian ice sculptor working on a masterpiece with a three-speed chainsaw. After a few more swings with the ax, Curtis held Quinn's arm back. Johnson's own yellow ARGO jumpsuit was now aglow with the ghostly neon-green piping.

"Jason." Johnson said softly. "First, it's probably too late. Second, if they were alive, we might injure them with the axes as we tried to dig them out. We'll just have to hope that they were clear of the slide."

"They weren't," Quinn said as he lowered the ice tool. "They were in the lunch tent, and that wasn't a slide. Jakes radioed and said he saw two guys on the Shan setting explosives. The avalanche was directed at us."

"What are we going to do?" Eva asked. Quinn was surprised to see that she didn't look scared; she just looked angry and determined.

"We can't dig out without risking injuring anyone still trapped in the snow, or mutilating their bodies, if they're already dead," Quinn was regaining his composure now, "Besides, it looks like at least fifteen feet to where the opening was. That would be a lot of digging."

"So we wait for rescue from the ARGO chopper tomorrow?" Curtis asked doubtfully.

"No. They might go after the chopper, and they might come looking for survivors too. Anyone determined enough to blow up a mountain to get Eva, would be determined enough to check for her body." Quinn looked lost in thought as he answered their questions.

"You mean you still think this is about me? The same people who crashed my plane?" Eva looked worried.

"Yes. It would likely be the same people. No proof yet, but then no one else is trying to kill ARGO people this week either. So, if we can't dig our way out, and we can't stay here, it looks like there's only one choice left, Curtis." Quinn's look had gone from a frustrated concentration to a look of small triumph.

"Digger?" asked Johnson.

"Digger." Quinn led the way toward the tunnel at the far end of the partially collapsed cavern.

CHAPTER 10

He led them down the tunnel. A few areas had caved in slightly, but each cave-in only took a few minutes to clear a space large enough to pass, with all three of them working to remove chunks of rock and ice. The tunnel was longer than Eva would have thought. It took them about twenty minutes of walking, after they had cleared the last cave-in, before they came to the end. At the end of the cave was Digger.

The technical name, Curtis told her, was an All-Terrain Heavy Hydraulic Coring Unit. Digger looked to Eva like a space-aged tank. The vehicle was *huge*. The body was roughly cylindrical, and at least ten feet in diameter. The bottom of the body was a few feet off the floor of the cave, supported by treads on each side that looked like tank treads. In fact, they were. The same size and kind of treads on the Abrams M-1A1 main battle tank, only Digger's treads were made of a special titanium alloy. Between the treads were what looked like rectangular scoops, which was exactly what they were. The scoops rotated under the body of the vehicle, scooping drilled debris under and behind the hulking mass. The scoops were made of the same alloy as the treads. At the business end of the thing was the most spectacular accessory. The drill on the front of the unit was roughly conical in shape, but with rotating bands that alternated in clockwise and anti-clockwise directions across the sides of the cone. The bands had their own spinning drill bits. The drill looked like a sadistic dentist's wet dream. It was capable of coring a twelve-foot diameter tunnel through solid rock, metal, or ice. ARGO had yet to run up against anything Digger couldn't get through with a running start. Eva thought the thing looked like a cross between a submarine and a tank.

"So we are going to drill our way out? Won't that hurt anyone who might be trapped in the snow even worse than an ice ax?" Eva asked, as Quinn helped her climb through the rear hatch of the massive vehicle.

"We're not going to go that way. We're going to aim for the side of the mountain." Quinn told her.

The inside of the vehicle was plush. There was room for three people to sit at the front of the vehicle in the cockpit. The rear of Digger had room for equipment and extra passengers. There were spare Yeti suits and all kinds of camping gear in the back on the sides of the aisle. The Lexan, polycarbonate windshield was covered by a metal shield to deflect debris spewed from the drill. Quinn took the pilot's seat with Johnson operating the drill. The vehicle was propelled forward by a 1500 horsepower Textron Lycoming diesel engine, which was specially designed for the vehicle, a one-of-a-kind drilling tank designed and owned by ARGO. The drill was powered by a separate 400 horsepower motor and powerful hydraulic pistons. Curtis brought the drill up to full speed and the tunnel was filled with a high-pitched whine. Inside Digger, there was only a small sound, as the entire cabin was soundproofed. The engine roared in the cave as Quinn kicked Digger into reverse, with the intention of ramming the cone-shaped indent in the rock wall in front of them.

"Drill?" Quinn asked.

"Up to speed and ready to ruin some rock." Curtis replied.

Digger jolted forward and the drill ripped into the rock with a tearing shudder. Eva was stunned at how quiet the interior of the cabin was, and said so.

"Wanna hear the external mic?" Johnson asked, and without waiting for an answer, he pressed a blue button on his side of the cockpit's console.

Suddenly the interior of the cabin was filled with an ear-splitting shriek of rock being ground to small chunks by metal. The speakers inside the cabin were only on for a second, but it was long enough for Eva to be glad the vehicle was soundproofed.

"How about some tunes instead?" Quinn asked.

Johnson activated the stereo, and the speakers started playing the sounds of the Rolling Stones. Eva watched the men work, as Quinn drove the vehicle and Johnson worked some controls to continually adjust the drill speed when it would hit on something too hard to be drilled on the first try. Occasionally, Quinn would have to back Digger up to try ramming again. The men were silent, each thinking of the friends lost in the attack on the camp.

Then the first tremor hit.

"What the hell was…" Johnson started.

Then another tremor, this one bigger.

"More charges, to make sure anyone in the cavern isn't still breathing. These guys don't quit do they?" Quinn said. He ground his teeth in a snarl.

The cave above them collapsed. What little light had been available between the metal shield and the windshield from Digger's cave lamps winked out.

"Oh my God." Eva cried.

"Don't worry. Digger can still crawl through the cave-in. As long as we have traction, diesel, and air, we're good." Quinn reassured her.

"How much air do we have?"

"Enough."

But he wasn't really sure they did have enough. Digger was designed to operate for 20 hours without external air supply. He had enough diesel on board in back to keep the treads rolling and the drill spinning. Also, Digger had been designed so that the fuel could be refilled from within the vehicle, so even in a complete cave-in they would still be able to refuel if necessary. But he had felt the treads slide more than once on ice and mud, and he wasn't sure how long it would take to get out of the mountain without any problems. And it looked like they were going to have plenty of problems.

Another tremor struck and chunks of rock knocked on the ceiling of the vehicle from the freshly dug tunnel's roof.

"These guys are really starting to get on my nerves," Curtis said with a calm coolness that made Eva suspect that when *he* got pissed off, he might be more dangerous than Quinn. "I'm going to have to have a discussion with them when we get out of here."

"Oh yes," said Quinn.

Eva assumed the machismo was mostly to calm her, and it was working, so she was grateful.

CHAPTER 11

Digger was tearing into the rock and crawling forward at a speed of about three miles an hour. The tremors from further explosives came at an interval of about 20 minutes. There had been about seven of them, and twice Digger had been completely caved-in. Even buried under tons of rock, soil, and ice, the drilling machine still kept lurching onward.

Its three passengers had been silent for an hour. Each thinking their thoughts, as Quinn worked the gas, and Johnson worked the drill. Each cringed when the tremors came, and Quinn silently cursed their would-be assassins. His own confidence as to whether they would make it out of the mountain was beginning to erode.

Then the biggest explosion yet, caused a complete cave-in just as Quinn was reversing Digger across a patch of slippery ice and mud. When he put the huge machine into forward, there was no purchase and the treads began to spin. He reversed again and then tried forward.

"Crap!" Quinn yelled, as he reversed again. The treads spun. He tried forward. Each time, the vehicle lurched with the shift in gear. The treads still spun freely across the ice without propelling Digger into the rock. Johnson was looking somberly at Quinn. He knew full well that if Quinn could not get the drill back into the rock, that they would all die inside Digger. They had enough air for about seventeen hours, and plenty of fuel. Food and water wouldn't be an issue when their air supply died. When the air stopped, they would be finished.

The two men worked frantically to free the vehicle from the cave-in. There was one more tremor, although it was a faint one. Digger would lurch forward and backward as Quinn worked the directional controls, but to no effect. The

RPMs were into the red on the dashboard gauge, and still the vehicle was stuck fast. Eventually Curtis gently placed his hand on Quinn's shoulder. Quinn understood. He was about to roast the hydraulic transmission. He eased off the throttle, and cut the engine. Not a word passed between them. They were both thinking furiously, searching for a way out of the situation.

Eva had moved to the back of the cabin and sat slumped on the floor. She knew that their ride had been canceled, and that they would die of asphyxiation. Curtis sat still staring forward at the metal shield outside the canopy. Quinn knew that his friend was working over all the possible solutions to their dilemma and dismissing them one by one. Quinn gave a deep sigh and got up from his seat and walked to the back of the cabin and sat on the floor next to Eva.

"We'll think of something," he said, not really believing the words.

She looked at him and stared into his green eyes. She could see the hurt in there. The deaths of his friends weighed on him. She also saw his disgust at failing, and something deeper, older. She wasn't sure what it was, but she had a hunch that it had something to do with a woman. *It's always a woman*, she thought. She leaned close to him, and he put his arm around her shoulders.

"I know you will, Jason."

They sat quietly. After about twenty minutes, Johnson sat across from them on the floor.

"At least they're done bombing us," he said.

"Considerate bastards, aren't they," Quinn smiled weakly.

"Ideas?" Johnson asked.

Quinn shook his head.

"You?"

Johnson didn't reply. Then the cabin was quiet again. Jason closed his eyes to think. After awhile, the other two also closed their eyes. It was still refreshingly cool in the cabin, but Eva knew that it would get stuffy and warm all too soon. She still couldn't see any reason why someone would want to kill her. Had they meant to kill Malcolm and David too, or were her colleagues just casualties in the attempt on her life, as the ARGO team had been? She didn't know. She just didn't know. Eventually, after how long she wasn't sure, she drifted into a fitful sleep, her head resting on Jason Quinn's shoulder.

CHAPTER 12

Curtis Drake Johnson was four years older than Quinn. Born in 1976 to Reginald Drake Johnson, a U.S. diplomat, and his wife Mary, Curtis spent his younger years in Pakistan, Nigeria, New Zealand, and Washington D.C., as his father's career kept the family on the move every two years or so. He finished high school in Switzerland, stayed on there to attend an Alpine school, and later became a guide in the Jungfrau region.

He had met Quinn in 1995, on a mountain in Switzerland. The fifteen-year-old Quinn saved Johnson's nineteen-year-old ass, on the Eiger. Ever since, they had been good friends and climbing partners. In 1998, Johnson returned to the U.S. and moved into his family's winter home in Vail, Colorado. After a few years of working with the Rocky Mountain Rescue Service, Johnson started working for ARGO. At the same time, he worked on a B.S. in civil engineering, with ARGO paying his tuition.

After a separation of nearly six years, Quinn showed up on Johnson's doorstep one day for a visit. The two spent weeks climbing in the Rockies. The whole time, Johnson talked up Alpine Research and Geographical Observation, trying to convince Quinn to stay in Colorado. In the end, Quinn agreed to meet with Marge Tower. That was all it took. Johnson had known that would be the case. He could be persuasive, but Marge was someone who could simply *not* be refused.

Quinn was on board with ARGO from 2004. Four years later, he was promoted to Director of Asian Projects. Johnson was also offered a promotion at the same time. Marge offered him the Director of European Projects (DEP) position, but he refused in favor of staying by Jason Quinn's side. Quinn was still unaware that Johnson had been offered the position and turned it down.

That was the way Johnson played things. Close to the vest, but loyal to the end. They were both making more money than either could spend, as a result of ARGO's enormous pay scale. The only thing Johnson would have gotten out of the promotion was more responsibility and separation from his friend, but even if they were being paid normal salaries and the promotion had been for a lot more money, he still would have turned it down. The two of them just had *too* much fun together. Curtis Drake Johnson couldn't think of any other way he would rather die than by the side of his friend, and he knew that Quinn felt the same way about him. They had been through some tough times together, but when they were together anything seemed possible, and all was laughter—or at least smart ass comments.

Johnson awoke with a start. Digger had just jolted again, and his first thought was that they were being bombed again. He looked across to where Jason and Eva had been to find them gone. Then he looked forward and saw that Quinn was in the driver's seat again. Eva stood a short distance behind his chair, watching with concern and holding a handrail on the cabin wall.

Quinn was ramming the vehicle from forward to reverse and back again. Johnson was about to say something about the transmission, when he realized that it really didn't matter if Quinn burned it out or not. They were stuck, and if they didn't get out, they would all die for sure. Johnson stood, holding the rail Eva clutched and walked up behind her silently.

Quinn was furious. He was revving the engine as high as it would go, and jamming on the gearshift lever with all of his strength. He looked as if he was mentally cursing the vehicle, the killers that had buried them alive, and any and all gods within hearing distance of his mind. Sweat was standing on his forehead, as he angrily worked the drive levers and the throttle.

Digger was jolting back and forth so quickly now that Curtis thought if it wasn't buried, it would look like a giant rocking horse. He actually had trouble holding on to the rail, as the vehicle bucked back and forth violently.

Just when Curtis thought it felt like the treads were maybe gripping a little, Quinn's fury let loose. The younger man was standing in front of the driver's seat, shoving the gear lever hard, as he began to yell at the top of his lungs.

The vehicle lurched and bucked hard and fast like a bull with a vise grip on its nuts and a foolish cowboy with a ten-gallon Stetson riding its back. *Forward. Backward. Forward.* Quinn flicked the switch to start the drill's rotations. *Forward. Backward. Forward. Backward. Forward.*

Eva and Curtis watched the man's mounting fury, wondering with open-mouthed horror, which would break first, Jason Quinn or the stubborn machine. Really, in the end it was no contest. Quinn worked the controls with blazing hatred, grunting, sweating, and cursing. Johnson knew he would not give up. His anger at the killers was driving him onward relentlessly. He would refuse to end up buried under a mountain in China. It just would not happen.

Johnson knew that Quinn would keep fighting, grunting, and struggling until he drew his last breath—the lapse in his effort earlier was a minor fling with defeat. Now that he had had a short while to rest, Quinn was attacking the problem with all of his energy and all of his relentless determination.

"Mother!"

Backward.

"Fucker!"

Forward.

"Must!"

Backward.

"Pay!"

Forward.

Digger lurched forward hard, throwing Eva to the floor, and Quinn into the windshield. Johnson heard it though. The familiar muted scrunching sound of the drill biting into the rock and tearing it asunder. Digger was on the move again! Johnson leapt over Eva and hopped into the co-pilot seat to adjust the speed of the drill. Now that they were moving, it would be ridiculous to blow the motor on the drill, and end up stuck again. Quinn lowered the RPMs and slumped into the driver's seat, with a determined angry scowl on his face. He pushed the vehicle forward at a steady sensible pace and the treads continued to grip the icy ground, and the drill chewed the rock as it had done earlier.

As Eva stood and cautiously approached the men, Quinn spoke to her calmly without looking at her.

"Are you okay, Eva?"

"Yeah. I'm fine." she told him.

"Then take a seat," he said. "We're on our way."

CHAPTER 13

The rest of the drilling went smoothly. There were no more bombings or tremors. No more cave collapses. Digger crawled on solidly. Even though they had just lost several friends in the senseless avalanche, the general mood inside of Digger's cabin was light, because everyone was feeling euphoric about Quinn's spectacular tread-freeing maneuver.

About two hours later, the mood was starting to dull as the monotony of the slow motion and seemingly unending drilling took its toll on their spirit. Then, as Eva was about to ask if they were ever going to get out from under the mountain, they did.

There was a lurching forward motion as Digger suddenly had no more resistance, and a blinding light came through the windscreen at the top, above the metal shield. Jason stopped the vehicle for a moment, then lowered the metal rock shield with a switch on the dashboard. It lowered slowly, showing the snow covered landscape of craggy mountains and plunging valleys. The sky was clear; the sun was shining brightly through the windshield. Johnson cut the power to the drill.

"Finally." Quinn voiced what they were all thinking. "Hang on a minute."

Quinn started Digger moving forward again, pulling the vehicle completely out of the mountain. Then he shut the engine off, and touched a button labeled PURGE. Air vents opened, and exchanged the cabin's air for clean air from outside. It was cold, but Eva thought it felt refreshing.

"Let's get out and stretch our legs," Quinn suggested.

The air was cold, but not too cold. The three got out and took a few steps around the drilling vehicle. They blinked at the brightness of the sun reflected off the snow around them. They each said their silent thanks at being free from the nightmare of being buried alive.

"Now what?" Eva asked. "Are the killers still around?"

"I don't think so. The explosions stopped a long time ago." Curtis said.

"Yeah. I agree." Quinn said. "Now we detach the drill assembly and turn Digger into an all terrain car and drive south."

"Where are we headed, Jason?" Eva felt confident that if anyone could get her to safety, Quinn would. He seemed determined not to let them die, no matter what.

"India. From there, back to the States. The last thing we want to do is show our faces in some little Chinese mountain town around here. If our bad guys *are* still around somewhere, it'll probably be in the nearby towns. So we drive until we run out of gas, then hike to the nearest road heading to India. Once we find a road, we should be able to hitch a ride on a truck."

"Jakes and Henrickson?" Curtis asked.

"If any of the others are still alive, they'll know to keep a low profile until the chopper comes or get out on foot. If we go back toward them now, we could be bringing more danger their way."

The men set to work separating the drill assembly from the rest of the vehicle, as Eva refueled Digger from the fuel cans inside. They were off in twenty minutes and heading south. Digger's powerful engine propelled them across the rough terrain at around 40 mph, now that it was free of the weight of the drill.

"I can't believe you're just going to leave the drill behind. Isn't that thing expensive?" Eva questioned Curtis.

"Like nobody's business, but we'd have a tough time driving with it. ARGO can always send a team to retrieve it later. Besides, we wouldn't be able to see where we were going with that thing in front of us." Johnson told her.

Eva had to admit to herself that it was nice to be able to see that they were moving now through the canopy windshield. Quinn was driving Digger across the rocks and snow as if he were on a Sunday drive. He seemed totally relaxed and in command. It was hard for Eva to believe that this was the man who looked like he was about to suffer from a nuclear meltdown only hours ago. But then she also had to admit that she didn't think his terrifying tantrum would have the results it did. She was glad now that he had gotten as mad as he did, or else they'd still be entombed in the mountains and slowly suffocating to death.

They drove through the rocky valleys between the mountains, heading south when the terrain allowed them to do so. Occasionally, they had to go well out of their way to get back to a path to the south. They had driven for four hours and still not come to any signs of civilization. Quinn was hoping for a road, because he knew he could make great time on a paved surface. Digger's top speed on asphalt was 60 mph, without the drill assembly.

"Note to self: Install GPS unit on Digger," Curtis said, with a grin.

"Yeah, no shit," Quinn smiled. "Would be nice to know where the hell we are. Can't believe we never thought of putting a global positioning unit on this thing. But then I never thought I'd be taking her for a spin through the uncharted Tibetan countryside."

"Well, it *is* a nice day for a drive."

"Too true. We should also get The North Face to add GPS software to the next Yeti Suits." Quinn said.

"Good idea," Johnson laughed. "How much fuel left?"

"Maybe a half hour. Any gas left in the cans, Eva?"

"No. I poured it all into the tank."

"That's it then. We walk in about half an hour," Quinn announced.

"I'll get some gear together." Curtis got up and headed into the rear of the cabin. He got them each a Yeti suit from a footlocker. Eva's was a bit too big, but Curtis told her it would work fine. He also packed a yellow backpack with a small stove, plastic packets that contained dehydrated food, and a tent. He grabbed another pack that had climbing gear in it: old-fashioned ice crampons, harnesses, nylon slings, a rope, and ice axes. Johnson wasn't sure if they would need to climb or not, but he thought it couldn't hurt. There was a lot of ground to cover between wherever they were and an airport in Northern India.

Johnson checked and rechecked their gear, then rejoined Quinn and Eva in the cockpit where they silently awaited the gurgling of the engine as it ran out of fuel.

CHAPTER 14

"Doesn't he look like a damn gunslinger?" Curtis asked Eva with a smile.

They had been hiking for a while. Johnson carried the backpack with the climbing gear, and Quinn was loaded up with the camping equipment, two ice axes hanging from the waist belt of his harness by short slings with carabiners. These axes had been specially designed for him with carbon-fiber blades made from Buckminster-Fullerene, a special form of carbon reputed to be harder than diamond. On his feet were huge clunky white plastic boots that looked to Eva like skiing boots, but these had metal teeth that retracted into the toes and soles. Eva knew what ice climbing crampons looked like, but she had never seen any that were a part of the shoe itself. Usually, she knew, they resembled a foot-shaped metal cage with teeth, and were attached to the bottom of climbing or hiking boots. What she didn't know was that the boots on Quinn's feet had also been made specifically for him, and to his own original design specs. The climbing crampon teeth were spring-loaded and could be ejected from the soles of the boots at the push of a button.

Eva had protested the fact that the men hadn't given her a pack to carry, but the men had looked at each other and then proclaimed that there wasn't anything left to carry—almost as if they had planned it that way.

"Yes. But he's a cute gunslinger. More young Clint Eastwood than Jack Palance," Eva replied, loud enough for Quinn to overhear as he walked slightly ahead of the other two.

"Hear that? She thinks I'm the cute one." Quinn added. "Guess that makes you scraggly ol' Lee Marvin."

They all chuckled at that one. They had been joking like this for a while, as the terrain was becoming more and more bleak and depressing. They had seen no signs of any kind of life. No plants or trees grew in this part of the Himalaya. The mountains were a palette of muted brown and gray colors— when they did actually show through the ice and snow. As they progressed along the barren winter landscape, they encountered the brown less frequently as the drifted snow became more difficult to negotiate, often getting waist deep.

After a night camping, they moved on again. By the middle of the day, the level of accumulated snow was decreasing, and the browns and grays were more apparent once again. The three lunched by a frozen river, and soaked in the sun, which was warming in spite of the altitude. The conversation focused on guessing the origin of their dehydrated packaged food.

When they had finished and Quinn and Johnson had packed the gear and hefted their backpacks, Eva sauntered off ahead of them as they neared the frozen river. Earlier, Johnson had suggested a way through the hills that followed a valley on the other side of the river. When Eva reached the edge of the stream, she took a tentative step on the surface of the ice, finding that it held her weight nicely.

"It should be fine. We'll go across one at a time though," Johnson told her.

She was about three quarters of the way across when Quinn and Johnson watched her plunge clean through the ice, and into the rushing waters below, disappearing instantaneously.

"Not good," Quinn said calmly as he began sprinting toward the ice. Curtis was right behind him, running hard. Quinn lunged from the shore landing on his knees on the ice about ten feet downstream of the spot where Eva had gone in. He frantically swept the snow aside to find that he was right on top of her. She was moving fast, being slid along the underside of the ice by the current. Quinn hacked at the ice above her with his ice ax, but the ice was too thick at this part of the river, and he was barely making a dent, as small chips and flakes of ice flew in an arc behind each swing. She was moving too fast.

"I can't get her, Curtis! She's getting away!" Quinn was nearly panicked. The strain in his voice was apparent to Johnson, who was already sprinting along the edge of the stream, past Quinn. Johnson was anticipating where the current would take Eva, and trying to get there first.

"Move your ass, Quinn!" Curtis yelled. Quinn was up and chasing Curtis along the bank. Curtis was well ahead by now, and removing his pack. He clipped a carabiner to his belt, and tossed the pack onto the ice as he kept running. Quinn could see that the neon green and pink climbing rope from the pack was spooling out as Curtis ran. The other end was now clipped to Johnson's belt. Then Quinn watched in awe of his friend, as Curtis leapt from the riverbank and pulled his knees to his chest in mid-air. Curtis Johnson executed a perfect *cannonball* directly into the center of the frozen stream, and crashed through the ice, leaving behind a nearly perfect, round hole in the surface. He disappeared and Quinn understood as the climbing rope quickly slithered into the hole.

"Got it," Quinn said, as he leapt headfirst out over the ice as if to dive into the shallow end of a swimming pool. He hit the ice smoothly and his yellow environment suit's nylon surface slid across the ice with little friction. He was moving fast, head first, across the ice toward the pack Curtis had dropped. But now the rope pulled taught on the other carabiner that secured the rope to the inside of the pack. The pack began to slide toward the hole at an amazing speed.

"Current's picked up. Damn it!" Quinn reached for the pack with his left hand and still clutched the ax in his right. He was a few feet from the hole when his finger felt a nylon strap. He clenched his fist and swung the ax down hard. It sank into the surface up to the shaft, and his body pivoted from the momentum. He clutched the pack firmly and let his body jerk to a hard stop. His shoulder felt torn, but he gripped the pack strap as hard as he could. He looked behind him to see that his feet were now dangling over the hole Curtis had made. Another second and they all might have been dead, their corpses washing ashore somewhere in India. Now Quinn pulled a leg up by the sunken head of the ice ax and clicked a plastic button on the side of his boot by smacking the boot on the ice. The spring-loaded climbing crampons extended with a snapping sound. Then he brought the boot down hard, digging the metal teeth into the ice. Next, he pulled the pack to his body, and wrapped the rope around his arm twice. Now he was an anchor. Curtis would have to do the rest.

It took a few seconds that seemed longer, before Quinn felt a steady pull on the rope. He waited. It seemed to take forever. His right arm ached, as he clutched the ax, and he prayed that the ice below him didn't crack. A minute passed, and still there was nothing.

Then she was there. Eva broke the surface with a gasp, sucking in air, and clinging to the pack that Quinn held. She was about to say something to Quinn, when to his surprise, she literally launched out of the hole, and over Quinn, where she landed on the ice in a crumpled wet mess. Quinn's eyes shot back to the hole where Johnson's arm was extended after having shoved Eva up and out of the water. From the position of the hand, Quinn guessed that it had been on Eva's backside, and he barked a harsh laugh, as Johnson hauled himself out of the hole and gulped in frigid mountain air.

"Good thinking," Quinn told him.

Johnson took in the scene with the pack, the ice ax, and the boot crampons, and nodded. "Good save."

"Good teamwork," Eva managed through her violent shivering. "Now let's get off this damn ice and get warm."

CHAPTER 15

Curtis thought Quinn's shoulder looked terrible. It was obviously dislocated. The flesh had turned purple from torn blood vessels, and the head of the humerus, the long bone in the upper arm, was now located about a fist's width to the front of Quinn's shoulder joint. In all their years of climbing together, it was the worst injury he had ever seen Jason Quinn sustain.

Curtis had always held a secret belief that Quinn was charmed with regard to personal injury. The man rarely got injured, and when he did, he tended to heal extremely fast. One time when climbing on Pinnacle Peak in Arizona, Johnson looked on in concern as Quinn showed the 6-inch gash to his forearm he received on a tough lieback crack called "Lizard's Lips." Quinn had wrapped it in gauze and they had headed home. The next day, Johnson was stunned to see Quinn's cut sealed, and a week later, it was gone, with hardly a trace of a scar. As a result, Johnson was rarely alarmed when Quinn got slightly injured. But this one looked *harsh*.

"Oh, it looks fine. I don't think we need to do anything with it," Curtis commented nonchalantly.

Quinn was lying on the snow-covered ground with the top of his environment suit off, and pulled down to his waist. He wore only a thin Capilene tank top, and he was already beginning to shiver from the cold.

"Can the sarcasm and just do it," he said.

"I can't watch this. This is just too gross." Eva said as she turned away.

Curtis held Quinn's outstretched hand, pulled the arm outward slightly, and raised the heel of his mountain boot. In one swift movement he brought his foot down on Quinn's disfigured shoulder joint, driving the head of the humerus down into the joint where it belonged. The sound reminded

Johnson of the report of a Colt 44 pistol. The crack was loud, and Quinn cringed at the pain but didn't cry out. He refused to let his pain do anything other than make him angrier at the killers who had murdered his team. His resolve to get answers and justice only grew stronger with the blaze of red and black that filled his vision as the pain vibrated through his whole skeleton.

After a moment of breathing heavily, Quinn got up and helped Johnson set up their tent. It was another garishly bright yellow TNF geodesic-dome tent. Quinn's pack contained a miniature version of the futuristic stove Eva had seen back at the Sunnydale camp. After it was set up in the tent, the heat from the stove took only a few minutes to dry Curtis's and Eva's still damp synthetic fiber clothing after Quinn had wrung the garments out. In the meantime, they huddled in compressible micro-fiber fleece blankets. Since he wasn't wet, Quinn hung his blanket from the gear loft near the tent's ceiling, effectively creating a wall separating the tent into two halves, so that Eva could undress in private.

They sat in silence. Eva thought about her deceased colleagues. Johnson thought about the seismologist Val, and how he was supposed to have had a date with her once they had all returned to the States. That wouldn't be happening now. Instead, he would be attending a lot of funerals—if they made it back to the States.

Quinn saw only a blistering haze of crimson as his thoughts turned repeatedly to revenge. He hadn't been truly involved in his heart or his head with Eva's mysterious plane crash, although he *was* attracted to her. He had been willing to believe that there was some explanation for the plane crash. But now there was no mystery. Someone had deliberately tried to kill Eva and the other two archeologists. And now the bastards that were after her had come back and tried again. Only this time they had murdered his entire team. Eight people whose lives were entrusted to him were dead, he himself had been buried alive three times in one day, and Johnson and Eva were nearly drowned.

Oh yes, he thought. *I am completely involved now.*

He went out of the tent and filled a small plastic re-sealable bag with snow and chunks of ice he carved out of the frozen ground with the retractable spikes on his boots. When the bag was full, he used a roll of neon-green duct tape to strap it to his aching shoulder and pulled his environment suit on over the improvised ice pack. He thought dark and grim thoughts the whole time. He wanted answers. He wanted names. He wanted to see someone bleed…

After Curtis and Eva were just finished dressing and Quinn had come back into the tent, Eva heard the sound.

"What's that noise?" she asked.

"Helicopter." Quinn frowned as he went back out again.

The other two followed him out and scanned the skies for the distant thumping sound. Snow was beginning to fall again. They were close to the river they had just escaped, and as Quinn searched the sky for a helicopter, he realized they were completely hemmed in on all sides by the dusty brown hills and brilliant blue and white snow covered mountains. They were in a valley, and they were sitting ducks if the chopper wasn't friendly. He was about to suggest they try to find some cover somewhere, but it was too late.

The twin-turbine Bell 214 helicopter came screaming over a low range of hills and into the valley. It was the regularly scheduled ARGO supply helicopter that was supposed to stop by the Sunnydale camp. The logo on the side of the white fuselage simply said *ARGO* with a stylized mountaineering ice ax underlining the acronym. But it was a day early, and it was moving way too fast.

"Crap on toast!" Johnson clearly understood the implications of the helicopter's untimely arrival.

They were all running in different directions when the angry sputtering blizzard of gunfire began. The line of fire ripped right through their tent, and the spot where they had all been standing just seconds before. Quinn recognized the sound. It was the almost leisurely cycle of an AK-47 assault rifle. The chopper blazed past on its first attack run, and Quinn caught a glimpse of both the unfamiliar Chinese pilot and the gunman in the open side cargo door with the Russian-designed weapon. Quinn continued his sprint back toward the river, hoping the helicopter would follow him.

Eva had changed her path to catch up with Curtis, and the two of them scrambled frantically for the cover of some small rocks and boulders. The helicopter had turned and was coming in fast and low, straight toward Quinn, since Johnson and Eva were now crouched down and out of sight. The rifle burst to life again, and a series of what looked like fountains of snow erupted straight up out of the ground, as bullets swept in a line toward Quinn. Just as the line of fire was about to rip him in half, he leapt up and sideways, landing hard in the snow, on his already injured shoulder. He swore, rolled, and sprinted in the other direction, back toward their camp. The helicopter banked sharply, and came at Quinn again. This time as the line of fire raked near to Quinn, he leapt into the air and performed an excellent back flip, landing in the snow on his stomach. The bullets grazed by close enough for him to smell the scorched air in their trail. He was getting tired and knew he had to do something about the shooter first.

As the helicopter raced skyward to perform another twisting banking maneuver, Quinn sprinted for all he was worth toward the frozen river, and dove head first into a slide across the ice. When he hit the other bank, he scooped up a rock the size of a melon, rolled, got to his feet, and stood perfectly still on the ice with an angry, defiant look on his face. The rock, held slightly behind his thigh, was concealed from the view of the approaching helicopter.

Quinn made no move and the approaching helicopter slowed. He could see the shooter replacing the curved magazine on the rifle, and chambering the first round. The helicopter slowed to a crawl, hovering over the frozen river, and turning broadside toward Quinn, so the open cargo door faced him head-on. The Chinese rifleman just looked slightly puzzled. Quinn didn't ˙ move. He just breathed in slowly, readying himself for the task ahead. Curtis and Eva looked on in frightened silence from their hiding place.

"What the hell is he doing?" Curtis asked.

When it happened, it was like a slow motion scene from a fast-paced Hong Kong action movie. Curtis could swear that both Quinn and the Chinese shooter moved in perfect unison like gun-fighters in the Old West. The shooter had switched to single-fire, leveled the rifle and fired a round in one fluid motion. Quinn sprung into the air horizontally, and launched his rock with his injured right arm. The bullet grazed Quinn's shoulder as he was in mid-leap. The plastic sack of snow and ice sprayed outwards away from Quinn's body, as did a small arcing spurt of blood. About a fraction of a second later, the rock smashed into the shooter's face, which burst in a geyser of twinkling maroon droplets. The man's body pitched forward, rifle and all, plunged downwards, crashed through the frozen surface of the river just a couple of feet below the helicopter, and disappeared from view completely. Quinn crashed into a crumpled heap in the snow on the bank, and Curtis came rushing toward him. Eva remained behind and watched as the confused helicopter pilot suddenly banked the craft hard and raced away from the scene. At first, it looked as if the man would completely retreat, but then the vehicle turned again, and launched forward as if fired from a large slingshot, only this time it was coming in at a steep bank, as if the pilot hoped to slice Quinn and Johnson to pieces with the rotor blades.

"Un-imaginative fuck," Quinn shouted. Curtis, who had just arrived as Quinn was getting to his feet, chuckled as he had been thinking the same thing when he saw the pilot dip the blades and launch his new action-movie-inspired attack. The men both dove in opposite directions into the snow to escape the roaring blades, as the craft shot over them.

"Nice move with the AK. Now what?" Curtis yelled over the roar or the attacking chopper, as they stumbled to their feet in preparation for the next pass.

"Keep him guessing."

Quinn sprinted away from Curtis, and the pilot now found he had to choose a target. He went for Johnson. As soon as Quinn saw, he shifted the direction of his run, back toward Johnson, and the helicopter bearing down on him. Johnson dove laterally into the snow and Quinn came into the pilot's view long enough to catch the pilot's eye. The chopper shifted direction wildly. Quinn sprinted again, and then dove to his right into a deep snowdrift as Johnson was again coming into the pilot's view. The tactic was working. The pilot couldn't decide who to chase and was getting frustrated. Finally, he decided on Quinn and stuck with him. Quinn knew it wouldn't take long. The dance between the slicing blades and the running man continued, and Johnson took advantage of his own brief respite to run toward the shredded campsite. He grabbed a climbing rope with an aluminum carabiner attached to it and began swinging it overhead like a lasso. He really didn't expect it to work, but thought: *What the hell?*

Johnson ran toward the battle scene, most of the rope trailing behind him, and a ten-foot long section of it swirling over his head with the weight of the aluminum *biner*. Eva thought momentarily that he looked like he was trying to become some kind of human helicopter, to battle the maddened pilot of the ARGO supply vehicle. As Quinn once again checked his running in time to dive away from the rotor blades, Johnson reached the distance he needed, and launched his makeshift bolas weapon. The rope sailed through the air, biner first, but as it approached the rotors, they sliced the rope into an array of short lengths, and the flight of the craft wasn't even affected.

The craft aimed at Johnson next, and Quinn just managed to escape the horrible blast of the blades. Quinn was up on his feet again and running toward the helicopter as it banked. This time the pilot banked so that the rotor blades were closer to the ground. He knew Quinn would try to leap aside at the last minute, and the pilot planned to yank hard on the control stick as soon as he detected which direction his quarry would turn—which is exactly why Quinn's plan worked. As the craft almost smashed head on into him, Quinn flung himself backwards onto the ground. He landed on his back with a bone-jarring thump, and the whirl of the blades was over his face almost instantly. A second later, Quinn reached up.

Then the world was flying by. He had grabbed the landing strut with both arms and gotten his left leg hooked around it as well. The timing was split second—but it had worked. Quinn was now hitching a free ride, just a few feet off the ground as the helicopter raced ahead and prepared to make its turn for the next attack run. As the craft began to gain altitude for its turn, Quinn released his grip. The ride had landed him on the hard packed snow close to the ruins of the campsite. Johnson saw the unusual stunt and ran a little slower, acting as a lure for the chopper. He suspected Quinn had something up his sleeve. He just hoped it worked and that it worked quickly.

Johnson and Quinn were in their 30s. Both men were at the peak of human fitness from mountaineering and non-stop training for their climbing trips. But even those in excellent physical shape can only take so much. Johnson was huffing and puffing heavily, as the sustained running and jumping had nearly worn him out. A plume of breath came out of his nose and mouth as he ran.

He scanned the ground and found what he was looking for. He lunged downward, scooped up his own good-sized rock, turned, and launched it toward the cockpit of the helicopter as it roared at him. The rock smashed into the Plexiglas and sent out fracture lines, but the pilot of the craft wasn't fazed. The damage was certainly not enough to be cause for ending the chase.

The pilot banked once again, and was planning to bring the rotor blades within inches of the ground. He was tiring of the game, and wanted the infidels to die already. As he brought the vehicle up to turn, Quinn was running away from the ruins of the camp and toward the chopper again. But this time his hands were full. In his left, he held the flare gun that had been in his pack, and in his right, he held the twin ice axes connected by the nylon webbing. He brought the flare gun up and fired it at the chopper during its bank. The flare went right into the cargo compartment. The interior burst into flame. There was no big Hollywood-style explosion as Eva had expected, as she watched the craziness from the shelter of her boulder. Just some small flames in the interior of the bird as it raced again at Quinn.

The pilot was distracted by the flame. Concerned, if not panicked. It was all Quinn had been hoping for. His next trick would be tough and would certainly be harder if the pilot was hell bent on killing him with the blades. Jason Quinn waited as long as he could. The helicopter was coming for him. Slower than it had been perhaps, but the rotor blades would carve him up at any speed. Instead of the bolas-style attack Curtis had used, Quinn just threw the axes straight at the rotor blades, aiming for the motor mount. The blades and the core of the ax shafts were made from one of the hardest substances known to man. *If they won't fuck up the damn blades, then I don't know what will.* He just stood still watching the damage unfold, waiting to see which direction he should dodge to avoid any shrapnel if there would be time. As it turned out, he decided to stand perfectly still.

The axes didn't glance off the blades as Quinn feared they might. They plunged right into the rotation of the blades, and ripped one of them right off the mount. The nose of the craft made a sudden dip and slammed straight downward into the frozen ground. The long rotor blades all slammed the ground at the side of the bird, digging deep into the ground before snapping off, one after the other. Naturally, it all happened in the blink of an eye. Again, no huge explosion. No shrapnel. No flying debris. Just a shriek of sound like a car accident and it was over. The craft sat crunched into the ground less than three feet in front of where Quinn stood bleeding and breathing hard.

CHAPTER 16

Quinn slumped to the ground in front of the crumpled helicopter and watched the trapped pilot burn to death in the flaming wreckage. It didn't take long. Quinn reached up with his hand and touched the tender wound to his already abused shoulder, and he discovered that it was a shallow slice out of the skin. The muscle underneath felt fine.

Eva and Curtis were running toward him and he decided that it was a good time to pass out. "Jason!" Curtis slid to a stop beside Quinn's body and quickly examined him.

"Is he okay?" Eva was right beside him.

"Yeah. Looks like he was just cut. He's passed out. Let's get him away from this thing in case it explodes," Curtis told her, and he began dragging Quinn away from the wreckage through the snow. Eva grabbed his feet and they managed to get about thirty feet away when the fuel tank on the Bell detonated. It wasn't very large as explosions go—the helicopter had been low on fuel after searching so long for them—but it was enough of an impacting thump to the air to knock them to the ground. The heat from the blast felt like someone had opened an oven while baking a turkey for Thanksgiving. The snow around them became slushy from the heat of the blast.

Quinn opened his eyes and looked directly at Eva. "Hi. Are you okay?"

Eva smiled and looked back at him. "You're the one we were worried about. How's your arm feel?"

"Anything less than a half a pound of flesh…" Quinn began with a smile.

Curtis finished for him. "…is just a nick. Old climbing slogan," he explained to Eva's questioning look.

"Who made that one up?" Eva asked with a shake of her head.

"Who knows," Quinn told her. "Probably an old movie we both saw or something."

"I think it was Lee Majors in The Fall Guy," Curtis said.

"Not likely," Quinn joked as he got up and shook snow and slush away from his body. "Anytime there's ever any doubt as to where a saying comes from, Lee here suggests The Fall Guy," Quinn raised his eyebrows at Eva as she laughed.

"It was a really good show," Curtis persisted. Eva laughed even harder.

They walked back to the ruins of the tent to salvage what they could. "Next time they send a helicopter after us—don't blow it up. We could use some transport, Quinn."

"Thanks for that sage advice, Fall Guy." Quinn frowned. "But we might have some transport, after all." Johnson followed Quinn's gaze to the top of a small ridge. There were three Buddhist monks in the reddish brown, red, and yellow robes of the region, standing serenely watching them. They stood next to two yaks, which were loaded up with a few bundles of brightly colored cloth.

"You're not going to kill a yak now are you?" Curtis said, as he touched Eva on the shoulder to point her attention toward the monks.

"Shut up, Curtis," Quinn smiled and began walking toward the monks. Curtis and Eva remained behind watching.

One of the monks was young. Quinn guessed him to be no more than sixteen. The other two were old but he couldn't even begin to guess how old. All three were deeply brown—a part of which was natural skin pigment and the other was years of exposure to sun at these high altitudes. They all wore prayer beads. The faces of the older two were wrinkled and leathery. All three had shaven heads and all three showed no emotion on their faces. No smile, no frown.

Quinn stopped about ten feet from the monks and brought his hands together as if in prayer. He smiled and offered a Tibetan greeting, "Tashi Delek."

The two elders seemed pleased, but their smiles were only a microscopic change in face patterns from the no-emotion look Quinn had first seen. Still, he knew it was a smile. They returned the greeting. The teenage monk's face lit up in a smile that showered Quinn with excitement.

"Are you guys Americans? Is that your helicopter? Did you crash? Cool!"

Now it was Quinn's turn to smile.

BOOK TWO:
THE CATHEDRAL

CHAPTER 17

Hong Kong, China

At any one time, 15 percent of the buildings in Hong Kong are being either demolished or rebuilt, renovated or restructured.
—Martin Booth

David Hong sat back from the window of the helicopter and relaxed against the plush leather of the chair he had occupied on the brief flight from his private runway at Lantau Island's Hong Kong International Airport. He liked the airport much better than the old Kai Tak—even if he did miss the low approach through the buildings of the city and the 47° banking maneuver before the abrupt landing. Lantau Island was more serene, but the facilities were far superior and arrivals were streamlined.

The lights of Hong Kong sparkled like a million multicolored jewels scattered across the horizon. Six times the size of Washington, D.C., the city sprawls over 200 islands and several steep-sloped peninsulas at the south of China. Although the *Special Administrative Region of Hong Kong* is roughly 600 square miles in size, most of the action actually centers around the southern part of the mainland—Kowloon Peninsula—and Hong Kong Island, which face each other across Victoria Harbor.

For a city its size, it should seem spacious. Just the opposite is true. London has the same number of people (about 7 million), but in Hong Kong they crowd into two-thirds the space. Yet, in spite of the rampant urbanization and crowding, Hong Kong still looks to be a vibrant green city from the air—and most of the greenery is undisturbed virgin forest. At night from the air, the city is a kaleidoscope of color. Green doesn't stand a chance.

David Hong glanced down to the low table bolted to the floor of the helicopter and saw the issue of Newsweek International. There he was on the cover, wearing the same Armani suit he wore now. "NEW SAVIOR?" The text asked. The stained glass window behind him had been digitally created. He was a tall man for an Asian—about six feet. His hair was jet black and slicked back over the top of his head. The smile said confident and the black eyes said "not only am I confident, but *you're screwed.*"

He had been interviewed about the cathedral again, because it was now just weeks from completion. The requests had been heating up, especially with the recent statements from Rome. *Just a few more weeks,* he told himself, *then the world will change.*

It was coming into view now. His crowning achievement to date. The Hong Cathedral. The spotlights on the ground blazed up at the towers and the rear spire. As powerful as the lights were, the tops of the spires were still in shadow. It was the biggest Gothic style cathedral in the world, and when it officially opened, it would be recognized as the tallest man-made structure in the world. The Sears Tower in Chicago had held the title for a number of years at 1,450 feet until the construction of the Petronas Towers in Kuala Lumpur had knocked it out of the running with an extra thirty-three feet in 1998. Then, the upstart Taipei 101 Tower in Taiwan had trumped them both in 2004, as the construction on the Hong Cathedral was beginning. 1,670 feet. Then, to add insult to injury, the Burg Kalifa building in Dubai had come in at 2,717 feet. After its unfortunate collapse in 2012, Hong was back in contention. He knew with several Asian cities all vying for the tallest building title, he would have to outdo all of them and by a significant margin. He had decided on 1,969 feet—or a round 600 meters. That way he conquered not only the World's Tallest Building race but also Tallest Towers, where the Canadian National Tower in Toronto had previously held sway at only 1,814 feet since the seventies.

The problem really was that it was a cathedral. No cathedral made the list of the top one hundred tallest buildings in the world. None came close. A few had been built taller than the Saint Peter's Basilica in Rome. However, with one exception they had all been built (or at least begun) before Saint Peter's. The exception was the Our Lady of Peace of Yamoussoukro Basilica, in the Ivory Coast. That had been built to be slightly smaller than Saint Peter's dome at Papal request, but the large gold cross on the top took it over the limit. The Pope hadn't been pleased and much backroom bargaining had gone on until Félix Houphouët-Boigny, the Iron Hand of the Ivory Coast, gave in and satiated the Pope's anger with a series of humanitarian gestures such as the construction of hospitals.

Hong's Cathedral project was a lot taller than any other place of worship in the world. To make matters worse, John Paul II had died in 2005, ruining all of Hong's delicate negotiations with the elderly Pope. Now, Hong had a new Pope to deal with. A man who was used to getting his own way and not willing to negotiate when he felt religious hubris was at play.

The helicopter was setting down gently on the helipad built into the roof of the massive structure. They were over 1600 feet up from the harbor and the widespread twinkle. The roof was mostly a steeply pitched affair with the exception of the overly large helipad just behind the front of the building. The twin crenellated towers were at the front and the giant spire reaching to the full 1,969 feet at the rear. The interior was dark and so Hong hadn't been able to see the extensive array of stained glass images around the building as he had approached. Now, the pilot escorted him to a reinforced steel door at the edge of the helipad leading into the structure. The winds at this height were often fierce, but tonight the air was relatively calm.

The pilot left and closed the door behind him. David Hong smoothed out his suit with one hand and set his laptop bag down with the other. He waited in the hallway at the top of the stairs for about thirty seconds when Jacob Lee arrived. Jacob was Hong's most trusted assistant, but more importantly, Lee was a true believer. Nearing sixty, with stylish white hair, slim gold-rimmed glasses and degrees in economics, political science, and sociology, Jacob Lee was the perfect resource for Hong's aspirations.

For his part, Jacob Lee could think of no man he would rather serve. He deeply believed in Hong's ability and mandate. His belief was further reinforced by Hong's asexual nature. Hong never abused his employees and seemed to use his power wisely. He was a successful shipping magnate who was genuinely interested in humanitarian efforts and philanthropy. The Cathedral Project would provide a more than deserving home for the Bishop but also community center services.

"My Lord," Lee greeted Hong and took the laptop case for him. They began the descent of the long spiral stair together.

"Jacob. How have things been while I was in Manila?" Hong asked unconcerned. It was more of a nicety. Hong knew that everything would be in perfect hands under Lee's care.

"Construction is slightly ahead of schedule. We could finish on the 15th if you wish. Rome has been contacted and they responded with curiosity as you suggested they would. Beijing is satisfied with their end of things. The Taiwanese are still incensed, but that won't matter soon. We still have sufficient people in Taipei. Finally, the masseuse is ready for you." Lee spoke in a slow smooth wave, which always soothed Hong like a lullaby.

"And the problem in Tibet?" Hong asked while rolling his neck to stretch after the long flight from the Philippines.

"That problem has moved from Tibet to America, My Lord." Lee hung his head slightly in shame.

Hong stopped walking and looked at Lee in surprise.

"Really? They escaped? Impressive." Hong was more interested in the improbability of the situation than in Lee's failure. Jacob Lee breathed an audible sigh of relief. "And you say he led them to the States?"

"Yes, Lord. It took some time for us to reacquire them. He somehow managed to fell the helicopter." Lee looked confused, as if he could scarcely believe a man could fight a helicopter and win.

Hong resumed the descent of the staircase. "Make sure the next attempt succeeds. We don't need any more interference from the Americans than we already have. No traces, Lee."

"Of Course, My Lord. Of Course."

CHAPTER 18

Jason Quinn loved Denver International Airport. There really wasn't any other competition. As far as Quinn was concerned, *all* airports sucked. The only exception was D.I.A. The massive tent-like tensile fiberglass ceiling to the main terminal was stretched into peaks and valleys, and as seen from a distance at night, all lit up, it resembled a small snow-covered mountain range. Quinn thought it was extremely fitting for the Rocky Mountain region, and he had years earlier joined legions of travelers in developing a particular loathing for Denver's former airport, Stapleton. The contrast of D.I.A.'s stunning main terminal with its huge indoor fountain, to Stapleton's claustrophobically low drop-ceiling corridors was like night and day.

Today, being in the arrivals terminal of D.I.A. brought him little joy. He was exhausted. He was still reliving the avalanche and the deaths of his friends whenever he shut his eyes, and as a result, he had slept little on the long series of flights from Bhutan. Sometimes in the nightmares, it would be Eva that was killed in the oncoming rush of snow. Sometimes it would be Curtis. Sometimes it was him. In each case, he had awakened with a jolt. He had given up on even allowing himself to try to sleep a few hours after they had boarded their connecting flight in London. Eva and Curtis had slept for much of the last leg from London, but they still looked tired from the ordeal in the mountains. It was around 12:30 in the afternoon, but Quinn thought it felt more like four in the morning. He had to admit to himself that he was as tired as his companions looked. They had all traveled with only carry-on bags and now approached the limo counter.

A short man with dark hair and a thick black mustache stood by the counter with a clipboard in hand. He was casually holding it like a signboard at his waist and the lettering simply said:

ARGO

He wore faded blue jeans, white Nikes, and a white nylon, windbreaker-style jacket with the ARGO text and mountaineering ice ax over the left breast.

"Mr. Quinn?" he asked preemptively.

"Yes."

"I'm Tony. I've been sent to give you a ride home," the man said. His accent spoke of an Italian heritage and a New York upbringing.

Quinn turned to Curtis and asked, "You want to go home yet or talk to the Old Lady first?"

"Let's get it over with," Johnson replied smiling.

Quinn turned back to Tony. "I think we're gonna want to stop by the office first, Tony. We need to talk with Marge."

"She said you'd say that. And if she ever heard you calling her *The Old Lady*..." Tony chuckled and left the sentence unfinished, as he walked them out of the terminal and toward an unmarked black stretch limousine.

Quinn smiled. Everyone at ARGO referred to his boss as The Old Lady. At least behind her back they did. Tony probably called her that himself. It was a term of endearment, as every employee at ARGO genuinely liked the boss, and Quinn had no doubt that Margaret Tower knew what people called her. Very little got past the woman. As everyone got comfortable in the spacious interior of the limo, Tony got them headed out onto Peña Boulevard toward I-70 through Denver.

Quinn's thoughts drifted for a while and he rubbed his sore shoulder, as Curtis acted like a tour guide pointing out the few sights for Eva, who had not been to Denver before. There really wasn't that much to see between the airport and the mountains, but it seemed that both Eva and Curtis were now awake, wired, and chatty. *Jet lag does funny things to people*, Quinn thought. *A minute ago, they were tired. Now they're nearly manic.* One thing he noticed was that Eva was checking him out less often. It was clear that she was interested in him, especially after the last few days in Bhutan and India.

They had traveled by land from the monastery to India. Then, they had caught an extremely long bus ride to New Delhi. At the U.S. Embassy, they had contacted Marge, and she had arranged transportation for them within two hours. They traveled on the same flights but not sitting together. They thought if someone was still looking for them, then those people would be looking for a woman and two men traveling together. Now in Denver, they felt safe enough to be seen together at last.

Through it all, Eva had been looking his direction a bit too much. When they had been together, she was always close. Now in the limo, he still noticed a furtive glance here and there, so he was confident that she hadn't lost interest entirely, but she was backing off some. He wondered if she was being cautious now after his tantrum in the Digger and the way he dealt with the assassins in the helicopter, or if she was just trying to give him some space. Quinn figured that Curtis had probably told her something of his past when the two of them had been alone in Bhutan at the monastery.

Quinn had to admit that Dr. Eva Rayjek was on his mind a lot too. He did like her. She was thoughtful, hard working, definitely smart, and stunningly beautiful, but Quinn suspected that there was more to Eva than just her work in archeology. She likely had deeper interests, and he hadn't really taken the time to get to know them. He had only known her a short time and really didn't know much about her. Because of that, and on some level the unresolved guilt over the death of his wife many years earlier, Quinn berated himself for his growing feelings. He had other things he needed to think about. He sorted through his plan for the next few days, and made a mental list of some things he needed for his place, and of some people he needed to contact now that he was back in the country. Marge would be able to help with a lot of things, and he figured she would already have contacted the Denver FBI branch office, to arrange for some protection for Eva.

His thoughts began to settle as the elongated Maybach 62 limousine cruised along the winding roads through the foothills of the Colorado Front Range. Eva and Curtis quieted eventually, and after about an hour on the road, they entered the small town of Empire, Colorado. Curtis often referred to the small ex-mining community as "that wide shit-splat in the road." The town had once been a thriving silver mining town, but had long since seen its better days when Margaret Tower had decided to relocate the headquarters of ARGO there in 1985. Now, the population of the town either worked directly for ARGO, or acted in a support capacity for the company in some fashion or other. As such, the town of Empire had developed significantly and no longer resembled the ghost town that Curtis joked about so sarcastically. The money ARGO had brought to Empire attracted other ventures, but mainly retail stores to take advantage of the vast sums of disposable income the well-paid employees spent each month. Quinn's personal favorite was the chain bookstore that had opened just prior to his departure for Tibet. As he was thinking about heading there sometime in the following week to pick up the large stack of reading he had ordered before his trip, the vehicle pulled up to the gates of ARGO.

A high set of primarily decorative iron gates stood open next to a small guard hut. The occupant of the hut didn't come out as the limo passed a low chunk of marble with a sign that read:

ALPINE RESEARCH & GEOGRAPHICAL OBSERVATION
Cartography • GIS • Geology • Vulcanology • Tectonics
Hydrology • Glaciology • Bio-Diversity
Civil Engineering • Product Development • Exploration

Quinn watched out the window as the limo cruised along the drive past rolling hills of lush well-tended grass, and approached the massive building. It resembled a large, squat, glass and steel pyramid, which had been upended and planted in the ground with its point buried straight down, under the ground. Tony dropped them at the front door and Quinn dismissed him, explaining that they would take a company car home when they were finished. Quinn led the group through the front doors and into the lobby of the building. They came to a security desk with an attractive female security guard named Samantha, who could have been a supermodel. Quinn knew that she had won several martial arts competitions and was a former Chicago cop. Quinn had no doubt that Samantha could kick his ass in a heartbeat. Curtis had been trying to get her to go out on a date for the last three years.

"Heya, Sam." Quinn greeted her with a tired smile.

"Jason. You guys look beat. I heard what happened. I'm really sorry." Samantha looked both glad to see Quinn and saddened at the loss of Quinn's team. She handed Quinn three security badges.

"Are you back for a while?" she asked him hopefully.

"Don't know yet."

"Well call me if you are. We'll get a beer."

"Yeah, alright. See ya." Quinn handed the others the badges, and as they pinned the plastic badges to their shirts, he led them to the elevators. Curtis had remained silent during the exchange—he was just too tired to hit on Samantha, as he usually did. He had been out with Quinn and Samantha drinking at a local pub called The Welshman a few times, but he hadn't ever been able to get her to go out on a date with just him. He was beginning to think the reason was that Samantha was more interested in Quinn than in him. Eva, however, noticed immediately that Samantha had the hots for Quinn. It was as clear as day to Eva that the pretty security guard had harbored a crush on Quinn for some time. She felt a quick pang of jealousy about it, but then started to become amused as she thought about the fact that Quinn was clearly oblivious to Samantha's feelings. Quinn noticed Eva was smiling and asked her, "What's so funny?"

"Nothing. So how many people actually work here? This place is huge."

"About 500," Quinn replied. "Although usually only about a hundred are here at any given time."

The elevator doors opened letting them out on the 25th and top-most floor. The elevator opened directly into a large oval meeting room with a large round table in the center. There were plush, overstuffed wingback armchairs surrounding it. The room was low-lit by recessed lights in the dark wood walls. There were no windows in the room, but the atmosphere was quite relaxing. As Quinn and the others entered the room, a door opened on the opposite side of the oval and Margaret Tower walked swiftly in.

"Jason. Curtis." she said, as she hurried toward the men and embraced each as if they were her sons.

"The others?" Quinn asked her quietly.

The woman sadly shook her head. "All gone. The Chinese will get the bodies back home."

Margaret Tower, known simply as "Marge" to ARGO employees, was a short woman. At 4 foot 11, she had to look up at every one of her employees. But that fact did not in any way diminish the respect they held for her. She was a well-dressed woman just into her sixties, and she held a keen interest in all of the projects ARGO was involved in. She also knew her employees on a first name basis and took an interest in their lives and families, as well as their work. Marge had furthered ARGO's investment portfolio and had introduced the current astronomical pay scale as well. Her missing and presumed dead husband, William Tower, would have been extremely proud of her ability to run his company. Although she had turned the company on its ear, she still believed in tradition. As such, there were only two decorations in the large oval meeting room. On one wall was an oil canvas portrait of ARGO's founder, Theodore Roosevelt, with a small brass plaque underneath it that read: "The life of strenuous endeavor." On the opposite side of the room, a portrait of the same size, of a significantly younger man, William Tower, and a brass plaque that read: "To the ends of the Earth," which had been the last thing he had said to Margaret before departing on his ill-fated Antarctic expedition.

"You must be Dr. Eva Rayjek." Marge turned up to face the tall blonde archeologist. "Come, sit. We have much to talk about."

CHAPTER 19

"That's quite a story," Marge said when the tale was finished.

"You don't believe us?" Eva began, but Marge cut her off.

"No, I believe every word. It's just amazing that in this day and age people still think they can commit murder and piracy and get away with it."

"Reminds me of that incident in the Pyrenees. Remember?" Johnson commented.

Marge nodded. "I've already contacted David Chambers at the FBI office in Denver. He's an old friend. He's coming out tomorrow, but he's not sure what he'll be able to do." Marge had a way of talking to people. Eva instantly relaxed and realized that this woman was only trying to help. "I do have a question though, Dr. Rayjek."

"Please, make it Eva."

"Alright Eva, what were you looking for at the dig site? There must be something that these people are after. They have been pretty tenacious in their intent to kill you." Marge held Eva's gaze with a serious look. She believed that Eva was withholding something. Silence filled the room for a moment, and Quinn and Johnson watched with interest.

"Okay. The site is near Xinning, in northwest China. Malcolm Brewer had stumbled upon it while he was looking for a different site. He was looking for a Qin Dynasty temple, but he came across our site instead. An entire unrecorded city in the desert. He asked David Arlon and me to come on board, and we got the dig up and running. We had the impression that the site was from the fifth century, but it had also been used as recently as the 1800s. That, and the fact that there was no historical evidence of the city's existence at all, is what piqued my interest. You see, I have a side project that

I work on from time to time, in addition to my work in Asian archeology."
Eva paused and took in a long slow breath.

"How many of you have heard of Sven Hedin?" she asked hesitantly, as if
she were an academic with a conspiracy theory she was used to being
ridiculed over, which was far from the truth, because she had kept this
particular theory a complete secret.

"The Swedish explorer? I think we're all pretty familiar with him here. He
explored and mapped most of Central Asia." Quinn answered, wondering
what could be coming next.

"Right. An amazing man and a hell of a writer. His books were phenomenally
popular. He studied geography and geology."

"Just like you, Quinn," Johnson interjected.

"He made four major expeditions to Central Asia between 1893 and 1935. He
helped to map the Xinjiang province of China, and he helped in the construction
of roads in the region by mapping the original Silk Road. He was good friends
with Field Marshall Carl Gustaf Emil Mannerheim, the Finnish war hero-cum-
President, and also with King Oscar II, of Sweden. He was the last person ever
knighted by Sweden in 1902. He was also initially an ardent supporter of Germany
in the days leading to World War II, but he soon lost faith in Hitler's plans as so
many other initial supporters did. He was mostly concerned about the Russians
invading Sweden via Finland. He had a lot of political interests in his latter years
and he wrote about his travels. Some 40 volumes. But he longed to go back to
Asia. He died in November of 1952, in his home, with a photograph of his old
love Mille Lindström on the table nearby."

"Okay. So?" Quinn was getting impatient with the history lesson.

"So I believe that he faked his own death." Eva replied, throwing her long
blonde hair over shoulder as she did.

"You think Sven Hedin is still alive?" Marge asked unbelieving.

"No. I imagine he's dead by now. But I don't think he died in '52. There
was too much to suggest that it was a cover-up. Mind you, the clues and hints
I found weren't all that obvious, but I've been a big fan of Hedin since I was
a little girl. Only a life-long Hedin scholar would have been able to piece
together all the things I have. But I was still on shaky ground with this

theory. The question was always *why*. I came to believe he wanted to go on one last journey into Asia, you see. He always wanted to see Lhasa. But there was a problem. He was a well renowned public figure. There was no way he could travel anonymously. Plus, there was the matter of the Soviets between him and his beloved Taklamakan Desert. So he needed to slip away somehow. Plus, there was the matter of his eyesight. He was partially blind in one eye since the 1890s, and in 1947, he had an operation that restored his vision. That was just five years before he would have left the country—when he supposedly died. Just long enough for him to do some serious planning for one last trip."

She paused seeing the looks of disbelief around her. "I know, I know. It sounds preposterous. But I eventually found the one piece of evidence I needed, to know that I was on the right track. I found one of his journals in a back street market in Lhasa."

"And?" Johnson wanted to know.

"It was dated *after* his supposed death. And yes, I am sure it was his. I have shown photocopied samples of his writing and samples from the journal to handwriting experts. They confirmed what I already knew. It was his writing. He slipped away in the dead of night from Sweden, allowed a friend of his to fake his death in the papers and arrange for a phony funeral, and he took off to Asia one last time."

"So how does this tie into the crazy tattooed assassins?" Marge asked, stunned at the revelation.

"I'm not sure. I was interested in the dig because I hoped it might be a place Hedin had visited on his last trip, but I didn't find anything there to indicate that he had. The journal only covered a period of six months after his departure from Sweden. He didn't write about his exit from Scandinavia either. He just started it in the middle of his journey to Tibet. He found Lhasa to be a pretty oppressive place with the Chinese freshly entrenched there. He was planning on heading north into the desert, in his last entry in the journal, and he was planning on starting another journal because he had run out of room."

Eva sat back in her chair as if her tale was done.

"So where is the journal now? Maybe that's what they're after." Quinn was putting the pieces together in his head but none of them fit quite right.

"I have it in a safe deposit box in San Francisco. But that can't be what they're after because no one knows I have it. You three are the only ones I ever told about it. So it's got to be something about the site itself I guess. So now what?" She seemed tired after explaining her pet theory. The strain of the last week was finally taking its toll, and Quinn could see that even the manic excitement he had seen in her and Curtis was now gone.

"We need some information. I know just the guy to get it for us," Quinn said with a smile.

CHAPTER 20

It was early still, and the sun was just beginning its crawl into the scattered clouds of the monsoon sky over the beaches of Sri Lanka. The beach near Weligama would remain mostly empty throughout the day except for the American man and his toys. He was young at 26, but not quite as young or as old as most of the predominantly German and British backpackers and package tourists that crowded the shores of the beach during the season. Also odd was the fact that he was here now, during a secondary monsoon the west coast suffered each year.

He was tall and lanky, yet he sat cross-legged and bent over, focusing on a wide array of electronic items splayed around him on a towel a few yards from the lapping waves of the Indian Ocean. He apparently had no concern for the effects of the salt-water spray on the delicate electronics. There were three computer monitor screens made from thin flexible sheets of transparent Plexiglas and handheld computers generations ahead of what was commercially available. Everything connected wirelessly and the keyboard the man tapped at was made from soft, rollable denim. Finally, the whole setup connected to a compromised NASA satellite.

When he was finished here at the beach for the day, everything would get folded, rolled, and twisted up into small packages—each not much larger than a packet of cigarettes. He would place them in the cargo pockets of his khaki shorts. Despite this immense portability, the array of computing equipment displayed before the man on this beach in Sri Lanka was enough for him to topple governments if he were so inclined. Some of the equipment he had designed himself, but much of it was stolen (although he liked to think of it as "appropriated").

The man was currently looting the bank accounts of several mafia figures in the United States and re-routing the funds across three satellites into the bank accounts of an orphanage in India, a soup kitchen in Florida, and a non-profit organization in Belgium devoted to stamping out malaria in South America. The money would not be traceable. Today, he didn't take any money for himself with his computer savvy. He had more than enough and he lived very cheaply.

He traveled mostly. All over the world. He had seen every continent and nearly two thirds of all the countries on the planet. He also traveled in any season. The weather did not seem to bother him. In many cases, he was glad to be in a place when the weather was considered poor, because there were fewer tourists and he preferred keeping to himself. And to his toys. Although the array of computer equipment would probably be worth close to a hundred thousand dollars (and the technology behind it would fetch him millions), he always thought of his equipment as "toys."

He was literally a genius, but he never let it go to his head. A true child prodigy, he had tested out of primary school at the age of six. He did a correspondence course for high school in two years and was admitted to the Massachusetts Institute of Technology at the age of nine. In four short years, he had earned dual PhDs in computer science and electronics. His parents had died in a fiery pile up on I-95 late in his final year at MIT, so when the Pentagon wanted to snatch him up to work in their Encryption Sciences Department, he happily went with them. He had no other relatives, but had a bright future in technology. At the age of 14, he was the youngest employee the Pentagon had ever hired. The U.S. government knew what a treasure they had, as he created all manner of advanced gadgets for them and revolutionized the way the department was run. But they didn't keep him interested enough in the work.

That was where all the trouble had started. Well, the Pentagon liked to consider it trouble, and he liked to think of it as *fun*.

After two years of employment, he erased every file the government had on him and quite literally disappeared without a trace. He also left behind a devious morphing computer virus that erased judicious portions of the Pentagon mainframes, every time they used their computers to look for him. The virus plagued the Pentagon for nearly three years before they were finally able to expunge it from their systems. Since he was able to hack into their most encrypted systems with ease, he e-mailed them a new virus the week after they had finally erased the original. This new one blacked out metropolitan Washington D.C. the first time they tried to search for him. Then it began broadcasting pornographic films to the home television of the Chairman of the Joint Chiefs, whose wife was understandably upset. At that point, it was decided to cease and desist all computer-related searches for the missing child prodigy. But the FBI and the CIA still had standing orders to seek the man out. They chased him all over the world, always remaining several steps behind him, and only because he allowed them to pick up on his trail. He didn't travel to escape his pursuit. He traveled because he loved it and couldn't imagine staying in one place.

He left the Pentagon at the age of 16, and it was now ten years later, during which time he had become a legendary bogey-man of the Internet. He was like a ghost. No one could find him, very few people knew him, and in the world of computers, he was nearly omnipotent. He hired out his legitimate services to governments and organizations around the world, never meeting with them in person. He had even performed jobs for the U.S. military twice during that time, which had particularly frustrated the Army generals who had lost him originally. They tried to trace the funds they sent to a bank account he had specified in Zurich, but he never collected the money. Instead, he withdrew the amount he was owed from a different and completely unrelated government account, and then he had the money they had sent to Switzerland on his behalf forwarded to the account he had burgled. They weren't able to trace any of it.

He also owed Jason Quinn his life.

As he checked an e-mail account he kept for business, he noticed a familiar sender: jquinn@argo.org. He immediately opened it and saw text that read simply: *Need to talk ASAP*. Mooky Jones wasted no time as he attached a portable webcam to his already extensive computing array. Within seconds, the connection was secured and he was seeing the ARGO boardroom on his monitor. Seated in front of the camera was his old friend Quinn, and the man did not look happy.

"J.Q.! How've you been, Man? You look pissed," he began.

"I am, Mooky. There's been a drama. Several Chinese bastards just tried to kill me over the last few days."

Mooky Jones issued a low whistle. "Damn. That's messed up. What do you need?"

Quinn didn't hesitate. "I'm sending you some photos I took of the killer's tats. I need you to find out what they mean. I'll send you all the info I have, which isn't much. I need to you find these guys. I need to know where they are and what they're after us for."

"They're after ARGO?"

"No, they're after her." Quinn said grimly and Eva stepped in front of the camera in the board room.

"And the lovely lady is…?" Mooky began, still trying to keep things as light as possible amidst the serious subject matter.

"All in the e-mail I'm sending you now." Quinn finished at the keyboard and hit 'send.' "Get back to me as soon as you can."

"You got it. I'm out." And then the mysterious cyber-ghost named Mooky Jones was gone.

CHAPTER 21

"And so who exactly was that?" Eva wanted to know.

"Mooky Jones. He's an old friend, and if there's anyone in the world who can dig up everything we need with the use of a computer, it's him." Quinn said, a bit more cheerful now, but still exhausted.

Marge stepped over to them both. "Jason, it'll likely be some time before your cagey Mr. Jones gets back to us. Why don't the three of you go home and get some rest. I'll beep you when we hear from him." She handed him an electronic pager. Marge Tower had twice before seen Jason Quinn rely on his electronic genius friend for ARGO's benefit, but even to her and her vast resources and network of informants, Jones remained a complete blank slate. She was both impressed and irked by that.

"It's a good idea Mr. Quinn. Let's get the lady to a safe haven and all of us get some shut-eye," Curtis said.

They said their goodbyes to Marge and headed out to the lobby. At the security desk, Samantha signed out an ARGO vehicle to them, and they returned to the elevators for the underground parking garage. Curtis, feeling much more awake after the meeting with Marge and a cup of coffee, volunteered to drive. Quinn climbed into the back of the Nissan X-terra SUV and sprawled out. He was asleep before they left the ARGO compound.

They dropped Curtis off at his apartment in Empire. Quinn reluctantly woke up and took the wheel of the ARGO vehicle. There was no discussion involved. Eva would be staying with Quinn. She thought that was perhaps a good sign, as she still found the man very attractive, but as she would soon come to find out, the decision was based primarily with her security in mind.

Quinn drove the Nissan onto an unpaved road right into the mountains. The going was slow but Eva felt too tired to ask questions or start a conversation. Eventually they came to the entrance to an old abandoned mine closed off with a huge rusted steel gate and a shiny new padlock. Above the entrance, a huge slab of granite stretched up to what Eva suspected must be a thousand feet. It was actually 350 feet and not quite vertical. Quinn had free-solo climbed it shortly after he had purchased the mine. There was a sign that had been shot up with a shotgun proclaiming the mine closed and that trespassers would be dealt with severely. There were narrow-gauge rails on the ground that led into the mine's opening; the SUV was so high that it cleared them with little difficulty. Eva assumed that they had once been for ore carts or something like that. Quinn had stopped the SUV about 20 feet from the opening and was now pressing the button on a garage door opener he had clipped to the sun visor when he had gotten into the driver's side of the car. Eva was stunned to see the entire gate swing open slowly. She noticed that the shiny new padlock was just camouflage, as it and the flange it was secured through swung out with the gate.

"Clever," she said.

"The mine leads to a bowl shaped valley in the mountains on the other side of this slab." Quinn began. "There's a house there that used to belong to the foreman. There's no way into the valley other than by foot over the mountains or through the mine."

He drove into the shaft and turned on the headlights as the rusted gate swung slowly shut after them. "I bought the place a number of years ago. The valley is beautiful, with lots of pine and juniper trees. No place for a helicopter to land." He smiled at her as he said the last part. She chuckled at him, remembering their encounter with the helicopter in what they had later found out was Bhutan.

"Basically, we thought my place would be more secure. It seems like they've lost us, but who knows. We need to keep a low profile. Curtis'll come by tomorrow." He added the last in case she was uncomfortable about spending time alone with him, but she didn't seem to mind. They drove on deeper into the mine for some time until they came to a dead end in the tunnel with metal rails chest high on the sides of the shaft.

"Now what?" Eva asked.

"Now we go down," he smiled and pressed another button on the remote. She realized immediately that the car was parked on an elevator. The metal rails she had seen were support structure for the platform, which slowly began to descend deeper into the mine. "The exit on the other side of the mountain is 85 feet lower than the entrance. It's a deep valley and snow covered for almost half of the year."

When they had finished their descent, Quinn drove straight off the platform and ahead about 50 feet until he reached a ten-foot wide chasm that had two metal planks stretched across it. He carefully aligned the SUV and proceeded over the chasm.

"How deep does that go?" she asked incredulously.

"Not sure. I plan on finding out some day," he said with a smile. Actually, he knew it went down 143 feet and narrowed as it went. He had explored every nook and cranny of the mines when he had purchased them. A moment or two later they came to another rusted gate that opened with the remote control. Quinn drove them out of the mine onto what Eva assumed to be a road. At least it was a space between the trees that looked like a path or road. The glare off the snow made Eva blink. She estimated that they had been underground for about 20 minutes and traveled only about 10 miles. Even though Quinn had said there was snow, she was unprepared for the winter landscape as most of Empire had only had scattered patches of melting snow on the ground. Now she saw a huge valley crammed tight with coniferous snow-weighted trees. Ahead at the end of the winding path between the trees, she could see the house, a sprawling, rambling white Victorian with slate gray trim. She tried to count gables and dormers but lost sight of the house as the road curved to the right and a clump of evergreens blocked her view for a moment. After another minute of Quinn expertly controlling the fishtailing SUV on the snow covered trail, they came to a stop in front of the house by the door.

Quinn killed the engine and got out. Eva got out and looked at the monstrosity of a home.

"Welcome to Storm Lodge." Quinn told her.

CHAPTER 22

"Must have been some foreman," Eva was saying as Quinn used a key he kept at ARGO when he left for abroad, to let them into the house. He deactivated a security system to the right of the door before answering her, "Well, actually he owned the mine but he was also the foreman. Eight bedrooms, five baths, three fireplaces, two secret passages, and a family of raccoons that keep deciding that it's *their* house."

She laughed.

"How the hell do you get your mail?" she wanted to know.

"I use ARGO as a mailing address. I'm overseas for much of the year anyway."

"I was going to say this must be a hell of a commute."

The entryway had a hardwood floor and a small table to the side where Quinn dumped his key into a small glass bowl full of change. He flicked on a light and Eva saw that most of the walls in the hallway had recessed bookcases with glass doors that were filled with all sorts of books. There was a staircase to the left and hundreds of candles on nearly every surface.

"Why all the candles?"

"Solar panels on the rear of the roof provide electricity for a few things like kitchen appliances and the computer, but I prefer natural light anyway, so I use lots of candles. A woman in Empire recycles the wax for me. I generally…" But Quinn stopped abruptly and held up his hand. Eva knew to stay silent. She wasn't sure what it was, but the intent look on Quinn's face let her know it was something serious. Quinn waited a moment, then quietly went to a bookcase and reached up under a shelf. He pulled out a Jericho 941 9 mm automatic. He ejected the magazine and pulled a box of cartridges from a different shelf behind some other books. He quickly loaded the weapon, chambered a round, and clicked the safety off. There was no point leaving the weapon loaded when he was gone for long stretches. The spring in a magazine could lose its power if it was left compressed for a long time. He motioned for Eva to stay by the door, then proceeded deeper into the house.

Quinn didn't believe in very many superstitious ideas, but he did know from experience that a house has a certain feeling to it when it's empty. He wasn't sure if that was a psychic thing or maybe there was some scientific explanation like too many or too few electrons. All he knew was you could usually tell when a house was empty. It also has a different feeling when someone is in it. Even if that person tries his or her best to remain silent, you can still tell if someone is there. Right now, Quinn's mental alarms were all going off. Even though the security system he had just deactivated had shown no sign that it had been set off, he was certain someone was in his house. He was also certain that it wasn't the raccoons—they were never this silent.

He crept further into the house, gun first. He checked the bathroom off the main hall, then crouched and went around the corner into the kitchen. Still nothing. He came back down the hall toward Eva, then slowly opened a door opposite the bathroom that led into a large lounge that Quinn used as an extension of the library that lined the hallway. Eva saw him relax somewhat, lower the gun, and enter the room. Then she began to follow him.

There was a man sitting comfortably in a plush leather armchair reading a book. A small reading lamp beside him on a table was on. The rest of the room was in shadow. He was wearing jeans and a leather jacket. Eva guessed him to be in his fifties. Cold gray eyes looked up at her and Quinn from under a high brow and short-cropped slightly receding dark brown hair. Then a smile lit up his wide face as he set the book aside and stood up. For a moment, Quinn's green eyes locked with the stranger's gray eyes. Then the man spoke.

"It's good to see you, Jason."

"I wish I could say the same," Quinn gestured to Eva then, "Dr. Eva Rayjek, Gene Quinn."

"A pleasure," the elder Quinn replied.

"You're Jason's father?" Eva asked.

"I am," the man said with obvious pride.

"We all have our crosses to bear," Jason said with disgust equal to his father's pride. "Why are you in my home, Gene?"

"Yeah, I noticed you put in an alarm system," the older man began. "I heard what happened in China." There was clearly some concern in his tone of voice.

Jason laid the Jericho on a side table with the safety catch applied. Then he took off his jacket and started out of the room toward the kitchen. "Beer?"

"Sure," Gene Quinn answered.

"Eva?" Jason asked. She indicated she wasn't thirsty. They all followed Jason to the kitchen and he turned on lights as he went instead of using the candles he would have preferred. The place was spacious and had sliding glass doors to the outside. Eva noticed another alarm keypad near the glass. The sun had already set and the sky was dark outside. "I imagine you *hear about* lots of stuff in your line of work. Why is the CIA watching me?"

Gene took the bottle of ice cold Guinness from his son and sat down at the small wooden table in the center of a rather large and very clean kitchen. Eva joined him at the table and Jason leaned back against the sink to look at the man.

"We aren't, son. But we hear things. I was worried. You two are in the shit, it seems. Do you even know who it is that's after you?"

"Isn't that what you came here to tell me, Gene?" Eva noticed heavy sarcasm each time Jason used his father's name.

"You know, if your mother was still alive, she wouldn't like seeing you be such an ass to me," Gene said and took a swig of the stout.

"If she were still alive, I doubt you'd know what she thought, 'cause she'd have divorced your ass years ago."

"That was low." the elder Quinn replied. But Eva sensed that the man wasn't really hurt but rather he seemed resigned to this kind of treatment.

She wondered what Gene had done to warrant this from his own son. Still, the man seemed determined to press on as if nothing had happened.

"The man's name is David Hong. You heard of him?" the elder Quinn asked.

"No." Now Jason seemed interested.

"He's a huge industrialist outta Hong Kong. Owns a company called Taiping Shipping. You've heard about the Hong Cathedral project in Wanchai, right?"

"Yeah. Giant complex with church and homeless shelters and things. Tallest building in the world now, after what happened in Dubai. Opens in a month or two, doesn't it?" Jason had read an article about the gigantic structure in Time magazine.

"That's the one. Hong's pet project. The Pope is pissed at him for building a church that's taller than St. Pete's, and for keeping it a secret project. Hong is the guy who is after you and Dr. Rayjek." Gene finished his beer and stood up.

"But why?" Eva felt it was time to jump into the conversation.

"That we don't know. A number of agencies around the world have suspected him of below-the-board sort of crap for years, but no one's been able to catch him in it. As it is, even the info we have on him being the one sending those suicidal bastards after you in the mountains is pretty sketchy. Not enough to hang him for it, but it is him. He's slippery and he's got more money than God. I just came by to let you know who he is and tell you both to be careful. We've been keeping an eye on him, and it doesn't seem like he's sending any more goons to this side of the pond. Still..."

Gene Quinn began to head for the door. Eva watched him go, and Jason picked up the empty beer bottles and began to wash them at the sink, knowing full well that his father knew the way out.

When she heard the door close, Eva turned to Quinn.

"That was a little... *tense*," she said softly.

"He's got a lot to answer for. But then I guess anyone in the CIA does." Jason said and gave her a soft smile to let her know that he wasn't as upset as he had seemed.

"He didn't really have that much information. Why didn't he just call you to tell you about this Hong guy? Seems a lot of work to break into your house and be all mysterious and shit."

Jason laughed. "He knows I'd hang up on him."

CHAPTER 23

"Well, now that Captain Mysterious has left, what do you say we each get a shower and then something to eat?" Quinn asked her with a smile.

"I was hoping for some sleep too. I'm beat."

"You got it. You like Italian? Anything you don't like?" he asked.

"Sounds good. Do you have anything I can wear?" He led her to the bathroom and then got her some fresh towels, sweatpants and an ARGO t-shirt to put on when she got out. She reappeared twenty minutes later, looking stunning with her wet blonde curls framing her face.

"Curtis'll be here with food in a half hour. He's jetlagged and can't sleep, and since I don't have much of anything here because we were supposed to be in China for another two months, I told him to come over. I'm gonna go grab a shower myself," he told her. "Help yourself to anything you want to drink."

She sat at the table awhile to make sure he was in the shower. Then she wandered around the house. She wanted to get a feel for what this man was like when he wasn't being hunted around the world. The house seemed to be filled to bursting with books. They covered all kinds of subjects from mountaineering and extreme sports to gardening and Buddhism. There were plenty of volumes on rock formations, volcanoes, glaciers, and (she was surprised to see) shelves and shelves of books about the planet Mars—both fiction and non-fiction. The room where Gene had been waiting was clearly just a library, as was the hall, and two other huge rooms on the ground floor.

The kitchen was large and filled with lots of health-food-aisle stuff from the grocery store, although most of it was stuff that would keep, as he was gone for months at a time abroad. She wondered if he was a vegetarian. She wasn't and liked her meat extremely rare. She hoped that wouldn't be a stumbling block. She'd dated a vegetarian in graduate school briefly, and the issue had always been a problem for them.

One room on the ground floor was a climbing gym with manufactured resin "rock" holds drilled into the walls and ceiling and thick gym mats on the floor. The whole room smelled of chalk dust, rubbing alcohol, and faintly of sweat. Another room held stacks of camping and climbing equipment. She guessed that room would have been a living room in an ordinary person's home. She smiled as she imagined Quinn's life. He clearly didn't do a lot of entertaining. There were two plush chairs in the library, the table and chairs in the kitchen, and literally nowhere else to sit on the whole massive ground floor.

Another room was wallpapered with maps and photos of mountains and crags, upon which he had drawn routes in red marker. There were files in stacks on the floor and some piles of rolled blueprints. Lots of white boxes were stacked along one wall with titles like "Engineering 403" and "Drafting." She guessed that this was stuff from his time in college. She remembered Curtis saying that Quinn had degrees in geography and geology.

A computer sat on a cherry wood desk in the corner of a small room upstairs with a huge plaque that contained the family coat of arms. It was a green shield with the top fourth a broad strip of yellow. There was a white winged horse on it. Above the shield was a knight's helmet in profile. The whole thing had fancy ribbons in gold and green to the sides and there was a ribbon below with the Latin motto: *Quae Sursum Volo Videri*. She had no idea what it meant. She had studied Greek in school, not Latin. She often regretted the choice.

There was a guest room with a bed and armoire, and his own room with just a bed and a walk in closet. Then, there were five completely empty rooms upstairs, a couple of bathrooms, and a stairway up to an attic that she didn't bother to look at. As he had told her, there were candles everywhere. It certainly seemed to Eva that this man spent most of his time away, and when he was here, he seemed to do a lot of reading. The extreme sports and climbing aside, it was pretty much what she had imagined for a bachelor who worked overseas.

She wandered back to the kitchen just as Quinn returned in shorts and an old beat up tank top with the logo: "Desert Moutain Sports & Climbing Magazine present *The 11th Phoenix Bouldering Contest.*" She was amused to notice that *mountain* had been misspelled. His shoulder length brown hair hung straight down with the weight of its dampness, and he was freshly shaved. The tank showed off his well-muscled torso. Eva smiled at him for what felt like the hundredth time. "Feel better?"

"Alive at least," he smiled back at her. Just then, the cell-phone Quinn had picked up at ARGO rang. Quinn answered it, said "Okay," then hung up and turned to Eva, "Food's here."

Eva woke the next day at nearly noon. She checked the clock on the armoire in the guest room, then got up and readied herself before heading downstairs. Curtis was in the kitchen making them both sandwiches. The previous night they had eaten Italian stromboli stuffed with Italian sausage and pepperoni, red onions and mushrooms. She needn't have worried about vegetarians. Not with this crowd. There was no sign of Quinn.

"Jason had some things to do and we didn't want to wake you. Hungry?" Johnson seemed pretty chipper.

"Yeah, thanks," she felt like she was starving, even after the huge meal the previous night.

They sat at the table and ate quietly. Then they spent the next few hours just shooting the breeze. He told her about his childhood overseas and how he got started climbing in New Zealand. She talked about her youth in California and her love of archeology. But no matter how long they talked around him, they both knew the talk would end up on Jason Quinn.

"So Curtis, what's Jason's story?" Eva asked when the conversation had lulled. By now, they had switched from tea to beers. Curtis sat back in his chair and sipped his Guinness. He seemed to be contemplating where to begin, but his steel gray eyes were boring into her. She felt slightly uncomfortable, and just as she was about to say something else to break the silence, he began.

"I was climbing in the Jungfrau region in Switzerland. This would have been in '95, now." He paused for another sip of stout. "My partner François and I were stuck in a bivouac at altitude. He had fallen about thirty feet and broken a leg. We had no idea how we were going to get him down the mountain, and anyway we had a snowstorm to wait out. It was a long night, let me tell you.

"The dawn finally broke and I stuck my head out the door of our tent. And there was Quinn. This cocky 15-year-old kid. He was climbing alone and he'd been on the mountain during the storm too. I couldn't believe it. But he and I got together and managed to get François to the ground and to a doctor. The leg never set properly though, and the man was done climbing. I was only 19 at the time myself. But I liked Quinn right off the bat. It didn't matter that he was a kid, you know. And I was out a climbing partner."

He paused again for another long moment. "So we started to hang out a lot and we climbed as often as we could. He was in school on some exchange program thingy, and I was working as an Alpine guide. I soon found out he was an awesome climber. Everything on the rock just seemed easy for him. He was a natural and quite a bit better than I was. But I started to catch up to him eventually. We were inseparable for about three years."

Another pause, and the man finished the beer off. Eva stayed silent. She could tell there would be a lot to this story.

"Her name was Sabrina," he said quietly. There was a long silence. "She was Swiss, and smart, and lovely in every way. I liked her a lot. She and Quinn were perfect for each other. He and Sabrina got engaged just before they graduated high school. His dad was working in Bolivia as a Foreign Service Officer at the time. The man got reassigned back to DC, and Quinn went with him to live in Baltimore at the family home. Sabrina went with them, and I headed to the States for the wedding a few months later."

Silence again. This time with Curtis gazing directly into her eyes. She met the gaze wondering where this was going. He seemed to see her working things out.

"He said you met Gene."

"Yes. Things seemed pretty strained between them," she said.

"Well, Gene Quinn was actually CIA. Had been for years. He was a Marine Corps pilot. Vietnam. Laos. Air America. The whole bit. He was a natural for the spook shit. The job took him all over the world and lots of times he was undercover as a diplomat at an embassy somewhere. The kids went with him sometimes, and other times stayed with the grandparents in Baltimore. Naturally they had no idea their old man was in the intel biz."

"Kids?" Eva wanted to know.

"Younger sister...Erica. I'm getting there. Anyway, seems like Gene got in a little of the special ops stuff over the course of the years. There were people looking for him. The wedding was this big elaborate affair with all the trimmings. Let's put it this way... it ended grim. Three assassins showed up gunning for Gene. He was armed and the resulting shoot-up—well, there were a lot of relatives and friends knocked off. The CIA hushed the whole thing up. Erica was among the dead."

He paused again. This time she understood the reason for all the long breaks. The man was collecting himself. She waited, letting the ramifications for Jason and Gene's relationship sink in.

"Sabrina was killed too."

He paused.

"In his arms, Eva. She didn't die quickly."

Eva felt a tear roll down her own cheek. She was horrified.

"The gunmen got away after the shootout. Jason disappeared. Literally. No one knew where he went. Not even Gene and his friends, *Christians In Action*, could find him. I moved here to Colorado to live in a house my family had inherited. I went to work for Rocky Mountain Rescue, and college too. Eventually I started at ARGO. Six years went by. No contact from him at all.

"Then one day, out of the blue, he shows up at my place. We stayed up all night drinking and he told me what he'd been up to. As far as I know, he never told anyone else, not even Marge."

Curtis got up and went to the kitchen cabinet to pour himself something a little stronger. He got out two highball glasses and poured a few fingers of Jack Daniels in each with three ice cubes apiece. He didn't bother to ask Eva if she wanted the drink. He knew she'd take it.

"Thanks," she said. Then she took a sip. The fire crept its way down her throat like a spelunker searching out a new tunnel.

"He's a dual citizen of the U.K. and the U.S. Did you know that? His mother was Thai, but she had an English passport. Quinn went to England and enlisted in the military there. You've heard of the Special Air Service?" Curtis waited for an answer, but Eva just shook her head. "They're England's Special Forces guys. Tough as hell and legendary. Generally considered to be the best of the best. Jason was attached to an anti-terrorism team. Not long, really. Just long enough to get the skills he would need. He said they give you all kinds of psychological tests as well as physical ones. Trying to weed out the nutcases and the people hell bent on vengeance like he was. But he passed them all.

"To make a long story short, he tracked down the three killers from the wedding. Each of them in a different part of the world. It took him a few years, but he did it." Johnson didn't say that Quinn had killed the men. He didn't need to. Eva understood. He didn't want to get into the details of what Quinn had told him he had done. Johnson himself didn't like to think about it.

He waited a bit to let that information sink in. Eva sat silently. "He got out of the service, and into Oxford then. Two degrees in two years. Magna cum laude and all that highbrow shit. Then he showed up on my doorstep here in Colorado and I got him a gig with ARGO. We started climbing again and went on jobs in Africa and Asia. He's gone on a few dates but nothing serious, Eva. Not for fifteen years. He likes you. A lot. I can tell. I've known him longer than just about anyone. But if it happens, it's gonna probably happen slowly, you understand? Slowly."

CHAPTER 24

Quinn was back an hour later and after a quick exchange, Curtis left. It was evening again and Quinn heated them up some canned soup. He told Eva he'd seen Marge again and that there was little the local FBI branch could do, unless there was an attack on U.S. soil. There still had been no word from Mooky either. They were to sit tight and check in the next day.

After they had eaten and Quinn was finishing up the dishes, Eva had an idea.

"Didn't you say this place had some fireplaces?" she asked slowly.

"There's one in the Library. Are you cold?" he seemed concerned. The house was heated by passive solar—the fireplaces were extra, but he rarely used them.

"A little."

They went into the library with the rest of the bottle of Chianti they'd had with dinner, and Quinn got the fire going. The chairs were too far away, so Eva just plopped down on the carpet near the hearth. Quinn joined her.

They sat and sipped the ruby liquid, then Quinn surprised her. "You never told me if you were seeing either of the guys on your dig."

"Hah. Malcolm or David? Not a chance. One was the epitome of *slut* and the other was the poster child for *prude*." she laughed. "No, not seeing anyone." Then, she decided to push her luck. "I didn't think you were interested."

A slow smile crept across Quinn's tanned face. His green eyes sparkled in the firelight. "You think I'd rescue just any damsel in distress?"

"Actually, yes. I do."

He laughed. Eva thought the laugh was more than a little nervous. "Okay, bad example. Yes, Eva. I'm interested. It's just been a long time. I haven't been involved with anyone for a while. Things are... I–"

"Jason," she cut him off. "It's okay. What say we take things slowly?"

His smile told her that she'd understood and saved him for a complicated and painful explanation. He set his wine glass down on the hearth and leaned in to kiss her slowly and fully. She set her own glass down and could feel the apprehension draining out of him as she caressed his face. She pulled him down on top of her. They laid by the fire for a while, listening to each other breathe, then fell asleep in each others arms by the fire.

Around five in the morning, Quinn woke up to an internal alarm clock. He'd always had the ability to wake up when he wanted. The fire had gone out and it was cooler in the house. He started to get up but Eva woke easily as soon as he moved. "Hi. Did you sleep alright?" he kissed her forehead.

"Yeah. I was really comfortable. I just wake up easily. Breakfast?"

"Sure. It's still early though." They wandered sleepily into the kitchen. It was still dark outside the glass doors. "Coffee or Tea?"

"Ooh, tea. Please."

Quinn put the kettle on, then turned to look at her as she was tying her long blonde hair back with a black scrunchy thing. There was a small red dot dead in the center of the 'O' of the ARGO logo on her breast. As the image was registering in his brain, his feet were already in motion.

He lunged at her, taking them both to the ground just as the sliding glass doors exploded inward, spraying shards of glass all over the room. She was screaming and bullets were lodging in the wall of his kitchen just over their heads. He started to crawl over the glass toward the hallway. "Stay down!"

As he reached the cover of the hall, he stood and began sprinting for the Jericho in the Library. At the other end of the hall, the front door burst open, splintering at the hinges. The man was in all-white snow fatigues and was armed with an Ingram MAC-10. The Ingram is a small, hand held semi-automatic weapon that fires a lot of bullets in a small amount of time. But as Quinn knew, they weren't very reliable, nor were they easy to aim. He dove left into the Library, grabbed the Jericho and just started firing at the wall. The bullets passed through the wall and into the hall. He didn't want to give the gunner time to reach Eva. He rolled onto the floor back into the hall firing as he came out of the roll. One of the shots through the Library wall had hit the gunner in the shoulder. The first shot Quinn fired from the hallway floor went into the man's eye, right through his snow goggles. The next shot Quinn fired hit the man dead center as he began his descent to the floor.

Quinn was still in motion heading toward Eva, who was lying on the floor and covering her head. The shooting had stopped but the shooter was probably still out there. Quinn kept his head down and asked if Eva was hit, but she was fine. The hallway was the perfect place to remain. He could see access to the house from the front or from the kitchen. He stayed where he was and waited it out. Eva didn't move.

After a minute, footsteps approached and Quinn heard exactly what he was hoping for. Curtis's voice shouting "All clear, Jason." Then, another crash as a snow fatigues-clad body crashed through the remains of the sliding glass door, the chest impaled by a fragment of glass, which had still stood in the frame. Curtis Johnson stood just outside the doors with a hunting rifle on his back and an M4A1 rifle with laser scope in his hands. He was covered from head to toe in white snow camouflage as well.

"Sorry man, it took me awhile to find the sneaky bastard. I had an idea he was out there an hour ago. Been looking for him ever since."

"Not a problem. I was busy with the other one. Anyone else?" Quinn asked, as he helped Eva up.

"Not yet, but where there's one of these fuckers..." Curtis began.

"There's ten more, I know. Get in here and cover the hall a minute." Quinn ran for the stairs to the second floor. Eva put on her shoes and grabbed her down coat from the rack in the hall. Curtis stood by Eva and kept his eyes on the splintered front door and the kitchen both. He and Quinn had been taking turns in snow camo watching the house from the woods. Just in case. Johnson was doing the nights while Quinn had been on the property most of the previous day. Quinn was thundering down the stairs a minute later with a black canvas bag slung over his shoulder and a silenced Heckler and Koch MP-5 in each hand. These were the types of weapon he had used in the service, and he had obtained them when he moved to Colorado. The attic Eva hadn't seen housed the weapons and a few other items Quinn had always kept in case they were ever needed. "Leave the rifles," he said. Curtis dropped them on the floor, and Quinn handed him one of the MP5s. They had both fired the weapons at the range in the sub-basement of ARGO.

"Time to go," Quinn said, leading the way to the door.

CHAPTER 25

Quinn led them to the ARGO Nissan, and they left Curtis's 2004 Ford Super Duty truck behind. They got in quickly with Quinn behind the wheel, Eva in back, and Curtis in the passenger side with the window down, and the MP-5 at the ready. Quinn started the engine, shoved the gear selector into drive, and slammed his foot on the gas. They raced off down the winding road toward the entrance to the mine but soon heard the staccato roar of the pursuing Kawasaki dirt bikes as the cycles leapt out of the trees with more white-clad riders. The bikes would have had a tough time making it over the mountains and into Quinn's valley, but Curtis saw that they had long snow spikes on the tires.

He loosed a volley of fire in their direction but missed. Quinn kept his foot on the floor, expertly negotiating the curves and the fishtailing of the rear end of the vehicle. He pressed the button on the garage door opener before the gate was even in sight. It was still dark out, but the sky was beginning to lighten in the East.

"Four bikes," Curtis told Quinn.

"We'll lose them in the mine," Quinn replied. "We'll—"

But Quinn was cut off as the sound of machine gun fire filled the air. Three of the riders had fallen behind. They were having a hard enough time with the slippery curves of the mountain road despite the winter tire spikes on their bikes. The bike in the lead had two riders, the added weight aiding in maneuverability. The second rider was armed with an AK-47 assault rifle and he fired over the shoulder of the driver. The sound shredded the morning calm. On the third burst, the rear window of the Nissan exploded inward, showering Eva with small square chunks of safety glass.

"Keep down, Eva!" Quinn yelled. She was already on her way into the foot well of the back seat. Curtis returned fire over her head and out the wide-open rear end of the vehicle. He hit the driver of the dirt bike and watched in satisfaction as the bike left the road, raced up a small hill and launched into the air. The rifleman leapt off the back and landed in a small evergreen tree. The driver's now limp body stayed with the bike until it crumpled into a small clearing between the trees.

The other three bikes were now catching up. The entrance to the mine came into the sight of the headlights and Curtis could see that it was fully open. He fired another burst out the rear of the truck, then turned forward to see the gate starting to close already as Quinn floored the Nissan through it. The first two bikes in pursuit made it inside the pitch-dark corridor. The third bike nearly made it, but the gate was made of unforgiving steel and the rider was crushed as his Kawasaki slammed into the wall of the cliff and the gate. The bike exploded from the impact, engulfing the entrance behind Quinn's Nissan in a ball of flame. He watched in the rear view mirror for just a second before returning his gaze to the road ahead of him through the mine.

Quinn raced ahead in the familiar tunnel, and as he made his way around a curve to the right and passed a support beam on the left, he began mentally counting and turned off the headlights. The tunnel plunged into darkness, then it was lit somewhat as the trailing bikes came around the curve in the distance behind them. Quinn raced on in the dark. When he reached a certain number in his head, he slowed suddenly to a near halt and turned on the parking lights. Just enough for him to see the quickly approaching chasm. He lined the SUV up with the planks and crossed. As soon as he was on the other side, he slammed on the brake, slipped the transmission into park, and leapt out of the truck and raced back to the chasm on foot. He crouched down and shoved the planks with all his strength. The iron planks were heavy but they slid. The first one dropped into the chasm and then the second. He was almost out of time. He was back in the Nissan and they were racing from the spot, just as the dirt bikes were coming to the chasm. The first of the two remaining riders was too late. He slammed on the brakes and the bike spun out from under him. He slid across the gravel road with the bike following him. Curtis watched in awe behind him as the rider slid right off the edge of the chasm and into the opposite wall of the gap. His trashed bike dug into the edge of the wall as if it were unwilling to take the plunge following its former rider. The second rider had seen what was going on and had actually sped up!

Curtis saw the man bring the bike up onto its rear wheel and ride up and over the first bike, then launch across the abyss. He landed safely on the other side and continued his pursuit. Then Curtis felt Quinn slamming on the brakes again. It was only a short distance from the chasm to the elevator. Quinn got out with the second MP-5 and walked toward the fast approaching motorcyclist. He switched the safety selector to single fire, raised the weapon with one arm outstretched toward the cyclist and fired at the man's face. Eva watched in horror as the man's head disappeared, the rider's body pitched backward and the bike came ramming into the wall very close to the back of the Nissan. She heard a wrenching tearing sound as the motorcycle was crushed against the unyielding stone. Then the elevator began to ascend. There was some scraping of metal as it began. But in the end, the freight elevator was more than a match for the small chunks of debris that had lodged into its workings from the remains of the bike.

Quinn walked back toward the Nissan from the edge of the elevator and got back into the driver's seat. "Fuckers just don't quit."

"What do we do now? Where can we go?" Eva sounded calm, but Quinn knew she was close to panicking.

"We'll go to ARGO. The cops and the FBI will be there by the time we get there. Don't worry. We're gonna get to the bottom of this shit." Quinn spoke softly but confidently. As he did, Curtis was taking the cell-phone from the glove compartment. He knew there'd be no signal this deep in the mountain, but as soon as they emerged from the other side, he had some dialing to do. Quinn turned to Curtis, "Then we take this fight to this Hong-moron's doorstep."

CHAPTER 26

Sure enough, as Quinn had promised, when he brought the bullet-ridden and battered Nissan tearing into the ARGO parking lot by the inverted pyramidal structure, several squad cars and more than a few unmarked government cars were waiting for them. They had been following a squad car that had been acting as an escort with lights flashing and siren screaming for the last quarter mile. Curtis observed perhaps twenty or more uniformed officers with combat shotguns waiting in the parking lot when they arrived. They hadn't seen any more white-clad assassins since they had emerged from the other side of the mine, but Marge apparently wasn't willing to take a chance after he'd called her and given her the scoop. She'd called David Chambers, and the federal agent had arranged for most of the state troopers, county police, and town cops from a thirty-mile radius to show up with guns drawn.

They got out of the perforated SUV and were met by a uniformed state trooper with a nametag that said "Dennings" and a mustache that said *frequently and finely cared for*. "You Jason Quinn?" he asked, all business.

"That's me. Curtis Johnson, Dr. Eva Rayjek." Quinn said, introducing the others. "Thanks for coming. Is Chambers here too?" Quinn shook the man's hand as he thanked him, then they began hurriedly walking toward the building's lobby. The others followed.

"He's inside with Ms. Tower. They're all waiting for you, son. From the sound of things, you three are lucky to be alive." Dennings escorted them into the lobby, where another dozen unfamiliar law enforcement officials of varying rank and service waited anxiously. Samantha was at the desk and looked relieved to see Quinn in one piece. She came out from behind the counter and rode with them in the elevator on their way to see Marge. No security badges this time. She escorted them personally with her hand resting on the .45 on her police belt the whole time. Dennings waited in the lobby. *Apparently, he wasn't one of the big-wigs. Must have just been one of the Empire cops*, Quinn thought. No one spoke on the ride up.

When the door opened on the boardroom Eva had seen the last time, a different sight greeted her. The room was full of people. Some in suits, some in uniform. The table was covered with files, telephones, laptops, radios, coffee mugs and a few open boxes of donuts. There was activity everywhere as they made their way past the people to the other end of the table. The assembled cops and agents looked up to see the trio with Samantha, but quickly went right back to work. Marge was speaking softly with David Chambers at the far end of the table. Chambers was about 35, with bleached blonde hair, a nice three-piece suit, and a characteristic bulge in his left armpit where his compact Glock 23 rested in its holster. Quinn and Johnson had met the man a few times, and although his demeanor was always friendly yet firm—all business, all the time—Quinn couldn't help thinking that the man's youthful appearance made him seem more like one of the snowboarding kids at Breckenridge than a decorated federal agent.

"Thank God, you're all right," Marge said as she hugged each of them. Then she got right down to business. "Eva, this is Agent David Chambers of the Federal Bureau of Investigation. He's not technically in charge here. That'd be Bill Hanks from Colorado Bureau of Investigations over there on the cell-phone."

Chambers jumped in, "He and I are old friends. I kick his ass in poker, Thursdays. At any rate, we're all doing what we can to get these bastards, Dr. Rayjek." Then he turned to Curtis, "What can you guys tell me?"

Curtis told the whole story starting with the incident in China, then explained how he and Quinn had taken turns in the woods watching the house and looking for signs of intruders. He detailed the fight and Quinn broke in with details of weapons and the style of dirt bike. Then, Chambers asked Eva to explain her theory on Hedin and everything she could remember about the dig site in China. By the time they were done, they had all had a few cups of coffee and a few donuts to go with it. A few hours had passed.

Hanks, the senior man in uniform had come over about halfway through and listened without interruption. He knew he was in way over his head. The man was sixty-one, with a receding hairline that was more like a *receded* hairline. What little hair left on his head was at the back and looked like an afterthought. The belly suggested that he spent far more time playing poker with Chambers than attending to serious crime. There wasn't a whole lot of serious crime in this part of the mountains. Between Denver and the ski resorts where Empire was situated, the most interesting thing to fall across the man's desk was usually the accident reports. Hanks was content to follow the FBI's lead on this case, jurisdiction or no. He received a report from another uniformed cop, and then finally spoke.

"We've got the body of the guy by the elevator in your mine shaft, Mr. Quinn. Strange tattoo on his chest. Looks like Chinese writing. No I.D. We lowered guys by cable to the house from a chopper. Nowhere to land, like you said earlier. They found the other bodies. All of 'em with ink. No sign of any more of the creeps. We're running their prints, but in all honesty, I'm not expecting we're gonna be able to do much more than offer protection for a while in case these nut-jobs try again."

"I appreciate it," Quinn said. Then he turned to Marge. "I need to see if Mooky has any news for us yet. Can I use the computer in your office?"

Marge nodded, and Quinn went into the octagonal office off the board room. The room was small, but contained a large teak desk with a slab of glass covering the whole of the wooden surface of the tabletop. There was a phone, a computer, and one silver framed photo of the long lost William Tower. Quinn sat in the plush leather chair and opened an e-mail account on Marge's computer. There was a new message from mjones@travelers.net. Quinn popped it open and saw a message that read only: "FTF ASAP."

It meant that Mooky had something for them. Quinn sent a reply and waited. He knew that there was not currently any software installed on Marge's computer that could handle the *face-to-face* video contact Mooky had requested, but he knew that wouldn't be a problem. Mooky would have it downloaded to Marge's computer momentarily, and he would hack into the closed circuit security camera in the corner of Marge's office ceiling as well.

Quinn knew that within five minutes Mooky's face would appear on the screen of Marge's monitor and Mooky would see him as well.

Quinn waited.

It took 90 seconds.

Mooky's tanned face appeared and a palm tree was swaying behind him. Quinn imagined him sitting on a beach somewhere.

"The tattoos read *Fu Huo,* which is mandarin for *resurrect.* I have plenty of info on who has used that phrase in Chinese history. Very few leads on what it might mean today, though. Unfortunately the best one I have is a serious stretch." Mooky was visibly disappointed to not be able to provide a more concrete answer to the mystery of who the killers were.

"I'll take what you can give me, buddy." Quinn replied with a smile.

"I've sent it all. There's also info on Lars Eriksson, the guy that helped Hedin fake his death."

"He's still alive?" Quinn was shocked.

"Yep. 86 years old and living in Helsinki. The address is there too. Listen, Quinn, I was monitoring police bands in your area. Are you guys okay?" Mooky had lost all semblance of his earlier grin, and was genuinely concerned for his friend.

"Yeah. They tried again, but we're fine. Listen, there's some things I'm gonna need you to arrange for me. It's time to get proactive."

CHAPTER 27

Quinn thought Helsinki was cold.

Damn cold.

Antarctica cold.

The city was in the icy clutches of its long dark winter by January, and this year they were seeing lows in the region of -13° Fahrenheit. Even with the frequent snow, Helsinki's cold was a dry cold, which tended to make it slightly more bearable.

Initially, Quinn had tried to get Eva to remain in Colorado, but she wouldn't hear of it. "I'm seeing this through to the end," she told him. Chambers drove them from ARGO's office to Wyoming, at first with them ducked down and Curtis riding in the trunk to make it appear that Chambers was alone in the car. Once they were a few miles away, they had given up on concealment for the sake of comfort. From Wyoming, they flew to New York and then on to Helsinki.

The flight from the U.S. had been uneventful, and there had been no indication that they were even being followed by more of the assassins. Quinn had explained his hopes that they could get to Lars Eriksson and obtain some useful info before the ever-present Chinese gunmen reared their heads again. However, he was leaving nothing to chance. He had arranged for two cars to be waiting for them at the airport in Finland. Quinn drove one with Eva and Johnson took the wheel of the other. Under the seat of the car Quinn had requested Mooky to secure for him, he found a small cloth-wrapped package that he slipped into his jacket when the others were not looking. Inside was a Russian-made 9 mm Yarygin PYa pistol that Quinn had no idea how Mooky had obtained, but he wasn't about to ask questions. Mooky wasn't taking any chances either, even if the gun laws in Finland were harsh.

They had also found an envelope containing Silja Line ferry tickets for the following day to take them from Turku across the Gulf of Bothnia to Stockholm in Sweden. There were also train tickets for the ride from Helsinki to Turku. All of this was conducted ahead of time as preparation, but in the hopes that they would not need this particular escape route from Finland, because they all already had return air tickets back to the States. *Just in case,* Quinn had told them. *It pays to have a Plan B.*

Johnson followed Quinn through the snowy city streets to a small street in a residential neighborhood. Quinn checked the street signs and a piece of paper he had written his destination on to make sure he had the right place. *Vanriki Stoolin Katu.* He pulled around behind the six story apartment blocks that lined the street and into an alleyway behind, where he parked the car, and Johnson did likewise with his Mercedes S-320 CDI sedan. They walked around to the front of the building and along the street to the appropriate door. Quinn rang the bell, and they all waited in the light falling snow for a full two minutes before a voice greeted them on the intercom in Finnish: "*Terve?*"

"Mr. Eriksson? Jason Quinn here. We spoke on the telephone yesterday?" Quinn replied in Finnish, leaning forward and pressing the return button on the intercom.

"Yes, of course. Please come in." The man had switched to a flawless English, and the gate buzzed briefly allowing them into a small courtyard on their way to the front door.

Lars Eriksson didn't look 86 years old. He was fit and trim, and could easily have passed for a man in his late fifties. His short-cropped hair was still more blonde than white, and his crystalline blue eyes radiated with clarity and a good humor that Quinn took to immediately. They shook hands warmly, and Quinn introduced the others. Eriksson invited them into his modest one bedroom, ground floor flat. Quinn began to remove his shoes as was generally the custom in many European homes, but Eriksson stopped him.

"No need to take your shoes off. The place is a bit drafty, and I find I need the extra warmth. So I keep mine on most of the day," he said. He invited them to sit, and then went off to the kitchen to fix them tea.

The flat was furnished with some simple and tasteful, yet inexpensive furniture and little in the way of decoration, besides the common items that indicate a well lived-in home. Quinn correctly guessed the man to be on a very small pension as his only source of income.

The man brought them tea and cookies on a tray and then sat in a chair facing the three as they all sat on a sofa across a low coffee table from him. He just sat quietly and looked at them. Eva looked to Quinn to do the talking but he also sat quietly, just looking at the older man. The man smiled briefly, just the hint of the corners of his mouth raising, and then he poured them each a cup of black tea and began his tale.

"He was famous by that point, you see. It was impossible for him to go anywhere or do anything, without the local newspapermen taking note." Lars Eriksson leaned back in his chair as if he were digging through files in his brain, looking for the appropriate manila folder. "He had been a few years before to the Vatican and had a private audience with the Pope. It was a trip he had undertaken in secret, and the whole time he was in Italy I was bringing bags of groceries to his house, and making it look like he was still at home.

"If that ruse had not been successful, I doubt if he would have tried anything else. But it worked. The press figured he was hard at work on his next book. Besides, with his support of Germany, he was not very popular with some people at the time. This trip to see the church would have been about five years before the end. I was the only one in Sweden who knew of his trip. When he came back, he was rejuvenated—truly alive. I had not seen him that way in the years we had known one another. But I recognized the look in his eyes as similar to the one he had whenever he would talk about his expeditions. That is how I knew he was planning another one. Even before he told me what transpired between Pope Pius the Twelfth and him."

The man sat forward and took a sip of his tea. He let the silence hang.

The others sat calmly and waited. It was clear that this man had an extraordinary tale to tell and he had held the secret for many years. It was a tale that had to be told correctly, and slowly.

"What do you know of the Taiping Rebellion in China, Mr. Quinn?" Eriksson asked.

Taiping Rebellion, Taiping Shipping, David Hong, son of a bitch, Quinn thought. Now he knew for certain who had sent the killers. He just didn't understand yet how all the pieces fit, but he was sure that it was Hong. *First Gene's CIA tip, then the longshot in the file Mooky had sent, and now Eva's Hedin theory. They were all falling into place.* "Mr. Eriksson, it seems that I am about to learn an awful lot more about it. But what I do know is that a man by the name of Hong Xiu Quan believed he was under a divine mandate from God to take over all of China. He was nearly successful, and his hold over China lasted about 14 years."

"Quite right, Mr. Quinn. Hong believed he was the younger brother of Jesus Christ himself. God's second child, as it were. He was a madman, of course, and today it is quite easy to recognize him as such when we look at the histories. But in the middle of the nineteenth century, the Vatican was a long way away from Southeast China. The missionaries in that region were at first confounded by this feverish man claiming to have had visions from God. But they quickly became true believers. These were well-respected men of the Catholic Church, you see. Their word held much weight in Rome."

The man paused to drink the last of his tea and rub at his temple slightly as if all of this turmoil in China a hundred and fifty years ago had affected him greatly.

"Pope Pius the Ninth bought into the insanity as well, and initially lent his support to the Taiping or *Heavenly* army in their bid to take over China in the name of Christianity. Eventually, he began to realize what a blood-crazed madman Hong was. The Vatican and the Western powers all pulled their support of the Taipings and threw in their weight with the Qing government instead, which quickly suppressed the revolution."

The man stopped talking again and this time let the silence hang longer, inviting questions.

Quinn took the bait. "And so one hundred years later, Sven Hedin, one of the greatest explorers of all time meets with a different Pope Pius, and learns…?"

"There was a document, you see. Signed by Pius the Ninth. Quite embarrassing if it should ever surface. After all, the Vatican put a spin on the story after withdrawing their support. They acted as if a few over-zealous missionaries were the only ones lending credence to Hong's divinity. Hedin was told that Vatican scholars suspected the document laid with Hong Xiu Quan in his tomb, the whereabouts of which were unknown, but rumored to be in the Taklamakan Desert."

Curtis wasn't sure yet where things were heading, but the others were fitting the pieces together.

Eva spoke up for the first time. "The Vatican asked Hedin to mount an expedition to find the document."

Eriksson nodded. "That was why he got the surgeries to fix his eyes. The faked death was to deflect any attention to the trip or its nature."

"He never came back though," Quinn offered. Eriksson just sadly shook his head. "And Hong Xiu Quan's tomb was never found. So when Eva came across an archeological site in China that was an unrecorded city in the desert—one that might have been the site of the tomb—someone tried to kill her. These men wear tattoos that read *resurrect*, and that was a rallying cry of Taiping soldiers during the final days of their rebellion. When Mooky told me the list of possible meanings for that word, that connection seemed the most far-fetched. But now I don't have any doubts. David Hong is a huge shipping magnate in Hong Kong. He owns a shipping fleet called *Taiping Huoyun*—or *Heavenly Freight*. He's built a gigantic cathedral on the Hong Kong waterfront. He's supposed to be a staunch Catholic. It seems he also wants to get his hands on the document."

"Mr. Eriksson," Eva began, "do you have any idea where Hedin was heading?"

"Sadly, no. He told me the purpose of the trip, and I arranged the details for his getaway. I handled the whole phony funeral, and the dealings with his estate. Naturally, I had to pay off a few people. But he left me no details of his plan. All I knew was the *Taklamakan*. He said it was for the best,

although I honestly thought at the time that he might not be sure himself."
Eriksson seemed deflated. He had given them helpful information, but not
enough information.

Quinn stood up and the others all followed his lead. He reached across the
table to shake the man's hand again. "You've been a great help, sir. I'd…"

Quinn's thanks were cut off as the front door exploded inwards and
bullets blasted into the apartment like a thousand tiny furious wasps.

CHAPTER 28

Quinn's hand grasped the old man's firmly and instead of shaking it, as he had originally intended, he yanked hard. He pulled the old man across the coffee table and into himself as he threw his weight backward sending them both tumbling over and behind the sofa. They landed in a pile right next to where Curtis had leaped with Eva.

Bullets still ripped into the walls near the entryway of the small apartment. Bits of plaster were spraying out of the entryway and into the living room. Quinn looked behind him to the kitchen, and found the door to the exterior of the apartment there.

"Curtis, take him and go!" Quinn shouted. He hustled Eva into the kitchen as well. "I'll hold them as long as I can."

"We're gone," Curtis said. He opened the rear door cautiously, checking for more gunmen, but they were all at the front of the place. He dragged the old man out and toward his Mercedes sedan.

Quinn stood near the door to the kitchen aiming the Russian pistol from behind the small refrigerator, which he had opened up to use as a small shield of sorts. He waited for the first sight of a body. He wasn't about to waste ammunition. He didn't have a fully automatic rifle like his opponents. He also figured they wouldn't be expecting him to be armed. He didn't want to give up that element of surprise yet. Then suddenly the deafening roar of uninterrupted automatic fire ceased. Quinn waited a beat. Nothing happened.

"Eva, get in the car. I'll be right there. Leave the driver's door open for me," Quinn whispered softly. She nodded at him, and slipped out the back door.

From where he was poised, Quinn had a good view of the end of the entryway to the apartment. He knew he'd be able to take out whoever came through first. But if they came through in a rush, he wasn't so sure.

Then it happened.

The tip of a silenced rifle came slowly into view, and Quinn understood.

Amateurs.

They would come in slowly and cautiously. It gave Quinn ideas. He glanced around and saw what he needed. A large cast iron frying pan was on the small stovetop range next to the refrigerator. Quinn pocketed the pistol and instead picked up the skillet. He cocked his arm back and waited until he saw a part of the assailant's arm. Then he launched the pan across the room. It knocked the gun from the man's hands and Quinn heard him cry out. But Quinn was already on his way out of the apartment. The others wouldn't be fooled so easily, but Quinn smiled anyway.

They still don't know I'm armed, and now they'll come quickly.

He sprinted out to the car and his smile widened as he took a small moment to appreciate the ferocious grace of the vehicle before him. The metallic silver 2005 Mercedes SLR McLaren. As he had asked, Eva had left the driver's side door in the up position, where it hovered both above the entrance to the car and swung outwards like an aircraft wing. Quinn took up position at the driver's side and aimed the Russian pistol across the roof of the coupé. He was glad that Curtis was already gone with the old man. The plan had always been for Quinn to act as a diversion should the need arise. That was why Quinn had arranged for the faster car.

As he had expected, two men came barreling out of the door immediately. They wore black ski masks, but Quinn had no doubt that they would both have Asian features underneath the wool. The men were dressed entirely in black and armed with Finnish Sako Rk.75 rifles with Reflex sound suppressors. Quinn recognized the weapons as Finnish rifles whose original design resembled a modified AK-47 assault rifle. Neither of the men got off a single shot. Quinn fired four shots, two to the center of each man's head. He was sliding into the McLaren and closing the door before either body hit concrete.

Jason Quinn didn't enjoy killing men. The smile he had felt when appraising his swift set of wheels had quickly faded.

"Seatbelt, Eva." he told her. She quickly attached the belt as he did his own.

Now, he used his thumb to flip a plastic lid off the top of the gear-shifting lever. He depressed the ignition switch for the car. The engine purred softly to life. Quinn stamped the accelerator pedal, and he had finished shifting to third by the time he left the alleyway. Just as he was turning back to Eriksson's street, he heard the report of small arms fire behind him.

There were more of them.

They would follow, he knew. He was just surprised at how quickly they pulled it together after he had taken two of them down. He was pulling onto Mannerheimintie, one of the more major streets of Helsinki, which was just around the corner from Eriksson's little suburban street, when a stream of midnight black BMW 645ci coupés raced after him. He counted six of them on his tail as he sped into the center of the city. There were too many of them. Quinn figured that they had to have been waiting in the cars. They were a backup team. Now he began to worry that Curtis might also have picked up a backup team. He would have to put all of that out of his mind for now.

Just focus on the driving.

Eva was looking over the back of her leather covered carbon-fiber bucket seat to count the chase cars.

"There's seven of them now," she said.

"Christ!" Quinn swore as he swerved between cars on the snowy road and then hung a sharp left toward the train station. He calmly controlled the fishtailing rear end of the sports car as if he had been driving on snow and ice all his life. He made straight for the huge station building, then abruptly switched gears, switched lanes, and took a right turn, south and away from the station. The maneuver lost the first of his pursuit cars, because that driver hadn't been fast enough to make the turn, but the other six cars were still with him.

Quinn quickly calculated a few advantages he had over the pursuers. He knew Helsinki like the back of his hand. His grandmother on his father's side was Finnish. He'd spent his summers for a number of years with his grandparents in

Helsinki. Then, he'd made it a point to visit at least once a year since. He liked the place and knew some of its secrets. He also could remember now that the top speed of the BMW 6 series was around 150 mph. His McLaren, which Mooky had obtained for him, would do more like 200 mph before its 5.5 liter supercharged V8 would begin to bitch and moan. But even though he had 617 horses at his disposal, he knew the crowded city streets of Helsinki wouldn't give him much of a speed advantage over his party crashers.

He'd need something more. He jerked the McLaren into a hard right-angle turn onto the *Pohjoisesplanadi* or the esplanade. *Against the one-way traffic.* This was one of the city's major shopping streets. One of the chase cars got nailed by an oncoming taxi as it came out of the small side street and the two vehicles smashed through the display windows of the famous Stockmann department store. The vehicles looked so twisted and intertwined that they might have once been one large vehicle.

Ouch, Quinn thought.

He wove skillfully through the traffic heading toward Katajanokka Island where he hoped he might be able to lose the rest of the pursuit cars. Quinn was thinking of the low center of gravity of the McLaren, and its *mid-front* engine configuration, which gave it a perfect 50/50 balance. And its carbon-fiber frame and crash tubes.

"Okay," he said. "Fuck it."

Eva was looking at him, wondering what next, when she was nearly thrown into him as he hung a sharp left turn heading for the Fisherman's Wharf. Another chase car raced past, not making the turn. It headed on into the crossing into Katajanokka.

That leaves four, Quinn counted.

Off to his left Quinn could see a concrete boat launch into the frozen Esteläsatama Bay. Quinn aimed the McLaren to the right of that, crashing through some small tables that had been set up for a fish market. He pushed the pedal to the floor and launched the car like a rocket at the edge of the concrete retaining wall and the flimsy chain—the only two things between Helsinki and the frozen sea.

CHAPTER 29

Seawater freezes at 28.6° Fahrenheit. Helsinki, the 'Summer City' of Finland, normally deals with temperatures in the mid teens in the winter. This year they were seeing temperatures in the -10 to -20 region. Not quite record lows, but close. The Esteläsatama Bay and even large sections of the Gulf of Finland routinely freeze in winter. Helsinki residents skate, walk, and even drive over its surface. Most often, they drive to the fortress island of Suomenlinna, just two miles off the coast of the city. That was what Quinn had been thinking when he set his jaw, slammed the accelerator pedal to the floor mat, and said "Fuck it."

The McLaren launched through the chain barricade and off the concrete end of the city's fish market. Eva braced herself against the dashboard of the car and winced, thinking her life was over. Quinn hung grimly onto the steering wheel, and slipped the transmission into neutral as the car arced smoothly through the air. The frozen bay spread out before them, covered in snow like the icing on some immaculate wedding cake. The chain of small islets at the end of the bay was visible in the distance. The horizon tilted slightly as the rear end of the car dipped a bit below the front end.

Then it was over.

The rear wheels slammed down onto the ice followed by the front wheels. The jolt was stunning and Quinn felt the steering try to rip from his grasp. He held on and slowly grinned. They were racing across the snow-covered ice of the bay.

"Oh my GOD!" Eva exhaled in a near scream.

Quinn shifted into third, matching their current velocity, then stepped on the gas and the McLaren sprinted ahead. Eva whipped her head around to see that their leap through the sky had taken them nearly 60 feet across the bay. As she watched, the first of the four pursuing black 'beamers' also attempted the jump. But the BMW 645ci doesn't have the same balanced frame as the Mercedes McLaren. As Eva watched, the nose of the black car dipped with the prodigious weight of its engine. It rammed into the ice nose first, in almost the exact spot where the McLaren had hit.

The spot that was already weakened from the first impact.

An ice floe of nearly fifteen feet in diameter ripped loose under the BMW and flipped over like a flapjack on a griddle. The nose of the BMW plunged into the frigid sea as the floe was flipping and the opposing side of it rammed down on top of the tail of the car a second later. The car was severed in half. The unoccupied rear half of the BMW skidded across the ice on its roof and on the lid of the trunk. The front half, with the driver and a companion gunman was lost beneath. The ice floe settled in almost where it had originally lain except that its exposed surface was now jagged with the spikes and waves of an undersea world.

Quinn had caught most of it in the rear view mirror and whistled softly now. "Hot damn!" He raced the Mercedes toward the island chain ahead and frequently looked back for the other pursuers that had chosen not to make the jump.

"Now what? The crazy jump worked, but I don't fancy driving across the ocean to Stockholm." Eva seemed exasperated, but Quinn could tell that she was impressed as all get out.

"First off, this is the Gulf of Finland, not the ocean. Second off, Stockholm is that way and we're not going there anymore." Quinn pointed to his right across her lap and then swerved the car a bit more to the left around the first island called Valkosaari Blekholmen. It was less than 900 feet in diameter.

"What do you mean? I thought we were supposed to be going to Stockholm. That's why we bought train tickets to the coast and ferry tickets to get us to Sweden." Now Eva was truly perplexed and she had lost the slightly charmed air.

"It was a false trail, Eva. We were never going to Sweden. We made a show of buying tickets so that if we were followed, they would think that's where we were headed next. We need to get ahead of these bastards. I'm tired of running for my life."

Eva was quiet for a moment while she absorbed this new information and dealt with the fact that Quinn and Johnson had not confided in her for this part of the plan. She felt left out but quickly realized that they had felt they were protecting her.

"Clever. Okay, so you mind letting me in on the plan?" The smile was almost back in Eva's eyes.

Quinn turned to look at her with a toothy grin. "We're going to Suomenlinna."

"Well that explains a lot. I—"

"Hang on!" Quinn wrenched the wheel to the side and the car began to skid to the left. Bullets perforated the rear driver's side of the Mercedes. The other three black cars roared across the ice after them. The lead car had a gunman leaning out the passenger side of the car firing his Finnish rifle non-stop.

The McLaren was straightening up and Quinn was lowering the driver's side window. He stepped on the gas and shifted up. He began to out distance the BMWs and then he reached into his waistband and pulled the Russian automatic out. He waited and slowed down just a bit so the slower BMWs could catch up. They were coming at him single file. *Probably afraid of falling into the sea,* he thought. It would have been better if they were side by side, but he would take what he could get.

Quinn slammed his foot on the brake, and cranked the wheel as a far as it would go. The McLaren began a 360° spin. He reached out the window with the Yarygin and began spraying 9mm bullets as the closest chase car came within range. He swept his arm from one side of the window to the other until the magazine had fed the last round into the chamber. Then he slowly withdrew his arm, raised the window, and pulled the Mercedes out of its spin with a burst of speed. Eva couldn't believe it. It had taken seconds, *or perhaps less*, she thought. Quinn had spun them in a complete circle and fired an entire clip of bullets as casually as if this sort of thing happened to him every day. To her it seemed that they were heading in exactly the same direction they had been before the spin.

The lead BMW's windshield had been shattered inwards and the gunman in the passenger side was hit in the shoulder. If the driver had maintained his cool, they both would have been fine. But the men chasing Jason and Eva were not professional soldiers. They were not even experienced in using weapons. Many of them were firing guns for the first time in their lives. The driver panicked and wrenched on the steering wheel. The BMW spun as Quinn's McLaren had, but one wheel smacked against an uneven ridge on the ice surface and the momentum rolled the car to its side in an instant. The second chase car was too close behind and rammed into the exposed gasoline tank of the first. Both vehicles were engulfed in a roaring ball of orange and black flame that reached high into the overcast sky.

The third and final car dodged to the right of the flaming wreckage. Even still, the driver could feel the pressure from the blast force his BMW across the ice several feet to the side. He regained control quickly and raced after the shining silver McLaren. The passenger leaned out the window and selected single fire on his suppressed rifle. He tried to take some shots at the Mercedes, but his own car was swerving too much, and his aim was poor to begin with. His shots didn't come close. He spoke to the driver in Mandarin as he slid back inside and shut the window.

"Get closer!"

CHAPTER 30

The sweeping fortress of Suomenlinna lies on a set of eight small islands just off the coast of Helsinki. Built in the 18th century during Swedish rule, the islands held one of the world's largest dry dock shipyards and were studded with serious fortifications that were often compared to mighty Gibraltar. It held a Finnish military garrison until 1973 and it still has a civilian population of about 850 hardy people. The wind-battered ramparts still hold many cannon today.

Quinn knew of Suomenlinna from visits as a child. He knew for instance, that the islands were pedestrian only—but there were roads for service vehicles. He also knew the roads were winding and narrow. He glanced in the rearview mirror for the final chase car as he drove the McLaren off the ice and up the concrete loading ramp at the main quay. The BMW was still in pursuit, but now Quinn could see several police vehicles close on its heels farther back on the treacherous ice. He was surprised that they had gotten in on the chase so soon. Now he knew his plan for evading the last of the assassins would work. The only trick was for Eva and him to actually escape the police afterward.

The speed limit for service vehicles on Suomenlinna was 20 Kilometers per hour (or about 10 mph), but Quinn decided to completely ignore the warning signs and took the turns and switchbacks as quickly as he could. In addition to the fortress walls and ramparts, the islands are home to nearly three hundred buildings that now serve as museums, restaurants, and housing for the people who call the islands home. These are all set upon gentle rolling hills encased by the massive stone walls. Quinn raced around buildings and darted the McLaren in and out of alleys. He soon lost sight of the bewildered

BMW driver who clearly was unfamiliar with the islands. As soon as Quinn couldn't see the BMW in pursuit any longer, he got back onto the one main road and headed straight toward the next island.

The BMW raced around the buildings on the main island of Suomenlinna looking in vain for its prey. The police vehicles were swarming around as well and soon blocked all egress. The Chinese driver of the BMW understood. He pulled the black car to a slow halt and turned off the engine. The passenger slowly lowered the Finnish rifle to the floor of the car. The police were dressed in navy blue with the word *Poliisi* in white across their backs and they were well armed. Several officers were screaming at the occupants of the BMW in Finnish, Swedish, and English. The Chinese men in the car did not get out. They did not roll down the windows or open the doors. The driver looked at the passenger and spoke in Mandarin. The passenger looked resigned and nodded. They looked forward out the windshield and did not move.

Finally, one of the police officers attempted to open the car door on the driver's side. It was locked. He told them to open the door. The Chinese men did not move from their stony gaze out the front of the vehicle, but they did each cross themselves slowly as if they were Catholics passing in front of the altar at a cathedral. Their hands steadily but slowly moved from head to heart, from shoulder to shoulder. The other police officers were still training their weapons on the car as the officer by the driver's side door took his police baton and smashed in the window of the BMW.

Of the fifteen police officers surrounding the BMW, only three would survive the devastating explosion that filled the air. One of those three would never walk again. The car was instantly shredded and the air was filled with shrapnel. Before stopping the car, the driver had activated a unique security feature all the BMWs in the chase had been equipped with—three pounds of C4 plastique. The two Chinese occupants of the vehicle were obliterated completely.

***

On the next island over, Quinn and Eva felt the shockwave of the blast. Quinn didn't know about the C4, but he understood that the Chinese men were dead and had taken others with them somehow. He quickly guessed that the men had used some kind of booby trap failsafe. He scowled as he turned the McLaren onto a small side road and headed for a tunnel entrance that was guarded by a chain link fence. He accelerated and shifted into third and smashed the front end into the chain link, which tore away as if it were paper. He knew the McLaren was ruined already from the bullet holes in the rear. More damage to the front end would be of little consequence. He turned on the headlights as he entered the tunnel. One of the beams splayed off at a grotesque angle from the collision damage to the front end. The car raced down the service tunnel. It had not been used in four years—had been all but forgotten by the Helsinki Police. Quinn knew it from his youth and he recalled that it led back under the sea to the heart of Helsinki.

A few minutes later Quinn approached another chain link fence. This one he stopped for. He got out of the car and walked up to it and examined the lock. Then, he noticed a side pedestrian gate that was not even locked. He went back to the car and told Eva, "They'll be looking for the car. We walk from here."

They gathered a bag from the trunk with some clothes in it and slipped away into the city of Helsinki on foot. He would contact Mooky later about the car. The gun he took with him.

CHAPTER 31

Hong Kong, China

The Hong Cathedral was nearly ready. Things were being arranged with the Pope. David Hong had been supremely confident of absolute success in his plans until he watched the footage of the shootout in Finland on BBC World News.

"Jacob!" Hong yelled for Jacob Lee from the leather chair in his office at the top of the 600-meter tall spire. The office was sparse. A smallish, circular room at the top of the spire. A desk, a chair, his laptop (he often took a second one with him on business trips) and an electronic media card reader that could handle a variety of formats and would check them for viruses and other infections before they were transferred to the laptop. David Hong relied exclusively on electronic files. No paperwork at all. Behind the desk, a large picture window looked out over the spine of the roof of the grand church toward Central District. The Cathedral was set right on the waterfront—technically on reclaimed land—in Wanchai. From one end of the widescreen window, Hong could see across the harbor to Kowloon, and from the other he could see up the slope to Victoria Peak and all the glorious skyscrapers of Hong Kong.

Jacob Lee entered the office. His own office was one floor down, because the tip of the spire was only large enough for the one office per level.

"My Lord?" Sweat was beading on his forehead.

"Quinn and the others. I just watched fascinating news footage from a helicopter over Helsinki. You have underestimated the man again," Hong frowned at the older man. "What have you planned next?"

"They intend to leave Finland via the ferry to Sweden."

"Perhaps, since Mr. Quinn has shown such resource in outwitting the faithful, it might be prudent to investigate all possibilities for departing Finland. And why they are in Finland in the first place." Now, Hong was less angry and again intrigued by the actions of the mountaineer that had thwarted every effort to silence him.

"They visited with a man named Eriksson, who was once in the employ of the Swedish Explorer. It seems that they are getting closer to finding the tomb, My Lord." Lee still stood in front of the desk. There were no chairs for visitors.

"Mmm. If Eriksson knew of Hedin's deception then they would have a reason to pursue Hedin to Asia. The question is whether or not the woman actually knows where to look," Hong glanced up at Lee. He smiled. "Jacob. We must also consider the possibility that Mr. Quinn might discover our connection to the attempts on him. He would then most likely come here. We should increase security for the grand opening and the remaining days leading up to it. We should prepare for the possibility of them coming into our web."

"It will be done. I have news from the Vatican as well."

Hong stood up with eager eyes.

"As you predicted. The Pope was not mollified by offers of humanitarian actions. He is very displeased by the construction of this Cathedral exceeding its original height specifications and acknowledges no prior arrangements with his predecessor. The offer of repatriating chest upon chest of Christian artifacts that have found their way to China over the years was met with significant interest though."

"And the coup de grâce?" Hong was smiling a large toothy grin.

"The offer to repatriate the spike used to nail Christ's feet to the cross? Carried to China in 1152 as a Holy Talisman by the mythical Prester John? Once I told them of the historically documented authenticity of the spike, I could hear their saliva dripping over the phone. They bought it hook, line, and sinker." Lee smiled a small smile.

Hong rushed around the desk and hugged the older man. "Fantastic! Outstanding, Jacob. Outstanding. I always knew that the records in the Vatican were sketchy on Prester John. They tried to find the man for centuries before giving up. But they never thought to search as far East as China, so the idea that he might have come here is perfectly plausible."

"Congratulations, My Lord. They have granted the audience. All progresses as you have planned."

"Excellent. Make the last-minute preparations. And Jacob…" Hong's face turned surly. "Make damned sure that Quinn doesn't make it to Hong Kong."

CHAPTER 32

Curtis Drake Johnson enjoyed driving quickly. He was pretty good at it too. He had dabbled with racetrack driving on occasion, but he really preferred to drive in the country and on switchbacks in the mountains. He had gathered a considerable number of speeding tickets in Colorado for his hobby, but since he was known to the police there from his days in the Rocky Mountain Rescue Service they tended to be fairly lenient with him. They just fined him. Repeatedly. But since his employment with ARGO, Johnson made more than enough money to laugh these tickets off.

Now though, he had to take the driving slowly because he was intentionally trying to stay under the radar of the local Finnish police and of the Chinese thugs that seemed to be dogging their steps across the world. He had safely deposited Eriksson with the U.S. embassy. The marines had been quite welcoming and the Regional Security Officer had been expecting them; Marge had made a few calls on their behalf to friends of hers with the State department. The RSO, an African-American guy named Ted Dean, had offered to safely get Mr. Eriksson to Sweden for a vacation with his niece there while things blew over with the Chinese. Plus, as Johnson had agreed with the man, Ted thought that it sounded like the Chinese were more concerned with Eva than with the old man—or they might have gone after him sooner. Johnson was pleased to report to Ted that all the chase cars had followed Quinn's distraction and he had not been followed. Nonetheless, Ted had insisted on swapping the Mercedes for Ted's own Audi sedan. Johnson liked the man immediately and promised no damage to his car, and a round of beers the next time he was in Helsinki. Ted promised to inform the local authorities of some of the nature of Quinn's actions in case they managed to capture him, and also to update Marge on the situation. Johnson and Dean had met briefly under the most unusual conditions of Dean's long career with the Foreign Service but they parted as fast friends.

Johnson eased the Audi into a parking lot at the ferry docks in Lappeenranta, about an hour's drive from Helsinki. He would take a ferry to St. Petersburg in Russia, and then rendezvous with Quinn and Dr. Rayjek on the Siberian Express train two days later.

He bought his ticket and showed his passport, then strolled onto the promenade deck in spite of the stiff winter breeze. His short-cropped blonde hair was buffeted in the gusts and his steel gray eyes swept the deck looking at the few passengers braving the outdoors prior to the ferry's departure. Then, he did a double take when he spotted one couple near the bow snuggling tight to each other. His face showed no emotion whatsoever as he casually strode over to the couple.

"Shouldn't you be in the steerage compartment, sir?" Johnson asked.

"First Class, actually, but we're slumming," Quinn replied. Eva turned away from the warmth of Quinn's chest where she had been snuggling and offered Curtis a warm smile. "Nice to see you, Curtis."

"You two must have been moving like bats out of hell to get here before me," Curtis replied and returned Eva's smile.

"That, or I might know the shortcuts. I did live here for a while. How did the embassy go?" Quinn asked, and took a step away from Eva. He became more business-like, Eva noticed, when Johnson was around the two of them. She wondered if he was trying to avoid any show of affection for her in Johnson's presence, so as not to make the man feel lonely without female companionship of his own. She had noticed the same at the ARGO building. Quinn had been more tactile with her outside the locker room when they had changed into ARGO clothing, than when anyone else was around. Then she wondered if perhaps it had less to do with Curtis's feelings than with his own discomfort with their budding relationship. She knew she was going to need to discuss some of these things with him.

Curtis was finishing talking to Quinn about the meeting with Ted when Eva refocused on the discussion.

"So is this trip to St. Petersburg another false trail then? I'd like to be kept in the loop this time if you don't mind," she told them.

"No false trail," Quinn told her. His long dark brown hair was whipping around his face and neck in the icy gusts. His green eyes took on a darker shade and his face lost the smile. "No. We're going to take this to China. We're only going by train because there's more room to maneuver than if we took a flight and these bastards strike again."

"So they followed when you left Eriksson's?" Curtis wanted to know. Quinn briefly related the car chase on the ice, and Eva noticed that he even downplayed all the extremely hairy moments. She wondered if it was modesty or just for the sake of brevity. Then they all went indoors to eat at the café there. The ride was a few hours long, so they parted, with Johnson going to the bar for a drink and the others going to their cabin.

Eva lay on the lower bunk and motioned for Quinn to join her. He took off his fleece jacket revealing a Capilene t-shirt pulled tight over his muscled torso and lay next to her. He looked deeply into her clear blue eyes and wondered if he was really ready to be as in love with this woman as he found himself to be falling.

"What are you thinking?" she asked him.

"I'm thinking about how slowly we should take this," he started.

"Why slowly? Are you worried that this might all be artificial because of the danger involved when we met? Or are you regretting getting involved with me?" Eva was not really concerned about these things. After her talk with Johnson about Quinn's past, she understood that this man was scarred by his past and reluctant to get deeply involved with anyone. But she also knew that since he had come so far already with her, he was possibly past the point of no return. Johnson had made it seem as if Quinn had had very few affairs over the years. She sensed Quinn was falling for her and battling his grief at the same time. She wanted to make it as easy for him to back out as possible if it was necessary for him to do so.

"No. No regrets," he told her, and slowly stroked her long curls of thick blonde hair. "I'm not really convinced that our attraction is tied to the adrenaline of the last few days either. I haven't really been involved with anyone for some time. I just want to ease into things if that's okay. I want to… I want to do things right."

She smiled softly for him, kissed him gently, pulled him close and whispered in his ear.

"Okay. And don't worry. So far, everything is right."

CHAPTER 33

The ferry had arrived in St. Petersburg without incident and they had a few hours to kill before the train departed for Moscow. They joined a tour group and saw some of the sights of the old city. The journey to Moscow was also uneventful, but Eva noticed that at any given time, either Curtis or Jason was busy looking around them with a constant vigilance. Although neither of them made it seem as if they were looking around for anything in particular. She only noticed because there were times when she would be speaking to one or the other of them and while they would respond, they wouldn't look in her direction as they did so. Eventually she realized they were involved in some kind of unspoken counter-surveillance routine.

At one point in the Moscow station, Quinn excused himself briefly to use an Internet café to contact Mooky. He was gone about fifteen minutes when he came back with four cups of hot chocolate. He sat at the table where Curtis and Eva had been waiting and distributed a cup to each of them and the fourth to the spot in front of the empty seat at their table.

"Are we having company?" Eva wanted to know.

"I was wondering if you'd spot him first," Curtis said directly to Quinn.

"I just picked him up. When did you spot him?" Quinn asked.

"Right before you left for the Internet café." Curtis turned to Eva. "Gene's here for a little chat, it seems." Then he turned back to Quinn with a large grin. "Try not to break any furniture this time."

"You're no fun."

It took a minute before Eva spotted the older man strolling toward their table from across the station. He had applied a fake bristle-brush style mustache, and had tinted his hair with gray highlights. It was a very minimal disguise, but effective. He walked right up to their table, slid out his chair and plopped into it as if he had been a part of their party all along. Eva wondered at what this man's long career in the spy game had been like—and if it was worth the loss of his son's affection and his daughter's life.

No one said anything for a moment. Eva noticed the man's eye color had changed too. *Contacts*, she supposed. Then, she wondered whether the eye color she was seeing here or in the house in Colorado was the real eye color. She quickly realized that puzzling out the intricacies of the spy game could give her a headache and she just gave up. Then Jason slid the cup of hot chocolate a little closer to Gene and smiled.

"More ominous news for us?" Jason asked.

"Just checking up on my only son. Not a crime, right?" The older Quinn asked with a grin.

"Just come from a Halloween Party, have you?" Jason countered.

"It's a disguise, son." Gene said with phony condescension.

"Not a very good one. You still look like an asshole."

"Ha, ha. Clever wit," Gene replied, "A half wit."

"You were about to say something before you left?" Jason asked, with menace beginning to creep into his voice.

"I just heard about Helsinki. Some impressive driving if I'm to believe the police reports I've seen. Lars Eriksson is resting comfortably in Stockholm. Says it was the most excitement he's ever even heard of. And David Hong is rumored to be making some kind of a deal to placate the Pope. Otherwise, no one's seen him. But he's assumed to be in Hong Kong. That's not where you're going is it?" Gene sipped his hot chocolate, which was now starting to cool.

"Thought we might pay a little visit to Mr. Hong, yeah." Jason said.

"Not really recommended. Of course, the Agency can't really tell you what to do since you're a civilian, but we can tell you that it's probably not a good idea. He's looking for you and right now you're off his radar."

"Probably not too far off it," Jason began. "You found us pretty easily, and

Hong's goons keep showing up every five minutes. I'm thinking if there's going to be some more rampant destruction of public property as he and I engage in another pissing contest, then it should be his property that gets ruined and we should do it in person instead of relying on his hit men."

Jason paused for effect and to stare his old man in the eye.

"Was there anything else, Gene?"

Gene Quinn just sat quietly looking at his son. Curtis and Eva sat quietly. Jason just stared back at Gene. Gene swallowed the rest of his chocolate, got up and left without a word.

"I've got a theory," Quinn began, ignoring his father's slightly glum departure. "Let's say that Hong wants to appease the Pope by trading the document that Hedin was searching for to get the Pope's blessing on his new Cathedral project in Hong Kong."

"Nah. He doesn't have the document. Eva wouldn't be a threat then," Curtis was picking up the thread of Quinn's thinking.

"Okay. Good point. He has a fake or a forgery or something. If Eva stumbles upon the real document, it could ruin his deal with Rome," Quinn concluded.

"So maybe Hedin found the document, and that's why Hong can't find it himself. So he thinks I have it, or I know where it is?" Eva asked.

"Exactly." Quinn said with a smile. "Which gives us leverage. Hong might not know for sure if you have it. He might not even have any idea where to look for it."

"So what now? Do we still go through with the trip to China? I was kind of looking forward to a long train ride." Eva said with a smile of her own.

"Yeah. We still go to China."

CHAPTER 34

Somewhere near the Ural Mountains in Russia, the landscape takes on a wondrous craggy design that looks as if the Earth herself had ruptured and flung fragments of stone and rocky ground into the air. Where the regurgitated geology had landed is where it had stayed, to be covered by centuries of snow and ice. At least that is what Quinn thought when he would occasionally glance out the window of the slow-moving Siberian Express train. Other times he would brave the cold and hang on to the handrail in the open doorway between his car and the next.

The last two days had been quiet. He and Curtis had shared the watch duty; keeping a cautious eye on the other passengers when they came near to their first-class compartments at the rear of the train and when they were forced to leave their cars for the dining car.

Curtis had been in good spirits even though there was little for him to do on his downtime. For Quinn, his downtime was spent with Eva in their compartment, and more often than not, they spent the time in bed getting wrapped up in each other's hearts and minds.

Quinn was enjoying getting to know Eva. He hoped that their interest in each other wouldn't be based solely on the thrill of the danger they had shared the last two weeks. He wanted more with her and hoped they would still want to dive into each other's eyes when the living became more mundane.

But then again, he chided himself, my life rarely gets mundane.

Between climbing with Curtis and working for ARGO, he was rarely home. His life was strange by comparison with most others. He wondered briefly if she would stay faithful to him with the long separations they would have to face between her job and his. He decided to put it out of his mind and take things slowly as he had said he wanted to do.

Quinn stared out the open door of the train at the fantastic winter landscape. He looked without smiling at three Chinese men dressed in drab colors as they shuffled past him down the corridor. Their clothes suggested that they wouldn't be able to afford to travel in first class, but they all seemed to be at least in their fifties. Quinn supposed there wouldn't be many of Hong's hired assassins that were over forty.

Still, he watched them move down the corridor and into the next car. Quinn knew that there was nothing at that end except the last first-class car. He kept his eye on the door at the other end of the corridor, waiting to see if the Chinese men were just being tourists and seeing what first class was like before returning to their own section. If they didn't come back in a few minutes he would go investigate. It was always possible that they did have the money for first class passage—or maybe they were hoping to squat in an empty compartment.

He was just thinking that he should tell Curtis before going to investigate, when the three men came back into the corridor. They began walking toward Quinn, and he kept his eyes on them. Then they slowed to a stop and looked at him.

They looked nervous. Older men, each losing his hair. They looked as if they could be related—maybe brothers. As they walked toward Quinn, they looked at the floor. Quinn was about to be convinced that they had been up to something in the first class car—but nothing to do with him or Hong— when one of them looked up again. The eyes were filled with hate.

Quinn felt hands grab him from behind. There were two more of them. Younger than the three older men and strong. They had come into the car from behind Quinn as he had focused his attention on the other end of the car. The noise of the train from the open door had prevented him from hearing them. Before Quinn could think to move, the men had pivoted and launched him out the open door.

Jason Quinn was horrified as he flew through the air toward a snow bank and away from the train. He crouched and braced for a hard impact against the rocks hidden under the snow. The impact was softer than he expected. He had landed in deep snow. He clawed himself out of the drift and watched the train recede into the distance. It wasn't moving fast, but there was no way he would catch it on foot.

He scrambled to the top of a small hill dotted with fir trees. He looked at the sweep of the tracks across the land ahead of the train. They curved to the right in the distance. Then they disappeared behind a small hill. His eyes crossed the hills where he thought the train might go and then he saw it. The train went through a tunnel, and it would have to make a few turns before it got to the tunnel.

Maybe. Just maybe.

Quinn started trudging through the snow and over the hills in as much of a straight line as he could and as fast as his body would take him. He had only one advantage over a train. He could go straight over the hills. As he knew all too well from his work on the tunnel in Tibet, trains couldn't easily go over mountains. They had to go through them or around them.

Quinn scrambled up the slope in front of him. For the most part, the snow pack was solid enough that he only sank up to the ankles of his climbing boots with the spring-loaded crampons. He kept the spikes retracted for the moment, because the surface snow was loose enough that they wouldn't make much difference in his traction. Only a few times did he sink into deep snow. He would curse and thrash until he got loose and was back on solid ground again.

He could see the train in the distance snaking around another curve. He realized he wouldn't catch the train before the tunnel.

Crap.

He would have to go over the looming peak ahead of him and hope he could go over it before the train could go through it. His one lone advantage was beginning to look like a disadvantage.

Quinn rushed down a valley and leapt a huge snowdrift that he spotted at the bottom. While in the air, he reached down and pressed the buttons to extend the ice crampons. He landed in a crouch on the other side of the drift with the Fullerite carbon spikes digging firmly into the ice. He began to sprint up the side of the mountain, barely using his hands—and only then for balance.

As he quickly neared the rounded summit, he glanced back and saw the train disappearing into the tunnel below him and several hundred yards away. He raced up and over the summit in the general direction where he assumed the train would come out on the other side. The summit was mostly flat and held a small grove of evergreens. He glanced at his Suunto wristwatch and switched it over to altimeter mode to see that he had climbed about 2,000 feet in less than ten minutes. His legs were throbbing with the exertion. The altitude didn't bother him because he was used to high altitudes, and the cold wasn't affecting him yet. He was sweating with the struggle of racing to the top of the peak. He wore only a fleece pair of pants and a Capilene t-shirt with his boots, but he was sweating profusely. It would only be if he couldn't catch the train that he would begin to feel the cold. And then he might die. But Quinn wasn't thinking of himself as he sprinted across the mountaintop.

He was thinking of Eva.

And he was thinking of his dead bride.

An unholy rage welled up within him and propelled him onwards with a second wind.

As he crested the other slope, he could see the tracks below. He had miscalculated slightly on the angle, but not by much. He could adjust for it. What pleased him most was that the train had not emerged yet from the tunnel.

Quinn raced down the slope, leaping and bounding over boulders, ice, and even small dwarf trees and snow-covered bushes. The train's engine emerged from the tunnel two thousand feet below him and he put on a burst of speed. Then, a sheet of ice snapped loose under him and he fell onto his back on it. He was racing down the hill now on what had become a makeshift sled. The train was more than halfway out of the tunnel when Quinn's sled began to drag off course. With no way to steer it, he simply pitched himself off it and hurtled down the slope. He slid down on his back with his legs in the air so his boots wouldn't snag the snow or ice and at the last second before he launched off the edge over the tunnel, he jammed the heels of his boots into the ice-crusted edge of the tunnel. The impact flipped his body over forward and he flew out over the roof of the train head first and looking down at it.

As he slammed down onto the roof, a quick glimpse toward his toes confirmed his fear—he had landed on the last car of the train and he was sliding. There was no room for error. His body slid across the slick rooftop, which was covered with a sheen of thin ice. He slid diagonally toward the edge of the roof. The train seemed to him to be moving much more quickly now that he was about to slide off its roof and into the narrow stream of rocks on either side of the tracks.

He tried to spin and dig in the crampons, but couldn't. As he went over the edge, he frantically scrabbled with hands and feet for any purchase. He was about to brace for the impact when he saw that the door to the compartment was open, as his had been when he had been thrown out of it. He stretched in the open doorway as he fell past it and was able to grab a fire ax that was secured on the wall. It ripped loose of its mooring and he twisted hard.

The ax lodged in the door crosswise and Quinn found himself dangling from the long wooden shaft with his feet just about to graze the ground, as the train picked up speed across the barren Russian countryside.

Quinn looked down at himself. No broken bones. He growled loudly, then hauled himself up and climbed into the doorway. He stood for a moment before setting off down the train corridor in search of the bastards.

He ground his teeth and took the ax with him.

CHAPTER 35

Curtis Johnson's nose was bleeding, and the blood was dripping into his mouth. Two young Chinese men were doing their best to kill him. Curtis had no idea where Quinn was. He assumed Eva and he were kicking it back in their compartment. But he did know one thing. It seemed that neither of the two Chinese men he was fighting were schooled in what he liked to call *That Chopsocky Crap*.

Johnson launched a powerful bar-brawler kick to the groin of the slightly smaller man. There was a cracking sound as the smaller man's pelvic bone shattered. The air was sucked out of the man's lungs and he crumpled to the floor of the compartment with a small squeaky noise. The second man had silky blue-black hair, which was longer than Quinn's, and it was tied into a ponytail. He looked with abject horror at the powerful kick Curtis had just dealt. Curtis was already thinking about how to get his hands on the other man's ponytail.

Curtis Johnson didn't enjoy fighting. But when he did it, he fought dirty and he fought to put the other guy in the hospital or the coroner's wagon.

He didn't think it was going to come to that with Pony-Tail though. The man threw a punch and Curtis ducked it, neatly grabbing a hold of the long black hair. Twisting his momentum in the same move, Curtis tugged the hair toward the door of his compartment with the intention of slamming the man's head against it.

At the moment when there should have been an impact, the door slid open and both Curtis and Pony-Tail continued on out into the corridor. Jason Quinn, ax in hand, quickly sidestepped the flailing bodies. There was a dull thunk as the Chinese man's head hit the window on the other side of the corridor. Curtis let go of the man's hair and the unconscious body slumped to the floor.

Curtis took in the sight of Quinn. His Capilene t-shirt was torn. He was drenched in sweat. There was a small cut on his cheek. He was wearing a climbing harness over his fleece pants, he had a rope bag slung over his shoulder, and he had a fire ax in his hands.

"Been having yourself some fun?" Curtis asked with a grin.

"Took a brief tour of the countryside. Eva's fine. Just checked on her. There are more of these guys. Three older men, and about six younger guys." Quinn began moving down the corridor as he spoke.

"Eleven men this time? We must be moving up in the world." Curtis commented as he followed Quinn down the passage.

"There were fourteen. Two of them are wandering Siberia on foot now." Quinn said casually over his shoulder as they moved into the next car.

"And the fourteenth?" Curtis asked with a chuckle.

Quinn's growling reply silenced any more joviality from his friend. "No longer has any feet."

Curtis glanced at the blade of the ax and saw blood there. As they entered the next car, he snatched a fire extinguisher from the wall to use as a projectile if necessary.

"We're leaving Eva unprotected as we go after these creeps," Curtis began.

"She's locked the compartment and I've swept the train from the rear forward," Quinn replied. "I want every last one of them off of my train."

As they exited the car, they caught a glimpse of a black-clad leg climbing up out of sight between the two cars.

"They're doubling back on the roof!" Quinn hissed.

"I'll take the high road," Curtis offered.

Quinn turned around and sprinted back toward the rear of the train. When he got to the very end, he slipped out the door onto a small balcony. He clipped a carabiner to the balcony rail. Attached to it was the colorful neon green and blue 11mm dry climbing rope in the bag on his back. As he climbed to the roof of the train car, the rope fed smoothly out of the bag behind him. The other end of the rope came out of the other end of the bag at his waist and attached to the front of his harness.

As Quinn arrived on the roof, he could see Curtis several cars up fighting two men. The other four young men were heading toward Quinn with speed. The older men were nowhere to be seen.

Quinn raced forward across the roof of the car. There was no ice on the roof now as his previous slide across it had dislodged it all. But Quinn thought there would likely be ice on the next car. He leapt the space between the last car and his own and ran headlong toward the four men coming at him. He dropped to the roof of the car on his side and swept his legs at the men. He slid with speed across the icy roof. Unable to stop abruptly on the ice, two of the Chinese men were felled by the leg sweep. One of them slid right off the roof and the other leaped over Quinn and tried unsuccessfully to grab him. Of the other two men, one leapt Quinn's leg sweep and landed safely on the other side of Quinn. The fourth had also tried a leap, but Quinn had simultaneously thrust the head of the ax upward and caught the man under the chin, launching him off the train completely.

Curtis was trading blows with his two opponents and all three of them were trying to gain footing on the slippery rooftop of the moving train. Curtis had managed to circle around his opponents so that they were now facing the rear of the train and Curtis's back was toward the fight Quinn was engaged in. There were huge evergreen trees very close to the edge of the train on both sides now. He thought he might be able to use the trees somehow when he saw something approaching from behind the two Chinese in the distance.

Curtis took a few tentative steps backward and then yelled with all his might, "Quinn! Low Bridge!"

Then, he threw his body backwards and landed on the roof of the train on his back a second before the wall above the tunnel mouth slammed into his opponents from behind. Then the roof of the tunnel was roaring over Curtis Johnson's head and body with only inches to spare.

Quinn had heard him but he hadn't needed to—he saw the tunnel coming and he saw that his remaining two assailants also saw it. They quickly dropped to their stomachs on the rooftop and ducked their heads. They had seen what happened to the two men that had been fighting Curtis. Quinn also dropped to his stomach. The jolt of the landing on the ice made him slide. In an effort to reach stability, he had to release his hold on the ax. Then the tunnel darkness swallowed them all.

Quinn was engulfed in blackness. He wondered briefly if he would be attacked in the dark from a prone position. Then, he wondered if maybe he should be the one making the tunnel attack. Before either could happen, he could see the light from the nearing opening of the tunnel. His last two opponents were still on their stomachs waiting for the train to clear the tunnel, but they were further away than they had been! They had scooted backward under cover of darkness. Now they would be able to get to their feet well before Quinn could. The two men were already getting to their feet as Quinn began to realize their advantage.

The two men rushed forward toward the receding tunnel and were on Quinn before he could gain his feet. Quinn activated one boot crampon and the spring-loaded metal thrust outwards as he delivered a vicious kick to one of the men in the stomach. The man screamed out in pain as the other yanked Quinn backward. Too late, Jason Quinn realized the danger.

He was being thrown off the train for the second time that day.

He was flying off the train to the side and smashed into a large fir. He slid quickly down the tree and then a huge dump of snow that had been resting on the branches fell on top of him. Quinn wasted no time thinking dark thoughts and instead leapt up and snapped the rope into the air to clear it of the branches. He raced toward the tracks but just missed the end of the train. He stood on the tracks and watched the train move on—trailing the rope he had attached to the balcony at the rear. He had originally hoped the rope might provide a small safety net from falling off the train. But now it would need to serve a different purpose. The rope was feeding smoothly and quickly out of his rope bag. He quickly removed the bag from the sling around his neck and back and held the bag loosely in front of him. He extended the other boot crampons and stood on the rail with both feet, one in front of the other. The teeth of the crampons fit smoothly over the rails except for the front points, which pointed downwards slightly and forced the boots to sit on the rail with the toes upwards a bit.

"This will either work or it'll kill me," Quinn spoke aloud. He was thinking about the slight elasticity of a climbing rope, meant to take the jarring stop out of a fall, and hoping it would help to keep his arms in the sockets when the train pulled the rope tight.

Quinn leaned back into a water-skiing stance just as the rope pulled taught and jerked him forward. He almost lost it immediately and fell over forward but caught himself just in time and settled back into a comfortable position. The crampons were gliding over the rail and the front points were spraying up an intense shower of sparks around Quinn's ankle in the specially designed boots. Slowly, Quinn lean back on his heels, lifting the front points up a bit—he didn't want them to stick in a groove between rail segments and send him flying. He began to reel himself in on the rope. He pulled arm over arm in a slow, careful motion, wrapping the loose rope he pulled in around his forearms. Most of his attention was on balancing on the rail at about forty miles an hour.

He had pulled himself about half the distance of the rope—Quinn quickly calculated it at 57 feet as the rope was 120, but some had been lost to the knots at the balcony and his waist—when he glanced up at the roof of the rail car and saw the last of the Chinese madmen he had been fighting. The man seemed shocked to see Quinn trailing along behind the train as if he were having the time of his life. Then the man quickly recovered and reached into his shirt and pulled out a folding knife, which he clicked open. Quinn doubled the speed of his arm-over-arm pulls. Then, knowing he would never make it in time before the man could drop to the balcony and cut his line, Quinn saw a foot smash into the man's groin from behind and launch him straight into the air. The train sped along and Quinn had to duck slightly as the rope pulled him right under the falling body of the knife wielder.

Quinn heard a dull thumping noise behind him as the Chinese man crashed onto the rails still gagging for breath. Quinn slowly pulled himself onward as Curtis Johnson dropped from the roof to the balcony on the last car of the train. He looked at Quinn's situation and then called out with a grin.

"Anything I can do for you here?"

Quinn smiled up at his friend. He knew Curtis was concerned for his life but would never let that creep into his voice. "Just pull me up when I get there. My arms are about beat."

"Will do," Curtis said, and he did just that a moment later.

"So what are you going to call that shit?" Curtis asked, pointing behind the train to where Quinn had been towed.

"What do you think about 'Rail-Skiing'? Been wanting to try that for ages," Quinn said with a straight face.

"Really?"

"No. I was scared shitless. Let's check on Eva then find the older guys," Quinn said, untying himself from the climbing rope.

The older men seemed to be experts at hiding. Or so Curtis suggested. The two mountaineers searched the whole train and could find no sign of the older men Quinn had been deceived by. It would take another day before they would have proof that the Chinese men never left the train. After a long day searching, the men were exhausted. They took turns on 'watch' as the other two slept throughout the night—this time all of them sharing Quinn and Eva's compartment.

Around dawn the next day, Curtis woke Quinn up. He'd been asleep for only an hour. The look on Curtis's face made Quinn snap awake and sit up. Curtis motioned for Quinn to remain silent and follow him out into the passageway.

"Problem. We stopped moving 20 minutes ago. I thought it might be another of the interminable stops we've had along the way..." Curtis began.

"But now you're suspicious." Quinn finished for him.

Quinn led the way down the passageway toward the front of the train. He opened the door between cars only to find the sweeping grasses of Mongolia for as far as the eye could see. The rest of the train was long gone. Their compartments had been at the end of the train. Quinn hissed between his teeth. The older Chinese. They must have detached the last car of the train and left them here.

"Okay," Quinn said.

"And now?" Curtis asked.

"We walk. Let's get Eva up and get our stuff together." Quinn turned grimly back for the compartment.

CHAPTER 36

Jason Quinn scanned the Hong Kong skyline from behind a pair of ATN NVB8-4 Night Vision binoculars. He was crouched low in the brush to the side of a pagoda up on Victoria Peak. His view took in all of the harbor side of Hong Kong Island. The multi-colored lights of the infamous skyline were dazzling. He shifted the binoculars into a regular view mode without the light enhancement and took in the sight. Then he shifted back to the night vision mode and swept the lenses back toward his target. At the base of the structure, Quinn knew he would be able to see several burly Chinese thugs wearing rented security officer costumes that were a bit too small. The men patrolled the church with the precision of former military and each was armed with a full-barrel Uzi. There was simply no way to get into the facility from the ground level.

It had taken him, Curtis, and Eva three days of hiking south through the Mongolian Steppe to find any people. The horsemen they met were thrilled to meet Westerners and had given them a ride to their village even further south. The village was little more than a ring of *yurts* or tents. They had partaken in a festival of sorts and enjoyed a hearty meal. Then, Quinn had used a combination of sign language, a few Chinese words, and charades to get their desires across. The Mongolians gladly escorted them south to the remains of the Great Wall of China in a part of the country where they were unlikely to encounter any human beings. Curtis quickly scaled the wall and lowered a rope for Eva. Quinn thanked the horsemen and they went off back to their nomadic village of portable tents.

Quinn had encouraged the others to take a moment to appreciate the magnificent structure that is the Great Wall and then they rappelled down the other side and into the People's Republic of China. A week of travel in trucks and on buses found them in Macao, where Curtis went into the back street gambling establishments to secure illegal transport into Hong Kong, which would bypass any unwanted scrutiny from immigration officials who might want to know how they had ended up in China without visas in their passports. Then they had gone to the ARGO branch office in Tsim Sha Tsui, on the Kowloon side, once they were in Hong Kong.

They had contacted Marge over a secure satellite phone and contacted Mooky for some satellite surveillance on the cathedral and Hong's other holdings. Quinn explained that he had a plan. Then, they grabbed all the gear they would need with the assistance of Margo Chen, the resident manager of the ARGO office in Hong Kong. Quinn had never met Chen, but because he was the Director of Asian Projects for ARGO, he had naturally spoken with her over the phone several times. It was good to put a face to the name.

Now, the small lithe Asian woman with the British accent and the soft brown eyes lay next to him in the bushes as he scanned the cathedral with the binoculars.

"All the gear is set to go. Last contact from Mooky suggests Hong is in Manila still. You should be able to get in and out without being noticed."

"Excellent. Thanks, Margo. You better get to the airport now. If this thing goes wrong I don't want it to touch you," Quinn shook her hand and gave her a brief smile. They left the bushes and went back up to the road.

He waited until she was safely on the road before he strapped the gear on and prepared for what was sure to be either the coolest thing he had ever done or the biggest nightmare of his life—and possibly the end of it.

He was dressed from head to toe in all black. He wore climbing shoes that he had spray-painted black earlier in the night. Previously they had been lime green FiveTens, like the ones Eva had seen in his house with *Quinn* written on the canvas in permanent marker, in case they got mixed up with other shoes at the rock gym in Denver. He wore a thick backpack, a rope bag, a chalk bag, and a thin nylon runner, which connected his climbing harness to the jet black, lightweight hang glider above him.

He gripped the control bar, raced across the road and leapt up onto the concrete safety fence, which thousands of tourists a day leaned over to get a perfect picture of Hong Kong. And then he was soaring down toward the skyscrapers of the city. Quinn pulled the control bar toward him and began to gather speed. He aimed himself to the northeast toward the Hong Cathedral. He was heading straight for the gap between two skyscrapers. The resulting boost in gust shot him through the gap and directly into a thermal updraft that launched him upwards and over the next skyscraper. He was now higher above sea level than he was when he began on the peak. He banked the hang glider to the right, swerving around another towering structure of glistening light steel and glass. He aimed for the Bank of China building.

Another gust took him unexpectedly downwards and he nearly thought his ride was over as he headed straight for the triangular designs on the side of one of I. M. Pei's most famous buildings. Then another thermal sent him upwards and around the building toward the harbor. He had been close enough to see in the windows of the building. Luckily, all the employees had gone home for the night.

Finally, he had a free stretch for the Cathedral's rooftop. He pulled the crossbar toward him and gained speed as he glided smoothly toward the building. He was a bit low and would have to land on crouched legs.

At least I'll be able to land, he thought.

Quinn thrust the crossbar away from him, driving the nose of the hang glider upwards and he began to run across the flat pad of the heliport. Just as he was about to stop, another gust of wind caught the glider from behind and began to drag him toward the edge of the roofline and a fall of 1600 feet. Quinn threw his weight downwards and landed on the heliport on his stomach, dragging the weight of the hang glider with him. He skidded slightly and then stopped completely. He sighed loudly, then began to unhook himself from the contraption.

There was a metal hook sticking out of the flat concrete slab at its edge and Quinn used a carabiner to connect the strap from the hang glider to the hook. Wind or no wind, the glider wasn't going anywhere. Quinn had once read that an aluminum carabiner could support the weight of a Volkswagen. He knew from his own climbing (and falling) that the things were extremely strong if not exactly indestructible.

He stood briefly and looked at the tower at the rear of the cathedral. Three hundred feet up from the ridgeline of the roof on the main structure. At the top was a large window. *Hong's office.* Quinn scowled and then raced across the helipad to the steep line of the pitched roof. He got down on his hands and knees and raced across the ridgeline to the base of the tower. He wasn't afraid of heights but he didn't look down. He was completely focused on the tower and before he knew it, he was at the base, looking up and contemplating the climb he was about to make.

Luckily, the tower was made from stone and concrete with lots of design niches and edges as the whole structure was in the Gothic style. Quinn dipped his hands in his chalk bag, placed his hands on the rock, and began climbing in a slow steady gait. It was almost as easy as climbing up a ladder to Quinn. He made the top in a few minutes. Then, balanced precariously on his feet alone, he pulled out a small handheld electric drill and drilled a hole to the right of his position and another to the left. He blew debris out of the holes and then ejected the hot drill bit and let it fall to the roofline below him. He wouldn't be needing it again and it was too hot to touch (or let it touch him). He clipped the drill to his harness. Then he pulled out a small bottlebrush and cleaned the holes. At all times, he kept one hand on the stone for balance, even though he didn't need the handhold for support. He worked out a bolt hanger and placed it on the hole on the right, one handed.

Then came the hammer and he pounded it home. Finally, a small wrench to tighten the bolt. He repeated the procedure for the second bolt. When he was sure that both bolts were solid, he clipped carabiners through them and hooked his harness to them. Then, using both hands he removed his rope bag and clipped the extra long climbing rope to an anchor he made with nylon webbing strung between the carabiners on both bolts. He let the rope fall. The center was attached to the anchor and the ends of the rope dangled just above the ridgeline, three hundred feet below. He examined his work, and then, satisfied, he checked that all the tools were secured in their original positions on his harness. Except the hammer. That he used to smash the large picture window that led to David Hong's personal office at the top of his tower in the sky.

CHAPTER 37

The computer was the last thing he checked. He had searched the whole office first and found basically no paperwork of any kind. Besides the laptop computer, there was a boxlike device with ports for USB and other media. Quinn recognized it as a device meant to check external material for viruses. There wasn't anything else in the office at all. Just the carpet, desk, and chair. It was sterile, with no decoration. It seemed that David Hong was in a completely paperless office. Luckily, Quinn was armed with a secret weapon—Mooky Jones. While Mooky had been unable to access Hong's computer because it wasn't connected to the Internet, he had been able to re-task a Russian spy satellite briefly the previous week. The pictures were enough for Mooky to reconstruct Hong's password as he typed it into his computer with the large picture window at his back.

Quinn typed in the password—*Resurrect*. He sneered as he did so. He still hadn't seen any proof that David Hong was behind the murders of his colleagues and the repeated attempts on Eva's life, but he knew. Oh yes, he knew. Besides, *Resurrect* was the word tattooed on the chests of the dead assassins.

Quinn knew.

He didn't have time to look for documents on the hard drive. He knew that Hong's security men could be by to check his office at any time. He inserted a keychain drive, which Mooky had designed, that held enough space for several hard drives and had a watertight housing, into a USB port and downloaded the whole of Hong's drive. It took twenty nerve-wracking minutes. Then he checked the belay device on his harness and the rope that was threaded through it and out the window. He slipped the keychain drive into a Velcro pouch on the side of his chalk bag, which swung from the rear of his harness. He usually used the pocket for his car keys when he went bouldering in Colorado. Finished. He was just about to smile…

The door to the office opened and there stood two of the overly muscled mercenary security guards. Each had an Uzi but neither had yet raised it. Quinn grabbed the rope at his side and held it loosely in his right hand as he flung his body backwards and out past the shattered remains of the window of the tower. Nineteen hundred feet above the ground.

He fell fast; the rope zipped through the Black Diamond "Air Traffic Controller" style belay device and through his loose fingers. He plummeted like a rock. He kicked off the tower with both feet and his descent arced out over the spine of the cathedral's roof. He tightened his grip slightly and began to pull the slack across his waist for extra friction just as the hail of bullets began to rain down.

Quinn wasn't going to make it to the helipad. He knew it too. The rope had arced him out about a quarter of the distance from the tower to the helipad. He let the rope slide free as he zipped down toward the harbor side of the pitched roof. He was starting to swing back toward the base of the tower. The ends of the rope raced free from the belay device and Quinn fell about 13 feet to the side of the steep roof. He crouched slightly for the impact. When he hit, his legs quickly compressed until he was in a full crouch. He should have at least broken an ankle, but he could tell that he had placed his feet perfectly. His legs absorbed the shock and he forced his muscles to extend his legs. He sprang off the side of the roof and into the air—literally flying—headfirst into the abyss off the side of the world's tallest building.

Bullets spattered the slate tiles on the steep side of the roof and Quinn could hear the subsonic ricochet as round after round chased him off into the night sky. Quinn aimed his body forward and downwards slightly with his arms at his sides, then spread his arms while activating his parachute. Quinn had only BASE-jumped once before in Colorado. He was by no means an expert at it, but he knew he had plenty of time. BASE-jumping (*BASE* being an acronym for Bridge, Antenna, Span, Earth) had been successfully done from heights as low as 200 feet. Quinn knew he had pulled the chute at probably no lower than 1,500 feet. He had the height. He was just worried that the only chute he had would fail. Most BASE-jumping parachute rigs didn't come with a back-up chute. In most cases, the person would be dead before they had the chance to pull a reserve chute if the first had failed. He was also worried about the bullets he could still hear slicing through the air around him. The canopy of the chute was painted black but in the dazzling night cityscape of lights all around him, it hardly acted as camouflage.

The wind was working for him and he steered the chute well out over Victoria Harbor. The harbor was one of the most polluted bodies of water on Earth and Quinn had no desire for a swim. He glanced around below him and spotted what he wanted. He toggled left, then released the toggle again. He swept in across the roof of the vessel and then tugged both toggles sharply, landing right in the center of the moving roof of the Star Ferry. The Star Ferry makes the trip across the harbor several times a day and its green and white color scheme is easily recognizable to millions of people.

Quinn detached himself from the harness and smiled. Home free. Then he turned around to look back toward the cathedral and saw five speedboats closing in on the ferry. All thoughts of getting out of a swim quickly left his head.

CHAPTER 38

Quinn dumped all of his gear on the roof of the ferry. He took the chalk bag's carabiner off his harness and clipped it through the nylon belt around his waist. Then he took off his sticky rubber climbing shoes and dumped them along with the harness on the roof as well. Now he wore only black tights, a black Capilene turtleneck, and the chalk bag with the drive. He ran to the side of the ferry and very carefully, in view of the pursuing speedboats, dramatically flipped off the side of the boat and into the harbor's ugly water.

He just hoped she would be on time.

He came up for air and started swimming away from the ferry, trying to draw the speedboats away from the innocent people on board. They were nearly on him when the high-pitched whine of a Yamaha FX personal watercraft roared as Dr. Eva Rayjek raced across his path nearly swamping him with its wake. She did a quick about face and slowed to a near stop right in front of him. The thing looked like a water motorcycle with wings. It was a garish blue and white and stood out on the black water like a neon sign but Quinn was much more pleased with its speed than its color. He climbed onto the back and before he was carefully seated, Eva was gunning the throttle and they were racing away toward the lights of Kowloon Peninsula, spewing a tight stream of water in the air behind them as they went.

The speedboats were closing fast and Quinn could only spot four of the five of them, as he tried to get a better hold on Eva so he wouldn't fall off the craft. He looked forward just in time to see the fifth boat arc across the bow of their craft. It had swept around the ferry and out of sight. Eva cranked the steering sharply away to avoid a crash. Quinn went flying off the back of the watercraft and back into the water. Eva smashed the watercraft broadside into the fifth speedboat and rolled off of it and right into the boat at the feet of three men all pointing their guns at her. A fourth man was behind the wheel and a fifth had actually fallen overboard from the collision and was climbing back aboard as the other four speedboats pulled up surrounding where Quinn had fallen in the water. The men on all the boats trained their Uzi submachine guns at the water but Quinn didn't surface.

"Where the hell is he?" one of the men on the boat with Eva asked. Eva was wondering the same thing. The ferry had now moved well away from the site of the speedboat collision. The pilot had no doubt seen the incident and would be contacting the harbor patrol. The men knew they didn't have a lot of time. They all looked in the water on both sides of the boats. When Quinn sprang out of the water at the stern of the boat Eva was on and smoothly leapt off the motor and into the boat, the man nearest to Quinn shrieked in surprise. Then he found himself flying into the water. Eva lunged against the man nearest to her and toppled him into the water as well. Quinn knocked the third off the boat, and he began to grapple with the fourth man.

The drivers of the other boats scrambled to the throttles of their respective boats to edge closer to the fight. The remaining men trained their guns on Eva and Quinn but did not fire. Quinn took a hard punch to the gut. The air blasted out of his lungs in a *whoop* sound. He doubled over in pain, then rammed his head upwards hard, despite the pain. The back of his head connected under the fourth man's jaw and launched him over the small Plexiglas windscreen of the boat onto the extended bow. Eva had slipped into the driver's seat and mashed the throttle forward. The boat sprinted ahead in a surge and Quinn was thrown onto his back just as one of the gunmen from one of the other boats fired his weapon. The bullets passed harmlessly overhead. Eva grabbed the steering wheel and unexpectedly cranked their boat into a 180° spin. Two of the other boats were right on them. The other two smashed their respective bows together and the collision sent both boats off course and away from the chase.

"You want the wheel?" Eva asked when Quinn managed to make his way forward.

"Not a chance. I don't think I could drive as well as you..." he smiled at her. "But I know you can't shoot like I can." He had picked up one of the Uzis. "Keep your head down."

Quinn lowered to a knee and took his time aiming. It wasn't easy. Either evasive speedboat steering came naturally to Eva or she had never driven one. Quinn told himself he would ask her if they made it out of this alive. The two boats in pursuit were holding their fire. They either wanted their prey alive or they were professional enough to know to wait until they were sure. The attempts on his life so far had seemed amateurish to Quinn, but when he had surveilled the cathedral, the men guarding it looked to have some bearing and skill. These were probably some of the same men. He guessed them to be ex-military or mercenaries. No. They wouldn't waste ammunition.

Quinn took aim for the driver of the pursuit boat on the right. He fired once on single-shot and the driver pitched over backward. The second pursuit boat broke away sharply. They hadn't expected to be fired upon.

That was when Quinn realized that he no longer saw the two boats that had initially fallen behind.

"Crap!" he yelled and whirled around to look for them to be flanking Eva. Sure enough, they came from the port side in his blind spot. They raced behind his boat firing their weapons at the motor, inches from where Quinn's head had been when he fired at the last pursuit boat. The motor was hit right away and exploded. The stern of the speedboat bolted into the air pitching Eva and Quinn over the windscreen and into the air. Most of the blast was directed away from the stern of the boat but Quinn could still feel the searing heat as his body flailed through the air at whatever ungodly speed Eva had been forcing out of the boat. Everything slowed down to a crawl as Jason Quinn's body twisted in the air over the harbor of Hong Kong. He watched the boat soar vertically into the sky with an expanding ball of orange growing off the back of it. Then it flipped over through the hellstorm and plunged sickeningly downwards. He lost sight of Eva and then he hit the water. He had no time to take a breath. He sucked in a lungful of the foul water and began to cough.

Then everything went black.

CHAPTER 39

Quinn felt cold. He opened his eyes slowly and took in the room. It was large and well designed, with dark wood walls and plush carpets. No windows. An interior room. Full bookshelves with leather-bound editions that looked new and never read. There was a small wet bar with a variety of bottle tops poking over the railing. The bottles looked full. Plush overstuffed leather chairs. The room looked like a room in an old men's club or a study in some millionaire's home. Quinn didn't care for the décor.

His arms hurt. He was tied with rope, his arms over his head and his feet barely on the floor but free to swing. His shirt was gone and his chest had been singed by the fire from the explosion. The chalk bag and nylon belt were gone. He wore only the black Lycra tights. He turned his head to the right and saw Eva tied up on the wall as he was. He was able to see the metal hooks extending from the wall near the ceiling. There would be no way to slip the loop of rope off them. The ceiling was too high. Eva looked fine. Her clothes were dry though. He had been unconscious for some time.

"You alright?" he asked her. Eva snapped her head around in his direction.

"You're awake! How are you? Are you hurt?" She was excited but didn't sound too nervous about being tied up. Quinn was continually amazed at the woman's fortitude.

"I'll be fine." Quinn asked her where they were, and she told him about what she had seen of the interior of the cathedral. They were in one of the upper levels. She guessed them to be near the roofline of the main structure. She also described a large warehouse-like room full of fancy sports cars and a giant stained glass window that looked out at the other buildings. Quinn guessed she must have been exaggerating. There were probably more like five or six Alpha Romeos and Ferraris—neither of which vehicles were an unusual sight in Hong Kong. The rest of the rooms she described looked either like typical church interiors or like the room they were tied up in. She told him that they had been alone for nearly an hour.

There was one other thing in the room.

The cart was metallic and it had two shelves. It was close to him but not close enough for him to reach it with his feet. It looked to Quinn like something he had seen in hospital rooms. The top tray had a black cloth that covered several lumpy and irregular shapes. He had a suspicion what might lay under that cloth. He had received some training in how to resist torture in the military, but he knew he wouldn't be able to deal with seeing Eva hurt. He closed his eyes for a moment and breathed regularly. His head was a little sore but overall he was not injured by the spectacular boat crash.

Quinn had only seen one door on the other side of the room. It opened now and an extremely tall and slender Chinese man entered holding Curtis Johnson at gunpoint. Curtis's arms were tied in front of him. The Chinese man had jet-black hair that was streaked with cherry red-colored dye. He wore a trendy black shirt and gray slacks that only added to the impression of him as being too tall for an Asian. Curtis looked unhurt as the Chinese man forced him across the room toward Eva and Quinn and proceeded to tie the man up. He was careful to stay on the other side of Curtis in case Quinn tried to attack him with his legs. Quinn took it all in calmly as Curtis didn't appear to be in any distress.

"So you heard about this place too? Is the food as good as they say?" Quinn remarked to Curtis with a grin.

Even as he was being roughly tied to a wall, Curtis didn't miss a beat and replied with his own grin. "The food is remarkable, but the service is a little slow and the maître d', is downright rude." Curtis looked directly at the tall Chinese as he said the last part with a cold look in his eyes. The Chinese man looked impassively back at Johnson. His eyes seemed lackluster as if he was on some kind of drug. Then he turned and walked over to one of the leather armchairs and sat down. His long, gangly limbs looked comical in the squat club chair. Quinn watched the man steadily even as he talked to Johnson.

"See the sights?"

"All of them. Nice architecture. Did you see the cars?" There was a hint of extreme jealously in Johnson's voice. He was a big automotive fan. Suddenly Quinn had the notion that Eva hadn't been exaggerating about the room with the cars.

"Do tell," Quinn replied. He wasn't really interested in the cars but he thought the idle chatter might wear down the attention of the Chinese man who was already starting to look elsewhere in the room from boredom.

"At least 100 in the collection. Rolls Royces, Alphas, Lams, and Ferraris. Even an SLR like you had in Finland but in black. Impressive. Wish I could have seen more."

At that moment, the door opened again and David Hong walked in. The tall Chinese with the cherry-streaked hair stood up. Quinn watched Hong now. He had seen pictures of the man before and he looked exactly like his pictures. Tall, but not as tall as the glazed-eye lackey. Hong wore a discreet charcoal colored suit with a gray and black striped tie. His hair was black and meticulously gelled back over his high, slightly tanned looking forehead. His eyes were smiling. He spoke to the henchman in Cantonese for a moment. Then he turned his gaze toward his three captives and strode over to them.

"Good evening Mr. Quinn, Mr. Johnson, Dr. Rayjek. I am delighted to finally have the chance to speak to all of you."

Quinn could not detect any hint of a Chinese or even a British accent in the man's speech. He could have been from Los Angeles, his speech sounded so American and neutral. Quinn said nothing and the others took their lead from him.

"I must compliment you on your amazing flight onto the roof of my cathedral, Mr. Quinn. And I hear that your attempted escape from the spire was thrilling. There were, of course, men on the Kowloon side awaiting you as well. You never really had a chance to escape, despite Dr. Rayjek's piloting skills with the watercraft."

Quinn kept his face neutral and did not respond.

"No witty banter? No clever comebacks? Come now Mr. Quinn, I have waited so long to speak with you. And I have instructed Chang to hold off on any torture until after we have had our discussion," Hong looked genuinely disappointed.

"You're right, Hong. You complimented my escape. I should return the compliment. But...well, I can't really compliment your assassins' attempts as they were all fairly clumsy. Your flunky over there looks like he's drugged out of his mind, and your suit is nice but is actually last season's fashion, isn't it? So I guess I could compliment you on the cathedral. The architecture is nice and the helipad was a helpful addition," Quinn smiled broadly.

"You raise interesting points, Mr. Quinn. Yes, the men sent after you were a bit clumsy. You must understand that while they were all highly dedicated to the cause, none of them were trained. They were all well-meaning amateurs. That knowledge might raise your respect level for them.

"And you are quite right; Chang is drugged nearly out of his mind. He lives for torture, you see. And when he is not at work on human flesh, he is in a state of abject misery. I allow him the drugs to keep him content during the down periods," Hong's own smile broadened. "As for my suit, I am ashamed to admit that you are correct there as well. I have been a bit too busy with my plans to do any shopping. I wouldn't have guessed you to be a man familiar with high men's fashion, but you surprise me yet again."

"What is it you want to know?" Quinn knew that even if they told Hong what he wanted, the torture would still commence. He was only stalling it as long as he could.

"Oh nothing, Mr. Quinn. I never needed any information from you. I just needed to prevent Dr. Rayjek from discovering the final resting place of the Swedish Explorer."

"Why?" Eva asked. "What difference could that possibly make to you?"

"I already know where it is you see. He's in the tomb of my ancestor." Hong replied to her with polite tones.

"Hong Xiu Quan. God's Chinese son," Quinn said.

"Of course, Mr. Quinn. The Swede was never of any real consequence except that he led Dr. Rayjek toward the tomb. Isn't that right doctor?"

"There were only two other sites left where I thought he might be," Eva said almost to herself.

"The true tomb is near Minfeng," Hong told her.

"So what if we found your relative's skeleton?" Curtis wanted to know.

"Do you know the present size of the Chinese Diaspora, Mr. Johnson?" Hong wasn't looking for an answer, and he continued in a polite but lecturing tone. "There are roughly 35 million of them. That number includes ethnic Chinese and other emigrants, of course. It's a large population though. How many of those would you guess were Christians, Mr. Quinn? I am told you are something of an amateur sinologist."

"Can't be more than ten percent," Quinn guessed.

"Actually, it is more. A lot more. The Chinese are essentially a non-traveling people, Mr. Quinn. Surely, you know that China has rarely engaged in colonial aggression. The Chinese believe that China is the center of the world. Why would they go anywhere else? I have read a vast amount of literature on China, and I am always surprised that no one has asked that question. How is it that nearly 35 million people, who could be called Chinese, are living outside of China? The answer is that most of them were told to," Hong paused and looked directly at Quinn. He could see that Quinn wasn't following and so he continued. "Mr. Quinn, at the end of the Taiping Uprising, my great grandfather, Hong Xiu Quan, was killed. His son, my grandfather, escaped the persecution of the Qing armies."

"I read that he was killed," Quinn interrupted.

"A necessary diversion. Not entirely unlike the Swedish explorer's own rumored demise. A double was killed in Grandfather's place, you see. He lived. And the vast majority of the Taiping loyalists were told to flee. To seek out other, more hospitable parts of the globe where they might await a new opportunity to seek control. They were to keep in touch with each other and to keep their faith a secret. This explains the presence of many so called *China Towns* around the world."

"Are you trying to tell us that every ethnic Chinese around the world is a sleeper agent for an uprising that died 150 years ago?" Quinn asked in disbelief.

"No, Mr. Quinn. I am trying to tell you that roughly 20 million of them are."

CHAPTER 40

Quinn's mouth hung open. "You can't be serious."

"Oh, but I am, Mr. Quinn. You've already met some of them in Colorado and again in Finland and Russia. There's no sinister cold war era brainwashing, I assure you. They are not *sleeper agents,* per se. They are merely dedicated and devoutly religious people—willing to kill for a cause," Hong's smile was genuinely pleased. Quinn had expected at least a trace of smugness but he saw none.

"It was necessary for Dr. Rayjek's discoveries to remain a secret. For now, the masses are hearing whispered rumors that the mighty Hong Xiu Quan has returned and will lead them all to greatness. I have people in most of the Chinese communities around the world who actually have some serious skills. The rest are all amateurs who will blindly follow the community leaders. Twenty million people, Mr. Quinn. They all believe with every ounce of their faith that they are destined for great things. This is, after all, what generations of their family and friends have been spouting. They all know my ancestor's prediction that he would rise up from the grave and return to lead them."

"Fu huo," Quinn said softly. "Resurrect. The tattoo we saw on the pilot in Tibet."

"Yes. Many of the absolute fanatics have taken to tattooing themselves with such quotes," Hong continued with near reverence. "They will do as they are told. They will rise up and soon they will be a dominant force the world over. The Ethnic Chinese have for years been infiltrating organizations like the FBI and the CIA in your country along with other such agencies around the world in the most powerful nations. And they wait, Mr. Quinn. Patiently. For the time when their savior returns to lead them to victory over the barbarians of the world that cruelly robbed them of victory in the 19th century."

"Okay," Quinn said trying to digest. "But why try to keep the location of the tomb hidden? It doesn't make sense. Besides, you can't really think your ancestor is going to miraculously spring to life."

"As far as the Chinese Christian Diaspora is concerned, Mr. Quinn, I *am* Hong Xiu Quan—reborn. It would be a simple thing to refute if someone were to show up dangling a dried up skeleton, though," Hong now let his grin creep into the range of smugness Quinn had been expecting earlier.

"So you're a religious wacko with an army. So what? Your 20 million will look like small potatoes compared to the rest of the world when they trounce your ass," Curtis explained pleasantly.

Hong laughed heartily. "Oh, Mr. Johnson. You make it sound like it will be a straightforward battle on a field of mud and soldiers. But you see, the battle is in fact one of blackmail. I have already long since alerted the security forces of the world that they have moles in their midst. I haven't revealed who, naturally. All I asked for is that they do not interfere in what I am about to do. They were all too glad to comply," his chuckling lingered.

Quinn felt something gnawing inside. Religious uprising. Sleeper fanatics. Blackmail. The world's security forces happy to sit back and watch.

"What are you about to do?" Quinn asked.

"I am going to do something the Italians have dreamed of since the time of Hong Xiu Quan. I am going to take the Vatican."

With that, David Hong turned and smoothly walked to the door and exited the room. The tall Chinese, Chang, stood. He looked at Quinn and then the other two. The glazed look in his eyes was gone now. His eyes gleamed with a hunger.

He walked over to the metallic tray table near the three captives hung by their wrists on the wall. He swept the black cloth off the cart, revealing several odd-shaped knives and metallic instruments. Many of them looked incredibly painful. He spent a moment arranging the instruments slightly, in some cases making miniscule movements to a tool until it met with his predetermined notion of how it should lay on the cart. Then he spent another moment just glancing at the instruments. Lost in thought. He turned back to look at Quinn once again, then left the room as Hong had done.

He came back in after what felt to Quinn like fifteen minutes. They hadn't spoken in his absence. They were each wrapped in their private thoughts thinking of the bombshell of intrigue that had just dropped into their laps. Quinn didn't know much about Vatican history. He did know that it was all that was left of a Papal state, which had previously taken up much more of Italy.

Chang swept in close to the three captives and landed a hard punch in Johnson's gut. The noise the air made as it burst forth from his lungs was like an explosion. Chang then hit Quinn equally as hard. Quinn saw it coming but had no time to do much other than tense his stomach muscles. It still hurt badly. When he raised his head, he could see Chang had moved toward Eva. The Chinese man turned to the cart, selected a long-handled scalpel, and turned quickly back toward Eva. He cut her down, hit her in the gut with his fist as he had done to Quinn and Johnson, and then dragged her from the room, still holding the scalpel.

CHAPTER 41

Quinn oozed rage. He had no idea where Chang had taken Eva, but he didn't have to wait long. Chang was back in under two minutes and Quinn calmed considerably, reasoning that there was not much in the way of torture that the man might have conducted in such a short time. She was obviously being saved for something else. Quinn hung his head as if he was overcome still by the blow to his stomach. It *was* still painful, but he was recovering.

Chang walked directly up to Curtis with a scalpel and slashed at his chest twice in quick succession. Quinn used his hands to grab the rope above his wrists and launched his legs up and toward Chang's head. He landed his calves around the tall man's neck and then twisted his body violently around 360°, while holding the rope for support. Chang's neck snapped loudly with a crack. Quinn held his legs tight around the gangly man's head and lowered the body to the carpet carefully. Then, he reached his bare foot out toward the dead man's hand, which still held the finely sharpened scalpel.

"You couldn't have done that before I became the fillet of the day?" Curtis asked as blood seeped down his black, long sleeved shirt.

"I've been trying to find the chance since I realized my legs were free. He didn't get close enough to me until just now, and Hong never came near enough either." As Quinn talked, he plucked the scalpel out of Chang's hand with the shaft of it lodged in the space between Quinn's first two toes. Then he took a calming breath and slowly raised his legs up toward Johnson's tied hands. His stomach still hurt, but his muscles were strong from inverted rock climbing and the recent excursions on the cavern ceiling in Tibet. He placed the scalpel near Johnson's fingers in one smooth leg lift. "Here. Get us down quick."

Curtis took the scalpel and made quick work of the rope holding him. Then he turned to Quinn and began sawing those ropes as well. As the last, frayed strings were tearing through, Quinn lunged away from the wall using his strength to tear through the last of his confinement. He made straight for the door.

Curtis took a moment to look down at the body of his would-be torturer. He still held the scalpel in his hand. He threw it down at the corpse. The tip of the blade stuck into the flesh and the handle wobbled as if it were a throwing knife stuck into a wooden log. He stood a second looking at what he had done and then thought better of it and pulled the blade out of the dead man and clutched it tightly. He picked up the black cloth that had been on the torture instruments and held it against the cuts on his chest. Then he turned and followed Quinn out of the room at a run.

Quinn raced down the corridor bare chested and barefoot. He blasted through the door at the end of the hallway into the warehouse with the car collection he had heard about. The others hadn't exaggerated. There were close to a hundred specimens including some of the most valuable cars in the world. Quinn noticed a Saleen S7, a French Bugatti Veyron 16.4, and an Aston Martin Vanquish. He also spotted some concept cars he had seen pictures of in Forbes back at the office in Denver. He only had a second to recognize the room and the cars. There were two large security guards near the middle of the room when Quinn burst in. He saw them almost immediately and continued straight for them. Curtis was right behind him.

The guards were startled. Even though they were both armed with Uzis, they did not have the weapons at the ready. Neither of them had expected to be charged by a half-naked man. They stood a moment and blinked in shock. Then the man closest to Quinn charged toward his attacker. The other man began to raise his weapon. Curtis watched the weapon raise as if in slow motion as he sprinted into the scene. He leapt up onto the hood of a Lamborghini and dove through the air toward the guard with the gun. The man watched Curtis streak through the air and continued to raise his weapon up toward Curtis and away from Quinn.

Quinn lowered his head at the last second and slammed it into the stomach of the rushing guard. The impact knocked them both backwards and they splayed on the floor. Quinn felt woozy and looked up just in time to see Curtis flying over him head first, arm outstretched as he threw something.

The scalpel sank deeply into the eye socket of the guard who had raised his weapon to track Johnson. The man's finger clenched in pain and the Uzi spat a continuous streak of bullets in an arc through the air, blasting cars, the wall, and finally one of the three fancy crystal chandeliers that lit the huge warehouse. Quinn watched fascinated as the giant glass and metal structure came plummeting down toward him. Then his field of vision was obscured as the guard stepped over him holding his stomach in pain and pointing his own Uzi directly at Quinn.

Quinn was in a sitting position looking upwards and rolled backward, his legs coming up over his head as the guard began to fire. The bullets ripped at the concrete as Quinn rolled over backward onto his feet and sprang upwards and back—just out of the radius of the chandelier that crashed into the guard in a monstrous tinkling and cracking noise as the glass shards sprayed everywhere. Quinn landed on his back on the hood of a BMW Z8 and stared at the crushed guard.

"Close," Curtis said as he stood and took up the Uzi from the man he had blinded.

"Too damn close," Quinn said. The crushed guard's weapon was under the wreckage. He left it and leapt over the hood of the Z8 and looked back at the giant stained glass window with its religious iconography in brilliant blues, greens, and reds, lit as it was from a spotlight below. They had come from a door by that side of the huge room and there was only one other. He raced toward it, skipping over fragments of crystal on the floor so he wouldn't carve up his feet. Curtis was by his side by the time they reached the door.

"How much time?" Quinn asked, as they burst through the door into an undefended corridor.

"Not much. Move it," Curtis replied without any mirth.

They followed the corridor to its end and a circular staircase cut from stone. Without hesitation Quinn began taking the stairs two at a time heading up. Curtis followed and checked how much ammunition he had left in the Uzi. Quinn could hear footsteps far above him up the steps.

They saw no one on the stairs, and at the top, breathing hard, Quinn motioned for the Uzi and Curtis handed it over. He knew he could hold his own in a fight but he knew Quinn was better and more ruthless. Quinn had once been trained for this sort of thing. Still, if Eva was in danger, Curtis would gladly throw himself into the fray. He had taken a liking to her and knew how Quinn was feeling about her. He would fight until his last breath.

Quinn slammed the heavy, metal and wood door open and sprayed the two standing guards with two bursts each and dropped the empty weapon. He was out the door and sprinting across the helipad before their bodies hit the concrete. The blue and white Hong Kong Express helicopter had already left the pad and was arcing away. Quinn could see Eva in the window looking down at him. She looked as if her last hope had just been answered as she saw Quinn arrive. He quickly mouthed three words to her: *I'll find you.* She seemed to make a nod but then the helicopter was too far away for them to see her any more.

"Another way," Curtis said, as he dragged Quinn by the arm and back through the doorway. He took the lead and began leaping down the circular stairs—seven to ten steps at a time—as many as the curvature of the stairwell would allow. Quinn followed him, hard on his heels. Curtis barely had time to think that if he stumbled Quinn would slam into him when Quinn grabbed the back of his shirt and yanked him to a stop.

"This way," Quinn was already diving through the door back into the corridor that led to the car showroom. "How much time?"

Curtis Johnson looked at his watch with a frown as he raced down the corridor behind Quinn. "Not enough! I hope you have a plan."

"Grand theft auto," Quinn replied, as he burst through the door into the showroom and made quickly for the Bugatti.

"What the hell..." Curtis began, but Quinn was sliding behind the driver's seat and starting the ignition with a roar. Curtis hopped into the passenger's side and strapped his seatbelt frantically. He hadn't buckled the thing when

Quinn had made the all-wheel drive vehicle jump forward, its wheels barking on the concrete showroom floor. He stamped on the accelerator and the sleek purple and black car blazed across the showroom floor toward the giant stained glass window.

"We're hundreds of feet up, Quinn!" Curtis buckled his belt.

"Got any other suggestions?" Jason Quinn stood on the pedal as the computer controlled transmission shifted through all seven gears in less than two seconds and the 1,000 horsepower sports car, all one million dollars of it, blasted through colored glass and lead into the Hong Kong skyline. They were about 1,300 feet up in the air and the explosives Curtis Johnson had planted in the basement crypts around the support structures, before being intentionally captured on an upper floor, were about to go off.

CHAPTER 42

In 1992, the Central Plaza skyscraper's construction was completed. It stands in the Wanchai District of Hong Kong Island at 1,227 feet with its spire. With 78 floors, it is mostly all office space. The most unusual feature of the building is that its footprint is triangular. The side that faces west lost its view of the city and the harbor because it was dwarfed when the Hong Cathedral was constructed.

Now, a night janitor named Micheal Woo was pausing from vacuuming the carpet in a plush executive office to stretch his sore muscles. He had worked it a bit too hard at the gym the two days previously and he was sore all over now. Especially his legs. He was looking at what he thought of as an amazingly gaudy stained glass window on the cathedral. It was maybe only 50 feet away. Just wide enough for the street below and the sidewalks filled with people during business hours.

As Woo watched, the window exploded outward and a purple and black sled of a car raced across the gap right toward him. It happened so fast he barely had time to move. He threw himself to the floor as the rocketing car ripped into the tinted glass window he had been standing at. The glass sprayed everywhere and the wind tore through the room. There was screeching and crashing of metal and glass. He stood with his weakened muscles shaking as he looked back into the office he had just been cleaning. There were tire tread marks streaked across the top of the cherry wood desktop next to him. The car had just barely cleared his head. Woo swallowed hard as he followed the trail of destruction with his eyes across the office and through the wreckage of the wall that used to lead to the hallway and the elevators. There were gouges in the deep carpet that were on fire from the friction, as the wide-bodied car had scraped its way through the building.

Woo began to rush to the hall and he followed the trail the car had left as it crushed everything in its path and spun into a crunched heap at the far side of the building—right at the point of the triangular building. It had burst through another executive office and the tail end had smashed through the pointed corner where two picture windows had met. The wind raced through Woo's longish black hair as he ran up to the thing that had nearly obliterated his life. Two men were climbing out of the thing. Woo had been a fan of the fancy cars he always saw in the windows of Hong Kong showrooms but he couldn't tell what the crushed vehicle had been. Not even close.

Then the rumbling started. The noise was deafening. Woo turned around and looked behind him. Something was wrong with the building with the shattered stained glass window. It looked liquid and warped. It was definitely moving. Without thinking about it, Woo raced back toward the shattered window and the wooden desk where he had nearly been smeared by a flying car. He stopped in time to see the giant spire of the Hong Cathedral come screaming past his view and then the rest of the building fall inward. The noise was like a jet aircraft engine Woo had heard when he took a trip to Bangkok years earlier. There was an immense amount of dust and creaking scraping noises along with a deep booming like a bass guitar amped up at a rock concert. Then there were crunching sounds and explosions. Woo ran away from the window and back into the shredded office. He fell to the floor and shook with the vibrations and rumbling that rattled the Central Plaza building and shattered some of its windows. When the noise stopped, Woo stood up and coughed from the dust and smoke. The carpet fire had stopped on its own, in the hall by the elevators. The two men that had emerged from the car were gone, and the Central Plaza building suddenly had its view of Hong Kong back. The mighty Hong Cathedral had collapsed.

BOOK THREE:
THE HOLY CITY

CHAPTER 43

I love St. Peter's church. The music that is heard in it is always good and the eye is always charmed. It is an ornament of the Earth.
—Ralph Waldo Emerson

The man named James Lau passed the metal detectors without notice. He was an average looking man of Chinese descent. He carried a disposable camera with 32 shots, three of which had already been used. He wore dark clothes but nothing ominous—just fashionable. He also carried a ceramic-composite serrated knife in his boot. The security guards at the detector manually searched through his small daypack and found nothing out of the ordinary. Some water in a bottle. Some snack food in plastic bags. A hooded pullover. Lau was allowed to proceed past the security station and move further on down the line toward the doors to the massive structure. He thanked the men in flawless Italian.

He looked up at the church he had visited so many times in the last year. It was late in the afternoon and the sun was falling behind the gigantic dome. Unlike the other visitors to the Basilica, James Lau and nine others who had entered at varying times of the day would be spending the night.

Lau wandered around the ground floor as if he were stunned by the beauty of the scenery. Just like all the other tourists did. He went into alcoves and took photos of the stained glass windows. Then he began to ascend the stairs toward the roof of the lower main structure. He knew he would find a small shop there and he would spend some time looking at postcards. He might even buy a keychain.

After wandering aimlessly for a half hour he continued up toward the top of the dome and the small circular balcony there to take some quick snaps before descending again. He knew he had to leave the balcony before the other tourists. He had to descend the stairs in relative isolation. It was close to closing time. The whole of the city would be closed to tourists the next day for security purposes—it always was for visiting dignitaries.

Lau descended some of the stairs toward the base of the dome. It was possible to look up the sides of the stairwell and see into the dark empty space between the outer dome and the inner dome. The space was considerable and the upper reaches of it were completely shrouded by shadows. There were no security cameras here. There was nothing of value here. Only a staircase that most people ascended huffing or descended quickly.

Lau glanced around to ensure that he was alone and then leapt over the metal handrail that accompanied the staircase. He clambered into the space between the upper and lower dome surfaces and quickly scrambled up into the shadows. It was tight near the top. Just enough room for his body. He removed an aluminum carabiner from his backpack and removed the car keys that had been hanging from it. The keys went back into the backpack. The carabiner got clipped to his nylon belt and attached to the metal ring that extended from the concrete of the dome. He then relaxed his muscles and lay down on his back with his backpack behind his head as a pillow.

He was completely comfortable and totally cloaked by shadows. His feet pointed down the slope of the dome toward the stairs. He watched patiently as tourists began to descend those stairs. They came in small groups and in twos and threes at first. Then they came in streams and he guessed that the announcement had been made that the building was closing. It took another twenty minutes until all the people had stopped streaming downwards. Many had looked up into the space where he reclined. No one had seen even a hint of him, with his dark clothes.

Then all the people were gone. Now was the questionable part. He knew that the guards didn't conduct any kind of a head count. With hundreds to thousands of visitors a day, it simply wasn't practical. There would be no way that they would know he hadn't exited the building.

The question was what kind of search they conducted for lingering tourists and lost children.

He waited.

Eventually, one of the guards came up the stairs slowly plodding along. He didn't even glance into the space between the inner and outer portions of the dome. The man had probably seen every part of the interior of the building. The architecture would hold no interest for him as it would for a tourist.

Lau waited. The guard had a long climb to the top of the dome. It felt like an hour by the time the guard returned down the stairs. Lau didn't know for sure. He didn't want to take the chance of activating the backlight on his Casio wristwatch only to light up his hiding space just as the guard returned. He had to content himself with estimating the time. As the guard walked slowly by, he seemed unconcerned.

Then, he glanced up into the space where James Lau lay in wait.

Lau held his breath. The guard continued his descent and turned his gaze back to the steps. After a minute, Lau heard the echo of a door closing and locking below him. He released his breath and relaxed. Now he just had to get some sleep. In ten hours, he and the other nine men hidden in niches and crevasses in the architecture would join their resurrected leader Hong Xiu Quan in taking over Saint Peter's Basilica in Vatican City.

CHAPTER 44

The private Lear jet had landed at Andrews Air Force base an hour previously. Margaret Tower was escorted directly to the waiting helicopter by two marines in full dress uniform. They helped her up the folding staircase and into the president's personal short-range rotary wing vehicle. The flight to the White House lawn was brief but was far too long for Marge. Every moment might count.

The moment the marines indicated she could get up from her seat, she sprang up toward the door. Harold Graines, the Deputy Chief of Staff met her on the lawn with an extended hand. She shook it quickly as he swept her away from the helicopter and toward the west wing. When they had reached an area of relative quiet, he spoke to her.

"Margaret, it's nice to see you. I understand you asked for five minutes. Something to do with an international terrorist act?" Graines was in his sixties and completely bald. His rumpled shirt and tie spoke of a busy day in what had been a busy term at the White House.

"Believe me, Harold. I wouldn't waste his time if I didn't think it was a grave situation." Marge unconsciously smoothed the front of her cream-colored suit in preparation for seeing the President, a man she had met only once before at a charity dinner.

"He'll be ready for you in about ten minutes. John will be there with you and General Shaw and a few others, okay?" Graines led her into the Oval Office where General Shaw, the Chairman of the Joint Chiefs was already waiting and discussing the collapse of the Cathedral with John

Conley, the White House Chief of Staff. Both men stood when Marge entered the room.

The president wasn't in the room yet. It looked almost exactly as she had expected from having seen the room in countless television shows and films. It was smaller than she had expected. The furniture was a bit more subdued than in the movies. She supposed the room was always done up in the most extravagant of colonial furniture in film to underscore the historical gravity of the place. She preferred President Gaffin's taste. Then again, maybe it was the taste of Mrs. Gaffin that Marge was sensing.

"Margaret," John Conley swept forward taking her hand. He was the consummate 'elder statesman'. Conservative brown suit. Perfectly groomed, practically shellacked, Washington haircut, a lovely shade of silver. "Nice to see you again."

"It's been too long since you've been to the mountains, John," Marge smiled at him as she referred to his last trip to ARGO, when the White House had requested some assistance with reconstruction work after an alpine earthquake in Chile. "This would be General Shaw."

She turned toward the huge bear of a man and firmly clasped his offered hand. The General was in Army dress green with a chest full of medals and ribbons. His head was nearly as bald as Harold's but it seemed more a choice of style than a full retreat of hair as in Harold's case. He was black with soft brown eyes that spoke of genuine warmth.

"Margaret, John, Harold," President Gaffin moved confidently into the room as the others all greeted him with the customary title of 'Mister President'. He came over to the sofas and plopped down into one, before crossing his legs. He was a short man but broad shouldered. His suit was gray and his tie was loosened at the neck even though it was not quite mid morning yet. "Can I get anyone something to drink?" They all replied negatively. "Okay. Let's hear it Margaret."

Marge proceeded to fill him in on the events of the past weeks starting with the attack on Eva Rayjek's flight and ending with Quinn's hurried phone call from the airport in Hong Kong when he had explained David Hong's stated goal of attacking the Vatican. She conveniently glossed over the fact that Quinn and Johnson were responsible for the destruction of the Cathedral, and she left the President and the others to fill in the blank in their own minds as to who was responsible for the act. Any negative acts attributed to David Hong only strengthened her case for the Vatican being in imminent danger.

When she had finished, President Gaffin leaned back on his sofa and sighed heavily. "We have a problem. I can't contact the Pope."

John Conley spoke up quickly. "Why not?"

The General answered. "Because the entire Vatican City is closed for Hong's arrival. No tourists and no outside communication. There's a total communications blackout. It's their standard operating procedure for visits from heads of state and other major dignitaries. It's one of their most outdated security protocols from before the Second World War The thinking is no one would be able to influence meetings with the Pope and heads of state. We can't reach them in time. There isn't a single mobile phone in the entire Vatican State working today."

"That is not good," Conley said. "Can we stop Hong at the airport in Rome?"

"We can contact the Italians. They might be able to detain him," the general was thinking hard.

"Let's make that happen," the President said. "Margaret, what about your two men? Did you say they're heading to Rome too?"

"Yes, Mr. President. If Quinn and Johnson can't stop Hong in Rome, then they'll follow him to the Vatican—"

"Hoping to rescue this woman, Dr. Rayjek?" the President interrupted her.

"Yes, sir."

"And who are these guys? Are they ex-military?"

Margaret gave the others a brief background on Quinn's military experience. She also mentioned that Gene Quinn, Jason's father, was with the CIA

"And you really think they'll try to break into the Vatican?" the President asked.

"I haven't asked them to do that, sir. But knowing them the way I do..."

"Yes, I see." The President sighed. "John, what else can we do?"

"We can just be ready, Mr. President. To act, when we can."

"Yeah."

CHAPTER 45

The morning sun had just peeked over the eastern walls of the Vatican as the helicopter swept over the western walls carrying David Hong and eight of his 'assistants'. Hong had declined the generous offer of the Pope to use the papal helicopter, because he had his own in Rome, ready for just such an occasion. The assistants were justified because of the four gold-decorated crates of Christian relics that Hong was repatriating to the Vatican. The helicopter arrival was justified because it was convenient, and because the Pope wanted to keep a total media blackout on the meeting. It was not uncommon for the Vatican to close its gates to tourists with a small sign at the gate declaring a private function. Hong claimed to have in his possession a relic that the Pope very much wanted to see and that he very much hoped would turn out to be genuine.

The helicopter settled lightly onto the private Vatican helipad and the pilot quickly shut down the engine. A small contingent awaited Hong's arrival—among them were four Swiss Guard in their colorful full dress uniforms. Their morion style gray helmets with brilliant red plumed feathers barely reflected the morning sun. Hong took pleasure in the fact that these men were dressed in regalia and not dressed for battle. Also among the group were a few holy men and Hong noticed there was a small paunchy man that he recognized as the Vatican Secretary of Relations with States, Archbishop Gioberto Silvano. This also pleased Hong, because Hong was not an official representative of China at all. Protocol was being broken here as a gesture toward Hong. He smiled widely as he stepped from the helicopter and approached Silvano with his outstretched hand. The archbishop grasped it and smiled warmly.

"Welcome to the Vatican, Mr. Hong."

"Archbishop Silvano, what a pleasure to meet you at last, Your Excellency," Hong looked in the man's face for any signs of insincerity, but it seemed that the Pope's outrage at the size of Hong Cathedral had either faded with the promise of the relics Hong was bringing, or else this man had never shared the Pontiff's displeasure. They briefly discussed the collapse of the cathedral in Hong Kong. Hong pointed to faulty architecture, tremors, or possibly terrorist action but assured Silvano that no lives were lost and the building would be reconstructed with far more personal oversight.

"We might also consider a smaller structure this time," Hong said with a small smile. Silvano seemed pleased. As they talked and Silvano led Hong to an open-topped Jeep parked at the side of the helipad, Hong's pilot took off his headset and joined the other seven men in loading the four decorated crates out of the helicopter and into the second and third Jeeps.

"Your request was highly unusual, you know," Silvano gently scolded, but he was smiling as he said it. "His Holiness usually meets dignitaries in his offices and not in the Basilica."

"I wanted our meeting to be as blessed by God as possible," Hong lied and the other man nodded his head as if that was precisely the reason he was expecting.

"I had suggested as much to His Holiness. Plus, considering the nature of the items you are bringing…" Silvano left the thought unfinished but Hong really knew that the Archbishop was thinking of one specific relic that Hong was supposedly bringing.

"I assure you that I have had it authenticated as much as is possible. Our written records in China go back before the birth of Christ. If the man bringing the item to China was telling the truth…" Hong left his own sentence unfinished to allow the Archbishop to come to exactly the conclusion Hong was hoping for.

"Our own records from the 11th and 12th centuries are sporadic at best and often quite vague or obtuse on matters pertaining to Asia," Silvano said slowly, "but most of our records suggest that Prester John was nothing more than a myth."

"I was quite skeptical at first, myself," Hong said as he watched the morning scenery of the Vatican gardens go by, as the driver slowly took the Jeep to the Basilica on small paved roads that were little more than pedestrian paths.

"There are certainly enough ridiculous legends surrounding the man, like the Fountain of Youth and so forth. I had not even heard of anything to suggest a connection between Prester John and the nail." There, he had said it. Hong glanced slyly at the old squat man to see his reaction when he said the words. The Archbishop winced as if he were projecting his mind back to the event and actually feeling the nail pounded into Christ's flesh.

"And your experts have dated the spike to the time of Our Lord's crucifixion?" Silvano asked as if he had not read the same reports the Pope had read.

"There is little doubt as to the age of the object. Only as to where it came from before it was brought to China. But I question why it would have been so revered if it were not authentic. The literature tells of a great golden box with jewels and inside a bed of soft velvet made from the hair of lambs. An army to protect the chest and an ever present crowd of faithful, praying day and night. It sounds like a long way to go for a scam in the 12th century." Hong contented himself with a small smirk as he was driven into the piazza in front of Saint Peter's Basilica. The jeep stopped near the front steps to the imposing structure, its dome reaching over 450 feet into the air from the pavement.

"We normally use an entrance on the side but I understand that this is your first visit to the Basilica. I thought you might want to see it from the piazza," the Archbishop said, as he stepped out of the Jeep and looked up at the stunning structure.

Hong was genuinely awed and did not need to fake his gratitude when he said, "I am very moved. Thank you for thinking of those kinds of details, Your Excellency."

CHAPTER 46

The secret compartment in the back of the helicopter was cramped. Eva could barely move. It was dark except for two round shafts of light that pierced the gloom. These were holes just large enough for fingers and were designed to allow a person to remove the false rear wall of the passenger compartment. Eva had seen the pilot of the craft remove the rear seats and then pull away the secret compartment wall. Hong's men had stuffed her into the compartment for the ride from the airport to the Vatican. Hong himself had patiently explained to her that the helicopter was soundproofed, so she could make all the noise she wanted and no one would hear her.

She looked again at the finger holes. They were also a source of air for her as well as a source of light. Her hands were tied in front of her with a soft and fairly flexible rope. She had been working at bending her wrists and flexing her arms for some time. She thought she might be making some headway but wasn't sure.

She did know she was tired. She thought of the helicopter flight away from the Hong Cathedral and the landing at what she guessed was Hong Kong's international airport. It was some kind of a private area of the field and she was quickly loaded onto a private Lear jet. She had looked for an opportunity to escape but had found none. At all times, alert, armed men loyal to Hong had surrounded her. They had loaded her on the plane and locked her in it while they had discussed something on the tarmac. Hong had seemed plenty pissed off in that discussion and seemed to be yelling at some of his men who quickly got on their mobile phones and began speaking rapidly. Eva had watched it all from the small windows of the lush plane but couldn't actually hear anything from inside the plane. She figured she would have to rely on her intuition anyway because the men were most likely speaking in Cantonese. She hoped that Hong's anger meant that Quinn and Johnson had escaped.

When Hong and the others had boarded the plane and it took off, she waited awhile and then attempted to bait the man.

"So what was all that about?"

"Be quiet," Hong told her softly.

"The boys threw a monkey wrench into your plans, didn't they?" Eva goaded the man. "Good."

"A minor inconvenience, Dr. Rayjek. One that I turn to my advantage. Now be quiet before I allow Lim to have his way with you."

Eva glanced at the man across the aisle from her. He was staring at her without blinking. She decided to be quiet. After a few minutes, Lim turned and looked out of his window. Eva kept an eye on him until he started reading a paperback novel.

She had slept a little on that flight, but her dreams were restless and she kept seeing the fight on Hong Kong harbor in her dreams—only with different endings. In some of them, she was killed or injured. In others, she watched Quinn being killed when his parachute took him into the water. Or it was Johnson on the chute but he landed on a boat that burst into flames. After several of these variations of her dreams, she woke and asked Hong's men for coffee, which they provided. She stayed awake for the rest of the flight to Italy, afraid more of her disturbing dreams than of her captors.

Hong and the others rarely spoke on the flight although they all stayed awake. Despite the fact that he was a religious nut (and the threat regarding Lim), Hong and his men had treated her fairly well. They had not been rough with her since their departure from the cathedral, allowed her to use the restroom at the rear of the plane, provided her meals, and even offered her a newspaper. When they landed in Italy, they had again transferred modes of transportation in a remote area of the airport reserved for private planes. This time they had tied her hands and gently escorted her into the secret compartment. Hong had assured her that she would not have to remain in the compartment for long and that there would be adequate air supply.

Eva pressed a button on the face of her wristwatch and the backlight feebly illuminated the small compartment. She judged that they had been on the ground for almost 20 minutes now and she had been left alone in the helicopter for the last ten. She didn't know how long it would be before Hong or one of his soldiers came back for her, but she was determined not to be there waiting in that compartment. She didn't know how to fly a helicopter, but she was fairly sure she could get out of it and get to help before anyone came for her.

She shifted her back and brought her wrists up to the narrow shafts of light from the finger holes and tried again to stretch her wrists. She flexed and twisted and then brought the knots of rope to her mouth. She used her tongue to count up the braids until she had the strand of rope she wanted clenched between her teeth. She pulled on the rope with her teeth and rotated her left hand as much as she could.

The rope was slipping!

She brought her hands to the light again to examine her work. Then she brought the rope to her mouth again. She did this several times until the cords were loose enough. She folded her thumb into her palm and pulled hard. Her right hand slid out of the knots. Then it was easy to pull the rope off her other hand.

Eva reached for the finger holes and pulled upwards while pushing out and the wall of the compartment cracked open allowing the sunlight to stream in.

She was blinded for just a moment until her eyes adjusted. Then, she shoved the panel away from her and found that it didn't move far enough. At first, her mind panicked. *Not far enough! I need to get out!*

Then she remembered the rear seats. Of course. They were still in place. Eva shifted in her compartment again so she could get her fingers under the lower edge of the now displaced panel. In one fluid motion, she launched the panel upwards and over the top of the rear seats and into the front of the passenger compartment of the helicopter. Now she had plenty of light but only a distance of four or five inches between the opening of her compartment and the back of the rear seats. Not enough room for her to squeeze out. She looked under the seats as well, but the space there was too narrow.

She would need to reach the release for the seats to move them out of the way. She was able to roll her body with the extra space she now had and flipped onto her stomach with her legs bent up behind her. She reached her left arm around the side of the chair on the left and tried to grab the release lever.

It was too far.

She stretched as much as she could and slid her hand all around the side of the seat but couldn't feel it. She couldn't see what she was doing but she could remember from when she had been loaded into the helicopter what it looked like. She just couldn't reach it.

Eva lay panting with effort for a moment and thought. Then, she retracted her arm and contorted her body around in an effort to spin around in the tight compartment. Then she stopped and breathed again. Now her head was where her feet had originally been. She tried the same tactic with the right-hand seat. She stretched her arm around the side of the seat and slid her hand around looking for the release lever on this side. Nothing.

"Damn it!"

Now what? Eva lay on her stomach looking under the seats into the freedom of the interior of the helicopter that was so close to her and so frustratingly out of reach. If only she had something to extend her reach. She looked under the seats for a tool kit or something. *What I wouldn't give for a wrench!*

Then, she remembered the rope that had been around her wrists. She twisted around and snatched at where she had left it on the floor of the compartment. She made a little loop and stretched her arm around the seat again—this time holding the loop. Instead of feeling around for the lever, she closed her eyes and visualized where it was. Then, she gently swung the loop of rope back and forth and then released it when it was on an upward swing. She grabbed the end and slowly tugged it. It pulled taut. She pulled harder and felt a resistance. Then, a click, and the seat moved forward. With a cry of triumph, Eva shoved the seat with her shoulder and it moved forward and fell over.

CHAPTER 47

The element of surprise was complete. A moment after the Pope entered the Basilica with another archbishop in tow, Hong's men effortlessly removed the lids of the ornate crates and removed the weapons contained within. Looks of astonishment were just beginning to emerge on the faces of Silvano and the Swiss Guards when Hong's men began spraying bullets.

The high-pitched electrical whine that emerged from the weapons filled the echoing spaces of the vast structure as a literal tornado of bullets perforated the guards, Silvano, and the extra archbishop. It was over almost immediately. The Pope was unmolested with the exception of a fine mist of red that had stained his Holy garments.

The Pope had never even heard of small arms that could fire off as many rounds so quickly and without much noise. The electronic whine was loud but the guns sounded suppressed even though he knew enough about weapons to see that these terrifying things that Hong's men wielded bore no silencing suppressors at the end of their barrels. It never occurred to him to be frightened for his life. The man was simply horrified that someone might bring rifles into the building and that they might slaughter his people without a thought.

Suddenly, more Chinese men emerged from various parts of the Basilica. One man even rappelled down a rope from the top of the dome. The Pontiff's mind was close to cracking. Finally, he stuttered a word in English.

"I-I-Impossible."

The ten men, who had sequestered themselves in dark alcoves and structural spaces under the dome, raced into the Nave, the main hall just inside the doors, and they headed directly toward the men standing over the crates. The tallest had a small scar over his left eyebrow. He began to bark orders in Chinese. Each man received a weapon from the crates. A few of the weapons required a quick and practiced assembly of parts. The Pope began to feel his knees weaken. He looked around the space at the bloodied bodies that hardly resembled humans any longer after receiving so many bullets. Silvano was dead. So was Archbishop Delano. Four of the Swiss Guards lay sprawled in a spreading pool of blood on the marble floor. He, himself, was covered in Delano's blood. Some of the quickly assembled weapons resembled sniper rifles and some even resembled 50 caliber heavy machine guns. The man with the scar over his eye kicked the crates over as they emptied. As each man received weapons and a few barked Chinese instructions, he would run off and out of the Nave. The Pope noticed that some of the crates, when kicked over, sprayed out gem-encrusted goblets and crosses of gold—camouflage for the weapons that had lain in hiding beneath—which skittered across the polished marble floor. Somehow the sight of a cross being used as a prop and then discarded with disdain triggered the Pope out of his horrified shock. Now his rage finally sank in.

"How dare you!" he shouted.

His voice echoed around the room and carried enough rage and volume that the Chinese men actually paused in their efforts for just a moment. They looked at him for a second, then glanced to Hong, who stood impassively to the side. He simply nodded and the men quickly resumed their rushed activity until the man with the scar was the last one left in the Nave with Hong and the Pope. He held one of the wickedly silent assault rifles and strode over to Hong's side where he stood and looked at the Pope.

"What in the name of all that is Holy are you doing, you…" the Pope struggled for a word and finally settled on "Bastard!"

David Hong calmly appraised the blood spattered Pontiff before replying.

"Your Holiness, I am David Hong, the great-grandson of the mighty Hong Xiu Quan, and I am doing something that has not occurred since the creation of the Kingdom of Italy—I am seizing the Vatican."

CHAPTER 48

The Vatican is home to just shy of 1,000 individuals. Precisely 101 of them are Swiss Guards. Although the current commander of the Corps of the Pontifical Swiss Guard, Colonel Johannes Andreas Werner, a stern, gaunt, tall gray man, was open to the idea of permitting women to serve in the Guard, to date, none had. All 101 of them are men, and despite their colorful, ceremonial uniforms with blue, red, yellow, and orange Renaissance stripes, the Swiss Guard are a well-trained military unit to a man.

Reports of gunfire came to Colonel Werner from five different sources just a moment after the sounds had echoed through the Basilica. Guards stationed near the Basilica were already investigating.

He radioed for additional men to go to each of the five publicly known entrances to the structure, and for others to go to the three secret underground entrances to the church. This was a decision he would later come to regret.

Since the sack of Rome in 1527, only two Swiss Guards had died while in service to the Vatican—a former Commander named Alois Estermann, who, along with his wife, was murdered under mysterious circumstances in 1998, by Cédric Tornay, another guard who turned his murderous weapon on himself after his brutal deed. After only two deaths in over four and a half centuries, today would be a shock to the Swiss Guard and to the world.

Just to the right of the front of St. Peter's square, as you face the Basilica, stands the Swiss Guard barracks. Colonel Werner was just leaving the barracks and heading along Via del Pelligrino past St. Anne's church toward the barracks of the Papal Gendarmes, and the office of the *Corpo della Gendarmeria dello Stato della Città del Vaticano*, also known as the Gendarme

Corps of the Vatican. The Gendarme were essentially the police and security officers of the Vatican—whereas the Swiss Guard served in more of a military capacity in the past and in the present day as bodyguards to the Pope.

For a brief moment, Werner considered turning toward the Basilica when he got the call but then changed his mind and ran as fast as he could toward his original destination. He reached the Gendarme office, which sat tucked away in the northeastern corner of the Vatican near the walls. As he entered the Security Office, the place was pure chaos. Just then, more gunfire had erupted at the church. As Werner was about to learn, his split-second decision to come to the Security Office, a kind of command center, instead of going to the church, had probably saved his life.

The room was filled with computers and large-screen monitors, all showing closed circuit camera footage of the exterior of the Basilica. Armed men in black, all with Asian features, were firing weapons out of the entrances. The Swiss Guards approaching those entrances were filled with so many bullet holes in so few seconds that no one in the room watching the scene on the monitors could believe their eyes. Some of the men in the room were rushing out with Heckler & Koch MP5A3 sub-machine guns as Werner stepped into the room and witnessed the commotion. Inspector General Thomas Giovanni, the Commander of the Gendarmes, was screaming at one of his lieutenants to mobilize all their remaining people and to get help from the Police in Rome.

Werner raced across the room to Giovanni, while Werner's own lieutenant, a man named Karl, was screaming to Werner about the massacre in Werner's earpiece. He ripped the small Bluetooth device out of his ear for the moment as he approached Giovanni.

"Tell me," Werner said.

Giovanni stopped instantly because Werner was who he really wanted to see at the moment. The Gendarme he was speaking to hurried off to contact the police in Rome.

"You saw?" Giovanni asked Werner. His face was pale.

"I did," Werner was equally grave. "How many?"

Although the meeting with Hong was scheduled for today, Werner had just signed on for the day. The relatively routine security for a visit from a dignitary was often overseen by the Gendarmes—and in this case, by Karl Schippers, Werner's lieutenant. Werner had no idea what was going on at the moment or how many enemies they might be facing.

"We assume it is David Hong's people—there wasn't anyone else in the building. Unless it's an outside force that entered the structure from underground. They have at least one of those weapons you saw on the screens at every entrance," Giovanni faltered for a moment. His eyes looked down. "I've never even heard of a weapon that could cut men down like that. It's like a portable 50 caliber or something."

"I've seen them before. They are manufactured by a company called Metal Storm," Werner began. "They fire rounds electronically, reducing the amount of moving parts in the weapon and allowing a rapid rate of fire."

"I've seen," Giovanni said. The man looked as if he might be ill.

"Hold your men back. There's no point in sending more bodies into the grinder," Werner placed the Bluetooth earpiece back in his ear and asked Karl to report. It took a moment and Werner was about to conclude that Karl had also fallen victim to the devastating stream of bullets that had been fired from one of the entrances to the Basilica.

"Colonel," Karl's voice sounded faint in Werner's earpiece. "I'm at Station Two. All dead here. Five men down."

Werner lowered his head and held the Bluetooth earpiece closer as he gestured to Giovanni with the other hand that he was seeking a quieter space, because most of the men in the room were shouting and talking simultaneously. He stepped into the nearest office and closed the glass door.

"And the others?" Werner asked without any trace of hope left in his voice.

"Station One is down. Six dead. I'm making my way to Station Three. From what I can tell, there were only one or two men at each Station." Karl Schippers was a huge bear of a man, but Werner appreciated the man's quiet intellect and surprising stealth. Karl was referring to the secret underground entrances to the Basilica, known to the Guard as *Stations* in a joking reference to the Stations of the Cross. Among the Guard—each a devoted Catholic—

such subtle humor was a show of comradery amongst themselves, yet each man took his duty very seriously.

"Pull any additional men down there back and out of range of those blasted Metal Storm rifles," Werner told him. "Keep a watch on all Stations but from a distance, Karl. We lost most of the men above ground. I'm sending medics now but I doubt if anyone is left alive. You keep them back, Karl. No heroics. Let's find out what these maniacs are after first. You understand me?"

"Yes, Sir." The signal was weak now that Karl was moving deeper underground toward Station Three.

Just as Werner was ending the call with Karl, Giovanni came into the glass walled office.

"Movement?" Werner wanted to know.

"Nothing. The medics are on their way to the slaughter," Giovanni looked less white now, but Werner had never seen the small Italian man look so grim.

"What else, Thomas?"

"They dumped bodies off of the roof," Giovanni began. "His Holiness was not among them."

"Who?"

"We assume the men stationed inside the Basilica. The only one we recognized was Silvano."

"God," Werner sighed under his breath.

"The medics should be reporting back any moment now. I've sent a runner to the police in Rome for reinforcements. My men are taking up positions around the building. More are heading toward the helipad and the rail station. The rest of the city seems to be secure," Giovanni hesitated for a moment.

"I'm not sure what else to do, Johannes. We train for terrorist attacks and assassination attempts. We don't practice what to do when an army takes over the Vatican and kidnaps the Pope."

Werner looked at him for a moment, then muttered "Well if we make it through this, we're going to have to upgrade our training."

CHAPTER 49

The traffic along Viale Vaticano had yet to thicken after the initial assault at the Basilica. The road to the north of the Vatican's walls is frequented primarily by those wishing to enter the Vatican Museums, and those folks are mostly paying so they can reach the sight at the end of the labyrinthine museums. The museums funnel their 10 million visitors a year through the corridors to their most appreciated sight, the Sistine Chapel.

As Curtis drove the ARGO provided minivan down the road and along the wall of the Vatican city-state, the only crowd that was beginning to form was ahead in the distance at the entrance to the museum.

"Pull over here," Quinn said.

Curtis maneuvered the minivan to the side of the road and Quinn quickly removed his shoes and pulled on a tight pair of turquoise FiveTen rock climbing shoes. Emblazoned across the lateral sides of the shoes, and written in a thick-tipped permanent marker was the word: QUINN. These shoes, unlike his older shoes that had seen many climbs and many rock-climbing gyms, were new, but he still had taken the time on the ride from the airport to write his name on the sides of them in permanent marker. It was habit, and it felt like a good luck maneuver.

"What's the plan?" Curtis asked.

"I'm inside, you're outside. Try to reach the Swiss Guard and give them whatever information and help you can." Quinn finished tying his shoes, strapped a chalk bag around his waist, pulled a sling over his shoulder that held a collapsed ice ax, and then pointed to a corner in the Vatican's wall. "Start moving and then slow as we reach that dihedral."

"Got it." Curtis started the van rolling again.

As the van reached the right angle in the Vatican's wall, Curtis slowed the vehicle and Jason Quinn opened the door and leaped out, taking several strides to reach the base of the wall. The van continued on and sped up.

Contrary to the way things are portrayed in films Quinn had seen, the few closed circuit video cameras mounted on the top of the Vatican's walls are in fact all stationary. They do not oscillate back and forth like a fan. The major disadvantage to these types of cameras is the possibility of a "blind spot" or an area with no coverage. The corner of the wall that Quinn had raced to was just one such corner because all the cameras in the area were placed to view the entrance to the museum and not the walls themselves. Why would they be placed to view the walls? The walls were mostly decorative in the 21st century, and the main gate that led into the plaza in front of the Basilica was nearly always open anyway.

The walls around the Vatican are made from brick and stone. In many places, they do not have enough mortar. In several places, mosses and even small trees grow out from between the cracks. The walls are angled inward at about a 75-degree angle. In other words, the wall was about as difficult for Jason Quinn to climb as the monkey bars at a playground. He raced up the wall to the top and was over it and into the gardens of the Vatican before anyone even had a chance to glance in his direction from the shops and cafés along the road.

The gardens are one of the most beautiful parts of the Vatican and also the most overlooked. In addition to trees, hedges, and shadowy footpaths, the gardens are adorned with several fountains and marble statues. Quinn was able to progress smoothly through them toward the rear of the Basilica without being seen—all eyes were on the Basilica itself and the gunmen that had seized the building. Only twice did Quinn see someone in the gardens and both were armed Gendarmes attempting to take up positions around the Basilica. They weren't looking for anyone to be in the gardens, and Quinn wondered if he had walked past the Gendarmes instead of hiding behind marble angels, whether they wouldn't have just rushed right past him. *Sloppy*, he thought, but then he told himself to give the men a break—their job was to police the drunken tourists and protect the Pope's bulletproof limo from assassins. They were most likely not very prepared for the assault that Hong's men had laid down today.

Quinn cut a wide swath to the west so he could approach the Basilica from the rear. As he did so, he caught a glimpse of someone moving toward the rear of the structure and doing so furtively. If the Guard were already attempting a military incursion of the structure, he'd have to recalculate his own plan significantly. Otherwise, he might end up riddled with bullets and suspected of being in cahoots with Hong's men.

He stayed hidden behind his hedge and waited for the other person to move again. The person was quick and darted from cover to cover. Whoever it was, he was far enough away that Quinn couldn't see the person clearly. He paralleled the creeping figure, moving only after the other moved. As he got closer, he caught a glimpse of the figure's hair and he knew who it was.

CHAPTER 50

Eva slipped out of the helicopter and across the Vatican's private and currently unguarded helipad. The helipad was formerly a tennis court and Pope John XXIII once referred to it as the Vatican's "helicoptorum." Eva knew she needed to find help and that she needed to alert someone about Hong's plans against the Vatican. What she did not know was that the first shots had already been fired inside the Basilica.

She sprinted across the tarmac of the helicopter pad to the edge of the gardens, looking frantically for someone she could alert and trying to stay as hidden as possible in case one of Hong's men was still around. A minute or two had passed when she heard the second volley of gunfire that cut down Werner's men at all of the entrances and exits of the Basilica. When Eva heard the gunfire, she dove down into the grass at the foot of a nearby hedge. She had no idea who was shooting or where—she was too far away from the Basilica to see Werner's men getting perforated. She thought Hong's men might be shooting at her. Almost as quickly as it had begun though, the shooting was over.

Eva cautiously crept from marble statue to hedge to tree, trying to stay hidden and trying to see what she could at the same time. She moved through the gardens, from cover to cover until she was near the rear of the Basilica. No further shots were fired, and she realized that Hong must have succeeded in his move against the security forces of the Vatican. It would make her job harder—getting past Hong's men and getting into the arms of the security forces. Plus, half of her job as she saw it—alerting the Swiss Guard of Hong's plans—was now probably pointless.

She could see the Basilica up close now, but she saw no sign of people. She would need to edge around the building, but she still remained in the shadows and cover of the gardens, as she started to circle the outer circumference of the huge building.

Eva was close enough to the building that she couldn't even see the dome. As with all such large structures, it becomes difficult to see the whole when up close to the base.

Consecrated in 1626, the Renaissance and Baroque structure looms as the centerpiece of the Vatican city-state. With a capacity of over 60,000 people and a length of 730 feet and a width of 500 feet, the Basilica is roughly the size of six football fields. While David Hong's cathedral project in Hong Kong had challenged it for tallest, it was still the *largest* Christian church in the world. The tomb of Saint Peter, one of the twelve apostles of Jesus, is rumored to be situated directly under the altar of the Basilica.

None of these things interested Eva as she slipped from tree to hedge to statue. She was concerned with a tingling feeling that she was being watched as she moved. She tried to be more erratic in her movements and timing as she went, and she searched around her both as she moved and as she hid behind cover. She saw no one, but her feeling of being watched only increased. She paused behind a low hedge and waited, looking at the windows of the Basilica, thinking that the sensation of being watched must be true. Surely, one of Hong's men was watching her from one of the windows at the rear of the building.

She waited and scanned the windows slowly but she still saw no movement. Then with an almost extrasensory knowledge, she turned her head to her left, and stared across the gardens and directly into the eyes of a man crouched behind a statue. He was staring directly at her. Eva almost shrieked at the shock of it. Then her sense of recognition set in.

It was *him*.

Somehow, beyond all likelihood, possibility, and logic, Jason Quinn had not only escaped his capture in Hong Kong, but he had also followed her to the Vatican and managed to be here within a half an hour of her arrival in Hong's helicopter. She couldn't believe it. Then, she wouldn't believe it. She thought her eyes were playing tricks on her. She rubbed them quickly and found Quinn still staring at her.

She could see that slow smile of his about to form on his face and then something happened. His entire crouched body tensed and his face darkened. She was about to call out to him or start to move toward him, when he ducked back behind the marble statue entirely.

The sensation that Eva had felt of being watched was back again and she whirled around to see one of Hong's men approaching her with a futuristic looking rifle. It was Lim. He had seen her. There was nowhere she could hide. The thought of running slipped through her mind for less than a fraction of a second and he was on her, grabbing her by the wrist and pulling her to her feet from her crouched stance. He wheeled about and pulled her toward the Basilica without a word, as if he had expected her to escape, and he had planned to corral her and bring her back. It was all in a day's work for Lim.

Eva went quietly and without struggle. Lim hadn't seen Quinn. She knew that Quinn would find a way to get to her. All she had to do was stay alive long enough. He was out there. He had followed her to Rome. He had infiltrated the Vatican. He was coming for her. She would do her part and not provide Hong's men with any further reasons to be angry with her. She was thankful that they had been so gentle with her thus far and hoped it lasted awhile longer. She wasn't sure why Hong wanted her alive and undamaged, but she was grateful for that much. If she saw a chance for an easy getaway, she'd take it. If not, she knew Quinn would come up with something. She felt the tingling on the back of her neck as Lim led her through a door into the mighty structure.

He was watching her.

CHAPTER 51

Quinn wasn't watching Eva. Someone else was.

Two of Werner's men were in the gardens and had spotted Eva. They hadn't seen Quinn, though. They were stunned to see a woman creeping through the garden when they were trying to stake out the men with the Metal Storm rifles, at the entrances to the Basilica. Kevin Miller was a Swiss-German who had been in the Guard for exactly four years. He was thrilled to be seeing some real action, terrified that he and his friends might all end up dead, and stunned to see this woman in the gardens. Miller turned to his partner in the gardens, Hans Wald, and was about to make a wisecrack about the unlikely blonde near the hedge, when Hans crouched lower, training his MP5 in the blonde's direction with both hands.

Miller turned quickly back toward the woman and saw one of the Chinese men, armed with a Metal Storm rifle, leading the woman back toward the Basilica. Miller aimed his own MP5 and listened in his earpiece as Wald was already calling it in to Schippers.

The Chinese man reached the door to the structure with the woman in tow and another two Chinese gunmen opened the door, both aiming their Metal Storm rifles out the door and attempting to cover all directions. Wald had seen the damned things in action, mowing down many of his friends.

"Now or never," he mumbled into his tactical throat mic.

"Stand down," came the order from Karl Schippers, the number two man in the Guard. Wald and Miller watched helplessly as the door closed and three enemies and the woman disappeared from sight. They knew that at this range, the Metal Storms would cut them down and they would hardly be able to hit a thing with the MP5s they held, but allowing the Chinese to take the woman, whoever she might be, didn't sit well with the men.

"Damn," Miller spoke aloud.

"Describe the woman and the whole scene. Leave nothing out. I'm passing every word you say on to Colonel Werner," Schippers told them in their earpieces. "And stay in position. We don't yet know what they hope to accomplish and if they make a break for it out that station, I want it covered. Stay sharp."

Schippers informed Colonel Werner in person about the mystery woman and the incident with the Chinese man capturing her.

"Strange," Werner mused. He was still in the command center and had set up his own group of men working in tandem with the Gendarmes.

"Anything yet on the support from the Italians?" he asked one lieutenant sitting at a computer terminal and watching a closed-circuit camera view of the lantern on the top of the Basilica's dome. A small Chinese man armed with a Metal Storm rifle appeared periodically and erratically on the tiny balcony there. He seemed charged with keeping an eye on all directions below at once. The lieutenant watching him, Fritdjhof Wiedermann ("Fritz" to his friends), had discovered only recently that the Chinese men did not seem to be using any communications equipment and had reported it to Werner.

"Still waiting to hear back from them, Sir, but we were told less than forty minutes for them to get authorization and get wheels in motion."

"Keep me informed, Fritz. Anything else on our Crow's Nest man?" Werner asked.

"It's the same man still. I've only seen the one Metal Storm rifle. No other armaments. Still no sign of a radio of any kind."

"No, there won't be," Werner scowled. "They knew about the communications blackout that we put into place when dignitaries visit. They will have assumed that we would block all radio communications. They will probably also assume that we don't have any. That gives us a slight advantage but not much of one.

"Fritz, keep a close eye on this guy. If they are somehow communicating using another system—a mirror, smoke signals, whatever—I want to know about it. If they can't communicate at all, then they will stick to a script and their expectations of what we would normally do. Which would mean they might have someone inside the Guard or the Gendarmes."

"God! You think they have someone in the Guard?" Karl Schippers said.

"Not out of the realm of possibility." Werner mumbled and looked closely at some of the other screens in the room and paid close attention to the screens displaying cameras on the different stations. The two underground stations especially. Werner secretly suspected that the entire operation by Hong was misdirection and they ultimately hoped to kidnap the Pope and take him out of the Vatican using the underground railway. Either way, Werner intended to break every rule and be as unpredictable in his response to Hong's men as possible.

He had mentally taken a survey of his men, and found that none were of any kind of Asian descent. The only common denominator in Hong's men was that they were all Chinese, all wore dark colors, and all seemed to have the blasted Metal Storm rifles. He knew that a mole was still a possibility though—Hong might have a blonde-haired, blue-eyed Swiss boy on his payroll. Or one of the Italian Gendarmes. Anything was possible.

Werner had figured out how Hong had done it. It was clever. Werner had compared the video footage of the helicopter landing with the faces of the men at the different stations. He had not ever *seen* more than eight men—the number Hong had brought on the helicopter. However, Werner had compared the faces and noticed that he wasn't seeing the same eight men at the stations. That, plus the dark clothes and the hooded sweatshirt and black cargo pants from a trendy fashion designer in Rome told him the rest. Some of Hong's men had slipped into the Basilica *before* Hong had arrived. Werner had already briefed his men and the Gendarmes that they might be facing a force larger than nine men.

Just then, a Guard who was acting as a runner to the front gate to communicate with the Italians arrived in the control room. He reported to

Schippers and then left the room to relieve himself. He would be back in a minute to receive new orders to take to the gate.

"Colonel," Schippers began.

"The Italians?"

"No. The Americans." When Werner's look expressed complete confusion, Schippers elaborated. "Apparently there is an American man at the Front Gate claiming he needs to speak to you and that he has urgent information for you about Hong's plans."

CHAPTER 52

Jason Quinn was the furthest thing from David Hong's mind as he led the Pope and a small group of his men under the Basilica to the crypt. The large man with the scar, Yang, shoved the Pope in the small of his back with the barrel of a Metal Storm rifle from time to time, to keep the old man moving along with them.

In short course, they came to a plate glass wall, beyond which was the reliquary below the Basilica's altar. They were at the tomb of Saint Peter. The reliquary gleamed under a spotlight with gold and jewels. Hong looked to the Pope, now an old man in a blood-spattered tunic, with hanging head and a look of defeat.

"Open it," Hong said while pointing at the glass.

"It doesn't open..." the Pope began.

"Yang. The glass." Hong barked.

Yang opened up on the plate glass wall with his Metal Storm rifle and the wall disintegrated into thousands of glinting shards that skittered across the floor of the crypt.

Hong turned slowly to the pontiff. "Did you think we might actually damage the *air* that's inside the fake reliquary? Do you want to open the pedestal or should we destroy it too?"

"No," the Pope said. "I'll open it." He stepped forward across the shattered glass and reached to the side of the reliquary chest on a raised pedestal. He depressed a hidden button and stepped backward as the pedestal swung smoothly to the side.

A small opening appeared under the moving pedestal. It contained a spiral stainless steel staircase, descending into a further level of the structure.

"After you, your Holiness."

***

James Lau was the small man on the balcony of the lantern at the top of the dome. He had been following instructions since he had left his hidden space between the inner and outer domes. He had gone down to the floor of the Nave and collected his Metal Storm rifle and other equipment. He had been furtive and unpredictable in his timing of when he appeared outside on the lantern's upper balcony and when he stepped inside. He crouched a lot—just in case the Swiss Guards had a sniper. He had kept an eye on all sides of the roof below the dome and the piazza below the roof beyond Maderno's façade. He had been searching for Guards in the gardens below him to the west and north. He hadn't partaken in the slaughter of the Guards at the entrances to the Basilica. He was too far away anyway. He hadn't seen anything in the gardens below and had only seen the occasional guard running somewhere far across the piazza.

Now, he checked his watch and knew that his part in the drama was about to begin. He stepped out on the balcony again and squatted down, this time searching the skies. Hong had anonymously tipped off a local Italian news service that they should get a helicopter over the piazza today for the story of their lives. Lau smiled a hard, cold smile. Hong certainly had a flair for the dramatic.

Lau waited for ten minutes, went inside and down to the lower balcony that circled the base of the lantern just atop the dome. He popped out here occasionally to scan the grounds for movement.

"They are late," he said aloud, in English.

Then he saw it. It would be awhile before he could hear it too. The helicopter was coming at the dome from the east, right along the road to the Vatican's front gate. Its present course and altitude would bring it right to Lau.

I couldn't ask for a better target, he thought.

James Lau waited another fifteen minutes, this time only peeking around the column behind which he hid twice, and both times to ensure that the helicopter was still coming right for him.

He waited until the helicopter broke Vatican law and crossed into Vatican airspace. The only vehicles ever allowed into or out of Vatican airspace were the Pope's personal helicopter and those of arriving dignitaries like the one Hong had arrived in.

The helicopter was moving slowly and hovered over the piazza a bit lower than the height at which Lau crouched. He knew that the reporter, cameraman, and even the pilot of the helicopter would all be focused on the piazza below them, looking for the story they had been promised.

Lau popped from behind the column and leveled his Metal Storm rifle at the helicopter. He hit it with an extended burst. The pilot and the two passengers were killed instantly. The pilot's hand fell from the collective and his feet no longer applied an even pressure on the pedals. The helicopter began to sway and spin. For target practice, James Lau continued to riddle the uncontrolled chopper as it descended. It then burst into flame and at the last second of its wild uncontrolled descent, pitched over and was impaled on the top of the 130 foot tall Egyptian obelisk. Lau expected it to slide down the length of "The Witness," as the 13th century BC spire was known. Instead, it lodged fast near the top and the only piece of debris that fell to the ground below was the large cross that had snapped off the top of the obelisk when the helicopter hit it.

Lau looked at his handiwork for just a moment and chuckled to himself before slipping into cover behind a column and then scooting inside the door. He went to the inner balcony and looked down over the edge into the center of the dome. Close to 400 feet below him, another Chinese man stood. Lau called down to him about the helicopter and the obelisk. The man ran off to pass the message to another and eventually the message would reach Hong down in the Crypt.

Lau went up to the upper balcony around the top of the lantern again and moved to the west side of the balcony, looking down into the gardens at the rear of the Basilica. Occasionally, when he went inside the lantern, he did so standing, so that anyone looking would only be aware of some of the times he went inside. The rest of the time, it would appear that he was simply taking cover and moving around the balcony to new vantage points. It made his job easier—he only needed to be outside some of the time—and it prevented the Guard from knowing where he was and what he was doing. Hong had been specific about that part. The goal was to keep the Guard guessing about their method of communication until proper communication was restored.

Lau had asked about that point and Hong had assured all the men that the communications blackout would be lifted in due course. Lau wasn't so sure. He couldn't see any tactical reason for doing so. True, it would allow the Guard to communicate with Hong, but it would also theoretically permit Lau and the others to communicate with each other and with the outside world.

Lau wondered how this new twist with the destroyed helicopter would change things.

CHAPTER 53

Jason Quinn had spotted the Chinese man approaching Eva and quickly calculated that he was too far away. He wanted to save her but he couldn't do it if he was riddled with bullets. He ducked behind his statue in the hopes that the man's attention on Eva meant he hadn't yet seen Quinn. He peeked around the other side of the statue and saw that this was indeed the case. The man grabbed Eva's wrist and quietly led her away toward the Basilica.

Quinn was about to make chase and hopefully take the man by surprise from behind. But then he paused. Some sixth sense told him he wasn't alone in the garden. He searched around the trees, hedges, and nearby fountains, and then he saw them. Two black-clad men with what might have been MP5s in the garden watching the Chinese man take Eva toward the Basilica's door.

Must be Swiss Guards, Quinn thought. He realized they were as likely to shoot him as help him. So he stayed put for a moment to see what they would do. They hadn't spotted him yet.

They had their weapons trained on Eva and the Chinese man as the two walked to the Basilica's door. Then they lowered their weapons. Quinn watched the door and saw the other two Chinese covering it as Eva was taken inside. He understood that the Guards were outgunned. He had seen the weapon the Chinese man was holding. He'd seen pictures of them but never seen one in the field. Electric Metal Storm rifles. Aptly named.

Quinn turned his attention back to the Guards to see if they would move on or if they were stationary. He waited five minutes and the two men showed no signs of interest in anything other than the door through which Eva had been taken.

Quinn silently moved off through the garden trees, away from the door and the two assigned Guards. After looking at the Basilica's lower level windows and thinking of his recent adventure in Hong Kong, Quinn was evaluating the building the way he would a climb in Colorado. He could see plentiful windows, ledges, and architectural nuances that would enable him to make the roof of the Basilica in no time. He wasn't normally in the habit of climbing buildings, but the more he thought about trying to gain access to the Basilica from the roof, the more it made sense. Hong's men wouldn't be expecting to be attacked from above.

He threaded his way through the garden to the very rear of the Basilica and slightly south of it, when he started to lose the cover of the trees as the garden dwindled. He spotted one other team keeping eyes on a door into the southern side of the building.

Quinn sat down on the grass, under the cover of a hedge. He evaluated the distance between this new group of spotters and the last he had encountered, and he knew the odds were good that one group or the other would see him as he tried his ascent.

He would have to hope that Curtis had gotten through to the Swiss Guard already. Even if he hadn't, Quinn wasn't about to sit still and watch the doors. He could be on the roof and taking out Hong's men one by one before the bureaucracy would ever decide on a counter attack. Unless Hong had paid off the Guards in the garden. Or unless the men were loyal to the Pope but became incensed that Quinn was climbing the Basilica. In either of those two scenarios, Quinn would end up with bullets in his spine before he reached the second window up.

He uncinched the chalk bag that was clipped to the rear of his nylon climbing trousers. Mooky had an ARGO rep and a supply bag waiting for them when they had landed in Rome. Quinn checked that his SOG Seal Pup knife was securely fastened to the right of his belt. He got to his feet in a crouch and then sprinted to the wall of the Basilica, just to the left of the westernmost door of the building. He slid his hands into the chalk as he ran, and as soon as he reached the building, he took a hold of the stone frame of a window and hoisted himself up onto it. Then he reached for the upper ledge of the window frame and pulled himself up further, his climbing shoes smearing their grippy rubber along the inner edge of the window frame. He repeated the move a few times and was at the upper portion of the building, where the upper story jutted out slightly, creating an overhanging lip. Quinn eyed the decorative cornice and considered whether it would support his weight. In a second, he decided against it and swung his right leg up and over his head, heel-hooking the lip of the extended upper portion of the building. He then pulled himself up and used a technique called mantling to stand on the lip adjacent to a small window. He crept laterally along the ledge, just the front half of his feet fitting on it, to the window, and he used his earlier technique to ascend the window's lower ledge and upper ledge, until he had a handhold on the roof. He peered up and over the edge, looking around and up on the dome. He spotted a Chinese man on the upper balcony of the lantern, atop the dome, and slowly lowered himself down again, so that just the tips of his fingers would be visible at the roof's edge. He literally hung by his fingers from one hand for just a second and slipped his other hand into the chalk pouch behind his waist.

After chalking up, he waited just a beat longer then peered up over the edge of the roof again. He checked around and glanced up at the lantern again. No sign of anyone.

He pulled himself up onto the roof and rolled smoothly away from the edge. The roof of the Basilica is actually lower than where Quinn was. Several smaller buildings lined the edge of the roof. He got to his feet and sprinted along the slanted tiles that covered the upper portion of one of these small buildings on the roof. Quinn had been to St. Peter's once before and recalled that that roof held a post office, shops, and so forth, all before the tourist throngs entered the one door into the base of the drum on which the dome sat.

He leaped down to the main roof from the roof of the small building he was on. He turned when he landed and saw that it was a gift shop, now closed up tight. He stepped left, crouched behind a large trashcan, and waited. If anyone was on the roof, they might have heard him leap down from the roof of the shop.

He waited.

No one came. He peered around the trash barrel and scanned the roof. He couldn't remember which side of the roof held the door to the lower section and which held the door to the dome. He'd have to explore.

Quinn moved cautiously around the rooftop, from the corner of a structure here to a doorway there. He found the door to the lower levels of the Basilica locked. Then, he found the door to the dome. It was also locked. He knew someone was up in the lantern though, so he stayed close to the base of the drum on which the dome sits, so he wouldn't be seen from above.

Then, he heard the helicopter and watched in horror as it was gunned down. When the shooting was over, he crept from his cover toward the façade at the front of the roof. Keeping an eye on the lantern and the dome behind him, he made his way forward and climbed to the low roof of the building in front of the rear of the façade. He crept up behind the huge statue of St. Andrew and viewed the devastation in the piazza for just a moment. He retraced his steps back to the main roof and took cover behind one of the skylight vents that looked to him like cylindrical phone booths, just as the shooter on the lantern came to the front edge of the upper balcony rail again. Quinn stared at the man and gritted his teeth while waiting. Sure enough, the man disappeared again in a minute. Quinn raced for the base of the drum and looked up the nearly 50-foot tall Corinthian columns that appeared to be supports for the ribs of the dome but were in fact merely decorative. With a sigh, Quinn dipped his hands in the chalk and stepped up between two close columns. He put his back against one and his feet and hands against the other and began to shimmy up between the columns.

It was going to be long damn day.

CHAPTER 54

Hong stepped down into the antechamber after the Pope, with Yang following him, and two others coming down the spiral stairs after. Next was a room with benches on each side and a small electronic control panel. Beyond it was an open doorway to a huge circular chamber that surrounded a small cylindrical room at its center. The floor of the great circular room seemed to be of gleaming stainless steel tiles, each about a yard square. The border of the circular area and the room in which they stood had a thick red line painted on the floor.

Hong turned to the Pope and smiled. "Would you like to cross that red line first, your Holiness?"

The old man looked at Hong with curiosity. "How did you know?"

"One of your Cardinals is on my payroll, of course."

Just then, Lim escorted Eva into the chamber from the spiral staircase.

"Ah, Doctor Rayjek, nice of you to join us. I figured you would eventually but your timing is perfect. Have you met the Pope? No, of course not." Hong bantered.

Before either Eva or the Pope had a chance to say anything more, Hong turned back to the Pope and said "Open the chamber with the boots."

Resigned, the Pope turned to the electronic control panel and punched in a key sequence. As he did so, the right wall of the room, and the bench that sat in front of it detached and recessed into the wall before sliding away, revealing four sets of gleaming metal boots that resembled skiing boots. Each boot had a small electronic control panel on it on the outer calf section.

Hong smiled and explained to the others what they were seeing.

"In the 1990s, the Vatican decided to invest in the world's most unusual security precaution for that little circular room you see over there," he pointed across the vast stainless steel floor plates. "Anyone stepping over this red line without a pair of these boots would activate the pressure plates hidden under all of those shiny floor sections out there. And that would set off a small micro explosion. Not large, mind you. Not enough to do damage to the room or the basilica above us. An explosion just large enough to kill a man or perhaps to take away his legs."

Eva was horrified.

The Pope stood silently and angrily looking at Hong as the man revealed one of the Vatican's most closely guarded secrets as if he had read about it in the tabloids.

Yang and the others had taken an involuntary step away from the circular chamber's thick red line. "And the boots?" Yang asked.

"The boots allow safe passage by electrically sending a signal that the person wearing them is not to be blown to bits. Isn't that right, your Holiness?" Hong elaborated.

"I have never used them, myself. I have no need to see the chamber. Some things are better left to faith." the pontiff stated.

"Ah, but you were quick to jump at my offer of repatriating the nail," Hong pointed out.

"Yes, to my shame." the Pope did not look at Hong.

"So what's in the room in the center?" Eva asked.

"I am so glad you asked, Doctor Rayjek. The small circular room at the center contains precisely two things. The one is the church's greatest treasure and the other is the church's greatest shame. But you will get to see them with your own eyes, because you will test out the boots for us." Hong told her. "Put a pair on."

"I simply can't find a pair in my size, Hong." Eva replied flippantly.

"You can try to make it across without the boots..." Hong began.

"Alright, alright, I'm putting them on."

Eva sat on the bench that hadn't moved and began putting the boots on her feet. When she was ready, she stood in front of the thick red line on the floor and looked out across the circular chamber to the room at its center.

"Any other security protocols once I reach the room? Nothing is going to cut me in half is it, your Holiness?" Eva wanted to know.

"You will be fine crossing the chamber, Doctor." the pontiff told her.

"Yang, you stay here with the Pope." Hong said as he began putting his own boots on.

He glanced up at Eva and saw that she was still standing in front of the red line on the floor.

"Do you require a shove?" he asked her.

Eva took a hesitant step forward and placed her foot down on the first stainless steel plate. She expected to feel the floor depress slightly like a key on a keyboard, but it felt to her like solid floor. She put her weight down on her foot.

She did not explode.

She walked rapidly toward the small circular room in the center and found another thick red line on the floor in the open doorway to it. She stepped over the line into the room and released the breath that she hadn't realized she had been holding as she crossed the 40-foot radius of explosive death.

The room held two simple objects. A large, dark piece of splintered lumber leaned against the wall as if left there when the artisans were wrapping up construction on the room. The other was a glass case lined in velvet, sitting on a small table. Inside was a thick envelope with a wax seal on it that bore the papal symbol of a tiara above two crossed keys. Eva looked down at the glass case. Around the glass was a wooden frame with a Latin inscription burned into the wood: *Nunquam Iteram*. She didn't read Latin. As she looked, she heard Hong step into the room in his own electronic metal boots.

"It says *Never Again*," he told her. "I would have thought you'd be more interested in that." Hong pointed to the piece of splintered lumber.

"Oh my God," Eva said as she understood that she was looking at a huge piece of the upright beam to the cross Christ was crucified on.

"Yes, exactly." Hong smiled.

Then, he punched his fist through the glass of the case and picked up the envelope, and walked out of the room and back across the exploding floor.

CHAPTER 55

Colonel Werner was receiving a report from Schippers, when Fritz Weidermann shouted out from across the room.

"He did what?"

All the Gendarmes and Guards in the room alike stopped talking and looked over at Weidermann. He saw that all eyes in the room were focused on him and turned immediately back to the man he'd been speaking with and said "Explain."

The young Guard cleared his throat and spoke loudly so that everyone in the room could hear.

"We have a report from Hans Wald that a Caucasian intruder was spotted in the Vatican's gardens." The Guard paused. "Before Wald could intercept the man, he ran from the cover of the gardens to the wall of the Basilica and climbed up to the roof like a monkey."

"Excuse me?" Werner spoke up from across the room.

"Yes, Colonel. That's what I said. Wald says the man was wearing rock-climbing shoes and had a chalk bag on his waist. He was up the side of the building and onto the roof before Wald and Miller could believe their eyes."

Werner strode across the room, his long legs carrying him there in just a few steps.

"Did this man look like he was working with Hong's men? Was he armed?" Werner asked.

"Wald says no, sir. I asked him and he said that the man paused before clearing the roof. It looked like he was trying to get in unobserved. Miller thinks he saw a knife on the man's belt but couldn't be sure. He was not dressed in black as Hong's men all appear to be."

Werner turned from the young Guard to Weidermann.

"Fritz, get Miller and Wald over here. Send two more to relieve them. I want all the details on this guy." Werner collapsed in a chair and rubbed his hand over his face. "What next?"

Inspector General Giovanni approached Werner and leaned on the edge of the desk. "First the woman, now a rock climber? What the heck is going on?"

"I am not sure, Thomas. He hasn't made any attempts to contact us yet, and I'm not about to send any more men up against those guns without some serious back up." Werner sighed and heaved his tall frame out of the chair. "Karl, any word yet from the Italians?"

"They are onboard. They should be at the gate in a few minutes." the huge man replied.

Just then, the young Guard that had reported on the rock climber reappeared in the room and called out.

"Sir, there's a helicopter heading for the front gate!"

"Front camera on the main screen, Fritz!" Werner called out.

The men in the room all watched as a white helicopter flew toward the front gate, about 200 feet off the ground.

"What is he doing?" Werner mumbled as he watched the helicopter. "They all know to stay out of our airspace."

"Sir," Fritz called out. He was the only one in the room watching a monitor that was not showing the helicopter. His monitor showed the balcony on the lantern portion of the dome. He was watching the Crow's Nest Man, as the men had dubbed the Chinese man on top of the dome. "Take a look at this."

Werner stepped over and looked over Fritz's shoulder as the Crow's Nest Man slipped inside. Fritz switched to another view and the men watched the Crow's Nest Man step out of the door on the lower balcony and slide behind the cover of a column.

"Oh no," Werner said.

The main view screen switched to another camera's view as the helicopter crossed the gate into the Vatican and flew over the piazza. The men in the room could all see the news crew markings on the side of the helicopter's tail.

Werner closed his eyes when he saw the Crow's Nest Man step from behind the column and level the Metal Storm rifle. Werner did not want to see what would come next. He heard the collective gasps around the room, then the deafening silence and could not keep his eyes closed.

He opened them and looked to the main view screen in the room, a flat-screen LCD panel approximately 20 feet across. He watched the sickening plunge of the helicopter as it impaled itself on the Egyptian obelisk.

No one spoke.

Finally, Werner was about to order some men to get a truck with a ladder to rescue anyone who might still be alive in the helicopter. Then the fire on it flared when it hit the fuel tank, and the entire structure of the helicopter burned. It didn't explode, but the whole thing was on fire. By the time anyone got up to it at the top of the obelisk, the people inside would be blackened husks if they hadn't died in the gunfire.

"Dear God," the Inspector General of the Gendarmes said. "Johannes?" he asked Werner.

"They'll be dead already. We'll get them down when this is all over." Werner's gray gaunt face now looked pale.

Then, Schippers came over and spoke quietly to Werner.

"This oughtta be good," he replied. Then Werner followed Schippers out of the command room to another office with a desk and three chairs. A tall American man with short-cropped blonde hair sat in one of the chairs.

Werner dropped into the desk's chair and peered across the desk at the man. Schippers stood by the door.

"I have good news and bad news for you Colonel," the American began.

"The good news first, please," Werner cut him off.

"You have a man inside."

"The climber?"

Curtis Johnson nodded.

"And the bad news?" Werner inquired.

"Your enemy is 20 million strong."

"I think you had better start from the beginning, Mr. Johnson."

CHAPTER 56

Quinn had carefully eyed the columns and the drum that holds the dome of the Basilica before ascending. He knew he'd get to the top of a column and his cover would evaporate. The gunman on the Lantern would be able to see him if the man just glanced down from either balcony on the lantern. Quinn knew he would have to race up the dome when the gunman was otherwise occupied.

Quinn had chosen the rear of the dome, which faced west, and then had moved two sets of columns over toward the south, thinking that the sunlight would be in the gunman's eyes on that side. He grunted and sweated his way up between the columns and then happily swung his body up toward the space above the columns and before the bottommost edge of the dome itself. The only cover on the dome would be just under the windows on it, but they were spaced between the ribs and Quinn thought the ribs would be the easiest and quickest way up, so he would have no cover at all.

He paused on his present perch, still invisible to the man up on the lantern. He twisted and placed his hands on the lip of the dome, automatically placing his thumbs on top of the second bones in his index and middle fingers, adding an additional 20% of strength to his grip—an old climber's trick. He was getting tired.

He pulled his head slowly past the lip and looked up to see the man on the lower balcony of the lantern. Quinn slowly lowered himself to his perch under the rim of the dome again and waited for a full two minutes.

Then he tried again. No sign of the bastard. He pulled himself up over the lip and then started climbing along one of the ribs of the dome. Spaced out about one every few feet were tiny wrought iron plates that had little spikes in their centers. They were left over from the days when the Basilica would be adorned with candles at night during festive seasons. But for Quinn they acted like stairs. He knew he couldn't linger on them long or they might snap clean off from his body weight, but he was in a hurry anyway. Only one candleholder was missing from the rib Quinn had chosen, but it was close enough to the top of the dome that it didn't even slow him down. By that point, he was pretty much just running up the surface of the dome.

He reached the railing around the lower balcony of the lantern and nimbly leaped over it and landed in a crouch. Then he quickly stepped behind a pair of columns, waiting to see if the gunman was on this level and would come running. He waited for just a moment. Then, he slid the collapsed ice ax out of its sheath on his back and quietly opened the blade into the locked position. It and the knife on his belt weren't much against rapid-fire machine guns but they were all he had.

Quinn stepped from behind the columns, ice ax in hand and crept counterclockwise around the balcony. He'd be approaching the east-facing door from the south. He figured the gunman would come out of the door and turn left—toward the shaded side of the lantern. Fifty-fifty chance on which way the man would turn and Quinn didn't want to have to run into the man inside. Column to column, staying as close as he could to the lantern, Quinn moved to the east, constantly looking in both directions around the lantern and up above him. If the gunman was on the upper balcony and looking down Quinn didn't want to be spotted from above and sprayed with projectiles. It took him longer to get to the columns nearest the door than it did for him to race up the dome.

Then he heard the scuff of a shoe on the concrete.

He cautiously glanced around his column and there the man was. Crouched by the railing and looking down into the east, into the piazza and his sick handiwork. He seemed oblivious to the idea that anyone might be up here with him.

Good, Quinn thought.

Quinn was about to step out from behind his column when two things happened at once. He realized he should have removed his climbing shoes now that he was done climbing. They weren't very comfortable to run in, and they would make loud footfalls. The thought stayed his movement and just in time. The gunman stood from his crouch and turned, planning as Quinn had suspected, to circle the lantern on the shadowed side. Pausing might have saved Quinn's life.

He squatted, set the ice ax down and quickly removed his shoes. He picked up the ax and stepped into the sunny side of the lantern's balcony. His shoes he left behind the column. If luck was with him again, the gunman would spend some time on the west side of the lantern and then return the way he had gone—on the shaded side.

But Quinn had gone just a few steps when he heard the scuff of shoes. Some weird instinct propelled him forward at a run instead of back or behind a column. In two steps, he saw the Chinese man, and in another the man saw Quinn.

The man tried to raise his rifle, but Quinn brought the ice ax down and across, slashing the man's forearm and causing him to drop the rifle. Quinn was bringing his left fist up in an uppercut as the man was looking down at his wounded arm and the fist connected squarely with James Lau's jaw. The blow lifted him off his feet and sent him crashing into the railing. Quinn was about to reach for his knife on his waist when he noticed that the Chinese man wasn't moving.

He stepped slowly toward the man and crouched to lift the head. It lolled sickeningly to the side. The impact with the railing had broken the Chinese man's neck. Quinn checked for a pulse but there wasn't one. The Chinese man was dead.

Quinn quickly checked the man for any personal effects but he didn't seem to have any. The rifle still had several rounds of ammunition and Quinn took it, placing his ax back in its sheath on his back. He pulled the body back behind a column and away from sight of the railing.

Then, the muzzle of the Metal Storm rifle leading, Quinn quickly circled the balcony and entered the Basilica's lantern.

CHAPTER 57

Eva got back to the room with the benches as Hong was taking off his metal boots. One of Hong's men had entered the room and whispered something to Yang. Yang dismissed the man and then turned to Hong.

"The news chopper." Yang grumbled.

Hong finished tying his shoes and stood. "And?"

"Impaled on the Egyptian obelisk." Yang reported without emotion.

"Oh my," Hong said gleefully. "Well, the world knows now." He switched to Cantonese and stood near the doorway to the spiral stairs, giving Yang instructions.

Eva sat on the bench next to the Pope and began to remove her metallic boots. She murmured when she sat up. "I'm sorry, your Holiness. Be patient. Rescue is on the way."

The Pope nodded so slightly that Eva nearly didn't see it.

Yang left the room and Hong turned to the Pope and Eva.

"What's in the envelope, Hong?" Eva wanted to keep him talking. *Got to stall him for whatever Jason might be planning*, she thought.

"This envelope is one of two identical envelopes in the world. The other is in that tomb in Minfeng that my operatives were trying to keep you from. I haven't seen it yet but I had to accelerate my plans for the Vatican when His Holiness was so receptive to my offer of repatriated Christian relics. The envelope contains a letter from Pope Pius IX, officially recognizing my great-grandfather as the second son of God. Christ's younger brother. The Vatican had a copy of the letter, and my ancestor had a copy of the letter, which went with him to his tomb."

"But why do you need that letter? Why all this?" Eva questioned.

"You see, I won't have any problem convincing the Chinese Diaspora. As I've already explained to you and the unfortunate Mr. Quinn in Hong Kong—I'm already the accepted resurrection of my ancestor for most of them. But the rest of the world? Well, most of them will never recognize me as the son of God. We're well past superstition and faith now in the 21st century. But with this letter, they will recognize me as the rightful head of the Catholic Church and of the Vatican."

Eva blinked. "You can't be serious. No one will let you stay here; you took the place over by force."

Hong smiled slowly. "You think that's what people told the Israelis when they carved off a slice of Arabian desert for themselves with massive bloodshed and loss of life? In any case, all I need to do is make one worldwide broadcast to the Chinese Diaspora and countless of my faithful will be ready to make war against Rome, London, Washington, Paris, and any other city I can pick out of a hat. The world's forces will stand down against a worldwide threat of terror attacks, especially when all I'll be asking them to do is stay out of something that isn't their business in the first place."

"You won't be able to broadcast anything," the Pope said calmly. "The security communications protocol is in effect. No signals into or out of the Vatican."

"Yes. I wonder how much longer that will go on. On your feet, we're heading upstairs." As they ascended the spiral stairs to the fake reliquary of St. Peter, Hong continued. "Now that the world's media has smelled what's going on inside the Vatican, how long do you think before the Swiss Guard are forced to turn off the communications scrambler? They will, after all, be wondering what our intentions are, because we have made no demands."

"What if they don't?" Eva goaded the man as he placed the envelope with the Papal seal into a Ziploc plastic bag and sealed it, then placed it inside another.

"Let's hope you don't have to find out Dr. Rayjek. It won't be pleasant."

They reached the Nave and walked toward the Narthex, the large entrance lobby, as Yang raced toward them. He stopped in front of Hong and took a deep breath.

"They've opened the front gate."

"Really? Let's go see."

When Hong reached the massive front door, one of his men had it ajar and was pointing his Metal Storm rifle out the opening. Sensing that his commander was near, but not taking his eyes from the sight across the piazza, the man spoke clearly.

"They are sending a tank against us."

CHAPTER 58

"Okay, Mr. Johnson. I think I get the picture. What I don't understand is what I'm supposed to do with a rock climber inside the Basilica that I can't even communicate with." Colonel Werner looked like he felt—like the day could not get any more bizarre.

"Quinn is ex-SAS. If he made it into the building, you can be sure that your number of terrorists is slowly dwindling," Johnson began.

"That doesn't help me much against 20 million does it?"

"Look, Colonel. I don't know how he plans to contact the masses of the faithful, but my best guess is that he's waiting for you to turn off the communications scrambler, from what you've told me. Don't. Just leave it on. You can get him a message the old fashion way. By a letter."

"Yes, and let my mailman get turned into red mist? I think not," the Colonel sighed.

"Use me," Johnson offered.

Schippers came back into the room.

"We are ready," he said. "Also, the U.S. Ambassador is at the gate and vouching for his story." Schippers pointed at Johnson.

"You are bringing him in, right?" Werner wanted to know.

"Of course."

"I might just use you after all, Mr. Johnson. But first we try our own technique to dwindle their numbers. Come with me."

They went into the command room and watched as an Italian Army armored personnel carrier (the "mini-tank" as Werner thought of it) rolled across the piazza on the main view screen. Werner, Schippers, and Johnson stood behind Fritz's desk, where Fritz was in communications with snipers placed around the piazza.

"Can those Metal Storm rifles fire armor-piercing rounds?" Johnson asked quietly.

"We are about to see."

The vehicle crawled slowly across the piazza, giving the obelisk and its grotesque new cap a wide berth.

"Fritz, where's the Crow's Nest Man?" Werner asked, pointing to a screen off to the side of the room showing the empty balcony of the Lantern.

"Sorry Sir, my attention was diverted with the preparations for the Italians. I'll run the recording backward so we can see how long he's been gone." Fritz replied. After a moment, his own monitor on his desk showed the lantern and the video footage shot backward too rapidly to make out any detail. Then, all four men watched as the Crow's Nest Man ducked inside the lantern and a moment later, Jason Quinn came creeping around the columns.

Schippers whispered to himself, "No, he did *not* just climb the dome."

They watched in silence as Quinn and the Crow's Nest Man performed their quick and violent battle. When Quinn disappeared into the lantern, Fritz fast forwarded the video file but at a slower pace so that they could see no one else emerged onto the balcony until the video footage caught up with the present time.

"Mr. Johnson, I retract my comment about the uselessness of a rock climber," Werner said.

On the main screen, the roomful of men watched as the mini-tank approached the façade of the Basilica. The front door opened and a Metal Storm rifle was pointed out of it. Then the rifle opened fire on the mini-tank. Then, another door opened and another man with another Metal Storm rifle appeared at that door and began firing. It was impossible to see from the angle of the camera whether the rounds were piercing the thick armored hide of the mini-tank, but all in the room could see that it was continuing toward the stairs unimpeded.

"Whenever they are ready, Fritz." Werner said.

"Take the shot," Fritz said into his microphone.

Then, all in the room watched as both men firing the Metal Storms took sniper shots and fell forward out of their respective doors.

"They got a little too cocky, didn't they?" Johnson said, although it was rhetorical.

They all watched as one body and then the other were pulled into their respective doors. Then, something streaked from out of one of the doors toward the mini-tank.

Johnson was about to shout out a warning but it was too late. The rocket-propelled grenade, or RPG, flashed out across the piazza and hit the pavement just below the front end of the mini-tank, tossing it end over end, to land on its roof and facing the gate of the piazza.

Now that the mini-tank had been dealt with, the front doors to the Narthex closed and all eyes in the command room could see that the Metal Storm rounds had in fact penetrated the armor (or at least the first few layers of it) on the flipped vehicle.

At that moment, the U.S. ambassador to Italy and the Vatican entered the room. John Henry Grimm was completely different from the image his name suggested. A short, round, sweaty man who resembled a used car salesman more than a public servant, he walked over to Colonel Werner and said, "So, that didn't look too good."

CHAPTER 59

Quinn carefully peered down into the interior of the dome. He saw a man standing in the Nave far below him. Then he stepped back from the edge and looked for the stairs leading down. He found them and descended to the base of the dome and peered again through to the interior of the dome and looked down. The man was no longer on the floor of the Basilica, and a rope was hung from the railing that led to the floor of the building hundreds of feet below him. On the floor of this inner balcony, next to the railing, Quinn found a harness and rappelling device he knew as an ATC. He looked over the railing again and was tempted but knew that he would be throwing away caution and stealth as anyone below would be able to see him long before he hit the floor.

Instead, he continued back down on the stairs, and at the base of the drum, he found the locked door he had seen from the roof of the Basilica. Hanging on a hook next to the door itself, was a set of keys. He took the keys and used them to unlock the door, carefully exiting onto the roof of the Basilica. He scanned the roof and satisfied himself that no additional men had come up. He then used the keys on the door that led to the stairs that would take him down to the main level of the Basilica.

As he began to open the door, the door began to move on its own, pushed from the other side. He heard a voice in Chinese and he knew he had just a second to figure out what to do. He pulled the door fast and rushed into the room, slamming his shoulder into the unsuspecting Chinese man who was coming out to the roof.

Both men lost their rifles as they crashed headlong to the floor. The Chinese man was faster as he nimbly got to his feet and swept Quinn's legs from under him with a swinging kick, just as Quinn had been getting to his feet. Quinn went down onto his back and rolled toward Hong's man, denying the tactic from working a second time. Quinn had stopped his roll on his stomach, pulled his legs up under him and sprang upward hitting the Chinese man in the stomach and forcing him back against a wall. The man punched out, hitting Quinn in the ribs.

Quinn spun away from the second punch, which missed, and threw himself to the wall adjacent to the man while bringing his foot up to stomp at the side of the smaller man's knee. The man suspected the attack and pivoted away just in time. Quinn stepped away from the wall as the small man with the dark eyes leaped at Quinn's face with a flying kick. Quinn was stunned at the speed and the distance the man could leap. He dodged just enough, and absorbed the blow to his shoulder, which spun him.

Quinn growled at the impact as the Chinese man landed neatly on his feet beyond Quinn and spun to face him again. They both paused, taking an assessment of the situation. They had crossed the room and the Chinese man now stood with his back to the stairs leading down into the Basilica, guarding it. Quinn's back was to the rest of the room and the Metal Storm rifles that had fallen to the floor. Quinn stepped closer to the man, not giving him room to attempt another flying kick. The man snapped a high kick up at Quinn, but Quinn leaned backward, away from the blow. He tilted his head and looked at the man with a look that said, "Uh oh, you're in the shit now."

Quinn kicked out with a hard powerful side kick and the Chinese man realized his folly. Being the shorter of the two, he couldn't reach Quinn, but Quinn's kicks could reach him. The man raised his arms and blocked the kick, but felt the sting of it in his forearms.

Quinn faked that he was going to kick again and the man raised his arms again, but instead Quinn rushed forward and simply pushed the man hard, just under his upraised arms. Then Quinn darted back.

The man tottered at the top of the stairs and Jason Quinn launched his own flying kick that connected cleanly with the Chinese man's middle and sent him flying backward down the staircase, while Quinn fell hard to the floor at the top of the stairs on his back once again.

Quinn got up and peered down the stairs to see the Chinese man moaning in a crumbled heap some distance down the curving staircase. Quinn went back to retrieve a rifle and headed down the stairs. When he reached the groaning man, Quinn set the rifle down next to him. One look suggested that the man had broken both legs and an arm in the fall. His head was bleeding from a gash on his forehead, and his lip was cut.

Quinn pulled his knife from its sheath on his belt and plunged it into the heart of the Chinese man with one smooth stab. The groaning stopped. Quinn pulled the knife out of the man and with a flick of his wrist wiped the blade on the man's black hooded sweatshirt. He then replaced it in its sheath, picked up his rifle and continued.

He didn't particularly want to kill the man, but he didn't want to chance that the man might recover enough to start screaming and alert any other men further down the stairway. The longer he could go without the shooting starting, Quinn figured, the better. Once the first shots were fired, things were going to get very messy.

CHAPTER 60

Yang closed the front door and turned to the man from whom he had snatched the RPG launcher and handed it back to him. He barked at the man to remove the bodies then turned back to Hong.

"What now?" he asked.

"They are starting to get sneaky now. The tank was just a diversion for their snipers. We don't have the manpower to afford getting picked off. Full sniper protocol. Alert every man to be mindful of keeping well back from the doors. There's no need for them to actually see what they are shooting with the Metal Storms. Those things will shred anything." Hong began walking back to the transept, where the Pope stood quietly waiting.

Yang sent the man with the RPG launcher to notify the man that had been designated their runner. The runner would visit each man at every entrance and the men on the dome to tell them the news.

"Get the camera and tripod set up. It won't be long now before they lift the communications scrambler." Hong told Yang. Then he looked around the spacious interior of the Basilica and spun around a few times.

"Where the hell is the woman, Yang?" he shouted.

The echoes of the shout seemed to last forever.

Yang ran off with another man and the two began searching the massive space. Hong walked up to the Pope. The man did not show even a hint of nervousness.

"Where did she go?" Hong demanded.

"I did not see. I was too busy watching your men fall dead in the doorway of this holy house." The Pope looked angry and not afraid of Hong at all.

"Have a seat on one of the pews, your Holiness, before I have Yang shoot you." Hong stormed off toward the altar to oversee one of his men assembling a tripod. After a moment, Yang came back and stood by his master's side.

"We haven't found her yet but there's no way she can get out. We have all the exits covered. But she can hide for a long time. There are hundreds of places she could hide. We don't have the men to search for her properly." Yang reported.

"Yes, okay. Send the runner to look for her once he's back from his rounds." Hong said. Then he turned and glared at the Pope, who was, as instructed, sitting in a pew.

Then something occurred to Hong.

"Why did we hear about the tank so late?"

"What?" Yang asked.

"The tank. Wu came to tell us he had seen it from the front door as they opened the main gates. Why didn't Lau send word of it? He would have seen it coming for over a mile." Hong mused.

Yang stood stonily, and waited.

"Get another man up to the roof and find out what's going on," he said quietly.

Yang ran to assign one of the men covering the northern entrance to join the runner on his way to the roof. He was concerned about the plan. They had lost two men at the front door, the woman was loose, the Pope wasn't cowed, their system for communicating took too long and wasn't working well.

Yang ran to the front of the Basilica and spoke quietly to the men at the doors, instructing them to be more vigilant in reporting anything they saw and to keep their heads down. He was about to sprint back to the transept when one of the men called his attention to the piazza. They could see armed men scurrying across the piazza at the far end. Then all was quiet. Yang waited another minute with the men at the doors. When nothing else could be seen, he started away.

"Okay. Stay sharp," Yang told them, and then he headed back down the ornately decorated Nave.

CHAPTER 61

Eva hid in the right arm of the transept in an architectural nook. She had seen the distraction at the front of the Basilica as the perfect moment to escape, because for just a moment, no one was watching her or the Pope. She had whispered to the old man to flee with her. He had whispered that he couldn't run very well and that she should go without him.

She had. It didn't take her long to get far enough away that she could start hiding. The frustrating thing was that she wanted to find something to use as a weapon and couldn't find anything that wasn't either attached to the building, or behind small gates or wrought iron bars.

In the end, she decided to just stay out of sight for a while. She knew Quinn was on the grounds but she didn't know how he would get into the Basilica, or for that matter if he had already gotten in. She also didn't know if she could or should go out. The first step would be to find a door on this side of the Basilica. She found a few small staircases that led to gilded balconies and considered them good hiding places. She climbed to one and used it to get a better view of the layout of the church.

She saw one man running toward a doorway on the opposite side of the transept that had a sign that read "Dome." She thought about trying to make it over that way but wasn't sure up was the direction she wanted when what she really wanted was out.

Then she heard him. Hong had discovered she was gone. His shout reverberated off the walls and echoed long after he stopped shouting. She instinctively ducked down behind the wall of her balcony. She slunk toward the stairs and worked her way down them toward the ground floor. She waited inside the doorway to her darkened stairwell for what seemed like forever. She was about to step out of it and search for a door again, when she spotted a man walking past her door and back toward the transept. She leaned slowly back into the darkness of the stairs and waited again. Then she inched her head around the doorframe looking after the man as he continued walking toward the altar.

Eva slipped out of the doorway the other direction and continued to use the complicated architecture of the building as cover as she made her way toward the end of the hallway. She found a door that was guarded by one man and a smaller hallway that led off to the right, which she slipped into.

How can I get him away from the door, she wondered. As she thought, she looked at a marble statue in a small alcove. She hoped it wasn't alarmed and ran her fingers over it. No noise, but the statue was attached at the base to the alcove. She pulled on it and it didn't budge. Eva scowled at it. The statue was about three and half feet tall and was clearly a saint of some sort. She placed her foot flat against the wall to the side of the alcove, placed her hands behind the shoulders of the figure, and pulled for all she was worth.

The resulting noise pleasantly surprised her. It wasn't the loud crack that she was fearing but a scraping "crunk" noise that was muffled enough to not attract attention. The statue broke across the legs of the figure, giving Eva a two and a half foot long weapon that weighed more than she thought it would. But she could heft it, and that was all that mattered.

She peered around the edge of the hallway to assure herself that she hadn't alerted anyone from the altar or the man at the door to her right. She moved slowly toward the man at the door, thinking he hadn't heard her at all, and as she raised her arms to smack the statue down on his head from behind, he started to speak to her in Cantonese and turn toward her. But the weight of the statue was enough to start its own descent and Eva brought her weight into it.

The statue crashed into the man's head, and he went down in a crumpled heap. Eva lost her balance and fell against him. The impact was mostly silent but the butt of the man's rifle hit the floor with an audible thunk.

Eva quickly got to her feet and moved to the side of the hallway with her statue. She thought for sure that the sound would bring people running but no one came. She moved back to the man slumped against the door and took his pulse on his wrist. He was alive but out cold.

She set her statue down on the floor and dragged the man away from the door to the side of the hallway. She was reaching for the door when she heard Hong's voice echo once again off the walls of the vast Basilica.

"Doctor Rayjek, I'd appreciate it if you would rejoin us. Otherwise, I'll have Yang shoot the Pope in the foot. I need him for my broadcast, but it'll be fine if he has a limp!"

Her hand was on the door handle. *Damn.* She couldn't let the Pope get shot, even in his foot, just so she could escape. She had her hand on the handle. *On the handle*, she thought.

She let go of the handle and started back toward the altar. Then she stopped, turned, and grabbed the handle again and opened the door just a crack. Then, she let go and turned on her way back to the altar. She wondered if Quinn would see the door cracked and be able to slip into the Basilica undetected. She sighed.

"Alright, Hong," she shouted. Her own voice echoed off the walls. "No need to be more of a bastard than you already are."

She walked down the right arm of the transept, then ducked into the stairway she had been in earlier. Then, she walked out of the stairway as if she had been hiding in the balcony the whole time, stepping into the light of the middle of the hallway where she could easily be seen by the men at the altar.

Jason, I hope you get here soon, she thought. She walked toward Hong, who was standing with his men, near a video camera on a tripod. He was smiling that smirk of his again. *I hope Jason wipes that smile off of your face, Scumbag*, she wished.

CHAPTER 62

Jason Quinn had killed three of Hong's men in the Vatican so far and was certain that Hong would soon notice the disappearances. The guy in the lantern, the flying kicker, and another man that seemed like he was coming to check on the two up at the roof. The final man Quinn had been able to hear running toward him. He simply stepped into the shadows of an alcove and then stepped out and slit the man's throat.

Now, Quinn approached the ground floor and inched out into the doorway. He saw some men near the altar, but he wasn't sure who they were. He also saw a man sitting in a pew and realized he was looking at the Pope.

Just then, Hong shouted out a warning to Eva that he would shoot the Pope in the foot if she didn't return. Quinn watched from the shadows until he heard Eva's reply and smiled. She was alright. Quinn considered using the rifle on Hong right then, but then he saw Eva approaching the altar from the other side. He couldn't risk a firefight with both the Pope and Eva in the way. *Damn*, he thought. He'd have to find another way to get to them.

Quinn crept out of the stairwell and moved slowly along the wall to another alcove where he could hide from those down in the transept. He watched as another man came up to Hong from the Nave. At about the same time, Eva arrived at the pews and Hong pointed at a spot near the Pope. Eva went over and sat next to the old man. *Good*, Quinn thought. *Just have to keep the bullets away from that pew. If they have any sense, they'll dive to the floor. Now if only I had a good distraction.*

Quinn was hoping for fewer of Hong's men around Eva and the Pope, but there were five men all clustered around them now, including the man that had arrived from the Nave. With the exception of Hong, the others all carried their own Metal Storm rifles.

"Watch them this time!" Hong was shouting at one of his men, and then he and three others all left and headed toward the front doors of the Basilica. Another headed off down the opposite arm of the transept. Only one man remained guarding Eva and the Pope. Now was Quinn's chance.

He left his alcove and crept along the gilded wall toward the transept and its domed roof. Quinn reached the end of his hallway and the remaining guard had still not looked in his direction. Quinn had trained his rifle on the man the entire time and was ready to shoot as soon as the man looked.

Quinn glanced around the corner toward the Nave and the Narthex at its end. Hong was heading to the front door with two men. No one else in sight. Now was the time. Quinn raised his rifle. He had set it to a single-fire setting. He wondered absently how many people had ever used that setting. Metal Storms were designed to shred things, not for accuracy. Still, he hoped the rifle was worthy enough for the shot he was about to take. He checked Eva and the Pope one last time, then fired the shot at the lone Chinese man's head, killing him instantly. The shot was fairly quiet but noisy enough in the Basilica.

Quinn started running toward the pews as the Chinese man's body slumped, as Eva and the Pope looked over to Quinn, and as he saw a look of urgency begin to cross Eva's face. Before he could react, he was smashed from his right.

Quinn went sprawling to the floor, and he lost the rifle. A tall Chinese man with a scar had hit him. Thankfully, he wasn't armed with a rifle, but he was approaching fast. Quinn scrambled to his feet and raced for the pews. Eva and the Pope were now crouching behind the pews. Quinn made for the pew where the body of the man he shot fell. He glanced back and saw that the scarred Chinese man was going for Quinn's fallen rifle. Hong and the others were running back from the far end of the Nave.

Quinn dove forward and down between the pews as a single shot ripped into the wood. He landed on the floor and slid a bit, but not far enough. He scrambled forward on his hands and knees and reached the rifle the dead man had been holding.

More shots splintered the top of the pew above Quinn. *He found the full-*

auto setting. Lovely, Quinn thought. Then Quinn returned fire with his own rifle on full auto. He sprayed the area where the scarred man had been and the hallway from which Quinn had come. Unfortunately, the shots only hit the walls and the ornamentation. The scarred man was gone.

Quinn twisted and fired a burst in Hong's direction. Hong and the two men running beside him hit the floor. Quinn dropped to the floor himself, looking under the pews trying to find the scarred man. He crawled to the end of his pew and stuck the rifle out into the aisle, business end facing the altar. He let a spray of bullets fly. Then he stood quickly, and he glanced around to find the scarred man nearby and holding his weapon trained on Quinn. Another man had reached the Pope and Eva and held his weapon on them.

Quinn lowered his rifle and turned back to face the scarred man, just as the butt of a rifle smashed into the left side of his face. Jason Quinn was rendered unconscious instantly and his body folded forward over the pew, his folded ice ax sliding out of its sheath and clattering to the floor.

CHAPTER 63

David Hong was losing his patience. First the mini-tank and the loss of his two men, then Rayjek's escape. The crumbling of his rudimentary communication scheme. The runner never returned from his job of alerting the others to the sniper danger. Then, Wu reported a man carrying a white flag and holding an envelope approaching the front doors. He had nearly been there when that damned fool Quinn had made his play. It was stunning to think that Jason Quinn had escaped the collapse of the cathedral in Hong Kong; that he was here in the Basilica!

"Yang!" Hong screamed. "Put the three of them in the chamber downstairs. Maybe surrounded by an exploding floor they won't be able to escape. Then, I want you to check each remaining man personally. Find the runner! Then, report back to me personally on how many men we might have lost to the American pig. Figure out how he got in here. If we have a security leak, we need to plug it. Now!"

He was sweating now from having worked himself into such a fit. Yang took the Pope and Eva, and he slung Quinn's inert body over his shoulder. As they headed for the stairs down to the crypt, David Hong turned back toward the other problem. The man with the white flag at the door to the Basilica.

"Wu!" he called as he strode to the Narthex. "Let him in and keep your gun trained on him. Don't get your damn head blown off by a sniper, either!"

As Hong continued the long trek down to the front doors, he saw Wu allow the man with the flag in and close the door. The man was tall and broad shouldered, with close-cropped blonde hair and ice blue eyes, in deep contrast to Quinn's wiry frame, long brown hair, and emerald eyes.

"I might have guessed," Hong said with disgust as he approached the man.

"Hiya, Dave. How ya been?" Curtis Drake Johnson asked.

"I should just kill you. You surely have some feeble plot in mind, like your friend did." Hong began. He noted no change in Johnson's expression, and he was thankful that he faced Johnson as an adversary in this and not in a game of cards. "Oh yes, we captured your moronic friend. You'll be joining him soon."

"Is that any way to treat a messenger?" Johnson asked and held up the envelope he carried with a message from Werner.

Hong snatched the letter from Johnson and opened it. The Swiss Guard wanted him to use Johnson as a messenger. They were still refusing to turn off the communications scrambler. They wanted to know his demands.

"So what was all that shooting, Dave? Did my buddy cap a few of you twerps?" Johnson quipped while Hong finished reading the letter.

"Your problem, Mr. Johnson," Hong began, "and Colonel Werner shares it, is that you both assume that I want to communicate with him. I don't. I want the scrambler turned off. Until that happens, I have nothing to say to your Colonel Werner."

Hong turned to Wu and spoke in Cantonese. He then turned back to Johnson as Wu began prodding Johnson in the back with his rifle to get Johnson to move deeper into the Basilica.

"I therefore have no reason to send you back out as a messenger. You'll make a better hostage than a messenger anyway. As a hostage, I can gag you and torture you."

"Didn't we already try the torture thing? It didn't take. Maybe you should just surrender. That Colonel seemed pretty patient. He might just be content to wait you out until you starve to death." Curtis kept up the talk, trying to seed some misdirection in as well. He knew damn well that Werner wouldn't wait and he wouldn't turn off the scrambler and give Hong what he wanted. Werner would mount a full assault next, hostages or not. They had discussed it at length, Johnson wanting to know what Plan B was when his messenger routine fell apart. Now, Johnson's job was to spread disinformation.

"You know the Swiss, Hong, they'll try diplomacy until they're blue in the face. Your little siege here could last weeks."

"No," Hong said. "It won't. Or I'll start sending out pieces of you, the woman, Quinn, and the Pope. I figure we won't get past thumbs before they turn off the scrambler."

Curtis Johnson hoped that Werner's team launched their assault before he lost the ability to type.

CHAPTER 64

Colonel Johannes Werner was strapping on his tactical gear. Each Gendarme had donned riot gear and the remaining Guards were all preparing to seize the Basilica. Fritz would remain behind in the control room alone. Ambassador Grimm had offered the official use of the U.S. Marines stationed at the embassy in Rome; the Italians had offered army troops. The remote-controlled mini-tank was a mess in the piazza. A helicopter was smashed down onto the obelisk, and David Hong still had a number of armed men holding the Basilica with an archeologist, His Holiness the Pope, and now an American engineer all held hostage. Possibly two American engineers.

Werner was in command of the whole mess and while things looked bleak, his men had sniped two of Hong's men. He was certain that he could breach the Basilica now.

There had been more shooting inside. His men in the garden to the north of the building had seen the door on that side opened just a crack and infrared revealed that the door was unguarded. The Crow's Nest Man still hadn't been replaced. Infrared now revealed that the front doors were guarded by only one man.

Johnson had been taken inside and hadn't come out again. That suggested to Werner one of three things: either Hong had captured Quinn and he was so pissed at the sight of Johnson, that he just took him, or he hadn't gotten Quinn but took Johnson for the hell of it, or that he just wasn't interested in communicating with the Guard until Werner turned off the scrambler.

Werner had no intention of turning off the scrambler.

No matter which way Werner looked at it, it seemed that Hong's force was dwindling. He lost two men at the front, and now that door was guarded by only one man who must have come from another post. The roof was clear. One of Werner's teams was going to get into Hong's helicopter and land it on the roof. The North station was completely unguarded and it made no sense. Plus the gunfire inside. Hong's plan was coming apart, Werner was certain of it.

"The press are going into a frenzy at the gate," Schippers advised.

"Let them. Damn fools should know better than to fly into our airspace. They are lucky *I* didn't shoot down their helicopter. Besides, if all goes well, this will be over soon and they can get the whole story—or at least the version we tell them—when David Hong is behind bars. With a little luck, His Holiness will make an exception to the Vatican's policy on capital punishment for the bastard."

Werner finished with his gear and picked up an MP5 submachine gun. "Keep in touch, Fritz."

"Yes, sir." Fritz replied from his monitor, where he would keep an eye on the assault and communicate with the Guards and Gendarmes through their own dedicated signal, which remained unaffected by the communications scrambler. Then, Fritz spoke to the teams on the microphone. "Helo team, you are go. Underground teams, move into place. North team: status report?"

"No movement near the door. The door is still ajar and infrared picks up no heat signature," Hans Wald reported from the garden.

Werner, Schippers, and the others left the command center and moved through the streets to the garden. Werner had sent a large contingent to each station, plus the helicopter team, but he was banking on the open door to the north. He suspected it was Quinn that had removed the guards from that door and left it ajar for Werner's men.

In a few moments, Werner's team met up with Kevin Miller and Hans Wald, who had both returned to their post watching the door. They had three other men already with them. Werner's team brought the strength of the group to ten.

He checked his watch. The attack would begin soon. The battle for St. Peter's Basilica.

CHAPTER 65

Jason Quinn awoke slowly. His head was throbbing. He couldn't feel the left side of his face. At first he dreamed that he was out camping somewhere in the mountains of Nepal with Curtis. His face had slipped off the Therm-a-Rest mattress and was lying directly on the pebbles under the floor of the tent. Then, he heard Eva's voice and wondered why she wasn't sleeping. It was night out, wasn't it?

He opened his eyes and the light of the room stabbed him in the eyes so hard that he squinted them shut quickly, causing a fresh burst of pain to dig into his skull.

"I think he's waking up," an unfamiliar voice said. It was an old man's voice.

Quinn opened his eyes more slowly this time and saw Curtis looking at him.

"Fancy meeting you here," he said.

"Always in the finest locales. Where the hell are we?" Quinn wanted to know as he tried to sit up.

"Take it slowly, man. And ixnay on the ellskay." Curtis said.

"That's quite alright, Mr. Johnson. I've heard worse in my time," the old man was saying, when Quinn put the voice with the face and realized he was in a small circular room with the Pope, Curtis, and Eva.

"How are you feeling, Mr. Quinn?" the pontiff asked.

"I'll live, Your Holiness. And I'm very sorry for the bloodshed in your church."

"Your rescue attempt was brave, if foolhardy. And yes, I'd appreciate it if you could keep the loss of life down."

"I'll see what I can do," Quinn mumbled as he staggered to his feet. Eva helped him up. He soon saw the open entrance from the small room into a larger space with a gleaming metal floor. He was taking his first steps toward the exit when Curtis grabbed his arm hard.

"Not another step, mon frere. See those pressure plates out there? The floor *explodes*." Curtis said.

Quinn turned slowly and eyed Johnson with a raised eyebrow. "It does *what?*"

The Pope at length explained how the security measures worked and then sighed, resigned to the present situation. Curtis then explained Werner's plan to use him as a messenger, and about how Hong hadn't taken the bait. Curtis then explained to Quinn that the Swiss would be mounting an attack in twenty minutes if they hadn't heard back from Johnson. He explained about the northern door, and Eva chimed in about how she had been about to escape through that door.

"I could have left," she said.

"You probably should have, my dear," the Pope told her, "but I thank you for looking after my feet for me." He smiled weakly at her. The strain of the day was taking its toll on him and he was close to a collapse. Quinn wasn't about to let the man rest just yet, though.

"Have you ever seen this floor tested, Your Holiness?" Quinn asked the man.

"Yes, actually. They test just one panel of the floor every year to ensure that the system still works. They replace the explosive charge behind that panel each time, though."

"Is there a delay before the explosive charge goes off?" Quinn asked.

"I don't think so. If there was, it was very short. Again, it is a small explosion, but quite frightening in this enclosed space. I never walked across the floor with the boots until today when we were placed here."

Quinn stood up and stared out at the explosive room. There was no way he could climb across the room, no way to reach the ceiling. No way to cross the floor. No way to get a pair of the boots kept in the room forty feet away from him.

The others sat on the floor and leaned against the cylindrical wall. No one spoke. Eva looked at her watch regularly. They all hoped to hear the sound of the Swiss Guards attacking upstairs—or better yet, that they would hear no attack sounds but that the Swiss Guard would arrive in the doorway of the room with the benches to tell them it was all over.

Instead, Yang arrived and he was wearing a pair of the metallic boots. Still, he paused on his side of the thick red, painted line that divided the bench room from the explosive chamber. He held Quinn's ice ax in one hand and stood staring at Quinn across the divide. Neither man spoke for a moment.

Then, Yang swung his arm back and threw the ice ax across the room at Quinn. Quinn stepped aside and yelled "Look out!"

The ax hit the wall of the small chamber and bounced to the floor. Curtis stopped its slide by stamping his foot on the ax, as if it were a fire he was trying to put out.

Quinn turned back to face the Chinese man with the scar.

"How much good will your fancy mountaineering equipment do you now, Mr. Quinn?" Yang taunted.

Quinn turned around and stalked across the small chamber to grab the large piece of dark splintered lumber.

"No!" Eva shouted.

Quinn stopped and faced her, pointing at the shattered table instead. She nodded and he picked it up. The broken glass inside the walls of the case tinkled as he held it above his head and threw it to the left of the door as far as he could. The desk hit the metal floor and a second later, a sharp explosion sounded, ringing in everyone's ears. The table fractured into small pieces that scattered, across the floor, each too light to set off another plate by themselves. When the smoke from the explosion cleared, Quinn could see that the pieces of wood that were intact were peppered with tiny holes from what he assumed were small metal fragments of the floor.

"Is that supposed to impress me?" Yang asked in ridicule.

One second, Quinn thought. *There's a delay of one second.*

"No," he called. He grabbed the ice ax and stood back at the wall of his circular prison cell, as far from the entrance as he could get. The others, standing now, leaned against the walls on the sides of the room, the Pope next to the salvaged portion of the Cross.

Quinn planted a foot against the wall behind him and sprinted out of the doorway and straight for Yang. And right onto the exploding floor.

CHAPTER 66

Jason Quinn was still barefoot from when he had removed his climbing shoes on the dome. He had always felt that he could run the fastest without any shoes on. Now it was time to find out. He had leaped the first panel and intentionally landed on the second panel's far edge. He moved as fast as he could but the panel still exploded behind him, sending small pieces of shrapnel into the back of his thighs.

He raced as fast as he ever had in his entire life and the shockwaves from each successive blast behind him helped to propel him to the point where he felt like he was flying.

From Yang's perspective, the crazy American was hauling ass straight toward him with gouts of flame and smoke erupting behind him with each step, so that Quinn looked like a crazed demon. Yang set his stance, prepared to block the man as he reached the line of safety—maybe even push him back into the explosions.

Quinn was covering perhaps five feet with each step, and had crossed most of the floor. His legs were bleeding, and his back was taking a pounding as if someone were repeatedly punching his spine. When he approached Yang, he could see that the Chinese man had set his stance to block Quinn. But Jason Quinn, the exploding sprinter, had no plans of crashing into Yang.

With his last leaping, exploding step, two panels away from Yang, Quinn leaped as high into the air as he could. His momentum was carrying him toward Yang's head, and Quinn's arm was pinwheeling through the air with the ice ax, which he buried into Yang's shoulder blade. Yang started to fall forward and Quinn released the handle of the ax, somersaulting down Yang's back, as the man fell.

Quinn's body sprawled inside the bench room at the same moment that Yang's head hit the last unexploded metal plate on the floor, just across the thick red line. The explosion, in such close proximity to Yang's head, simply turned the man's skull and brain to paste.

Quinn lay where he was for a moment, wondering how badly injured his legs and back were. He felt a lot of small cuts and aches, but he could move. He stood slowly, leaning on a bench for support as he did. The explosion from each plate was aimed primarily upward, so he had caught very little of each blast by moving as quickly as he did. Likewise, he expected that by clearing the first panel at the start of his run, none of the blast would have gone backward into the chamber where the others still waited.

He looked down at Yang's headless body as smoke from the chamber began to clear.

"No," he croaked to the corpse. "You were supposed to be impressed by *that*. Prick."

Finally, the smoke from the room cleared enough that Quinn could see three stunned faces looking at him from across the forty feet of destruction.

"You might just be the craziest fucker alive," Johnson shouted. "Sorry, Your Holiness."

The old man shouted right back, "Seconded." The profanity had not bothered him in the slightest.

All of them had ringing in their ears.

"What can I say," Quinn shouted back. "He pissed me off."

Curtis smiled, and Eva just shook her head.

Quinn quickly squatted and took the metallic boots from Yang's dead feet and put them on his own feet. Not the right size but they would do for now. He grabbed three more sets of boots from the floor—they hadn't been put away properly. Then, he crossed the exploded panels in a direct line back to the room. The others each put on their boots and crossed back to safety with Quinn.

Curtis looked down as he went. Just two unexploded panels between the center and Yang's body. He whistled but it sounded far away in his ears.

"I'd like you out of my church as soon as possible, Mr. Quinn," the Pope shouted as he looked at the remains of the scarred Chinese man on the floor. The man's ears were still ringing.

"Understood sir, understood."

They felt another rumble and each understood that the battle upstairs had also begun.

CHAPTER 67

Werner's men fired tear gas canisters into the open northern door of the Basilica and then rushed inside, wearing small tactical gas masks. The helo team would be landing on the roof right now and would be coming barreling down the stairs on the left arm of the transept, guns blazing. He had teams in hiding at the other doors, should Hong's men try to escape. His team was coming in the right arm of the transept. The hope was to pin Hong down in a crossfire.

There was just one problem. Hong and his men were nowhere near the altar. In fact, they were nowhere to be seen.

Then, Werner's team was ripped apart by Metal Storm fire from above. One of Hong's men, wearing a gas mask, was situated up in the balcony across the transept. Werner's team pulled back but too late. His ten men were now just three fully functional men and one wounded in the leg. They huddled in a hallway, and tended to Wald's bloody leg. Miller was sprawled in the blood of his fellow Guards up near the altar.

Schippers tied a quick tourniquet on Wald and left the man as their rear defense. He moved to the stairway of the balcony on this side of the altar—the same one Eva had visited earlier in the day. Werner moved to an alcove on the eastern side of the hallway. No one took any shots at him as he moved. The third man, Claus Fellman by name, moved along the right edge of the hallway back toward the altar, watching the balconies, alcoves, and niches as he went. He also watched the altar in case men might be behind it. He heard gunfire elsewhere in the building and assumed it was the helo team making their way down the steps.

Fellman reached the end of the hallway and the end of cover, but still the man on the balcony did not appear again. Werner moved up and covered the stairs that led to that balcony, in case the man tried to come down the stairs.

Fellman raced out into the open, past the fallen bodies of his comrades and made for the pews as loudly as he could. The man in the balcony popped up, ready to spray the transept with bullets, but Karl Schippers was standing in the balcony directly across the transept from him and neatly put two shots into the Chinese man's forehead. The body fell down into the balcony and all was quiet for the moment.

Fellman got to his feet from where he had slid behind the cover of the pews and made his way back to the fallen Guards. He began checking them for signs of life along with Colonel Werner. Schippers remained in the balcony, covering them. All of the fallen were dead. Werner passed the message to Schippers through his lip microphone. Then, he called for the helo team.

"Helo team? Andreas?" he called quietly. "Fritz? Anything on Helo?"

"They entered the stairs. That's all I know. No movement at the other stations yet." Fritz replied in Werner's ear.

"Wait," he said. "Station Three is opening its door. Standard one man, peeking out."

"Send them in," Werner said.

Fritz ordered the team outside the underground entrance to the Basilica to fire their gas canisters and their weapons. Werner listened to the command and then heard two words that were like sweet music to him from the underground team's commanding officer in his earpiece, "All clear."

Finally, some good news, Werner thought.

Then, Metal Storm fire hit near his position, and he was forced back into the right arm of the transept.

Karl Schippers, the huge man in the balcony, was riddled with electronically fired rounds, and his massive body tumbled forward out of the balcony and down to the Basilica's floor. His MP5 fired the whole time, as his body was jerked and stabbed by the metal projectiles and as his body fell.

Hans Wald had pulled himself along the floor to support Werner and was firing blindly across the transept, laying down a suppressing fire when he caught one of the buzzing bullets tearing the air apart.

Werner was alone now on this side of the Basilica. And the gunfire was coming from where his helo team should have been.

So quickly, everything had come apart.

CHAPTER 68

Quinn and Johnson raced up the stairs to the main floor of the Basilica, Quinn holding Yang's Metal Storm rifle, which he'd found in the bench room. Eva was slowly escorting the Pope up as well, but Quinn and Johnson were far ahead.

As they approached the top of the stairs, they could hear that the battle most likely wasn't going well for the good guys—Metal Storm rifles were blazing like angry hornets but no MP5s were returning fire. They soon saw why. They came out of the stairwell and realized that they had come in behind Hong's men in the left arm of the transept. He had additional men in the Nave and both groups were pinning down the right arm of the transept.

Quinn didn't waste time. He blasted all four of Hong's men in the left arm of the transept. Then he was out of ammunition. He dropped his rifle and picked up one from the men he had just shot, as Curtis was scooping up his own rifle. Now both of them opened fire on the men in the Nave. MP5 fire could be heard coming out of the right arm of the transept now. The men in the Nave were forced to retreat slightly, and they had to divide their fire now between right and left.

Curtis recognized Colonel Werner in the right arm of the transept, now advanced up to the corner to lay down fire into the Nave. He was bleeding from one leg and his right arm had been grazed as well. He looked fine otherwise. Just angry. Curtis waved to the man and he gave Johnson a quick salute in return.

Now, fire seemed to be coming from two of Hong's groups in the Nave and Quinn and Johnson were hard pressed. Werner was trying to communicate with Johnson across the transept. He was holding his hand up and then pointed to his ear. Johnson held a thumb up to acknowledge that he understood.

"Fall back," he said to Quinn, tapping him on the shoulder. "The Cavalry is on the way."

Both men moved back and away from the corner as the withering Metal Storm fire continued to blast away chunks of stone from the wall. Suddenly the fire stopped—or at least it stopped coming at them. Quinn and Johnson returned to the corner, hearing the fire continuing, but now they could see that Hong's men were firing at another group of Guards that had entered the Basilica from the eastern end, from side halls.

"Must be another way in," Quinn said. Then he switched his rifle to single-fire and tried to choose individual targets, avoiding overshooting and risking the Swiss taking the shot at the far end of the Nave. Curtis did the same. After a moment, Quinn glanced over and saw that Werner was also picking targets carefully.

Then, one of Hong's men fired an RPG at the Guards near the Narthex. The explosion echoed forever and seemed to take the fight out of the Guards.

Then, the Metal Storm fire was more concentrated back on Werner's position and he had to retreat again into the transept. Quinn and Johnson tried to return fire but their position was peppered with bullets. They too had to pull back.

Hong's men were advancing toward the transept, while Johnson was collecting another weapon from the men he and Quinn had killed when emerging from the stairs. Quinn glanced back to the stairs and saw Eva peeking around the doorframe. He held up his hand telling her to stay back.

"Cover," he shouted to Johnson.

"Awww, shit!" Johnson replied. He knew Quinn was up to something but he didn't know what. He laid down a heavy burst of fire into the Nave.

Jason Quinn sprinted for the altar, spraying bullets into the Nave as he ran. Between the fire from the three positions—Quinn moving to the center, Werner on the right, and Johnson on the left—Hong's men were hit multiple times.

Then, Quinn saw the man with the RPG launcher readying to fire on

Johnson's position. He stopped running and concentrated his blasts directly at that man, standing out in the open and yelling, "Nooooooo."

The man fired the rocket at the same time that the bullets tore his body into tatters. The gunfire stopped and everyone left alive watched in a kind of sluggish slow motion as the man's aim had been knocked off and the rocket's trajectory went up instead of left. The rocket left a trail of smoke behind it as it raced up past the pews and into the transept.

And up into the dome of St. Peter's Basilica.

CHAPTER 69

There was no other place it could go.

The rocket hit the dome. Above the drum and at the very base of the dome. Almost exactly on the opposite side of the dome from where Quinn had started his run up its side hours earlier.

The explosion seemed huge in the echoing transept and all gunfire had ceased as everyone watched in horror as the explosion moved in a slow-paced sludge-like motion. The wall of the dome seemed to explode inward (although people watching from the outside would later recall having seen the wall explode outward). The size of the hole that the explosion created wasn't apparent at first due to the smoke, but then Quinn saw daylight at the top edge of the hole and felt a tremor in the floor.

He ran back behind the altar and as far as he could go into the apse. He never saw what the others saw—only its aftermath. With a great grinding sound, the entire weight of the dome, now no longer supported on a full quarter of the diameter of its base, wrenched free from its supporting sides at the base and slowly began to topple toward its wounded side.

The noise was deafening and the air filled with concrete and marble dust. Masonry and brick came crashing to the ground in successive explosions, thunderclap after thunderclap. The booms echoing long after their occurrences.

To the credit of the architects that designed the dome and the successive waves of architects and engineers that tended to it since its completion in 1590, the dome stayed mostly intact. It did not shatter or break into tiny pieces; it simply shifted and fell over. The lantern stayed attached to the top of the dome, and it was what saved the entire structure from collapse.

As Fritz Weidermann saw from his monitor in the control room, the dome fell over with the lantern leaning to the north, over the garden side of the Basilica. The lower edge of the dome, much of it destroyed in the rocket impact, slid down into the drum, and the lantern hit the edge of the drum, looking very much now like the business end of a ball turret gun on a B-24 bomber. The southern end of the bottom of the dome was now raised in the air, giving the entire structure the look of an umbrella that has been laid on edge to dry.

Masonry dust plumed up and away through the gaping hole left by the absence of the dome over the southern side of its original resting place. Dust also blew out the open northern door to the Basilica. As engineers would later find, the main portion of the Basilica building was entirely intact except for the minor damage caused by bullets all over the interior and the rocket damage to one of the doors and a portion of the Narthex, near the front doors.

It would be hours before all the bodies were found. Hong's men had ambushed the helo team as they had descended the stairs. Nearly all of Werner's men had been killed. Out of 101 men, he was left with just seven, including himself and Fritz. Werner had only minor injuries. Many of the Gendarmes had been killed but many had not participated in the assault, so fewer of their number had been taken. They assisted in the rescue efforts.

The Pope was completely uninjured, as was Doctor Eva Rayjek. People would later say that God had protected him, and he wouldn't have argued with them, but the Pope always pointed out that Dr. Rayjek had been God's instrument in that protection. She had shielded His Holiness from a small piece of falling masonry and had managed to get the old man out of the Basilica before the choking dust did his lungs any lasting damage. She had also found the envelope Hong had stolen, still wrapped in its double plastic baggies. Days later, when the rescue efforts were over and the rebuilding had begun, she presented the envelope to the Pope, when he spoke with her personally. He was very grateful.

Curtis Johnson suffered a broken leg from falling masonry but was expected to make a quick and simple recovery. Jason Quinn had multiple cuts, bruises, abrasions, shrapnel wounds, and two new bullet holes in his body. He was concerned only about the well-being of his friends, the Pope, and the Swiss Guards. He assisted in the rescue work for hours and visually checked each dead body.

The Battle for the Basilica was over. Neither Hong's men nor the Swiss Guard won. The Basilica itself lost.

David Hong was not found.

BOOK FOUR:
THE LOST TOMB

CHAPTER 70

Minfeng, China

The Taklamakan is the worst and most dangerous desert in the world.
—Sven Hedin

The road to Minfeng from the town of Golmud in Qinghai was one of the worst that Jason Quinn and Eva Rayjek had ever been on. The journey took them *days*. However, they both made light of it and had a great time, while those around them grumbled. They had traveled on public transport, taking it slow and easy, in no particular hurry to reach the town, because it would be at least a week of resting there before they set out with camels across the desert to find Hong Xiu Quan's tomb.

They had flown to Golmud from Hong Kong in an ARGO jet, and gotten out of the town of Golmud (a town that Quinn refused to refer to as anything other than "that shithole where you get the bus to Lhasa" as a result of his previous experiences in the town years earlier) as quickly as they could. They took a bus that had 30 people on board. It broke down nearly every two hours or so. Each passenger would disembark and push the bus until the driver could get the engine going again, then they would all quickly hop aboard through the bus door, as it slowly rolled down the road.

The road itself was paved for about 100 yards and then a mountain of gravel would be dumped right in the middle of the road, forcing the bus to go off-road for nearly a mile of unfinished, unpaved road. Then, it would get back on the paved surface, then it would break down again, and then they would start all over. Quinn guessed that had the conditions been equivalent to those on U.S. roads, they might have made it to Minfeng in a single day of traveling.

Roughly 500 miles from Kashgar and the westernmost border of China, Minfeng, a city of 30,000, sits in a Uyghur ethnic region of mostly desert and tree lined oasis roads, just to the north of the Kunlun Mountains. An Islamic area, the town sports a colorful bazaar and a traditional mosque with minarets. Like much of the rest of China, asphalt and concrete are abundant. Ornately carved jade is one of the region's specialties.

Quinn and Eva spent their days in Minfeng wandering the market and eating primarily at the ethnic restaurants, where they found the food to be quite tasty. They drank water only from special bottles that filtered the water as they drank it, eliminating viruses and bacteria alike. Quinn arranged for some camels to take them part of the way into the Kunlun Mountains, before they would have to begin hiking. He suggested that Eva check out the local library for more clues on Sven Hedin and his possibly final journey to this region, looking for Hong Xiu Quan's tomb.

"After the tomb," she assured him. Although secretly she hoped that the tomb would contain some clues to Hedin's having passed through.

After a week, they were both pretty bored with Minfeng and ready to get on their way. Eva joked though, that after a week in the mountains, eating camping rations, they'd be glad to get back to the Uyghur restaurants. Quinn laughed and agreed.

They laughed often and loud, discussing the craziness of the past weeks with David Hong's men attacking them around the world. His die-hard forces had mostly been killed or had fled. Intelligence communities were on the lookout for the man himself and a few terrorist cells of devoted followers. Hong's business ventures were a shambles in Hong Kong and elsewhere. The Vatican was reconstructing the dome of the Basilica and the Swiss Guard were extensively revising their security practices.

Eva had regaled Quinn with her story of escaping from Hong's helicopter, her near escape from the Basilica, and her time with the Pope. Quinn had filled her in on his ascent of the Basilica with Eva laughing hysterically the whole time and amazed at his audacity. They had spent a few weeks in Rome, interviewed by the Vatican, the Swiss Guard, and other security forces. They also helped with the reconstruction efforts.

Curtis and Werner became drinking buddies, telling stories and chatting up the Italian ladies throughout Rome for a few weeks while they both recuperated from their wounds. By the time Quinn and Eva were ready to leave for Hong Kong, Curtis had his leg cast removed and was walking with a cane. Their parting was warm and happy, with Curtis quietly wishing Eva the best with her growing relationship with Quinn and telling her that she was making Quinn happier than Johnson had seen the man in quite some time.

Eva had to admit that Quinn had come a long way out of his distant shell from when she had met him and he had avoided her in the tunnels at the Sunnydale camp. Their nights in Rome had been full of passion and their days had been full of fun and laughter. Hong Kong, just before they flew to Qinghai Province had been the same. Now, however, she began to see yet another side of Jason Quinn, as he planned and organized for their expedition into the mountains. He was more serious and determined to get everything just right. He would leave her for short periods of time to go pick up various things from different parts of the market. She never saw him with a written list of any kind, but he always had just one more thing he was looking for. Sometimes it was something simple like a length of cord 20 feet long, and other times he seemed to be looking for things he couldn't find, but he would then improvise something from smaller parts.

The day they set off, they had two guides, five camels, and food and water to last them to the mountains, for weeks in the mountains, and for back to Minfeng again. After all of Quinn's careful preparation, she was stunned that his mountaineering pack was smaller than hers.

"Where's all that stuff you've been buying?" she wanted to know.

"It's in here," he told her with a small smile.

"No way."

"Yep," he told her, his smile growing to a grin.

"When we get back, you have got to show me how to pack better. I thought with all my experience on the road and at digs, I had it all down, but you mountain boys have got some skills." She laughed, but inside she was slightly irked that it was possible he could pack better than her.

"Wait til you see the kitchen sink that I packed in here."

"Shut up." Then they were laughing again, and the caravan began to move out, south, toward the mountains, and the long-lost tomb of a Chinese man who had believed himself to be the second son of God.

As their caravan left town, they were observed.

CHAPTER 71

Quinn's thoughts drifted on the long camel journey into the dry and desolate mountains. He had been in this part of the world before for climbing expeditions and three different projects with ARGO, including the doomed Sunnydale project. The landscape was cold and gray, with flecks of brown and tan. In the distance, the snowcapped peaks looked like balls of cotton clouds fallen out of the blue sky and finally resting on the tops of the dirty mountains. Still, he was grateful for the view after being in the city for a week and the dull ride across the windswept sands and grasses.

The Kunlun range is one of the longest mountain chains in Asia. From Tajikistan to the east, the Kunluns form the natural boundary between the ethnic stew of the Xinjiang Autonomous Region of China's northwest and the region formerly known only as Tibet to its south. Today, Tibet is another so-called *Autonomous Region.* Quinn also knew that the treeless Kunlun Mountains were believed to be a Taoist paradise of sorts. For Quinn it was a kind of paradise as well—he just loved to be in the mountains, even if he had no plans to climb any.

His slightly smelly Bactrian camel swayed smoothly as it plodded along after the guide's camel in front of it. Quinn's body rocked back and forth between the camel's two humps as his thoughts floated away. He didn't sleep on the beast, but he did review what he had learned about Hong Xiu Quan, David Hong's plans, this part of the world, and the time with Eva in the last weeks since the battle at the Basilica.

His love for Eva was growing from a panicked thought at the loss of her into more of a comfortable presence that he regarded like a warm blanket around him on a chilly Colorado night by the fireplace. He had felt a bit of the strain of the journey on their relationship, but it had been minor. He had always believed that a couple's ability to travel together without turning on each other was the defining characteristic of a relationship with legs. However, he also knew that relationships begun in unusual circumstances and under duress often failed. He'd spent the first few weeks after the Basilica incident enjoying his time with Eva but telling himself that it might end at any time, and he should be prepared for it. After all, she had her own life as an archeologist, and David Hong's bizarre machinations had kept her from it. As the weeks had gone on however, she had showed no sign of wanting to leave his side and Quinn's feelings for her had deepened.

What Quinn enjoyed most was that Eva could surprise him with cunning, resources of strength, and brash humor. He was still surprised that she had found the document that Hong had been after and that she had given it back to the Pope—but only after hanging on to it for a few days. Days after the destruction of the Dome of the Basilica, the Pope had requested a private meeting with each of the three of them. He had spoken with Johnson first, then Eva, and then before they had a chance to speak with each other after her meeting, he had seen Quinn.

The Vatican gates had remained closed to the general public as the reconstruction efforts had begun. The Pope asked to meet with Quinn in a book-lined study in his private quarters. Not the Pope's normal audience chamber, as Quinn was informed when the Camerlengo, a cardinal appointed with overseeing administrative tasks at the Vatican, led him in to see the Pontiff.

"He has requested none of the usual formalities be observed. You need not worry about protocol or traditions." The fifty-something man in a black robe with crimson red trim glanced at Quinn's recently purchased Italian suit. He seemed to understand that while the suit looked very good on Jason Quinn, it wasn't his normal mode of attire. "You address him as *Your Holiness*."

"Thank you," Quinn said as he was led into the book-lined room and the Camerlengo indicated that he take a seat on a battered leather sofa. The older man left and Quinn took in the room. It was peaceful, with a nice view from its many windows—bulletproofed, Quinn was certain. He noted that many of the books in this room were fiction hardcovers from a variety of genres, but in very few instances did it seem that the Pontiff read any given author for more than a novel or two. *Perhaps he reads for references to the Church*, he thought.

The room was dark wood but showed little of the pomp and glory to be found elsewhere in the small city-state. The sofa on which Quinn sat seemed well worn and he wondered how many naps the Pope might have taken on the couch. Then, he wondered if other Popes had napped on it. There was a simple wooden coffee table. Also a plush armchair that Quinn suspected was in fact a *La-Z-Boy* recliner. A nearby desk was clear of things like a phone or a computer and instead had a small pile of leather-bound books on it. A framed map of the world was on one wall, but Quinn noticed that it was the standard World Map that National Geographic sent out with their subscriptions.

Does he have to pay for that subscription, he wondered, or do they give him a complimentary lifetime membership?

After a few moments, the door opened and the Pope entered. He wore his white robes with the white trim but no hat. Quinn rose from his seated position but the Pope quickly stopped him.

"Please, please, sit."

He walked over to the armchair and plopped into it with all the grace of a lumberjack sliding into a favored chair for a weekend of Budweiser and National League football. Quinn suppressed a smirk as the old man reached over to the side of the chair Quinn hadn't seen, pulled the lever, and reclined the chair. *It is a La-Z-Boy*. Quinn restrained himself from smirking.

"May I call you Jason?" the Pope asked. His eyes were partially closed as if he had just finished a very wearying day, which Quinn supposed he had. The man probably felt that way every day.

"Of course, Your Holiness."

"Roberto told you that in this room, for today, we would not be observing any formalities, yes?" Before Quinn could reply, the man went on. "I suppose he also instructed you to call me Your Holiness. But in this room, today, I'll be pleased to have you call me Joseph."

Quinn was unsure of what to say but the Pope needed to say more, so Quinn simply nodded his head.

"I understand that you feel horribly responsible for the destruction at my Basilica because your bullet was responsible for the death of the man holding the rocket launcher." Now the man leaned forward in his recliner and looked directly at Quinn. "I strongly disagree, Jason. Officially, I am abhorrent of the entire affair in my church and every bit of bloodshed that occurred on all sides of the battle. Personally, I believe that you were solely responsible for salvaging the situation, saving many lives, and possibly saving the entire Holy Church from ruinous scandal."

The man paused and watched Quinn in silence for some time. Neither man spoke.

"I see the doubt in your eyes, Jason." The man leaned back in his easy chair. "You were in a tough position, as were all Werner's men in the Swiss Guard. You believe that you should carry the guilt in your heart for the destruction of the dome because you killed the man who fired the rocket. Do you think if you hadn't killed that man that I would be happier because that maniac had succeeded and his lackey had fired a rocket through the altar?" The Pope smiled a do-you-get-the-parable smile at Quinn.

It was hard to not return it. The man was charismatic, and he got to Quinn.

"Cast off that guilt, Jason. It did not end the way I would have wished, but you are in no way responsible for the actions of David Hong and his fanatics. Officially, I am praising the works of the Swiss Guard in attempting to end the terrorist situation in the Vatican. The actions of a determined terrorist resulted in the partial destruction of the dome, but the perpetrators have been brought to justice, and I am confident that God will oversee and bless the reconstruction of the Basilica." He paused again.

"Unofficially, I am grateful that you and Mr. Johnson and Dr. Rayjek were present, I am impressed beyond belief that you scaled the Basilica, and I am stunned that God's plan did not call for you to smite David Hong."

Quinn's smiled widened.

"Of course, I'll deny that I ever said that."

"Of course," Jason said as the old man lapsed into thoughtful silence again.

"We're going to be offering the three of you honorary Vatican citizenship, but you'll understand if people will be a bit tense should you choose to live here in the near future."

Quinn laughed and the smile crinkles around the Pope's eyes intensified as the man chuckled at his own joke.

"Is there anything I can offer you by way of thanks, Jason? Anything you need or desire?" Now, the man's face had taken on a more serious look.

"No, sir—I mean, Joseph." Quinn was shocked that the Pope would offer him anything. Then, before the old man could speak, he said, "Your forgiveness for my part in the loss of life and the destruction of two of your churches is enough."

"Ah yes, the Cathedral in Hong Kong. I had almost forgotten." The smile was back in his eyes. "Probably for the best, that one. I understand no civilians were injured in the collapse."

Then the man lapsed into a long silence. Quinn was content to let the man spin it out. At first, he seemed to be considering how to phrase something but after awhile, it seemed more like he was drifting off to sleep. Quinn was about to make a polite noise in his throat before attempting to slip out the door if the man didn't wake up. The Pope turned his head abruptly and fixed his gaze on Quinn. He still seemed tired, but now he held determination in his look.

"You know about the letter that Hong was after?"

"Yes."

"There were two copies of that letter. One stayed here at the Vatican—it was the copy Hong was after and which Dr. Rayjek so politely returned to me today. The *other* copy of that letter was sent by courier to Asia in the middle of the 19th century. It went to Hong Xiu Quan himself. In those days, the Church was looking for a miracle and thought we had found it in China. It seems silly today to think that a man might claim he was the second son of God and everyone around him would believe it. In those days, however, it was far more plausible. The distance from here to there in the days before air travel and the Internet? It was measured in years, you understand. By the time we heard any news of the savagery that man was capable of, it was far too late. We had lent him our official sanction as the second child of God Almighty."

The Pope paused for a moment and shook his head at 19th century Vatican gullibility. Quinn let his thoughts wander to what life must have been like in that time. He knew a little about the Taiping Rebellion and the challenges that faced China at that time with continual struggles against the British Navy and internecine strife between warlords in the fringes of the Chinese Empire.

"Hong mentioned that the location of his ancestor's tomb was near a town called Minfeng," the old man began.

"Yes, Eva is convinced it lies in the Kunlun Mountains to the south of Minfeng. She had narrowed the tomb down to three possible locations when all of this began for her with Hong's men crashing her plane." Quinn suspected where the Pope was going with this approach. "We plan to go look for it next."

"I was hoping you would say that, Jason. If you do find the tomb, I suspect that you will also find the second letter from Pope Pius IX, or at least the remnants of it. I have doubts as to whether the paper would have survived well, out in the deserts of China, outside of proper archival conditions. I would appreciate it very much, if you do find it, if you could return it to me. I'll be happy to finance the expedition..."

"I appreciate that, but it really isn't necessary. Eva and I will go alone first. A chance to get away from the craziness of the last few weeks. We'll make it into a sort of vacation-expedition hybrid. If we find anything significant and it requires excavation, then she'll spend the time setting up the dig. But I understand that she's already spoken with my boss about financing for the dig."

"Ah yes, Mrs. Tower and I have met. A very robust woman." the Pope smiled again.

"That's the one. In any case, if we find the letter, we'll be glad to return it."

The Pope eased the footrest of his chair down and slowly stood. Quinn also rose to his feet, suspecting that his brief audience with the Pope was over. The Pope walked with him toward the door of the study, but before they reached it, he gently laid his hand on Quinn's upper arm. Quinn turned to face the man who was much shorter than Quinn's six feet.

"Jason, if he's alive out there somewhere, you know that he will be coming for you at some point. During your journey to this tomb? Well, that would seem an optimal time, strategically. Do be careful. And take good care of Dr. Rayjek. She's a wonderful and briskly intelligent woman. I would hate to hear that anything had happened to either of you." Then the man had hugged Quinn and wished him good luck.

Now, lazily swaying on the back of a two-humped desert beast, Jason Quinn remembered the old man and his warning. He scanned the foothills around them for any sign of life, but their caravan of camels and equipment was the only thing moving. Quinn had been vigilant ever since the end of the affair at the Vatican and would have been even without the Pope's warning. He probably would have returned the second letter from Pope Pius IX anyway, even without the Pope's request as well. *If we even find it*, he told himself.

He was surprised that the Pope had absolved him of all guilt associated with the destruction of the dome and although he wasn't Catholic—he was a non-practicing Episcopalian with non-practicing Buddhist leanings—he did feel a weight lift from his heart after the blessing of the Pope. What he found more interesting though, was that before asking Quinn to undertake the expedition to Hong's tomb, the old man had first attempted to gauge Quinn's level of avarice by essentially offering him anything he wanted. Quinn had understood on some level in the Pope's study that the offer was both sincere and a test. But that level hadn't been close enough to consciousness for Quinn when he had replied that he didn't need anything more. It was just a gut reaction.

Later that night, Quinn had asked Johnson about his own audience with the Pope. Curtis said that it was briefer than Quinn's visit, that the man had genuinely thanked Johnson for his part in stopping David Hong, and that he had also been offered anything he might desire.

"What did you ask for?" Quinn wanted to know.

"I told him a good bottle of single malt would cover it nicely."

"You didn't?" Quinn was aghast and amused at the same time.

"The old boy had a courier send over a 1968 bottle of 41-year-old Bunnahabhain. The man has *taste*."

"*Nice*," Quinn commented.

"I'm trying to decide whether to open it or keep it." Curtis chuckled.

Later still that evening, back in his hotel room in Rome with Eva by his side in bed, Quinn asked her about her own visit with the Pope.

"Yes, he also asked me to name my reward." Then she got quiet.

"You asked for something didn't you?"

"I had to," she said playfully.

"What was it?"

"Did you know that the birth rate in the Vatican is officially zero?" She rolled on her side to look at him. The candlelight from the table in their hotel suite glimmered in her blonde hair like a halo. "No child has ever been born inside the walls of the Vatican. Lots of people, both men and women, live there, but no one has ever been born there. Well, I asked him, if I ever got pregnant—in wedlock, of course—if my child could be the first one born in the Vatican."

Quinn barked out laughter and Eva joined him. He laughed so hard that tears were coming from the corners of his eyes and no sound was coming from his mouth. When the giggles began to subside enough that he could speak, he gasped, "What did he say?"

"He laughed his ass off just like you did."

Quinn laughed harder and Eva's voice hitched as she fought for breath between bursts of her own laughter.

"Then he said *Yes*."

CHAPTER 72

They had made a final camp before bidding farewell to their guides. The men would wait one week to rendezvous with Quinn and Eva. Quinn had promised them more than they had earned on the way into the mountains and had paid them for waiting the week. But he had instructed them to leave after a week if he and Eva hadn't returned from the mountains by then. The two Uyghur men, each over sixty but stout and strong, seemed content to wait for the week and eager to collect the money Quinn promised them if they would act as guides on the return journey to Minfeng.

The Uyghurs set up yurts, like the guides to the northeast in Mongolia did. They tended to the camels and went about their business while Quinn and Eva readied their packs for the final part of their journey. The camels could not continue on, because the ground became too uneven and rugged. They were finally into the actual mountains and the guides were really only comfortable in the foothills—neither of them had any experience in the mountains, according to the one that spoke enough English for Quinn to deal with him.

"You okay with the weight of that?" Quinn asked Eva as they were setting out from the camp, their leather hiking boots slipping on the rock scree along the base of the hill.

"My pack might be bigger, but yours is heavier," she said poking him in the rib.

"Somebody had to carry that kitchen sink," he said, recoiling from her tickling.

They hiked for hours that first day but made little distance because the route was mostly up and down low hills that filled the valley they followed through some larger snowcapped peaks. Late in the afternoon, Quinn set up his brilliant yellow expedition-quality tent. He broke out a camp stove and heated some water for some hot chocolate. Eva sat nearby, removed her hiking boots, and massaged her feet. The boots were well worn, but she still wasn't used to hiking in mountainous terrain with extra weight on her back. She was sore but had no blisters on her feet and considered that a good sign.

The chocolate in a camp mug in her hand, she sipped it and smiled at Quinn, as he sat holding his own mug and looking at her intently.

"What?" she smiled at him.

"Just thinking about how my life has changed so radically in the last few months. And about what's next."

"I imagine that Margaret will be looking to get you back to work soon," she said.

"Yeah. You need to get back to being a working archeologist too."

"The Smithsonian will be happy to see me back in the field. I e-mailed my boss and he's thinking of getting a dig going in Cambodia. My French is a lot better than my Chinese, so it sounds like just the thing." Then, she realized that he was talking about their relationship. "You mean us."

"I mean us." he said and smiled.

"I think that we shouldn't complicate things. You have your life, I have mine. When our trajectories match or can be made to match, I'd like to spend as much time with you as possible. Sound good?" She had been thinking about this subject for a week and had been grumpy about it as a result. Now she just blurted it out and hoped that this was what Quinn wanted too. If he wanted to hold on to her too tightly, it would feel constricting and it would probably interrupt her career, which was going along just fine.

But his reaction was completely unexpected. He was laughing. Again. She wanted to be irritated because she had put so much fretting into this statement but his good nature caused her to smile as well.

"I was going to suggest the exact same thing. Curtis and I have a lot of mountains to climb still and the work with ARGO keeps me on the road for a lot of the year." He was still smiling, his green eyes sparkling as he looked at her.

She moved closer and snuggled up against him. "Let's just make sure that the times apart don't last too long."

He put his arm around her and squeezed and said, "You got it, Doc." They sat for a while watching dusk fall over the mountains and talked little. After awhile, they ate and then Eva said she wanted to get to sleep and he encouraged her to go in and he would be in the tent in a little while. He stayed seated in front of the camp stove and made another cup of hot chocolate for himself.

The stars were out but the moon wasn't up yet. His eyes adjusted to the dim starlight and he finished his drink. Then, he removed his boots and donned a pair of Vibram Five Fingers shoes. They looked like slippers with individual compartments for each toe on his feet. Sort of like gloves for his feet with a thin rubber sole. He pulled on a fleece jacket and moved away from the camp, heading back the way they had come but ascending the side of a steep hill as he went.

He gained altitude quickly and soon found what he was looking for. He could see the guide yurt well in the distance, little more than a speck, lit by the Coleman lanterns the Uyghurs had liked so much, which Quinn had offered them as gifts along with the generous salary he was paying them.

Then, he slowly let his eyes follow his own trail, from the guides to where Eva slept, in the yellow tent behind him. He missed what he was looking for the first time he followed their trail with his eyes, but when he let his eyes start to head back in the direction of the guides again, he found what he had suspected he might.

Another camp. Low light. Maybe a small LED lantern. It was too far away for him to see how many people, but the likelihood that someone else was in these mountains in this area was slim. He wished for a good set of night vision goggles, but wasn't sure at this distance he'd be able to make out individual heat sources or if they would blur together.

Regardless of how many, they were clearly following Quinn.

CHAPTER 73

The morning was cold and gray, and when Eva popped her head out of the tent, Quinn was already up and breaking camp. A small pan of instant oatmeal was staying warm on the camp stove and waiting for her. Quinn packed up smoothly and efficiently, and Eva wondered if she dallied at all with her oatmeal if he would end up doing all the work, packing things up around her as she ate. She felt a little guilty but then looked at her watch and saw that he must have been up much earlier than she—dawn couldn't have been long ago.

"Good morning," she said, as she crawled out of the tent toward the oatmeal.

"There's coffee in the thermos," Quinn said, but he didn't slow his packing as he spoke. "You okay with getting an early start today? I figure there's not much else to do here, and we didn't get in too much distance yesterday."

Eva nodded her agreement as she ate. When she swallowed the mouthful of oatmeal, she said "I feel bad that you're doing all the work breaking camp."

"Don't worry about it. I woke early and wanted to keep busy."

They set out within the hour. Quinn deliberately led their trail into more challenging mountainous terrain, instead of following the easier trail along the valley floors and over the lower hills. When asked, he explained that the reason was that he wanted to be able to visually search for the tomb. He told her that it couldn't be more than a day's hike from their current location. Secretly, he also thought that the higher terrain would pose a problem for the team following them. If their pursuers hoped to not be seen following Quinn and Eva, then their movements would be hindered by possibly being seen whenever

Quinn turned around and looked back the way they had come—which he did frequently. If the pursuers wanted to keep their perceived element of surprise, they would be forced to dive for cover every time they spotted Quinn looking at his back trail. The other possibility was that the pursuers wouldn't be concerned with being spotted, counting on their numbers and speed. As the day went on though, Quinn was assured that his pursuers were more concerned with stealth. He didn't spot them once during the day.

Both Quinn and Eva were getting into their strides on this second full day of hiking. They took breaks occasionally and snacked on PowerBars and instant camping food. Toward the end of the useful hiking hours, Quinn took them again back down into the valleys and lower hills, giving up on keeping an eye out for his pursuers. In any case, they were far behind Quinn and Eva, and he would again search for them at night by starlight.

They stopped for a long break so Eva could consult her GPS, a topographic map, and her own notes in a miniature leather-bound journal. "We must be quite close to the tomb at this point. Should we press on and risk making a camp for the night in the dark?"

"I'm up for it if you are," Quinn said with a good-hearted grin.

Quinn consulted his own GPS unit and noted exactly how far they were from the tomb. He'd contacted Mooky Jones, who had retasked a few satellites and had run several computer simulations and analysis programs before declaring to Quinn with absolute certainty, the precise location of the tomb to within fifteen feet. Quinn had kept this information from Eva, correctly deducing that she wanted to discover its location both on her own and from her own research. Still, he had no intention of letting that go on for too long if she was way off in her calculations. He'd seen her work and discussed her theories with her. She was in the right neighborhood, so he wasn't too concerned, but now that he knew they were being shadowed, he was glad he'd thought to make some preparations, including getting Mooky's extensive computing prowess to work on the tomb's precise location.

They were close enough that within an hour or two, they could be there, although the opening of the tomb would have to wait until the following day. They continued deeper into the mountains, Quinn letting Eva guide them in the direction she suspected would lead them to the long lost tomb of Hong Xiu Quan, Christianity's fallen Chinese son.

The sun was low in the sky but not quite gone behind the gray rock strewn mountains to their right when Eva announced that they should be close enough to see the temple, or at least to see some sign of an underground structure.

Quinn, knowing what he was looking for after seeing detailed satellite imagery that Mooky had e-mailed him back in Rome, suggested that in this kind of landscape, perhaps the tomb was built into the side of a mountain, like a mineshaft.

"That's a great idea," Eva said. "No one is really sure what kind of tomb this might have been. Remember that the Taipings were on the run for their lives from the alliance the West had made with the Qing emperor, to crush the uprising. Their messiah had died in 1864 from illness—although some sources suggest he did himself in with poison. The Qing forces had killed a man they believed to be Hong's son, *Hong Tianguifu*, but who was actually a decoy lookalike. Loyal supporters had been ordered to take Hong's body to a special place in *paradise*, where the Qing wouldn't find it."

"Didn't a Qing general claim that he'd found Hong's body in Nanjing?" Quinn asked.

"Li Chendian. He was the second general to search the sacked city of Nanjing for Hong Xiu Quan at the end of the Taiping rebellion. He didn't find a body either at first, but they later found a hidden chamber in the ground that had a body holding a cross, wearing only a loincloth. The body was so badly decomposed that little of it was left. Still, Li proclaimed it as Hong's body. Others were a bit skeptical. Nearly a hundred years later, some surviving Taiping documents were discovered that suggested the Taipings had whisked Hong's body out of the city and under cover of darkness before Nanjing was sacked. I did quite a bit of research in Rome. I was able to talk with a few Taiping scholars as well."

"So after the switcheroo with Hong's body, it makes perfect sense that they would pull the same trick with his kid, David Hong's great-granddaddy," Quinn summarized.

"Exactly. I narrowed down the location of this tomb to a couple of possible sites from my research before all this craziness began, and this area was the third possibility. But I have no idea what this tomb would look like. It could just be a simple cave covered over with a boulder, or it could be a gleaming golden temple—but I'm leaning more toward the former. The Taipings were on the run. The only way this place could be in any way elaborate, was if Hong Xiu Quan had had it prepared long before his death."

Eva stopped walking, and Quinn, not paying attention, walked right into her backpack.

"What is it?" he asked.

She pointed across the valley to the other side and toward a small rectangular stone doorframe built into the side of a hill.

"Looks like your mine shaft theory was sound. That's gotta be the place," she said. "Let's go."

Eva raced down the rocky slope toward the valley floor so she could cross to the opposite hill and make her way up to the door. Quinn scanned around them from his place on the hill. He looked at the hills and mountains around them, paying close attention to the direction from which their pursuers would be coming. He looked at the valley and across the small lake below him. He determined the best spots for an ambush—both an ambush set by him and one set by his pursuers. He quickly sought out possible ways into and out of the valley, and also where they should set their camp for the night. The sun was down behind the western ridge of peaks now.

He felt that the pursuers were still far enough behind. The attack wouldn't come tonight. It would be tomorrow or tomorrow night at the latest. That gave him time to plan a few surprises and get the tomb open. Maybe even time for him and Eva to get what they needed and get out of the valley entirely.

It was going to be close.

CHAPTER 74

They reached the stone door and realized that it was massive in size. Perhaps 13 feet in height and half that in width, the door was a single giant slab of gray stone. Upon closer inspection, Quinn thought it might be an unpolished marble—clearly not a stone taken from the surrounding valley. Around the edge of the door were thick gray, rectangular granite slabs, forming a doorframe. There was no writing; there was no ornamentation of any kind. The path leading up the hillside to the doors was nothing more than the scree and boulders of the natural hillside. No actual pathway was apparent. Because this valley was far away from the traditional paths followed north and south through the Kunlun range, Quinn guessed that they might be the first people to see this door since the 1860s when Hong Xiu Quan had been laid to rest here—well, aside from Sven Hedin, if Eva's theory about the man's secret expedition held any water.

The rock face of the mountain was nearly vertical above the doorframe, as Quinn suspected it would be from the satellite pictures he'd seen. As far as he could tell, the massive slab of a door went *up* somehow. It might be easier to break through it depending on how thick it was, but he didn't think Eva would go for that.

"Set up camp or commence Operation Grave Robber?" he asked her.

"Bite your tongue—I'm a trained professional archeologist. We don't rob graves. We *relocate* them." She turned away from where she had been running her hands over the smooth stone door and grinned at him. "Let's see if we can get in without damaging too much. If we can, we can set up camp inside if it's large enough, which it looks like it will be. I was way off, thinking that this might be a cave. This place must have been in the works from shortly after Hong's uprising came into power, if not since before then."

Eva produced a small hand trowel from her pack and began scraping the small scree away from the bottom of the great stone door. Quinn lugged a few heavy rocks out of the way. In just a few minutes, Eva sighed. "That's what I was afraid of. The frame stones go all the way around the slab. No way to tunnel in under. We'll have to figure out how to open the slab but it looks like it goes up. I don't know about you, but I'm not strong enough to lift a piece of stone that big."

"No one is," Quinn said, as he sat and rummaged through his own pack. "There must be some kind of mechanism for raising the slab up. Take a look around the sides of the doors and see if you can find something, but I don't think you will."

"Why not?"

"This place was meant to be a one-way trip for Hong Xiu Quan. No one was going to be stopping by for a visit. My guess would be that the mechanism for the door was not meant to work again after it was sealed shut. You're the archeologist—does that make sense?"

"Yeah," she admitted with defeat. "In fact, it's pretty darned likely. I wonder what Hedin would have done when faced with this slab?"

Quinn was laying a small tarp on the ground. From his pack, he produced a straight pry bar the length of his arm, a small hammer with a wide head, and then the pieces of a disassembled Hi-Lift brand mechanical jack.

"Wow," Eva stared in shock. "The kitchen sink?"

"I had a suspicion that it might come in handy," he told her as he assembled the steel handle with cotter pins.

"We'll have to cut into the base of the door a bit so you can get the edge of that in there," she said. "That goes against all my training as an archeologist, you know."

"That's why I'll do all the hammering. We'll only need to cut out a portion of the stone the size of your hand to fit the jack into place," he told her, as he finished putting the jack together and picked up the pry bar and the hammer. "Besides, the interior contents of the tomb are the find, right? Not the door. Without any pretty golden inlaid designs, it's not like any museum is going to want to display the door."

As he set to work on chipping a small hole in the stone at the base of the door with the pry bar and the hammer, he called over his shoulder. "My Plan B is to smash the door to pieces with that thing after having to lug it this far, so let's hope this works."

"You will not be welcomed to the Society of East Asian Archeology's fundraiser dinners, defiler," she told him.

"Is there such a society?" he grunted.

"Of course. Luckily for you, I am not a member."

She busied herself with looking around the door at nondescript rocks and boulders, hoping beyond hope that she might find a clever catch or lever that would raise the tomb door, but she agreed with Quinn's assessment that the door was always meant to be sealed and remain closed thereafter.

The sky was darkening when Quinn had finished his chiseling work. He donned an LED headlamp and shone it on the small hole he'd carved into the base of the door. It was about the height and width of his outstretched hand and only the depth of his fingers. The few inches of depth hadn't reached the other side of the door and Quinn now silently reconsidered attempting to smash the door down—the marble could possibly be feet thick.

"We're ready," he told Eva as he fitted the jack into place, with its base lodged in a thin crack under the door and above the stone frame, and the lifting ledge of the device snug against the upper edge of the roughly rectangular hole he had cut away. He had to shove the jack and kick it a few times to get it tightly into place. "Do you say any special words or anything before you tomb raid?"

"Nope. Crack that sucker."

Quinn began to pump the handle of the jack, silently praying that it could handle the weight of the slab and that the whole thing didn't just explode into a few hundred pieces of shiny steel shrapnel. It wasn't easy to pump the handle, but it was far easier than he had thought it would be.

The jack bit into the marble and the door raised just a crack. They heard a whooshing noise as the air pressure inside the tomb adjusted to that outside of the door. Some dust blew out from the crack at the base of the door. Quinn had expected some rancid hideous smell to blast out of that crack, but the air just felt a bit stale, like the forced air on a long airplane ride. Stale and dusty. He coughed a few times at the dust and then resumed working the handle of the jack up and down. The upright on the jack was about four feet tall—it had only just fit in his large mountaineering backpack. He hoped to get the door up a good three feet before he stopped.

Night was falling now, and Eva set a small LED lantern at the opening of the door and lay down on the ground next to the jack as Quinn pumped the door up.

"Don't get too close," he cautioned her. "And don't get too comfortable down there, it's gonna be your turn soon." He wiped the sweat from his brow and stood back to give his hands a break. He could feel a blister wanting to start on his left hand, and the door was maybe only six inches up off the ground.

Eva stood and took hold of the handle on the jack. "Sorry. I'll take a turn. I was getting carried away." She began heaving on the steel rod and the jack slowly click-clacked away.

Quinn lay down in the spot where Eva had been and shined his headlamp in the opening, but he still couldn't see much, beyond the fact that the interior space went deeper than his headlamp could penetrate.

"Don't go in without me," Eva said.

"I don't think we should go in until we get that door up to about three feet." he told her, standing.

Eva heaved the handle and grunted. "Gonna take awhile."

"Maybe a half an hour. Your curiosity can wait."

She worked the lever for another five minutes and then stepped back panting and sweating. Quinn took over and managed to get the door up high enough for them to crawl into, in about another ten minutes. The sky was fully dark by then, and the cloud cover prevented them from seeing anything by starlight.

Quinn lodged his straight pry bar in the crack at the side of the door. If the jack snapped, the pry bar likely wouldn't help to keep the door open but it was all he had. He slid both of their backpacks under the door, past the jack, and into the tomb. Then, he looked at Eva, the brilliant white light from his LED headlamp making her blonde hair shine as if it had an aura. She was almost tingling with anticipation.

"Ready?" he asked her.

She smiled at him, then dropped to her knees and scooted under the stone slab and into the tomb.

CHAPTER 75

Quinn emerged on the other side of the jacked up marble slab into a huge space. The chamber seemed to him the size of a ballroom in a modern hotel. He scanned the room with his hand held flashlight as well as with his headlamp. Eva was walking across the length of the room. The space, although cavernous, was not decorated in any fashion that Quinn could see. It was just a vast space carved from the side of the mountain. He saw a few slumped and seated skeletons around the edges of the space. They each wore the same kind of robes. The cloth had not yet deteriorated in the hundred and fifty years it had been sealed in the room, but the fabric was worn and had holes in many places. He suspected that more than a bit of it had been consumed by insects that would have feasted on the flesh of the dead.

There was nothing else to see in this part of the tomb, so Quinn picked up a sword from a skeleton, glanced at it, and was surprised to see that it had not rusted during its time in the cavern. He swung the blade a few times, and then quickly followed Eva at the far end of the space.

At the far back wall of the room, she had found another smaller door, marked with a large bronze cross. The door was wood and had simple hinges set into the stone wall of the room. The door was ajar, and Eva was beginning to open it as Quinn arrived at her side. Inside was a small room, just large enough to be a bedroom. Along the far wall was a raised platform with a stone casket. The lid on it was slid aside. Seated in front of the casket on the floor of the room, was a single skeleton dressed in heavy layers of wool and wearing small round spectacles. Beside it on one side, was a small leather-bound book, and on the other side was a small leather backpack.

Quinn heard Eva gasp as she reverently stepped forward and knelt before the remains of Central Asia's greatest explorer, Sven Hedin. She just looked at him for a moment, not touching anything. Quinn stood nearby, respectfully allowing her this moment of discovery. After a few minutes, she pulled out her digital camera and took several photos of the room, the remains of Hedin, his equipment, the book, and the casket. Still without having touched anything, she motioned Quinn over and they approached the casket and peered in.

Inside was another skeleton—this time with long, flowing white hair, and it was clothed only in a loincloth. The hands were crossed over the breastbone and held a crucifix. At the side of the remains, along the wall of the casket, was a sword with a jeweled handle. On the other side of the casket, at waist height, was a small wooden box with an inlaid gold cross in the lid. It had no latch.

Eva took several more photos of the remains in the casket and close-ups of the box, the sword, and the crucifix. Then, she delicately reached for the box. Without moving the box itself, she slowly raised its lid.

Inside the box were two things. One was a lock of hair tied with a brilliant red ribbon, still looking as fresh as the day it was dyed crimson. The other thing was an envelope, faded to yellow with age. Across the edge of the flap, was a broken, deep ruby colored, wax seal that bore the Papal symbol of the crossed keys and *triregnum* or triple crown.

"The letter must have been one of his most prized possessions, particularly after the tide of battle began to turn when the West threw its aid behind the Qing emperor." Eva pulled some gallon-sized Ziploc plastic bags from her pack and delicately picked up the envelope and slid it into one of the bags. Then, like David Hong had done in Europe, she double bagged it. She carefully slid the double-bagged envelope into a small plastic Tupperware case she had brought along for just such a purpose. There was no way that the letter would get wet now.

She took out the camera again and photographed the casket again now with everything exactly as it was but with the envelope no longer there—as if it never was. This would be the photo she would share with colleagues and with the government in Beijing. As far as the rest of the world would know, the letter from the Vatican would not have been found among the remains of

Hong Xiu Quan. She and Quinn would return it to the Vatican on their way back to the U.S.

She packaged the lock of hair similarly to the way she had the letter, then gently removed the wooden box and handed it to Quinn. He held it while she removed some soft cloth from her bag. She then wrapped the wooden box and placed it in her pack as well.

She used another long piece of cloth to wrap up the sword and asked Quinn to hold it. She then took additional photos of the skeleton. She then very gently removed the crucifix from its hands. It took her a long time to do so, gently sliding the metal one tiny bit at a time so as not to vibrate the bones of the fingers. The skeleton wasn't old enough to turn to dust if jostled too hard, but neither did she want to fracture one of the phalanges or metacarpals.

"It's a shame we can't take the skeletons on this trip too, but at least we can remove any temptation for any grave robbers that might find this site before we get a team in from Beijing."

"Most likely no one will be in this valley for the next hundred years other than the Beijing academics," Quinn observed.

"You'd be surprised at how quickly the scavengers hear about a dig and how often they manage to get there just before the archeologists." Eva frowned and then squatted down to examine Hedin's remains again.

She very gently picked up the leather journal, even though it was only slightly older than 50 years. There was no chance it would turn to ash before her eyes, but she still treated it as if it were delicate porcelain.

Then, she gently probed the pockets of the dead man, looking for anything that would go to the Sven Hedin Foundation. The man had nothing in his pockets but a pencil. She left it and delicately removed his spectacles and placed them in another little plastic container that she had brought along.

After she had packed away the man's glasses, she stood and faced Quinn. She hugged him tightly and he hugged her back. There were tears in her eyes.

"We did it!" she said.

"You did it," he said, and hugged her back tightly before releasing her and looking into her eyes.

Their kiss was long and slow, and even though it had been days since they had been able to shower, she still smelled fresh to Quinn's nose and he drank in her smell and buried his face in her hair for another hug.

When they parted, he let his thoughts return to their pursuers and asked how much time she wanted to spend in the tomb before they departed.

"Frankly, I've done most of what I can do here. We can take off tomorrow, bringing Mr. Hedin's pack with us, as well as the other things I've already tucked away. I'll need to get in touch with Beijing, of course. Then, I'll come back with the team that does the dig—assuming that the government lackeys in the vast Chinese bureaucracy allow it—you never know what they'll do. But hopefully when they see that I'm willing to give them the artifacts from Hong's casket, they'll be more receptive."

"And the Hedin possessions?" Quinn asked her.

"Oh, they'll go to the Sven Hedin Foundation in Stockholm. After I've had a chance to catalog everything and read the journal, naturally," she told him with a giddy schoolgirl grin.

"Naturally," he conceded. "Well, in that case, allow me to make a small suggestion, and one that your tired legs most likely will not appreciate."

"What is it?" she turned to him now with a look of mild concern. Her legs were very tired, and she had been looking forward to pouring over the journal until her eyes tired out or until the LED light in her headlamp dimmed— whichever came first.

"Well, I didn't want to tell you this before and worry you, but we were followed into the mountains. They're pretty far behind us. I doubt we'll run into them tonight, but I still think it would be a good idea for us to get out of the tomb and away from it before dawn. Just to be on the safe side."

"You don't think it could be..."

"Not really sure what to think. Not sure how many of them there are or who it is. But one thing we can be sure of. They're not in this part of the mountains by sheer coincidence. Whether they're bandits or some of Hong's men, the only thing we know is that they are not planning on being friendly."

"Of that you can be certain, Mr. Quinn." The voice came from the small doorway to the room leading back into the cavern. In stepped two men, dressed in dark fleece clothes and hiking boots. The first was a tall, muscular Chinese man who could easily have passed as a professional wrestler with his long, sweaty, unkempt hair. The second man was smaller in stature, and while he was equally sweaty, he was immeasurably more refined in his look, with a trimmed goatee and an expensive haircut.

The man was David Hong.

"Thank you very much for discovering my ancestor's tomb as your last act on this Earth."

CHAPTER 76

Hong stepped fully into the small room. Quinn saw that both Hong and his henchman had night vision goggles around their necks. Now he understood that they were sweaty because they had been far behind but had hustled to catch up to Quinn and Eva and had most likely hiked through the night.

"The letter, please, Dr. Rayjek." Hong held out his hand, but still maintained his position well behind the muscled assistant.

"What letter?" Eva asked haughtily.

"Oh come now, Dr. Rayjek. Don't make me ask Xiao Jia here to tear your arms out." Hong crossed his own arms as he made this threat. Almost as if he had seen the hulking man in front of him do just that very thing to someone.

"Xiao Jia?" Quinn asked. "Really? *Little Jade?* A sissy name like that for such a big boy?" Quinn goaded the giant, seeing correctly that although the muscled Chinese was tired from his long and hurried hike, he was also spoiling for a fight. Quinn stood stock still, the blanket wrapped sword held vertically behind him and hidden by Quinn's leg from Hong's view.

Xiao Jia glanced back at Hong for approval and Hong nodded almost imperceptibly. The huge man turned back toward Quinn and lumbered at Quinn across the confined room.

Quinn waited until the last second and then whipped up the wrapped sword, poking the package at Xiao Jia's face. The impact made a dull thunking noise and the giant's onrush was halted. He stumbled backward and smashed into Hong, knocking the smaller man out of the small room and back into the larger cavern.

Then, without more than a shake of his head, as if to clear it, the huge man launched himself at Quinn again, and to Quinn's astonishment, Xiao Jia came on in exactly the same way. It was as if the man had always been able to solve problems by charging them like a bull and simply didn't need any other strategies.

Quinn thrust the wrapped sword again, in exactly the same way, and harder this time. The vibration from the impact shot up his arm, and as Quinn pulled the package back from his thrust, he saw that this time, the tip of the blade had punctured the end of the microfiber blanket and was coated in blood.

Xiao Jia staggered slightly sideways this time. His left eye socket was gushing crimson blood that glinted in the light from the lantern Eva had set in the room earlier. Again, the man shook his head, as if to clear it, but this time it wouldn't clear. His vision was blurred and the big man didn't seem to know why. He shook his head again and a gout of blood arced across the room from side to side, the way water would from a dog shaking its body to dry off after a swim.

Quinn swung his arm a few times, unraveling the blanket from the blade of the sword, but it still hung from the hole that had been punctured in it. Quinn grabbed the blanket and tugged. It ripped free just as the partially blinded man began his third charge.

Eva had moved to the side of the room, wearing her own pack and holding Hedin's leather sack. She was quiet and she was edging closer to the door on Xiao Jia's blinded side. She glanced at Quinn, and he nodded that her plan was a good one. He eyed the door warily and knew that she understood that David Hong would still be out there. Then, he saw that she was clutching a small camp knife they had picked up in Minfeng. *Good girl*, he thought.

Xiao Jia rushed in. At the last moment, Quinn ducked under the behemoth's encircling arms and dodged to the opposite side of the room from where Eva was. Eva darted for the door. Xiao Jia crashed headlong into the stone casket at the back of the room, his enormous foot stepping through the chest and ribcage of the remains of the Swedish explorer on the floor.

Quinn stepped forward and thrust the sword into Xiao Jia's lower spine. The man let out an inhuman howl and began to spin. Quinn retracted the blade just before the tip snapped off. As he stepped backward toward the door, he raised the blade and saw that it had been bent near the tip. *Bent, but not unusable.*

Xiao Jia again launched an attack, but it was slower this time, and the skeletal remains stubbornly wrapped around his leg confounded his footing. Quinn began his own run forward toward the huge man, lending more momentum to his thrust. He stabbed the bent sword deep into Xiao Jia's chest, where the man's heart should have been. Quinn drove the blade in deep until his arm thumped with the impact of the hilt cramming into Xiao Jia's chest.

But the gigantic, wounded man was still not dead yet. He wrapped his meaty fingers around Quinn's throat. Quinn was stunned to discover that with a sword buried in his heart, this monstrosity of a Chinese man was effectively choking the air out of him.

Quinn struggled to pry to larger man's fingers from his throat to no avail. He was losing air already and dark spots were forming at the edge of his vision. He raised his left hand over the giant's forearm and jabbed his thumb deeply into Xiao Jia's remaining good eye, twisting and digging until the man was shrieking in pain. The tightness on Quinn's throat lessened, and he was able to pry the fingers loose.

He stepped back for a second and watched the man claw at his face as if he could replace his sight by doing so. Quinn lunged forward and took hold of the hilt of the sword and twisted it hard. He heard Xiao Jia grunt but there was little effort in it. Quinn stepped back and launched a kick at the hilt of the sword with his hiking boot. The heel of the boot connected, driving the blade just slightly deeper, before snapping the hilt cleanly off of the blade. Xiao Jia's body tilted for a second, as if the man would still stand despite this onslaught. But he was dead. His body slowly fell backward, cracking the corpse's skull against the edge of the stone casket that held Hong Xiu Quan and chipping the stone.

Quinn whirled to face the larger room on the other side of the door. He had no idea how much time had passed since his fight with Xiao Jia had begun. His body was filled with adrenalin and the blood was rushing in his ears. He listened for Hong and Eva, but he heard nothing as he approached the door. He was concerned that Hong might be lying in wait for him in the shadows, but he was standing in the center of the room, holding Eva in front of him, her knife in his hand and held to her throat.

"All that money from your shipping business, Hong, you should really invest in some better help." Quinn quipped.

"There will be plenty of time to do so after you are dead, Mr. Quinn. Not another step, by the way." Hong's hand was shaking slightly. Quinn wasn't sure how the fight had gone with Eva, but he could see from Hong's shakes that the man had his own adrenalin flowing.

Then, Quinn saw that Eva was holding something in her hand in front of her, away from Hong's line of sight in the darkened cavern. Quinn looked her in the eye and nodded his head just slightly. He adjusted his stance and took in a breath.

Eva snapped open the blade to a second knife she had concealed on her— a Spyderco folding serrated knife that could be opened and closed one-handed. The blade was open and she was smashing her head backward into Hong's nose. Quinn was running toward them. Eva flipped the blade in her hand and drove the knife backward and into Hong's upper thigh. He launched backward toward the floor screaming, and she scrabbled on the floor for the Hedin pack to her side.

Quinn leapt over her and landed a kick to Hong's chest, driving the air out of the man in a loud burst. Quinn rolled on the ground on the other side of Hong as he landed and spun to face the man.

Eva was already near the jacked-up door and throwing the packs out before she scooted out herself. Hong was scrabbling to his feet and pulling the folding knife from his leg. The wound wasn't deep, but it would cause a limp and hurt like the devil.

Quinn moved between Hong and the door, still twenty feet away and faced the madman. Hong held up the knife and looked at it for a second before flinging it at Quinn. Quinn dodged slightly and the knife flew across the room to clatter harmlessly against a far wall.

Hong's body posture suggested a new attack of some kind, but the man didn't move. Quinn was ready for anything but noted that both of them were panting and in little shape for a prolonged battle. Quinn expected him to say something, but the rage that coursed through the Asian man's dark eyes looked like it was consuming him.

Quinn took a tentative step back toward the door. Then, he saw Hong's hand moving for the zipper of his fleece jacket. *Sonofabitch*, Quinn thought, *the bastard has a gun after all.*

Quinn turned then and sprinted for the huge marble slab of a door. He was three quarters of the way there when a shot rang out in the echoing cavern, and a small chunk of the stone wall fragmented to the left of the doorway. A second shot came, and then a third. Quinn was rolling on the floor in a clumsy somersault. He rolled through the open doorway, and as he went, he reached out and grabbed the base of the jack with his hand. His foot snagged the pry bar away as he rolled. His momentum pulled him though the doorway and out into the moonlight. His shoulder pulled tight and the jack came away, the giant slab of a marble door rumbling down, and scraping stone as it came.

Quinn heard David Hong scream.

"Noooooooooooooooooo..."

And then the ground shaking thunder of the tremor as the marble door slammed shut on its stone frame, sealing the tomb of Hong Xiu Quan with his descendant in it.

Quinn's body tumbled down the scree and boulders of the hillside until it reached the bottom, near the small lake. He left a trail of blood the whole way. It looked inky black in the moonlight.

CHAPTER 77

Eva reached Quinn's still body in the valley. She thought he was dead. He hadn't moved since he reached the bottom of the hill. She had been standing to the side of the door and had seen him plunge after she heard the gunshots. She had raced down the hill after his tumbling body, tripping and scraping her shin as she went.

His head was bloody and he had left a blood trail the whole way down, but she didn't think it had come from his head. She knelt down and reached tentatively and gently to his neck to feel for a pulse, certain that there was no way he could be alive.

"Damn, I'm hungry," he rasped, startling her as she retracted her hand.

"Oh my God, Jason Quinn! I thought you were dead." she began to cry.

"No way on Earth that death could hurt like this," he said.

She began to tend to his wounds, first running back up the hill to grab the packs, and then ripping open the Velcro-sealed first aid kit. The gash on his head wasn't too serious. They thought that perhaps the steel jack had scraped his head as he had tumbled and before he had let it go. His shoulder was dislocated again and she set it the way she had seen Curtis do. He had been shot three times, once a glancing blow to his left calf, taking a small bit of muscle, another grazing the shoulder blade on the side of his dislocated shoulder. That one had only taken a small slice of skin, the bone effectively helping the bullet to ricochet.

The serious wound was a shot through his lower right side, which had thankfully passed clean through and missed all kinds of arteries and organs. Eva used up nearly all of the gauze in their kit, wrapping the other wounds and then packing the serious one from his back right through to his stomach.

She had to use some sticky moleskin strips in the kit to seal the wound in front and back, and while the wound would require medical attention, Quinn felt certain that it could wait until they made it back to Minfeng. After she had patched him, she helped him to his feet.

He stood a little shakily, but after lightly testing his leg, found that he could walk, albeit with a limp. He glanced up at the door to the tomb, now gloriously lit by moonlight. Then, he began the slow hike up the slope, following his own trail of blood, to the door. Eva walked with him. When they reached the giant marble slab, Quinn placed his hand on the door.

"Will he be able to get out?" she asked quietly.

"No," Quinn said with certainty.

"No chance?"

"Hedin didn't get out. Now that I think of it, I wonder how the hell Hedin got in."

"I'm sure the journal will tell us," she said and gently laid a hand on Quinn's back.

"You got it right? Because I'm not going back inside for it."

Eva laughed a small tired laugh. "Yes, I got it."

"As tired as I am, I don't think I want to camp in this valley tonight," he told her.

"Seconded."

They packed up their possessions, Eva redistributing the contents of Hedin's pack between their two nylon packs and finally rolling up Hedin's empty leather bag and strapping it to the outside of her own pack. Quinn told her he could carry the weight of his own pack just fine, but she still placed heavier items in her own pack. In any case, she thought, Quinn's bag would be lighter without the jack, which they planned to leave. Although Eva buried it first, to prevent any bandits from getting ideas, should they discover the valley.

They snacked on some energy bars and left the valley, headed back the way they had come. They walked in silence for a time, each lost in their own thoughts.

"I have all the important contents of that tomb. It goes against my professional training, but I think I don't want to announce the location any time soon now."

Quinn looked at her with concern. "You gonna be okay with that?"

"Yes. That man was a maniac and a menace. I can't even keep track of how many people died because of him. He might live long enough for us to reach Minfeng and report him to the authorities there, and for them to get back here and crack him out of the tomb."

"He might. Or he might not. And the police in Minfeng might just as soon arrest us."

"I've thought of that," Eva said gloomily.

"So what about the Hedin finds? How can you reconcile them without a location, if you don't announce the find?"

"Oh, I'll probably announce it. I just don't see any reason to rush."

Quinn smiled. "He'll be dead long before we get to Minfeng. He was bleeding too and he had no pack with him—no food, no supplies."

"Are we wrong not to go back and try to get him out?"

"I *am* going to go back and get him out. How does this time next year sound to you?"

"Do you think the tomb will remain undiscovered that long?" she asked, walking along a valley floor toward the base of a hill.

"No one will be coming this way."

They made it back to the guides and the camels in two days of strong hiking, Quinn's side killing him, but his leg wound bothering him less and less. The guides tended to his side wound with fresh gauze; they later got him to a doctor in Minfeng that asked no questions for American dollars. The next day Eva Rayjek and Jason Quinn got into a truck headed for the border with Pakistan.

Customs agents never bothered searching them, and they smuggled out the artifacts from the greatest Asian explorer who ever lived and the self-professed *second child* of God.

Jason Quinn will return in
FROZEN

ABOUT THE AUTHOR

Kane Gilmour has lived all over the world. He has worked as a physical therapy assistant in the US Air Force, as a clerk in various retail positions, as a human trash compactor for a freight company, and as a teacher, a teacher-trainer, and a teacher of teacher-trainers. Recently, he has worked as an editor for an IT firm and as a freelance editor for thriller authors.

RESURRECT is his first novel. His novella with Jeremy Robinson, CALLSIGN: DEEP BLUE is also available. Kane lives with his wife, son, and newborn daughter in the wilds of Central Vermont.